KEYS TO ERRAVILLA

Book 1

Hosts of Erravilla

Reba A. Ritchie

"Hosts of Erravilla is not a book one easily takes a break from. Reba A. Ritchie captivated me with her creativity in this beautifully written story. Hosts of Erravilla is a delightful story filled with romance, intrigue and drama about a group of people who rediscover themselves, while learning that love and forgiveness will bring them closer, and trust can seal that loving bond."

Michelle Stanley, Readers' Favorite - 5 Stars

Dedication

For My Boys:
Brooklyn, Toby & Caleb
You Will Always Be My Babies…

Contents

Acknowledgements

Firstly, a huge thank you to Tony, for being the greatest husband a girl could want and a fabulous father to our boys. Thank you for the years you persevered with me. I'll always be grateful that you married me.

Thank you to my Mum, Jennie, for teaching me to find my voice.

An enormous thank you to my big sister, Trish, for always believing in me and without whose early feedback Maisy and Walter's story would have never been told.

Lots of love to my Grandmother, Cath Challinor, for your constant encouragement and support.

To my fellow author, Emma Whale, whose early input and love of fiction encouraged me to never give up on my dream.

A huge thank you to Jesika Carey, whose artistic genius has provided the first visual insight into Erravilla's gates. You are amazing!

Thank you to Bruce McCabe, for inspiring me as a writer!

To Karen at Serenity Press Publishing, thank you for helping my dream become a reality so smoothly.

Finally, to my besties, Amanda West and Sandra Wolf, thank you both for loving your little monkey! Chiang gang for life.

Prologue

April 12, 1917, rural Gloucester, England
Sir Walter Finnegan, last Earl of Erravilla Court

The inscriptions had read: "Till Death Do Us Part".

For fifty-eight years I had not realised the truth of my feelings for Maisy. Not until death had approached her did I finally give flight to the love that I had repressed, hidden somewhere between my heart and the fleshy tissue beneath the surface of my skin. Only in those final fleeting moments had she known the truth, just before death claimed her.

Maisy went to be with her Maker this morning at 06:55, at the noble age of seventy-six years. She died peacefully in her sleep, in her twin bed across from mine. At the very moment that her heart ceased to beat, the rings that had held us united for nearly six decades had finally thawed from the ice-blue and cracked open, springing from her hand and mine, which were held as one, onto the bed covers below.

Just before the bright hues of the rings had wavered and died with her, both the rings had seared with a fierce shade of burgundy: signifying the true love that coursed through her veins and mine, one for the other. I had smiled at this realisation, knowing that she had died, with the knowledge of my deep commitment and affection for her.

I had positioned the rings together in the small keepsake that I had created for her all those years ago, and laid them in their resting place until the next set of hands should come upon them.

The steps up to the old attic were steeper than I had remembered, and I had had to pause many times before reaching the landing, rubbing these old knees as I journeyed.

I had kissed the ceramic box with the hand-sculptured designs before laying it upon her mother's vanity desk for the final time, beside the heavy glory box with her wedding gown. I had not lingered in the cold attic, instead made my way back down the iron steps, passing closed-off drawing rooms and the magnificent dining hall, which was now shrouded in large white sheets.

The world is on the brink of war, and my time at Erravilla is at an end. I will follow her soon enough.

Before I sign off for the final time, bidding whoever reads this journal a fervent prayer and fond farewell, I feel I must tell of our story, so that those upon whose destinies befall the rings will understand their plight...

Sir Walter, S. Finnegan

Summer, Modern Day,
Audenlea Manse,
Blue Mountians, Sydney, Australia

April Falls

The scent of freshly cooked lamb in rosemary and red wine lingered through the living area, causing my stomach to rumble in anticipation. The table was set with napkins, wine glasses, the best silverware and candelabras; the lights were dimmed to a low haze, like the sun slipping behind the horizon before twilight. A cool summer breeze cruised gently through the back door from the grey gums beyond the patio; all was quiet except for the mid-summer crickets, which sang to the setting sun in a pink painted sky.

The evening was perfect.

I paced through the kitchen like an impatient house-pet at meal time, looking for any final patches on the wooden benches that I had neglected to spot clean already, or any premature washing up that I had missed in the last three meanderings around the dining area. All was clean and tidy…perfectly so. I pressed my floral seasonal dress with the palms of my hands, admiring the way it sat firmly beneath my bust-line, and then fell lightly to my knees, impressed by the natural brown glow that kissed my smooth legs each summer.

I glanced at the mantel clock in the lounge room again. Hugh was forty-five minutes late for dinner. This wasn't completely out of the ordinary: except that he usually called when he left work late, or if the traffic was heavy. I tried his mobile number again, and was greeted by a message indicating that Hugh's phone was either out of service range, or switched off.

I knew that I often worried unnecessarily. I often assumed the worst of outcomes, based on little supporting evidence. I also knew that Hugh would arrive, or call, as soon as he could, knowing how prone I was to unwarranted concern on his behalf.

I smiled to myself, imagining Hugh's deep brown eyes dancing in amusement as he waltzed through the door and I chastised him for being late to dinner. Hugh always visited me after work and stayed for dinner. It had been my idea that we live separately before we were married. But not for long; in one month and one day, Hugh and I will be married. Until then, we agreed that I would live in the comfortable old colonial house that we had mortgaged together just three months ago on our engagement, and Hugh would move in after our wedding.

While I knew Hugh would have liked us to have started living together earlier, and perhaps waited much too long to have gotten engaged, I couldn't explain why I had insisted otherwise. Hugh was kind, patient, gentle and every parent's dream son-in-law. I loved his community dedication, hard work ethics and high morals. He was gifted at almost everything he tried his lean fingers at.

Nevertheless, I was hesitant to give myself completely to him or any other man; and I felt I had to do things the *right* way this time: getting married *before* committing myself heart and soul and body. There were things from my past that would haunt me forever if I did things otherwise…things I hoped I would never have to tell another living soul about.

The mantel clock struck again and I lurched back from my furrowing. I pondered calling Hugh's family-owned printing company, a successful publishing house, which Hugh's parents had built and worked for forty years, and that Hugh managed and directed personally. But I knew that he would have already phoned if he had stayed late.

I stared longingly at the roast, still warming in the oven, wary at the thought that the meat would dry out, and my efforts would be in vain. I knew that Hugh would be grateful for my efforts; ever supportive, and ever uplifting. I wanted this night to be memorable, to toast that the wait to begin our lives together was almost over.

I propped myself in front of my laptop, hoping for a distraction by working on a fictional piece I was devising, and determined not to allow my wallowing over the scorched meal to ruin an otherwise perfectly fine evening.

An hour passed. I closed the screen with a sigh; no luck there. Then I tucked my legs beneath my crumpled dress before letting my white-strapped shoes fall to the wooden floor with two loud claps. I gazed anxiously at the magnificent blue sapphire on my left hand, admiring its crystal clear perfection, and the way the white gold band sat flawlessly around the narrow of my finger.

A slow knock resounded at the front door and I leapt to answer it, pushing aside the scolding that I would give to Hugh after I had taken him in my arms for my usual evening embrace.

I felt the heart-warming smile on my lips fade to a taut line at the sight of Mr and Mrs Grady, Hugh's parents. Mr Grady stood beneath the porch, anguish funnelling his facial features together as though they were going to implode and with his arm absently placed around his wife's erratically moving shoulders. Mrs Grady wouldn't even look at me: her eyes and nose were veiled by a tear-soaked handkerchief.

I stared at the conservative but usually spirited couple, knowing that etiquette obliged me to invite them inside. A hole had begun to rip at the insides of my heart: the feeling you get when you don't realise in halves what they had come to deliver. I could not ask them to come in; I did not want to hear their explanation; I could not even ask them the question.

"April, dear April," Mr Grady began, his eyes searching the sandstone stoop for an incomprehensible rationalization. "We thought we would deliver the news in person...I know Hugh would have wanted as much."

His use of past tense was more than I could bear to hear...and more than I needed to confirm what I already knew. I also knew that Hugh's family were founded upon a deep spiritual faith; but they appeared as void and as hopeless as an effigy.

"There's been an accident," Mr Grady's ageing voice wavered as his deep familiar brown eyes travelled to meet mine. Utter despair journeyed through his deeply lined face, his mouth dipping to form a half moon crest. "He won't be visiting today: he's already gone home."

And I knew at that moment my penance had begun: *an eye for an eye*. One life taken from me, for the life I had taken two years before.

Part 1

Signs of the End of an Age

1. Origins

Autumn, Two Years Later

He had always been there. He, who had created the Heavens and the Earth, had always been there: sometimes I just forgot that He was…

Commuting home from the city was always the longest part of my day. I resented the rowdy passengers and school children; the stench of over-worked sweaty business men and women in suits; the constant stop-start of the engine at each station, and the shoving of human bodies as they jostled for a place to sit or stand in the crowded carriage.

By the time the train began the climb up the hills on the north-western outskirts of the city, the train had become void of human voices, just the steady rhythm of the carriage wheels rotating around somewhere beneath me, keeping me patient until my station. Houses had become scarce and the rugged bush terrain had begun to creep up against the edges of the train-tracks as though desperate for human company.

I was in a mindless daydream when my mobile startled me into reality, *Scissor Sisters* blearing out at me and earning me a glare from the purple-haired lady sitting across from me, who mumbled something about "*rude young people today*".

I squinted at the woman, taking offence at her jibe, because at twenty-two, I no longer considered myself as a "*young person*" anymore. Teenagers were young people. People who hadn't endured what I already had.

"Hi, Alex, what's up?" I drawled.

"Are you still on the train, April?"

"Yes."

"Seriously, it's almost seven-thirty! Are you nearly home?"

I gazed out of the carriage window at the looming shadows beyond the brush.

"Yes, Alex."

I huffed loudly and hoped my voice portrayed the rolling of my eyes, which, when stationary again, met the cold stare of Purple Hair opposite.

"There should be laws that prevent people from getting home after six on a Friday!" Alex objected.

"You know that if I leave work after five-thirty, I get the slow train."

"Who has deadlines on a Friday anyway?"

"I'm a journalist, my life consists of deadlines."

"You need a different job."

Here it comes.

"Well, it's Friday night," Alex hedged.

"As you've just reminded me."

"April, come on. Stop playing so hard to get! I'm your sister. Some of the girls and I just want you to have some fun! Like the old days."

The *old days*: the days before the accident. What did she want me to say to that? I sighed, hoping she could hear how taught my voice had become and back off.

"I have a major feature article to write, Alex. I need to ring cousin Joel and see what contacts he made at the German film festival last year. I need an A-Lister to interview to keep my job next year."

"It's Friday night for heaven's sake, April. Can't it wait till Monday for once?" Alex persisted. "I mean: you could humour those that care about you and say yes every now and then. That's all I'm asking," she pressed, suppressing what sounded like a huff herself.

I drew in a deep breath and slowly released it, letting all my impatience drain between my teeth with the breath. "What's doing?"

"You'll come?" She rushed on before giving me a chance to answer. "Nothing big. Just me and some of the girls are going out to a movie. It won't be late and you can drive."

I moaned long and loud, like a steam train running on empty and climbing a steep slope. "What movie?"

"The latest Lucas Forrester film. He's said to be even more Greek god-like in this one – like it's possible!" she screeched.

I flinched and held the phone away from my ear like it had just slapped me. "So, you've become one of the cult followers too?"

"I'm the damn president! So you'll come?" Alex giggled. "Hey, and Andy left another message on the machine," she offered hesitantly, her tone dropping a notch.

I instantly grabbed at my stomach as though I was about to lurch from my chair: his very name caused a metallic taste to form in my mouth and my belly to feel immediately ill.

"No, I won't go; I'll wait till it's out on Blu Ray. And if Andy doesn't leave me alone, I'm going to take out an AVO. For real this time. I can't believe he's still trying to contact me after all this time."

I felt my body tremble like I was in the aftermath of a windstorm and blinked away the memories that stalked me like a stray cat.

"You broke his heart good and well, April," Alex said, proceeding cautiously.

"Don't you *dare* defend him! You have no idea what I went through for him!" I gasped so loudly that Purple Hair glared like a Siamese cat about to pounce on her prey.

Alex didn't know the quarter of it. And she never would. No one would.

"Oh, that's really grown-up of you, Apes."

"I am not a pre-historic animal. Please don't call me one."

I held the phone out from my ear again as Alex sulked into the receiver. "I'll see you at home…party pooper."

Why did she have to mention Andy? Why couldn't she just have erased the message and I would never have known? How did he get my new number anyway? Couldn't he just disappear once and for all!

I sighed again as I involuntarily recalled an old proverb my Dad had always said when I was a kid. It's the one he used to say after I had confessed my guilt over being caught doing something I knew I shouldn't have been: reminding me that we all fall down sometimes. Unfortunately, I seemed to have fallen further than most…

I closed my eyes and sheepishly allowed an image of Lucas Forrester's emerald green eyes drift to the forefront of my vision. His face was in every media publication or on every screen I looked at and I was finding the image as forgetful as the sweet taste of chocolate at Easter.

The known human world had been given to fits of hyperventilation since the tall, tousle-haired Lucas Forrester had graced the screen stage with his presence in this blockbuster saga my sister had spoken of. He had been twenty-two when he had landed the lead roll in the first of the blockbusters and was an overnight success, landing him on the top of every "most popular male" and best actor awards in the media globe. You only had to glance at a magazine stand to experience the global impact his stardom had created.

Forrester had been acclaimed for his outstanding portrayal of several literary characters and received industry recognition as Britain's most outstanding screen talent in a decade. The trail of crazed followers multiplied daily, heightened by the release of each new film.

From my entertainment research the now twenty-eight year old Forrester continued to release features and sign film contracts at a rate previously unparalleled by an actor as young. His success could only be admired, whatever you thought of Forrester on-screen or off.

And here was I: feeling past my used date before I'd even hit twenty-five! Talk about living in the afterglow…

I had always wanted to write. Since my fingers could curl around a coloured pastel I would drift off into another place on the page, taking me wherever those words were travelling. Throughout school I won every writing competition and book review running. It was the one thing I was certain that I loved and the one niche in life I knew for certain I was good at.

And then the highlight of my early career happened: I won the National Young Writers Fiction Award, scoring myself a publishing contract for the short work of fiction I had entered and won. I was interviewed for all the major newspapers in the country and fulfilled another dream in the making: I met my favourite Australian author of choice in a live-recorded documentary.

I soared for the twelve months following the acclaim, earning myself a place in the best Creative Writing/Journalism course in the country, and a cadetship with News Limited in Sydney.

I thought the piece of fiction I wrote in Year 12 would launch me into some kind of creative frenzy, expelling book after book for as long as I lived.

But writer's block is real.

Or maybe it's just life that's real: I know a part of me had died that day when I'd taken another life.

Creative energy, at least where fiction writing is concerned, doesn't quite work on demand for everyone, every time. I can't quite seem to separate the real from the non-real.

I haven't been able to write another book.

And I worry.

I worry that my creativity and time to succeed, along with Hugh and that small part of me, has all been and gone.

Audenlea Manse, Blue Mountains

At nine 'o' clock the following morning my phone rang.

"April? Are you going to get that?" Alex called from the lounge room. "It could be Andy returning your call."

My knuckles clenched and paled in frustration.

Do I answer the phone or not? Was it going to be Joel or Andy? My palms began to sweat as the mobile continued to buzz.

"Just pick it up and tell him not to call again or you'll call the cops," Alex called from the lounge room.

"That's what I told him years ago!" I returned, staring at my phone like it was about to explode.

"April Falls speaking," I announced breathlessly, hoping I would hold my nerves together either way.

"April Falls? Listen, my name's Gerry Ottoman. I spoke with Joel Falls today, your cousin, I think. Anyway, he told me you're looking for a subject to write about and emailed me copies of some of your university works. And that *book* you wrote in high school . . ."

I inhaled sharply, feeling my eyes dilate in alarm at Joel's prerogative.

"...and you know, I think this could be just the thing Lucas needs right now, you know a bit of...*sound* publicity. He's had some flack recently, bollocks really despite his success rate growing every day and all—"

"Lucas?" I interrupted. "Lucas who?"

"Forrester of course! I'm his agent, naturally. I met your cousin at the German film festival last year. Fabulously talented director, for a small budget film an' all, your cousin Joel. Anyway, I'm sure we can work at an angle that his publicist and I are happy with. We'd like to publish your work on Lucas here, in Britain."

"My work on Lucas?" I repeated, holding my fist to my heart in case it failed on me completely.

"But listen, you must understand, Lucas is a very busy man right now. He has gigs here, there and everywhere...and I mean *everywhere*! He's in between filming and has major publicity do's at the moment. Which means you won't be able to talk with him so much as...*observe* him. You can research as much as possible, you know, we'll give you a list of contacts and that sort of thing; you know we want people from his past and all sorts of people who can sing his praises, remind the public why they like him so much, you know? Let them see more of the *conservative* private side of Lucas, and all. So we'll tell you what you can and can't publish, what angle to spin the work from, so to speak. And one more thing...April?"

I tapped on my chest twice to make sure I was still alive and not dreaming...I would have to write a piece of literature so compelling as to leave there no option but to have the truth, the whole truth and nothing but the truth told, no matter what the research revealed. Lucas Forrester couldn't be in that much trouble with the media...could he?

"April?"

"Yes, I'm here," I said finally.

I squeezed the band on my left ring finger with a force that made me flinch, desperately wanting to know what the man who had given me this ring three years ago would advise me to do right now. My flippant heart knew with certainty before my logical mind could argue.

"Okay, Mr. Ottoman, you have yourself a writer," I accepted.

"You know, April, you might just be the answer that we, at camp Forrester, have been looking for. You see, we couldn't have some half-crazed journalist running around after Lucas, could we? We won't have to worry about you at all. You'll be invisible. Forrester won't even know you're there. We're expecting you this Thursday evening at Heathrow Airport," Ottoman announced matter-of-factly.

Evidently, this was not a man who ever heard "no". Or much of anything other than his own voice!

<u>*Summer, 1859, rural Gloucester, England*</u>
<u>*Sir Walter Finnegan, last Earl of Erravilla Court*</u>

The beginning is always the best place to start: for it reveals the truth behind all things to come: the perspective that is found only at a later time, in contemplation of days gone by.

The beginning was our wedding.

I remember standing beneath the pergola of Erravilla's majestic green lawns, surrounded by a thousand English summer roses and warmed through by the light breeze blowing in from beyond the pine forest. I had arrived by carriage the day before, after alighting from the ferry at Hollyhead in Wales. The boat trip had only taken a few hours from Dublin, across the choppy seas that separated the two islands.

I met her briefly upon my arrival the day before. She looked but a child compared to me. I was told she was in fact legal: she having turned eighteen one month before. The same day I had received the post message asking for my assistance.

And here I was, about to wed the lass. I was fourteen years her senior; and looked every one of those years and more. For though hers had been a fine upbringing, mine had been fraught with hard work, long days and early mornings, and barely two coins to scratch together.

The decision to respond to the letter I had received had been a heart-wrenching choice, but a swift one none the less. For, though I was planning on proposing to my own Rosie from county Galway in Ireland, on the great island that was home, I had nothing to give to her; nothing that we could call home, except for the barns I slept in during harvest time on the potato plantations.

Although she was the love of my heart, I knew that Rosie could do better than the likes of me. She never accepted this notion, however, even as she tearfully bid me farewell from the boardwalk of the Dublin jetty. The letter had said little other than that I was to inherit a stable property in rural London,

England, regrettably, as the sole surviving relative of one Sir Harrison Bishop, Earl of Erravilla Court.

I had responded immediately, initially thinking that upon the death of my distant relative, I should inherit enough finances to ferry Rosie across soon after, where we would be married and live out our happier and more refined lives together. But alas, the correspondence had indicated none other than a conditional inheritance: that I was in fact to wed the sole surviving daughter of the terminally ill Earl of Erravilla.

My naïve and evil mind immediately conspired to plot a civil divorce proceeding when the time seemed fit; and to take my rightful share of the inheritance back to county Galway and marry Rosie as planned.

The vows were issued and I placed a chaste kiss upon the cheeks of my new bride, who did not seem at all at odds with the marriage proceedings. However, my initial memories of Miss Maisy Bishop, thereafter Mrs Walter Finnegan, were of a quiet young woman, who smiled bashfully each time I happened to have to look upon her to recite my vows before the Good Reverend of Canterbury. Her father had smiled a strangely shaded grimace as the two unique gold bands were placed upon our fingers. A strange pinching sensation followed, as though the ring was resizing itself to match my finger-width perfectly.

Innocent that she was, Miss Maisy Bishop had aspired for nothing more than her God-given station required of her: to be married as soon as possible and to provide an heir apparent for Erravilla Court. The estate was her ancestral legacy, passed down through her father, and now her husband. I barely felt any guilt at what was to come for the girl; maintaining only a thought for my sweet Rosie of Ireland.

I chaperoned my prized wife for the duration of the ceremony and festivities that were held at the large property; far greater an economic treasure than I could have imagined. My evil mind plotted further about ways in which I could ferry

Rosie across to the Court, in the guise of hired help until such a time as we could be together. At least she would see out her days in comfort.

I delayed the inevitable for as long as possible, waiting until my expectant bride's eyelids were almost closed before taking her up to the bridal suite on the second floor. My plan had worked indeed: Maisy's eyelids had closed before I had to follow through on my legal duties...

In no time at all, I would be rightfully bestowed upon with the title Earl of Erravilla Court. Until then, I had decided, I would refuse all marital obligations with the stranger who was now my wife. There would be no union until I legally held that inheritance.

2. Erravilla Court

Current Day: St Petersburg, Russia

Emerus Forrester

I placed the empty shot glass back on the ledge of the bar a little firmer than was perhaps necessary, and ordered another Russian Twist.

One more for the road and no more.

I'd need something to keep me company, and I'd learnt long ago that nothing warmed a man like a shot of Russian Whiskey.

Eleven p.m. It was still early for the Russians, even though everyone at home would be in bed by now on a Thursday night.

Another blonde sidled up to me at the bar and held up a finger to the barman to indicate that she would have one of whatever I was drinking. She placed a daring arm around my shoulder and I examined her from the corner of my eye as the barman placed two shots before us. I held the petit glass up in salute before tilting my head back and drowning the fiery liquid quickly, shaking my head as it burned into the pit of my stomach.

She placed her empty glass down on the ledge at the same time as me and smiled triumphantly. *These Russian women sure knew how to drink.* The blonde was the fourth who'd shared a drink with me this evening, each one taking the same approach to the lone Englishman at the bar; and each one leaving in the same manner. Women were the same the world over. I'd learnt long ago that they all wanted one thing, and it wasn't to give you their heart. And only to warm your bed if it led to them getting something financial from you.

"You are English, no?" she began, sliding her finger across my jaw-line before allowing it to linger at the nape of my neck-tie. "A business man?"

Another gold digger.

"I am Sonja," she announced boldly, loosening the knot in my tie a little.

Sure. They were all called Sonja around here.

"It's nice to meet you, *Sonja*." I'd play along for a short while; let them have their five minutes. Besides, sometimes the company was better than drinking alone.

The brazen blonde eyed me critically. She knew I had called her bluff. "And you are?"

"Emerus."

"Yah! You are the man from the paper," she said, her English suddenly becoming more fluent. "You are very important man."

I laughed outright at her suggestion and watched as her eyes grew wide with genuine interest, as though she'd just swung a round at a slot machine and come up a winner.

"I wouldn't go that far," I laughed, indicating to the bartender that I would go one more round.

"Yah, I have read about you. You are the Forrester man. You deal with very…" She lowered her eyelids and stared becomingly into my eyes. "…Big…" She then traced the collar of my shirt and ran her blood-red fingernail down behind my tie, the entire way to my belt, where I swiftly caught her hand and jerked it away. "…Fish."

I thought of the meeting I had finalised with the Russian Ambassador an hour ago in the restaurant upstairs. Another successful project underway. I held up the shot and saluted my companion for the final time, slamming the glass down upon the ledge and nodding as I stood to leave. She made a move to protest as I placed more than enough Ruble on the bench before me. She eyed the currency with intrigue and smiled as I walked through the double doors.

I marvelled at the architectural brilliance of the eighteenth Century European city, a unique masterpiece of historical inspiration, and my favourite European city for that reason.

I watched my icy breath appear in a white mist before me as I held up my arm to hail a taxi for the airport. No more drinks tonight: I had a date with home.

<u>The Atlantic Ocean</u>
<u>Destination: London, England</u>

<u>April Falls</u>

I run and I walk from You; but You always find me…

"Dad, Dad! This is the actor I told you about, the one I'm going to write my piece work on," I said, unable to hide the excitement in my voice. I grabbed my father's arm in case he really hadn't heard me. I knew he must have because the snowy-haired man across the isle glared at me, again.

We were on the Singapore leg of our flight to London, from Sydney. What was with older people glaring at me anyway?

My father glanced over the top of his spectacles, down his broad tanned nose, and squinted at the small television screen in front of me. This was the third time in half an hour that I'd managed to interrupt his perusal of client data on his laptop.

"Yes, well, he's a fine looking man, April," my father mused, clearly not interested, but he seemed hardly annoyed by my interruptions.

"You have no idea who he is, do you Dad?"

He shook his head in mock defeat. "Sorry, precious. If it's any consolation, he doesn't look like the conservative-looking type you usually go for."

By "usually go for", he meant Hugh…

I stiffened at his remark and he placed a hand on my wrist. "Even if he was, you'd never approve. Okay, no more interruptions. I promise."

"It is nice to see a smile on my daughter's beautiful face at long last," he said, holding my gaze momentarily. Before returning to his work he bravely allowed his eyes to linger momentarily on the Sapphire ring on my finger, which I twisted with my thumb self-consciously.

I managed a half smile as Dominic Falls lightly kissed my forehead, pushed his spectacles up his nose a notch and continued to examine his files. My father never seemed annoyed by my strange behaviours, even when the rest of the world seemed to be. I glanced across the isle to where the hard-lipped man had begun to snore softly, like the warming up of a tried and tested engine.

My father would say that there were no such things as coincidences. But I found it strange all the same that my father and I happened to both be flying to the United Kingdom at the same time, both for business purposes. I had not been on an aeroplane since I was seventeen, five years ago; and had not travelled with my father since I was eight years old. I had definitely never flown Business class before.

It made sense, however, that we booked seats together; and my father, who flew regularly, never flew "cattle" class, as he called the Economy class. Dad believed that everything was for a reason: part of a greater plan that we mere mortals could never comprehend. I hoped he was right, that there was a rhyme and reason to this great and potentially risky adventure I was embarking on. There certainly hadn't seemed any rhyme or reason for Hugh's death; or for the Hell I had endured with Andy…

I decided to leave my father in peace for the remaining nine or so hours of our British Airways flight and settled back into my seat to watch the first in-flight film with a sly smile weaving itself across my lips. The film just happened to be the newest release for Britain's infamous new acting talent: the same film I'd told Alex I'd see at a later date. And here I was not only seeing the film before it had been released on Blu Ray, but on my way to interview him! *No such thing as a coincidence?*

Still absently fiddling with the ring on my left hand, I wanted to pinch myself for the fifteenth time today at my incredible fortune. I was beginning to wonder, ever so slightly, whether I was purely excited about writing the potential story of my life, as I had been telling myself for a week now; or whether I was becoming just a little overwhelmed at the thought of meeting Lucas Forrester in person.

<u>Heathrow Airport, London</u>

Parting with my father was harder than I had imagined it would be. I had known that my father would be too taken with his work to visit me during his short stay and so I had not even asked. He had initially offered to wait with me until my ride arrived, but I had refused. This was a step I had to take on my own. No more safety nets.

I had never travelled on my own before, nor did I know my way around London. But this did not frighten me. And yet an unidentifiable feeling of fear had gripped me as I watched my father stride away from me, out into the brisk London air and hail a taxi.

Standing there alone in the baggage lounge, I felt an overwhelming sense of danger. I was used to living alone at home now, and knew that this was not a sense of *physical* danger.

And then, like the gusty westerly wind back home, the knowledge swept straight through me: if I was to embrace this new and unknown chapter in my life – to take my first real steps forward in twenty-six months – there were chains that needed to be severed. Every decision in these next few months would significantly alter my future. I was me – me alone – again for the first time in years. There was no one here with me anymore from the past – just the fumes left behind from my father's taxicab.

I decided at that moment to remove the ring that should have left my hand two years ago, gently laying it inside its silky pouch and tucking it deep into the safe recesses of my handbag.

Gazing ahead, I saw my future waiting for me. It was as though the past had handed me over to the future, like a father offers over his daughter on her wedding day. Through hazy eyes I noticed a shortish man holding up a sign with my name neatly written on it. I swiped at my eyes with the back of my hand and managed a shaky smile. I do not know how much of this private moment the man had witnessed. He simply nodded.

I closed the gap between the stranger and me with several easy strides, realising that he would not know me by sight. He acknowledged me again with a curt nod upon my approach, folded the sign and placed it inside his suit jacket. The slightly balding gentleman was dressed as a driver of his station would be: in a grey suit and outdated wide tie. His poker face would have disturbed me had I not seen the shadow of kindness in his faded smoky-grey eyes.

"Miss Falls, I presume? I'm Erravilla Court's House Master, Mr Urland Chisholm," he said holding his unusually large hands out to take my luggage. "Will this be all today, or is there more to be collected?" He tilted his head ever so slightly to one side and peered around me as though expecting another pile of cases.

"It's nice to meet you, Mr Chisholm. This will be all, thank you."

I was pleased with myself at how lightly I had packed for an extended trip. I did plan, of course, to replace my outdated wardrobe during my stay. I suppressed a smile at the memory of Alex, as she had begged me to bring her back her own latest London wardrobe after she had heard about the retail "research" I was planning on doing here.

We began to head out of London and a sudden panic overwhelmed me. "Mr Chisholm? Mr Chisholm, you are going the wrong way! I'm to stay at Ms Mary-Anne Brothwell's apartment in London central."

The old man's warm grey eyes met mine in the rear view mirror. "I'm sorry, Miss Falls, but there has been a change of plans. I'm to take you directly to Mr Forrester's estate out of London. I was under the impression that Mr Gerry Ottoman had informed you of this?"

"No! He certainly has not. Why must I go there now? *I* was under the impression that Lucas Forrester was out of town for a few days."

"He is, Miss Falls. But Ms Brothwell has relatives staying at her apartment," Mr Chisholm's calm voice replied.

"At her apartment? I was told the relatives were staying at her house! Where am I to stay?" I asked, finding it difficult to breathe as the anxiety grew by the second.

"It is my understanding that you are to stay at Erravilla until Mr Lucas Forrester returns."

"What's Erravilla?" I asked bluntly.

"Why, it's the Forrester estate in rural Gloucester," he replied matter-of-factly.

I inhaled a large breath to steady my heart palpitations. "And then where am I to go, Mr Chisholm?"

I had made it perfectly clear to *Mr* Gerry Ottoman that I was not going to stay with Forrester.

I let out a deep breath. No use shooting the messenger. I would have to bide my time to speak with Ottoman and demand he find an alternative arrangement.

As we headed out of London I was somewhat glad to be leaving the city, if only for a short period of time, and the busyness and emptiness that often came with large cities. Driving through the outskirts of an almost ever-grey British sky in London and approaching the suddenly sparse countryside of wild grass and hedges, low-lying stone fences and sheep farms, I was fondly reminded of the previous two visits I had had to Britain.

I recalled an image of my vivacious mother, born in Brighton on the southern coast of England and who had immigrated to Australia in her twenties. Heather Canon had been the black sheep of her family and had flown the English nest in search of something more exciting than her rather ordinary, conservative parents and two sisters. My young mother had met the debonair entrepreneur Dominic Falls at an inter-church fundraiser, which his business had financially supported at the time, and the two had apparently been inseparable.

Marrying hastily, "rather too hastily," my paternal grandmother had confided to me some years past; my mother had been thirty and my father thirty-five when I was born. Alex had been a surprise, eighteen months later. "Both of them had been thrilled," my grandmother's crimson voice echoed through my memory.

I smiled at the image of my rather stoic father in comparison, whose business had taken off rapidly and began taking him around the world for weeks at a time. My mother, still feeling young and desiring more children, became isolated and withdrawn with him away so frequently. By the time I was five my mother had fled the family home with Alex and me in tow.

My father never completely recovered from our desertion, and although still enthralled with his work, has never been settled enough to remarry, despite the occasional short-term relationship. I knew he still blamed himself for the divorce, and for the fact that my mother had remarried so quickly after the split.

I closed my eyes at the memory of my mother on her second wedding day, the only one from the year that I turned seven; and then the memory of the day my youngest sister was born, four years later.

Urland Chisholm and I had been travelling along a narrow gravelled road for miles now through the flat Cotswold countryside. We were somewhere between Oxford and Gloucester, closer to the latter if my bearings were correct. I had ventured near to this part of the country on my previous visit to England and had admired the fresh air and blue skies as much as I did now. Rows of pointed green pine trees lined the sides of the lane as we approached an intersection. I noticed that the road was worn slightly more to the left turn off as we continued straight along the occasionally bumpy road.

As we approached the end of the pine gallery, I caught my breath, as the regal Rolls Royce came to a patient halt at a grand gateway, which opened slowly for us to roll through. I gasped as the vintage car swept along a pebbled driveway, which led half a mile through a brightly manicured green lawn, lined with a low-lying hedge, and almost sang with the adorning pink, white and red springtime roses.

"She's a beauty, is she not?" Mr Chisholm caught my eye and boldly winked at me in the car's rear view mirror. His voice suddenly cut through my reverie and forced me to respond.

"Yes, indeed, Mr Chisholm, breathtaking," I replied.

The Rolls had pulled to a stop in front of a wide flight of stone steps, leading up to a magnificent set of oak doors, flagged by two white stone Greek statues and bordered by a trellis of climbing red English roses.

Urland Chisholm had already retrieved my cases, opened my door and beckoned to me at the bottom of the short staircase with an outstretched arm.

"Welcome to Erravilla Court, Miss Falls," the House Master said simply, the ghost of a smile shimmering across his aged features. "Mr Forrester is not expected home for a few days. Mr Gerry Ottoman has asked me to leave you a copy of your schedule, which I have placed upon your desk in your suite."

In my suite?

"Thank you, Mr Chisholm," I returned, also noting the word *schedule* and intending to return to it after I had finished taking in the remainder of the House. "How long has Mr Forrester lived here?"

"Mr Forrester invested in Erravilla Court, a deceased estate at the time, about three years ago, Miss Falls," he responded, offering no further information. It was clearly not going to be an easy task to elicit much information from Urland Chisholm.

"And when was the house built?" I asked, not intending to sound nosey as I lifted my eyes to drink in the magnificent three-storey grey and white sandstone residence.

"I believe Erravilla was built circa 1604, Miss Falls," he said placing my luggage by the entrance and pressing with both forearms against the centre. Then he nudged the doors wide open, revealing a spacious parlour, complete with low hanging chandelier and a wide, prominent wooden staircase.

Once again I attempted to restrain the gasp that escaped from my lips as he began to lead me up the winding staircase, allowing myself to filter off some of the angst as I examined the ascending row of modern artwork that lined the supporting wall of the stairs. I allowed my imagination to come to conclusions about the history, significance and genius behind the strange joining of history and modernity that adorned the great house.

Was this Forrester's doing? If so, I admitted with slight reluctance, I had a newfound admiration for the young owner, whose taste both surprised and impressed me.

"The kitchen is down the hallway off the foyer you just entered, should you need anything before dinner," Mr Chisholm offered. "You are free to wander any room of the house which is not locked. Breakfast is at eight o' clock."

The House Master ushered me directly up to the third floor, across a wide landing to a set of large white wooden doors, which he promptly opened and strode through.

I could only imagine that a penthouse apartment at a prominent hotel in Sydney would not have captivated the eye of its beholder as this suite caught mine. The room was completely modern with sunflower coloured walls, large and exquisitely laced curtains which hung, tied and ribboned, from the fringes of the cathedral height ceilings, to the warm coloured carpeted floors. The curtains framed the corners of the two far walls, which were glass from floor to cornice, revealing a panoramic view of more rolling green lawns and immaculate gardens, framed by a dense pine forest, and shadowed by a large, setting orange sun, which cast shadows across the landscape as it continued to descend behind the horizon as I watched.

Surely no man could depict a more inspiring sight as the one I held before me now…

I crossed the room and lightly touched the large red mahogany corner desk, which sat positioned in front of where the two glass panes met. A simple pile of stapled papers sat atop the desk, and my irritation flared anew as I comprehended the *schedule* left for me by Gerry Ottoman.

I pushed Ottoman out of my mind momentarily as I came to terms with the beautiful surrounds where I was to "*do my work*" and spend my free time. I felt a twinge of guilt at my sudden longing to stay in this moment forever and never have to leave it. I wanted to lock myself in time, my first conscious feeling in over two years of really feeling alive, and revelling in the fact. For a moment it seemed I never wanted to return to anywhere that would remind me of anything past. Just to stay right here, where no one could reach me.

It was then that I remembered I was not alone and spun around as I realised for the second time today that a very private piece of me had been shared, unrolled like a table dressing and put on display.

But as I faced the entrance, Urland Chisholm was gone. I didn't know when he had left, as silently as the mist rolling in across the orchard below. A surge of relief washed through me and I turned to once again behold the setting English sun, only to encounter a hazy twilight that remained in its wake.

I closed the curtains, then searched for a light switch, and realised that the remaining two walls were adorned with tasteful petit lamps, which Mr Chisholm must have switched on before he left. A large mantel clock hung above an open fireplace, which framed an array of lightly burning flames.

Six o'clock.

A wave a fatigue suddenly overwhelmed me as I made my way over to a grand four-poster bed at the far end of the room. Allowing my head to rest upon the large cushions beneath my body, I gave in to the deep weariness.

I woke, immediately remembering where I was, and a smile ran across my lips as I recalled that my fantasy evening had not been a dream. The mantel clock read ten o' clock, and although I was still tired and probably suffering from jet lag, I was momentarily too stimulated by my surroundings to continue sleeping. The fire still burned well below the mantel. I noted that someone, probably Mr Chisholm, wondering why I had not made an appearance at dinner, had re-stoked the flames.

I felt warm, but uncomfortable in the clothes I had now been wearing for two days and decided to venture through a small archway near my bed, which turned out to be a walk-in wardrobe, larger than my dining room back in Australia. A second archway led through to an ensuite bathroom, complete with two French windows, a large corner spa, laundry chute and a suede lounge suite.

Whatever am I going to use a lounge suite in a bathroom for?

I ran a warm bubble bath and relaxed for a short eternity, soaking up the sweet aromas of the bath crystals. I could definitely do this forever.

I decided that it was safe to don pyjamas and a dressing gown to venture through the house at this hour. After all, no one was home except Mr Chisholm, and maybe a cook or maid – I really had no experience with the functions of a house such as this or who lived here on a regular basis.

As quietly as possible I made my way back down the elaborate stairwell, my light step only landing on two squeaky floorboards on the way. I padded lightly across the cold tiled floor like a jaded Cheshire cat and realised too late that I had forgotten my slippers. The wide hallway off the foyer was lit with wall lamps the same as in my room and led directly to the large, industrial style kitchen beyond another grand oak door.

I found the fridge and poured myself a glass of milk, heating it in the microwave before continuing to explore the fridge for a sign of leftovers. I discovered a large pot of beef stew and served myself a portion, also heating it before perching myself at a low wooden bench.

The stew was unlike any I had ever eaten and I suddenly found myself looking forward to breakfast. I wondered how long it had been since I had sat down to a heart-warming home-cooked meal. It surely beat the bland sandwiches I had become accustomed to at Audenlea.

I washed, dried and replaced the bowl and eating utensils and then stood in the middle of the kitchen ready to down the remainder of my milk, when the large oak door swung open, allowing me to be momentarily lit up like a deer in headlights. The sudden blinding light startled me, and I dropped the glass and its remaining contents from my hand before it reached my mouth.

3. Star-Struck

About me: I am the worst sinner of them all…

"Shoot!" I let out a cry and hunkered to the floor balancing on my feet to start collecting the larger pieces of broken glass. "I'm so sorry Mr Chisholm, if you just direct me to a mop and broom, I'll clean this mess up right away."

"April Falls?" a strangely familiar voice interrupted my hasty glass gathering. "Don't move. I'll turn on the light."

Before I could protest and beg him to just leave me be in my utter embarrassment, a light flickered on and I craned my neck up slowly to lock eyes with the one, the only, Lucas Forrester: *who was not supposed to be here*!

He looked like he'd just stepped out of a runway shoot for the latest *Spence & Carriage* catalogue as he stood there raking a hand through his tousled hair.

I couldn't have looked worse: my hair hung in a tangled mess around my shoulder blades; I was wearing an old pair of pyjamas and a worn dressing gown, with no shoes; and was surrounded by a giant mess, which I had created in *his* kitchen. I wanted to disappear into one of the enormous cupboards behind me.

Instead, I was momentarily star-struck by the celebrity standing in all his six-foot-something glory before me: Lucas Forrester was easily as bewitching in reality as he was on screen. His bright green eyes shimmered almost translucently beneath dark eyebrows and a shock of sun-streaked brown hair. He was cleanly shaven, forcing an observer to notice his defined masculine lips and high cheekbones. A slender neck trailed down to a half-opened dark blue button-up shirt and fitted denim jeans. How did someone look like that at this hour of the night?

I looked away from him and silently scolded myself for allowing the crazed inner teenager to escape my mind for the first time in years. I knew it had been too late when I turned my face away: he had seen the brief expression cross my features. Tomorrow I would be out of a job when he realised that I was no better than the screaming horde of fans outside his London apartment.

I had lost the one thing I had been priding myself on for years: the ability to stay *professional* under all circumstances. And in one moment of weakness I had thrown it all away!

"Just don't move, okay? You don't have shoes on," he observed as though aware of the fact for the first time and slightly mystified at the same time. He stood there in thought before slowly stepping through the milk and glass until his feet, leather shoe clad were within close proximity of my still fumbling hands.

Without glancing up I handed him a pile of larger glass fragments, which he took and placed on the ledge above my head.

"What do you want me to do?" I asked, still staring at my horrifyingly hairy toes.

"Um, you need to stand up," his resonating British accent replied.

I did so very cautiously, lest I cause some other catastrophe. I fumbled with my hands, and let out a deep breath.

"Are you hurt?" he asked cautiously. He was probably worried about litigation.

"No, no, I'm fine, just a bit shaky," I replied. "I'm so sorry. I kind of slept through dinner and I didn't think anyone would hear me in the kitchen. I hope you don't mind."

The kitchen door suddenly swung open, giving me an excuse to look away from my hands. A young woman, who looked about thirty, stood in the doorway, clad in a fluffy dressing gown and slippers, and squinted into the light.

Great, another household member who I did not know existed, and I had woken her up too!

"Somethin' the ma'er, Lucas?" she asked sleepily, her broad northern English accent barely decipherable to me at this late hour.

"Ah, Geraldine, this is April Falls, who your father picked up from the airport this afternoon," he waved an arm in her direction. "April, this is Geraldine Chisholm, Urland's daughter."

"Nice to be mee'in' you, April. Did you have an acciden'?" she asked, motioning to the spilt milk covering the floor like a bleeding wound. Before I could answer she turned and left the room, muttering over her shoulder. "I'll jus' ge' the mop."

I stared after her for several moments, horridly aware that the attention would shift back to me. Lucas Forrester looked down to me, then to my bare feet and then to the remaining shards of glass scattered in front of me.

"I'm going to take you out of here," he said matter-of-factly.

"Oh, no, I want to help Geraldine clean up this mess," I fumbled, glancing up at his intimidatingly close face, frantically begging him to do nothing of the sort. "Sh- she shouldn't have to clean this up. I'm okay, really. I won't cry over the spilt milk if you don't," I fumbled, too shaken to actually find it funny.

"You don't have shoes on," he stated simply, a hint of a grin tracing the corners of his mouth. "Just hold on."

Without further warning Forrester delicately swooped over and gathered me to his chest, my legs dangling over his arm like a child sitting in a chair one size too big. I hoped to heaven that he didn't notice my sudden intake of breath as he nudged the great oak door ajar and carried me through to the hallway. He casually danced side step on the large white tiles in the hallway past Geraldine, who was armed with a mop and bucket.

"Thanks, Geraldine," Lucas said with a tilt of his blonde head.

I could only manage a faint smile of gratitude for Geraldine, who eyed me briefly and returned Lucas' nod.

My host carried me through another set of thick white French doors off the foyer and into a grand lounge room. He gently placed me before an enormous fireplace, which snaked up to the ceilings thirty feet above our heads, cradling a lively fire within its stone walls. The wall supporting the chimney was made of grey stone, and stood in perfect contrast to the modern leather lounge suit, European coffee tables, lamps, colourful Persian rugs and framed art works which decorated the room like a Sultan's Palace.

A series of glass windows ran the length of the wall several stories high and I could view an almost shimmering barricade of glass above. A beautiful German piano stood in front of an enormous window, the elaborate bordering curtains now closed for the evening.

I had been silent long enough. Masking my face with the best poker-face expression I could master, I turned around, basking my back in the warmth of the open fire, and looked Lucas Forrester directly in the eye.

"I'm April Falls, as you now know. I'm also incredibly sorry for the mess I caused back there. I had no idea I was going to be staying here and—"

I stopped abruptly as a strange smile crept over his lovely features, causing my brain to momentarily forget why it was that I had ventured into the kitchen in the first place.

"It's fine, really," his rich voice echoed from beneath the nod of his head as he spoke. "I suppose I should introduce *my*self. My name is E—"

"Whoa! You weren't just going to introduce yourself as . . ."

A broad grin swept across his bemused face.

He was toying with me! Lucas Forrester was about to introduce himself as his heart-throb alter-ego Ethan, and in the same debonair way he had done in the first *Seasons* film no less. I was done for if he ever tried that again. There would be no going back.

He laughed quietly into his chest before he continued. "You know who I am. I was just playing. So we'll skip the introductions and let's just forget about your little accident. I mean, I was to blame really, sneaking up on you like that. I was sitting in here listening to a recording of my brother's band, and heard the microwave. I'm the only one here who eats during the night and I was curious."

Forrester didn't appear to mind my disturbance. To my renewed horror he grinned in amusement, running a hand through his thick hair again. Did he think I was going to eat him out of house and home every evening after the lights went out?

"I don't usually eat at night…anymore. It's just that I slept through dinner. I think I may be slightly jet-lagged," I offered, trying my utmost to retain the poker face.

He returned a lop-sided grin and sat himself comfortably into a niche of the leather lounge, like Santa in a shopping mall, waiting for the next in line.

"So, you'll be writing some heart-winning stories about me I hear," he said, returning my gaze.

I managed a sly smile, determined to meet his appraisal as colleagues, not movie star and fan club member.

"That's the aim. My cousin Joel suggested the idea to your manager, who he'd met in Germany last year," I explained, trying to keep my voice even as I spoke of Ottoman.

Forrester nodded in acknowledgment, his eyebrows now piqued in interest, which had the affect of enlarging those already too distracting green eyes. What had I got myself into? How was I ever going to write about him from a purely professional point of view?

"Gerry said as much. He and my publicist, Mary-Anne, are interested in seeing more of your cousin's scripts." Lucas casually placed his spider-long legs onto the bench ottoman and reclined with the grace of a cheetah. "So, you're from a family of writers?"

"Just Joel and I," I said, smiling now at the thought of my rogue of a cousin, whom I didn't know whether to punch or hug at this moment for getting me into this extraordinary situation. "He's the talented one. I'm just a glorified cadet at the moment."

"Not true."

Forrester's serious tone caught me by surprise as his entire face shifted with a force that suddenly transported me to the privacy of one of his films: his eyes and lips bore the same hypnotic expression that I had viewed countless times from the screen and I became truly aware of his heightened power for the first time.

"I've read some of your stories and that book you wrote in school," he continued, a rueful smile playing upon his lips as he noted my surprise. "I wouldn't have agreed to this without doing some research of my own, you know."

The award-winning book suddenly felt like the lamest thing I'd ever done and I felt the heat surge into my cheeks.

"Forgive my ignorance, but I assumed that only managers and publicists did the, ah, leg work," I managed, unable to tear my eyes away as he lured me closer with his voice.

He responded with a loud, resonating laugh, which had the same effect on me as it would on a cinema audience; my entire being relaxed, relishing in his attention.

It dawned on me that Lucas Forrester was as much a businessman as an actor, apparently deeply involved in his work, to the core. He was not simply a pretty public face, whose life was dictated by the choices of others.

"It's not ignorance, April."

My name seemed to echo off the stone walls as it rang from his voice, as though it had been shouted, and remained the only sound in the world.

His features became knitted together in earnestness. "Most publicists and managers do that part of the work in the beginning. But now, I can be picky, and I'd rather know who is going to be following me around."

The final part caught me off guard and I wondered if he had been against the idea initially.

"I came home early to meet you, but, as you already said, you slept through dinner." A light grin crept back onto his masculine features. "I hope you've found everything to your liking?"

"Yes, thank you, everything is…"

Breathtakingly beautiful? Beyond a dream?

I held his unearthly green eyes for a moment longer before replying. "Perfectly comfortable."

A slow wide smile spread across his features again and I exhaled silently, knowing that my response had pleased him.

"Thank you again for saving my feet in there," I motioned with my head towards the thick French doors. "It's a real honour to meet you. I'll leave you to continue listening to your brother's music, and try not to make a nuisance of myself while I'm your guest. Hopefully that won't be long, either."

He stared at me suddenly, as though confused by my response. "You don't want to stay at Erravilla?"

I fumbled awkwardly, racing through the thoughts in my mind. *Of course I now wanted to stay at Erravilla! Who wouldn't?* But it just wasn't proper if I wanted respectability as a writer. If anyone found out I was here my career would end before it began!

"It's not that. I—" I swallowed hard, unable to meet his eye any longer. I couldn't believe that *I* was about to tell *Lucas Forrester* that I didn't want to stay at his home.

"You're welcome at Erravilla as long as you want, April Falls," he said.

I gave an awkward nod with my head, daring for one more moment to observe his all-too-perfect face before crossing the carpet and reaching for the filigree door handle.

My heart hammered as I took the great wooden staircase two steps at a time, streaking across the landing in a cat-like movement. Upon reaching my desk I ran my eyes over the full schedule in front of me, and held the paper to my chest. I closed my eyes offering a silent prayer of thanks that I would be able to *closely* observe Lucas Forrester, perhaps even interview him formerly.

I looked out into the darkness. I had forgotten to close the billowing curtains after twilight. From my window I noticed that my room was higher than any other, which gave me a view to the west of the entire back of the house. I could see directly through a series of glass windows, which ran the span of the western wing of the house, with smoke curtailing out of a chimney from the tiled roof just below my room.

I realised suddenly that it was the lounge room I had just left: my large glass walls were the shimmering glass I had noticed from the lounge. I could see directly into the lounge room, where the Lord of the Manor, Lucas Forrester, remained, reclining with his eyes closed, listening to his music.

Did he know that I could see him? Did he know that if he opened his eyes at this very moment he would see me, staring directly at him with the same deer-in-headlights expression he had first seen on my face?

I closed the curtains with urgency, noting that from now on, I would only open the southern curtains, which looked out onto the back lawns. How strange to design a house with such little privacy. I sat down at the desk and began typing some notes. Notes that were already beginning to depict a different Lucas Forrester to the one I had created in my head after reading the tabloids.

The fire still burned in the hearth, creating an English warmth I could not recall from my previous visits. I switched off the lamps and snuggled in under the luxurious feather down doona. Momentarily I went to remove the ring from my finger, as I had done every night for the last few years. A sudden panic overwhelmed me as I realised the ring was gone. I sat upright before remembering that I had tucked it safely away into my handbag at the airport.

I breathed a sigh of relief, allowed the ring to remain resting in its safe enclosure nearby, but gently patting the place it used to be on my finger.

I phoned Alex, not knowing whether to laugh or cry at my adventures so far; and repeatedly asked her whether I was in over my head this time. My dear sister laughed hysterically at my plight in the kitchen before telling me how jealous she was that I was living under the same roof as the recurringly labelled *World's Sexiest Man*. I knew she wasn't jealous. Alex was just being sisterly, encouraging me to lift my chin and soldier on. She never doubted my abilities. In fact, sometimes she liked to punch me when I was down just so that I learnt to soldier on even in defeat.

4. Ghosts of Erravilla Court

Emerus Forrester

I arrived early at Erravilla to catch Lucas, who I hadn't caught up with in weeks due to overlapping schedules. *Were we always this busy?* I wondered, walking in to the dining room for breakfast with the Chisholms.

"Good morning, Emerus," Mr Chisholm greeted, waving his spoon through the air. "You've just missed the morning blessing."

His daughter lowered her eyes as she always did when she addressed me. "Good morning, Mr Emerus," she said timidly.

"Urland, Geraldine," I greeted. "Not to mind, Urland."

I smiled and sat down across from them, giving a silent prayer of my own that I had survived another trip full of weird women, strange drinks and fat businessmen. Geraldine handed me the *London Times,* always careful not to make contact with me, and I set about reading the latest of English social effects.

"No Lucas this morning?" I pondered aloud.

"'e's been an' gone, Mr Emerus," Geraldine replied quietly, still not looking up to meet my inquiry.

"Been and gone?" I mused. "I thought he was coming home yesterday?"

"He came home early…to meet the guest," Geraldine replied.

"The guest?" I asked, staring over the top of the large paper.

"Yes sir, I picked her up from the airport on Thursday," Urland Chisholm replied, placing his spoon in his empty bowl.

"Her?" I asked, completely confused.

"You know…that writer from Australia," Geraldine said, peering at me from the corner of her eye.

"Her name's April. April Falls," Urland supplied.

"She's staying *here*?" I balked. "Why on earth for?"

I put the paper down harder than I had meant to. *Of all the stupid things…!*

"Why would he risk a *stranger* in the house?" I asked, almost to myself. "Has he even met her yet?"

"Yes, sir, and she made quite a *breaking* impression on him. He's told her to stay on for as long as she likes," Geraldine supplied.

I didn't even hide the frustration I felt at Lucas' impulsive behaviour. "That boy's going to get himself killed one day."

"She's hardly the axe-murderin' type from the looks o' her," Urland volunteered.

"Maybe not. But she could be the *stalking* type, Urland," I replied bluntly. "She could be anyone."

April Falls

I woke to the sound of curtains being pulled across supporting wooden rungs and the faint hum of a woman's voice. I battled my eyelids, which did not want to wake just yet. My view adjusted quickly, for the weather was overcast with a light mist. I remembered instantly where I was and smiled. The woman approached me as the clock above the mantle chimed in a sweet low lullaby. Nine o' clock.

I sat up suddenly remembering that Urland Chisholm had announced yesterday that breakfast would be served at eight. I would need an alarm clock until I broke in the jet lag.

"No need to worry, you jus' take your time," came the soft croon of a thick British accent. I recognised the chestnut-haired woman from last night and I squinted up at her in the lit room.

"Geraldine?"

The fair young woman gave me a curt smile and nod as she stood beside my bed. "Aye. I've unpacked all of your things into the robe through there." She gave a quick flick of her head indicating the walk-in robe through the archway.

Her efficiency only fuelled my embarrassment. I was a private person, not used to others handling my possessions. And I was already late for breakfast on my first day; and Geraldine had mopped up *my* spilt milk and broken glass!

"Geraldine, I am so sorry about last night…and being late for breakfast," I rambled feebly.

"Tha' wasna' las' nigh'. It's Saturday. You've been asleep for nearly two days," she chuckled, tucking a stray strand of blonde hair into the neat bun at the nape of her head. "Thare's naugh' to worry abou' though, April, you go on now and dress. Your little phone's been singing for days too. I think someone's trying to reach you. Lucas said to tell you tha' 'e's gone to London for a couple of days. 'e'll be back tomorrow."

Geraldine gave me a curt nod and left the fire-warmed room.

I reached for my phone, recalling vague recollections of *Scissor Sisters: I don't feel like dancing* and *Michael Jackson's: Thriller* playing through my mind as I had dreamt. I had several missed calls from Alex, and several more from mother. I returned Alex's amusing and nosey calls, assuring her that I had not secretly eloped with a movie star; and asked Alex to pass on the same to mother.

I spent the morning taking notes of my journey so far and observations of my new surroundings in my room before I set off towards the kitchen. Geraldine had tea and coffee brewing, as well as an array of home-baked cookies and scones. I didn't hear anyone else nearby, so I decided to head on out the back doors of the industrial kitchen and followed a dimly lit corridor. A dozen or so closed doors branched off the wide tiled walkway before I reached a flight of descending stairs, which looked far too dark and uninviting, sort of Elm Street style. Ahead lay the end of the corridor, and a narrow flight of stairs, spiralling up into a small hole in the ceiling, which reminded me more fondly of Charlie and the Chocolate Factory.

I barely fit between the iron railings as I ascended the creaking stairwell. I arrived into a long room with floorboards and an empty fireplace at one end, and a small window at the end close to the landing. Three walls were lined to the ceiling with shelves of dusty books. A desk sat in front of the barren fireplace, complete with an old wooden chair and desk lamp.

Above me the ancient looking stairwell ascended through another circular hole in the high ceiling. Maybe I was going to step through into a different land, like in the Magic Faraway Tree. I went to look out the window and saw that I was looking out from the second floor window at the far end of the old house, viewing out onto the edge of the front lawn, watching the mist retreat from the fringes of the rose garden.

The aged library was cold, unlike the other heated rooms within Erravilla's sandstone walls; and I wished that I had worn a jacket over my thin long sleeve shirt. The library was uninviting, lit only by the dull glow from the window, but looked as though it could be a place of solace and tranquillity when lit and warmed accordingly.

I decided to continue up the windy rickety stairs, holding on to the arm rails for fear that the stairs might give way beneath me at any moment and I would end up in the rabbit's burrow like Alice in her Wonderland. I was glad when my feet made contact with a stable landing. I had reached the roof of the old house, the attic, which must be on the same level as my suite. I looked out the sole window to the still mist-shrouded gardens below, seeing only the peaks of the pine trees lining the boundary of the yard, although the fog was becoming lighter by the minute.

The attic was lighter than the library had been, thanks to a series of square glass panes in the cathedral style panelled roof. It had to be the only room in Erravilla Court completely untouched since its original construction. The triangular room was as long as the library, laying safe harbour to a plethora of antique items, covered in thick dust and cobwebs, which glowed in the rays of light shooting through from the glass above.

I had only read about such places, mythical-like, holding the secrets of those who had lived in another time. I slowly wandered the length of the forgotten room, wanting to touch the once-treasured objects, but not daring to disturb them. There were boxes of stored items which seemed to contain photos, documents and diaries; a turn of the century pram, with pretty laced edges and moth-eaten, crocheted blankets; a wooden rocking horse with faded brown paint and a matted mane; a tall reading lamp, trimmed with lace and cobwebs; a vanity unit, displaying a beautiful crystal mirror; an endless amount of furniture; and personal items including a hair brush, butterfly hairpins and necklace.

There was one item that caught my attention, not because of the delicate hand carvings on the outside of the little round box, but because it seemed to be the only object with life still visible across its facade, as though it had been the last item to be placed in this crypt. It looked like some kind of ceramic music box, brightly painted in every shade able to be held by the human eye. I gently picked up the keepsake and took it back to the window for a better inspection.

I unclipped the delicate pin clasp and the lid immediately flipped open with the shrill chiming of an unfamiliar tune. The sound was eerie in the silent dimness and, after quickly examining the contents stored, I closed the lid, finding the high-pitched noise unbearable as it ricocheted off the wooden walls, like somebody was screaming to be released from within.

I hurried back down the stairs, feeling more and more like Alice as I stumbled down the narrow flight of spiral stairs, the things around me shrinking as they whizzed past, and the smell of the stagnate attic yapping at my heels.

My breath was still heavy in my throat and my heart was still trying to catch up with the pace as I quick-stepped along the corridor and through the kitchen, blowing from door to door before finally careening into a firm wall of body mass.

In an instant strong arms were around me, steadying me on my feet as they threatened to wilt beneath me from my plight. A calm breathing sounded in my ears, like the coursing of the wind as it leapt over the edge of a cliff pallet. "Whoa there! You look like the devil's after you!"

"For a second I thought he was," I mused between deep breaths. "Or maybe it was the Queen of Hearts!"

I burst out laughing, my voice sounding on the verge of mild hysteria.

It was then that I looked up to meet the stranger who held me, and my chest tightened in awe at the face looking down at me. He was familiar in a handsome way, and yet I knew I had never met this person before. The man was slightly older than Lucas and stood at about the same height, only broader. He had light brown wavy hair that fell to his shoulders like light webbing. His eyes were a piercing blue; his skin was smooth and defined around his jaw and cheeks, like Lucas'; and his skin held a slightly darker shade of olive.

"April Falls, I presume. I'm Emerus Forrester," he said releasing me tentatively and held out his hand for me to take, squeezing mine gently as I accepted the gesture. His gaze pierced me as though he were reading my very soul.

"April Falls. Nice to meet you, Emerus. Thanks for the catch," I mused, still staring at the strangely familiar face before me.

"Are you sure you're all right?" he asked after a moment. "You're shaking," he said, tightening his hold around my hand ever so slightly.

"It's just adrenaline," I replied, still clutching the delicate box. "I'm okay."

He didn't release me.

"Really," I assured.

"Have you had something to eat?" he asked casually, after unwinding his large hand from mine. He held an apple in one open palm and one of Geraldine's mouth-watering cookies in the other, the image of a human Justice Scales.

"I already ate," I replied, not trusting my fluttery stomach to eat at this moment. The adrenaline was surely taking its time to leave my system.

"What's with the box?" he asked curiously.

I instinctively wrapped my arm tighter around the box, not sure whether it was to protect the box or conceal it.

"I hope you don't think I'm a great snoop, but I found this in the attic and I was curious to see what was inside," I replied, eyeing Justice cautiously and deciding that the truth was best.

"Well, you are a journalist, so snooping would be within your nature, I suppose," he said thoughtfully and then grinned. "So let's see what's in there."

"Can we go somewhere?" I listened intently to make sure we were alone. "In private?"

A strange sensation had overtaken my body, as though the contents of this box were private – to be shared by a select few only.

I hadn't intended on sharing my discovery with anyone, but I didn't really have a choice now. After all, the contents belonged to the Forrester family, not me.

"Do you want to take a walk out back?" he asked, his accent undiscernible, as though he had learned to speak across several continents.

I hesitated, wondering whether I should be taking a walk with a stranger, despite feeling as though I already knew this man. My curiosity won in the end, and I agreed to the walk, remembering that the mist was lifting.

"I'll just get my jacket," I said, almost running to my room, grabbing a backpack and coat, before gliding down the stairs with the music box safely inside the pack.

Justice was packing a satchel of supplies, including lunch I noticed. I smiled at his thoughtfulness, suddenly grateful to have someone to share my excitement, which, I cautioned myself, might lead to nothing exciting at all.

He left a note in the kitchen for Geraldine, explaining that we were going for a walk and wouldn't be back for lunch.

We walked in silence until we reached the boundary of the pine forest, which opened before us into the woods. Emerus started down a well-worn path, the fog lifting with every step we took and allowing me to glimpse the small woodland animals that scurried along the ground and across low hanging tree branches above. The pine needles were covered in a thin layer of moisture from the morning dew, glistening as the early rays of sunshine penetrated through the higher layers of mist.

We walked mostly in silence, marvelling occasionally at the forest's wild flora and fauna. Emerus seemed completely at ease with the trek, a smile permanently settling upon his smooth olive face as he hummed intermittently.

We had walked less than a kilometre when the tree line vanished and was replaced by long grass and reeds that retreated into the depths of a large pond, about the size of an indoor ice-skating rink.

"Does it freeze in winter?" I asked loudly, my voice echoing across the still waters. I instinctively cringed at the shrill sound of my noisy voice in the serene forest. "Can you skate on it?"

My companion laughed throatily and I felt as though I were twelve and asking for an ice cream. "Yes, we skate out here often during the winter. You should see it; it's like Christmastime all winter long."

He pulled a blanket from his satchel and placed it over the grass and plonked himself down, retrieving two sandwiches and handing one to me.

"Thankyou, you're very thoughtful, Emerus. It must be nice to have an older brother," I said simply, with a grateful nod of my head.

"Well, the others might not think so all the time," he mused. He inhaled a deep breath before proceeding, as though deciding something important in his mind. "Call me "M". Like the letter."

"Are you sure?" I asked instinctively. Something about his reserve told me he allowed only a select few to call him "M".

"Positive," he replied with a nod of his head. "I take it you don't have any brothers?"

"Two sisters. One's still a kid," I replied, thinking fondly of Steph. "So, you're the famous architect?"

M laughed heartily again. "I don't know about *famous*. But yes, I'm a designer. And you're the reporter who's going to be following Lucas around for a while?"

"I guess so," I said with a shrug, hoping to give off the impression that being at Erravilla was all business and no pleasure.

But something about the way Justice stared straight into my eyes when he spoke told me he was no fool when it came to food *or* people.

"Do you want to eat first, or open the box?" M asked, his eyes narrowing and his mouth tipped to a smile as he studied my face. "Stupid question. Let's see what's in the mysterious box from the attic!" he joked in a melodramatic voice.

The lid flipped back as it had done in the attic, the music playing instantly as though we were listening to an old gramophone. The music did not sound eerie in the woods, just a soft, soothing lullaby. I placed the box on the blanket and gently snaked my hand into the hull of the keepsake, retrieving a small satin covered ring box.

M peered over my shoulder as he watched me open the delicate blue satin lid, revealing a set of gold wedding bands. We each picked one up, reading aloud the inscription engraved underneath.

"*Till death do us part*," we read in unison.

"These are unique designs," M said instantly, running his finger around the gold filigree design on the outside of the ring he held.

"They're beautiful," I replied, daring to push the ring ever so slightly down the shaft of my left ring finger, halting when it reached my knuckle. My hand shook slightly as I gazed at the foreign treasure upon my finger, trying not to remember the other ring that should have been resting upon the same one.

"This one looks as though it's been cracked and welded back together a couple of times," M said, squinting at the thin band. "Strange, the design is still perfectly intact, despite the fusing."

"This one's the same. I can see tiny little cracks up the inside," I replied, lifting the ring for M to examine.

"I thought old gold was supposed to be the toughest," M mused, holding the two rings up to the sky to inspect. His hands slowly drifted closer together, and as though they had turned to lead, the rings flew together like magnets, clinking lightly as they met.

"What did you do?" I asked, rising onto my knees to view the rings better.

"Nothing, they just…drew to each other. Strange," he replied, using quite a grip to pry the metals apart and then gave the smaller one back to me.

"What will we do with them?" I asked, still studying the peculiar ring.

"I don't suppose Lucas will find them terribly interesting. Mother and Geraldine might get a kick out of them," he said thoughtfully and then turned to me and smiled. "Nice find."

"Can I keep them in my room for a while?" I asked, glancing up into his pensive face.

"I don't see why not," he replied, with a thoughtful look upon his face.

"I'm just curious, that's all," I said, answering the question in his eyes.

"If you want to, April, go ahead. It's not like they're going to be missed by anybody. They've probably been up there for a hundred years, maybe more."

"The box isn't as dusty as the other things up there," I pondered out loud. "If I didn't know any better I'd say they've been handled recently."

"I highly doubt it. No one would go up into that old attic. I've never been up there. I doubt even Lucas has. Maybe you should ask Urland Chisholm. He's been around for a while." He thought for a minute and then smiled. "It's probably haunted."

"I wonder if the rings would do what they just did, if they were being worn?" I pondered, semi-alarmed at the thought of the attic and its ghosts.

"I don't see the harm in testing them. You might lose a finger though," he joked.

We both laughed at the ludicrous suggestion, although I placed the ring upon my finger ever so carefully, and at a safe distance from M, who did the same. I gasped slightly as the ring seemed to pull slightly, almost pinching my skin and then releasing quickly to sit snug upon my finger.

"Wow, this is weird," M said, studying the polished gold band upon his left hand. "It fits exactly, slightly snug."

I smiled weakly, feeling strange having a ring upon the sacred finger; when it wasn't the ring that was supposed to have been there.

"Are you ready?" he asked, a playful mysterious tone lacing his words.

I nodded. A thrilling anticipation crept through my body in anticipation as we faced each other, and I slowly moved the palm of my hand towards M's. With a couple of inches between us, my hand began to tremble slightly, as though it were being led by an invisible force to meet the hand opposite mine, and in an instant we were joined tightly, metal to metal, skin to skin.

"I can't move my hand," I whispered, staring at the moulded statue our hands had become.

"Well, I can't say that I've seen gold do that before. Not even in Africa and India… There must be another metal component in the rings. Here, I'll pry them apart again. Sorry if it hurts," he said, wincing as he wedged his free hand between the rings with force.

I immediately attempted to take the ring off my finger, but it refused to budge. "It's stuck!"

M tried to take his off, but with the same difficulty. Then he tried to yank mine off, but it remained firmly planted on my left hand. "I think we need detergent or something," he said, his brown eyebrows knitting together in consternation. "We'll deal with it when we get back to the house. Just, ah, keep your sandwich over there a little."

We enjoyed our lunch by the pond, chatting away intermittently, and soaking up the solitude of the forest in between, before heading back to the house.

Detergent did not help to take the rings off. Nor did vaseline, or anything else we could think of. M assured me that he would find a solution before the afternoon was over.

I spent the afternoon in my room storming ideas for an approach to an idea I had for a story, and taking notes about Erravilla and its occupants. Try as I may though, I could not shake the thoughts about the curious pair of rings and what they signified, pausing every so often to examine the thin band. I had placed the music box in the drawer beside my four-poster, and wondered whether there was more in the attic that would tell me about the previous owners of the rings. For some reason, I wanted to know their story, to know if it had a happy ending. The words of the inscription rippled through my mind: *Till death do us part*. It sent an icy shiver through my warm body.

M hadn't discovered a solution to the mystery of the immovable rings by evening, when he announced that he had to return to his apartment in London. His oval face was apologetic as he bid me farewell, promising me that he would work on finding a solution, even if it meant severing the rings with a pair of bolt cutters. I didn't think such drastic measures were called for just yet, assuring M in return that I could wait for him to find a safer solution.

Autumn, 1859, rural Gloucester, England
Sir Walter Finnegan, last Earl of Erravilla Court

Maisy lived out her days during those first few weeks attentive to her father's every need; fixing a false smile upon her face as she nursed the old Earl to his death. She spent her evenings and nights trying to stifle her tears after reading her Bible to her father and praying; which became unbearable for me, and I moved into the adjoining suite on the second floor. I wasn't sure if her many tears were for her father, or from being denied the one thing she strangely seemed to desire the most: my physical comfort.

I knew the ever faithful daughter Maisy would never disclose to her dying father the distant manner in which I treated her. It bothered me that she continued to pray for both her father's soul and mine unceasingly – like I ever asked for it or needed it...

The old Earl passed four weeks later; and she spent the next month crying a renewed floodgate of tears. After that she left me alone and stopped praying out loud to her God. She ceased her futile attempts to bid me an overly long good-night; she even stopped blushing and fluttering her eyelids every time I walked into the room she happened to be occupying. In fact she ceased to speak to me at all; and promptly left me to my own devices if she happened to walk into a room that I occupied.

This suited me fine, despite the small amount of pity I felt for the girl at what was to become of her life now that her father had passed. I spent my days pondering the length of time that etiquette permitted me to mourn for my late father-in-law before putting into action my plans for the future. The late Earl had bestowed upon me the generic title upon his deathbed. It was the only time I had visited the late Earl Bishop before his death.

And there was the remaining issue of fulfilling my legal marital duties with my estranged wife. I no longer felt it necessary to oblige the young Maisy, distant as she was herself now-days, and preoccupied with the affairs of the estate. I had been quietly surprised at the efficiency and competency with which the new Lady of Erravilla was managing the assets and finances. Her father had educated her well. She would perhaps be a useful asset herself until I could employ a bookkeeper; someone unrelated who would maintain the privacy of the plans I had for the estate's resources...

Three months into the marriage, Maisy had become so withdrawn that it took me an eternity to find her every time I needed to ask her something about the estate that she alone held the keys to or knew the answers for. I considered learning the art of managing the funds myself; but I had never been formerly schooled as a lad, working for a living from the time I could carry my own pack.

I became increasingly irritated by her frequent disappearances whenever I begrudgingly required her assistance; and when I finally did come upon her, usually by the pond in the forest, I realised much later, I was at my wit's end and I only served the hopeful young face a dish of my frustration. In time that hope also faded from her as she learnt to expect to receive nothing at all from me. Nor could I see any deliverance for her from the God she prayed to.

I fulfilled my social role as best as I could, in the hope that I might learn from the other aristocrats the social etiquettes and financial know-hows of my new station. I became quite apt to equalling the other young Lords and Earls at their cards and darts, their political theory and sporting prowess, as well as becoming the lively asset to social balls and parties, and a host to many an evening that they would speak of for months to follow.

My token wife dutifully smiled and prettied herself up for the entertainments and functions we attended, leaving me to the gentlemen and my own devices once the introductions and formal services were completed, and playing a rather deceivingly cheerful hostess at Erravilla, serving my imported fine wines without the scowl of disapproval that I knew lingered close to the surface of her face.

This life-style was suiting me quite nicely. I had begun to believe that it was what I was born to do and more. When one had access to money, the trade markets were an exciting and adventurous prospect, especially when the finances were from one's own and unlimited funds.

Maisy still cried herself to sleep most nights. I would try to banish the sound from my ears with pillows, but could never sleep until she was silent. There was something unnerving about the sound of a woman in distress. It reminded me of when I was a wee child and I would lay awake at night listening to my mother, bless her soul, as she cried herself to sleep at the hopelessness of her life...

There was just one thing that bothered me the most, and I would confront my delicate wife about it post-haste: was it my imagination, or did the golden ring upon my finger sometimes lend itself to spells of heat? I could swear that the very metal warmed at times – enough to irk me irritably. Was it to do with the climate? Or some other metal that reacted to my skin like an allergy? If so, I would inform her immediately that a new ring was to be ordered, custom made, and spun from only the finest pure gold.

5. Small Talk and Chance

April Falls

If I had been born an April Fool, would you still have loved me?

"You'd better wake up now. Lucas said 'e's leaving for London soon," Geraldine cautioned through the thick haze that had become my mind.

Lucas? Leave for London?

I remembered my busy schedule for the day and leapt out of bed, almost bowling a surprised Geraldine into the wooden stand beside the bed.

"Oh! Geraldine, I'm so sorry! I'm not usually like this, really. I think I've still got a bit of jet-lag!"

A familiar light danced in her smoky eyes as she tried to hide her amusement on my behalf, and I recalled how her father's eyes had done the same at the airport.

"Please send my apologies to Lucas!" I called, making my way through to the bathroom behind the walk-in robe. "I'll be there in a minute!"

I heard a faint scoff, and then the door opened and closed as the mysterious Geraldine left me to my privacy.

One glance in the mirror and I decided a hasty shower was in order. Today would be a big day and the dark shadows beneath my eyes were testament to the fact that I was still enduring a bad dose of jet lag.

I dressed in the most appropriate seasonal English casuals I could dig out from my limited wardrobe, noting that on my first available day I would hit the London fashion stores. I tucked a knee-length grey coat over my arm as I surveyed myself one last time in the mirror. I decided on grey boots, fitted jeans and shirt, and finally the only fashion belt I owned. It would have to do, for now. I sighed, twisting the gold band on my finger. How was I going to explain the ring to Lucas? Would he think I was a snoop?

I couldn't remember the last time I had been overly concerned about my appearance. Maybe it had been that fateful night two years ago…In this case I was trailing a movie star and may well be snapped in photographs in the background. Of course, I would be avoiding this at all costs so that I could stay *invisible*.

I realised that I hadn't been shown to the dining room and I became slightly flustered at my already late arrival. I'd noticed two doors leading off the kitchen last night and another two sets of French doors leading off from the central lounge room as well. While I hesitated beneath the chandelier in the foyer I deduced that surely guests wouldn't be ushered through the kitchen to be seated, and decided to try my chances through the wide French doors.

In the lounge room I silently debated which direction I should go in first. A grandfather clock in the far corner near the grand piano chimed once, reminding me that I was now half an hour late for breakfast. I hastily took the doors facing west, the same direction the kitchen was, and strode down a corridor. I halted abruptly when I heard voices coming from behind a closed door.

"She's had a few days sleep now, but she's still very tired," Geraldine's voice echoed. *Another stone tiled floor*, I surmised. "Don' think she slept much on the plane."

"Hmm," came a loud, reverberating reply. *Lucas Forrester*. "Maybe I should tell Mary-Anne and Gerry to lay off her for a while. I mean…we've got months ahead of us."

A loud noise erupted, as though two china plates had been knocked together accidentally.

"Are you alright, Geraldine?" Forrester asked, his voice alarmed.

"Yes. Beg pardon, Lucas. The silly teapot slipped from my hands…I think tha' could be wise," Geraldine returned. "You know, she's a lo' younger than I was expectin'. I though' maybe she would be…older, more experienced. It's unlike Gerry to allow anyone near you, you know, with the threats and everything tha's goin' on."

"That's exactly why Gerry *is* allowing her here," Lucas said matter-of-factly. "With her *in*-experience, Gerry's hoping she can spin me some nice publicity, his way. Not that I agree it will work for long. The rags will always find something to jump on me about." He paused. "And there'll always be threats, Geraldine. I don't pay any attention to them, and nor should you."

Inexperience? Threats? What was this?

There was a moment of silence followed by the trickle of water, which could have only been the sound of Geraldine refilling a cup with tea. I was about to enter, when the woman continued.

"She's quite…pre'y, Lucas, don'ya think?"

I heard the tickle in his throat before he cleared it, and pictured his mouth upturned uncomfortably. I chose that moment to grace the room with my presence, loudly opening the door before gliding in as gracefully as I could manage, feigning ignorance to their conversation as though I had just blown in from downstairs.

I was once again overcome with the exquisite décor of the otherworldly spacious dining hall. Deep maroon middle-eastern carpets covered the centre floor beneath the great banquet table; the high walls and ceiling were painted a deep burgundy and were trimmed in a delicate white architrave; red velvet covered chairs lined two walls facing one another; while two polished wooden low tables were placed comfortably in either corner, supporting two Victorian looking lace-trimmed lamps.

"Good morning Lucas, Geraldine, again," I smiled as I continued to peruse the fine room. "I'm so sorry again that I'm late for breakfast, Lucas."

I didn't look at him for a reply as I seated myself at the only remaining place, which happened to be directly opposite Lucas. He sat back casually in his chair, a little way out from the ornate oak table. He held the *British Times* in one hand and replaced his steaming mug down beside a delicate porcelain teapot with the other. He went as though to stand, motioning with his hands, paper and all, as if he meant to assist me.

His gesture took me by surprise, and he clearly looked uncomfortable, almost apologetic. I had caught him off guard with my cavalier entrance.

Geraldine returned my smile with a grimace of her own before leaving through a narrow swinging door half way down the banquet room.

"Um, would you like some tea, April?" he asked gesturing towards the teapot with his free arm.

"Please," I replied simply, meeting his inquiring gaze with a decidedly neutral one of my own. He poured me a cup and then went to spoon a cube of sugar. "No sugar, thank you. Milk would be great," I added, suddenly sounding far calmer than I felt.

Lucas handed me the delicate teacup on a saucer and sat back down. I grinned to myself at his familiar upturned mouth and baffled expression.

"Anything interesting in there?" I asked, sipping my tea and motioning with my head to the paper, which had found its way from his hand to the table, and now back into his hand. He also drank from a large mug, which seemed out of place among the other delicacies around us.

"Um, just the usual. The world financial crisis, terrorism, politics, the usual media circus," he offered, flashing an amused grin which displayed a row of impeccably straight, white teeth.

I returned his smile with one of my own, amused that he found humour at his own expense. "I'm bound to be in here somewhere," he said light-heartedly.

Geraldine re-entered the room, carrying a large, covered tray and placed it down before me on the table. She removed the lid and I had to withhold gawking, as my eyes grew wide at the sight in front of me.

"Thank you, Geraldine. I'm not entirely sure I will get through this in one sitting," I retorted, as politely as possible. "This looks amazing. Wow! I don't know where to start."

I heard a stifled chuckle and looked up to see Lucas watching me with intense amusement, the enormous grin spread across his handsome features. Geraldine took her leave again.

"Did you eat all this?" I asked, incredulous, returning my gaze to the generous serve of English breakfast under my nose.

"Of course," he replied simply, continuing to flash his bemused grin.

"Every day?" I asked finally picking up my fork and stabbing at a piece of sausage.

"No, only when I'm here," he replied, opening the giant newspaper again. He didn't appear to be rude, but rather using the paper as a means of politely leaving me to eat. "When I stay in the flat it's just me. So I usually order breakfast or eat leftovers."

"Oh," I said, thinking as I chewed. "How often do you stay in the flat?"

Before I gave him a chance to reply I pulled out my new dicta phone that I had fiddled with on the plane long enough to know how to record a conversation. "Do you mind?" I asked, indicating to the device as I placed it on the table. "Just tell me if it's off the record and it won't go past you and me…and that great mantle clock over there," I said attempting humour.

"Sure," he replied slowly, his jaw tensing as he chewed the idea over in his mind.

"I swear, Mary-Anne will read everything before it goes to print," I promised, sensing his unease.

"It's not Mary-Anne you have to worry about," he returned cautiously, a warning perhaps. "Being at the flat…depends what's on the schedule for the day. If I have several gigs in the city or if I finish late, I stay at the flat." He seemed to be lost momentarily in thought, gazing off past me without looking at me. "I'll show you the flat," he said decidedly, skimming my eyes with his own. "But anything about the flat is off the record. Only family know where it is."

I didn't know what to say. This was more than I had hoped for – to see inside his personal life and be able to write with far greater perspective than I had hoped for.

"Absolutely," I replied, masking my astonishment and managing to still look him in the eye.

I took a moment to recover from my head rush, feigning sudden interest in a mushroom, which I only ate on occasions to be polite, and to hide my immense dislike for the glorified fungus on my plate.

"So, you have an official opening this afternoon in London?" I decided to talk business. "What's it about?"

"I am opening the start of the theatre season at the *Globe*," he replied with a grin. "It's kind of an annual thing. My previous manager runs the show there now. He got the job because of me. But he was the first one to land me a lead stage role, which led to a film role the following year. So I still feel like I owe him. Plus, he's an absolute card!"

I smiled and paused the dicta phone, wanting the conversation to flow as naturally as possible. "I visited the *Globe* when I was in London five years ago. But it was the off-season. I would die to see a live play there," I said allowing my heightened excitement some freedom. "What's playing?" I asked, flicking the recorder on.

"They always open with a comedy. Probably *A Midsummer Nights Dream*," he said thoughtfully. "So, you're into theatre?"

His personal inquiry caught me by surprise again: *I* was supposed to be interviewing *him*. I paused the phone again.

"Yes, I've always been fond of the theatre, any kind of entertainment, really," I replied, replacing my knife and fork neatly to indicate I was finished eating.

"Ever tried your hand at acting?"

I smiled thoughtfully before replying.

"Only very, very amateur, like school productions, that sort of thing."

"Any leads?"

I wasn't used to talking about myself: mostly I focussed questions on others to get them talking about themselves for a while. Perhaps Lucas Forrester was momentarily bored with the attention on himself. After all, I pondered, he would repeat himself on a daily basis with all the interviews and press releases he was involved with…

I grimaced, wondering where his questions were leading.

"Yes. But as I said, they were small time school productions. Nothing flashy or exciting."

"Don't worry, I'm not going to dob you in for theatre sports this afternoon," he chuckled, clearly sensing my hesitation.

"You lead theatre sports…at the *Globe*?"

Lucas expelled an enormous laugh, which I realised meant that he had been joking. I hated feeling like the fool. Forrester had got me twice! I would have to watch myself, or else I'd end up Erravilla's court jester.

I returned his smile and had to admit that it was infectious. I was warming more than a little towards my host's appealing sense of humour. The way his green eyes almost squinted at the ends and his nose wrinkled when he laughed! The way that he flashed every one of his glowing white teeth and his full lips gently curled up above his mouth!

Could I write about those things in my book?

"Okay, okay, I'm a little slow today," I admitted, making no attempt to hide from my shame. "When do we leave?"

"As soon as you're ready," Lucas said, indicating with a slight nod of his head to the large Victorian clock stationed above the mantel. The large numerals indicated a few minutes to nine.

I stood up abruptly, grabbing the recording device off the table ledge and throwing my chair out noisily across the polished boards, alarmed that I wasn't quite ready to leave yet.

Lucas' brows knitted together in alarm as he rose to help me.

"Is everything all right?" he asked concerned, but without losing the constant amusement in his eyes.

"Yes, just wait. I need to get a few things from upstairs," I said replacing my chair under the table.

He remained standing as I walked to the doors.

"One more thing," his deep British voice rooted me to the spot. His eyes narrowed in thought before he spoke. "My brother's band is playing at the *Dungeon* tonight. It's invitation only. I don't know what kind of music you're into, but you said you like *any kind of entertainment*," he said tunefully mimicking my earlier comment.

I allowed a subtle smile to creep across my face, a shadow of the one resonating through my entire being. This wasn't on the *schedule*. He was taking a risk. I nodded absently before accepting his invitation. "That would be great."

"Um, some of my family will be there too," he offered slowly. "You can meet them, if it helps with your research."

I nodded and grinned weakly, unable to trust the heightened pitch in my voice any longer; then I turned and left it behind with his presence.

6. Park Lane

Within minutes I had my coat, scarf and shoulder bag, complete with notebook, pens and my trusty hand-held recorder. I descended the stairwell to the foyer, as light on my feet as I felt in my mind.

Lucas stood there waiting for me as I glided down the stairs, his presence captured like a statue of Neptune or Venus, watching my every move with a casual expression on his face. It bothered me that I could not read him easily. I would need a lot of time and careful consideration before deciding how to approach my first story.

Then I had three months to perfect the art of telling who Lucas Forrester is…

Today he was dressed with a grungy, artistic flare that I had seen him wear in countless interviews: fitted black jeans, wrapped by a silver threaded chain-link belt, heavyset boots, and a stylish dark grey tweed jacket shoved over a loose fitting long sleeve shirt. The top three buttons were left open, revealing the peak of a muscular chest. His tousled sun-streaked hair had the perfected look of neglect, although we all knew the style itself probably took considerable work to look as fascinating as it did on Lucas – to frame such a perfect looking face.

I felt like Ugly Betty beside my fashionable companion. I would definitely need some retail therapy before meeting the band and family tonight.

We stepped out into the cool March morning and I had the sensation to stop and bask in the rays of the sun, aware that London city would probably be wrapped in an overcast rain jacket. Seeing the sun caused a sudden surge of longing for home, which was almost always the colour of sunflower petals during the day.

I blinked and strangled a gasp as I watched Lucas descend into a lowered ice blue Porsche Carrera GT. The convertible roof and windows of the two-door roadster were lowered, revealing a completely leather interior driving dream. I had never been near a motor vehicle like this, and knew even less about its mechanics, but I could identify a Porsche when I saw one.

A proud smile lit up his features at my fascination. "You like it?" he said with a creamy-smooth approval.

"I can appreciate a Porsche when I see one," I replied, almost too scared to close the door once I had joined him in the cabin, afraid I would slam it too hard; I knew how much some people treasured their motor children.

"Good. Then hold on!" he warned with a mischievous grin.

He slid the car into gear and headed out at a steady speed down the white-pebbled drive. He barely slowed for the iron gate as it opened leisurely at our approach.

Feeling the caress of the sun on my upturned face I had a sudden urge to raise my hands to the sky and allow the cool breeze to wash right over me. I did, momentarily, until I had to grab at my fly away scarf. I settled for hugging my bag instead and watching the English countryside stroll happily past my window like a passing out parade in spring.

I felt wild, rebellious and completely free for the first time in years. I had no boundaries, no limitations or restrictions on who I wanted to be and where I wanted to go. I could change my life's direction with no consequences to anyone; and there was no one holding me back anymore. I found myself looking forward to the future with curious anticipation. I felt joyful and terrified simultaneously, like I could take either road at its fork and not look back to regret my decision.

"Are you afraid?" Lucas' hypnotic voice suddenly cut into my reverie.

I met my companion's gaze and saw a wide grin scattered across his face with the confronting wind as he eyed the road steadily. I laughed at his banter, recognising a well-known line from the first *Seasons* film.

"I'm not afraid of you," I replied smoothly.

"You should be," he grinned, unbelievably, as he kept playing with the lines from the film.

"Then the papers are right about you," I mused in reply to his banter. "But I'll figure you out yet, Lucas Forrester."

He smiled at my determination.

"And I can quote as well as you can – even your own lines! But you aren't your character, Ethan, you know. You aren't supernatural, Lucas."

And you can die if you're not careful…

In that instant my heart blackened and folded over like a pocket-handkerchief guarding a keep-safe as I thought of Hugh. Why did Lucas have to pick *that* line? The line in the movie that would have had any mortal killed upon impact.

I turned to see if he had noticed my withdrawal. He had his eyes fixed on the road, with a warm smile still upon his face.

"So, you're as crazy about *Seasons* as every other girl on the planet then?" he pressed.

"Ha! I was once, yes," I replied softly, trying to maintain an even voice. "I fell in love with the books, even though I didn't really identify with any of the characters."

"Not even Violet's?" he asked surprised.

"Not really…maybe in some respects. She was intelligent…but a klutz. She was daring and brave…but not sensible or logical. She kind of drove me crazy."

"I thought every girl wanted to be her," he said shaking his head, probably picturing the months of crazed fan-worship following the release of the first *Seasons* film, which had been Lucas' first blockbuster lead role.

"No, every girl just wanted someone to love them in a death-defying way. Oh, and it probably helps if they find him out-of-this-world irresistible," I said before I had time to catch myself.

The words were out before I could take them back. I feigned a sudden interest in a passing oak tree outside the window.

"You know, I meant that the character, Ethan, was out-of-this-world irresistible," I said quickly.

I stole a glance at the silent passenger beside me and saw a lingering half-smile on his face. I hoped that I hadn't offended him, or given the impression that I was one of the crazed fan-worshipers.

"So, why were you so immune to Ethan's 'irresistibility' as you call it?" he asked, a curious edge to his voice.

I didn't know where he was going with this, and my guard rose automatically. How much did he want to know?

"Because at the time that I read the books and saw the first film of *Seasons*, I was nearly eighteen years old and didn't believe that someone like Ethan really existed." Could he tell that I had answered cautiously?

Lucas also took his time formulating his next question, his eyes never leaving the road ahead.

"And now that you're older and wiser?" he grinned at his shrewdness.

"I do believe that men such as Ethan exist. But they are a rare breed," I replied, satisfied with my response. I thought of Hugh again and I wanted to choke out the phrase *a rare and dying breed*, but I refrained.

"Do you always hold back this much, April?" he asked suddenly.

"Well, it is *I* who is supposed to be interviewing *you*, Lucas Forrester, not the other way around," I half scolded, feeling like an old school matron. I decided to take a lighter tone, calmly and casually changing the subject. "So, what's the new and revised *schedule* for today?"

"Well, I have a reading this morning."

"A reading?" *That* wasn't on the schedule.

"Yes, I have accepted a part in a film that's to start filming in L.A. in June, but I can't get there, busy schedule and all that…so Miramax have sent the three female potentials here to their London studios so that they can audition with me, while I read my part. A lot of producers and casting managers do that so that they can get a feel for, you know, on-screen chemistry and that sort of thing," he said matter-of-factly. "Producers like to keep tight-lipped on this sort of thing though."

"Oh," I muttered, suddenly wanting to know why I couldn't be privy to this exciting part of his working life. "And I gather Gerry doesn't want me around too much, does he?"

Lucas' chest heaved as he took in a deep breath and pondered for a moment. "Gerry's wary of everyone at the moment."

Just wait until I finally meet this man…and then he'll have something to be wary about!

"And you?" I dared to ask balling my hands into fists; then wished I hadn't pressed the issue. I was angry that he didn't trust me yet. *And why should he? We're practically strangers!*

"It's not always up to me. I know you want to get all the info, but that'll have to come in time."

Trust. That's what he was talking about. There must be something else going on here that I didn't know about. I made a mental note to look further into it later…

"I thought I'd drop you at the apartment and you can wander London for an hour or so…it won't take long," he volunteered.

I decided to steal another glance at Lucas' profile as he drove, a wrinkled expression creasing his brow.

I thought of Hugh fleetingly and automatically began comparing him to Lucas, as I was prone to do with any man I met. Once I had decided that Hugh was the one for me to spend my life with, the idea of monogamy had been an easy one. Every man who I compared to Hugh fell short in some way. It wasn't that Hugh was perfect, but he was the rational, sensible choice compared to most men, who usually weren't interested in a life partner, or had a one-track mind.

An image of Andy and I played suddenly in my mind, as though someone had hit play on a remote control and a scene slowly emerged before my eyes: we were lying across Andy's sofa and laughing deeply, as we used to do often in high school. He had one arm outstretched behind my shoulders as I leant into him, as close friends tended to do. We were innocent old friends then, as old as the lungs that expelled the heady breath from our bodies, and as innocent in our feelings for one another as the weeds growing up between the cracks in the pavement.

I drew up short and switched the remote off, closing my eyes to the haunting memories that Andy had left in his wake.

Hugh had accepted me, for me, a couple of years later, despite the bundle of damaged goods I had thrown at his feet when we met. Hugh, careful and patient, soothing and kind, had been willing to take each step at *my* pace.

I glanced at Lucas, proud and confident; and doubted very much that someone like him would have even the slightest interest in the type of relationship that suited me.

"April?" Lucas' voice echoed, as though he was an ocean away and not within the simple grasp of my fingertips. "I said 'do you know your way around London well enough'?"

"Huh? Oh, sure. I'll find my way," I replied, pasting an over-confident smile on my face, knowing full well that I didn't have a clue about London's blueprints. I would stay clear of the underground, lest I end up in France or something.

He examined me blatantly then, feeling his way with his eyes, deep into my own, clouded ones, a troubled expression scrambling across his lovely features.

"You have a mobile on you?" he pressed.

"Yes, and your manager kindly left your number for me," I said, careful not to say Gerry's name in case he sensed my loathing for the man. "He said to register it under the name *Henry*," I continued as this baffling existence of Lucas' was becoming clearer by the hour.

"Good." He was silent again as he watched the road, slowing gradually as we began to reach the more populated roadways of London's outskirts. His dark brows creased again, as though he were silently debating with himself. "Will you be… all right?"

"Do you mean: *will I be safe*?" I supplied.

"I mean, do you know your way around well enough…and yes, be careful, April," he replied, with a wary smile upon his handsome face.

His mood lightened suddenly and he laughed softly. "I would hate for you to have to write a piece about how bad a host I am if anything were to happen to you."

I grinned to myself as I thought of my Karate Ghi hanging in Erravilla's walk-in robe on the third floor: I would be a lot safer walking around London than *he* would be.

"I know how to look after myself," I replied simply, turning to meet his gaze.

"I don't want to scare you April, but there's been some bad press associated with me lately…some threats as well," Lucas volunteered.

"I know about the bad press. That's why I'm here, aren't I?" I asked abruptly, gazing back out the heavily tinted window, which Lucas had automatically wound up when we had left the Cotswolds. I knew I sounded smug, but I was making no attempt to hide my bruised pride from overhearing his conversation with Geraldine at breakfast: it was my *in*-experience that had landed me this job after all.

"You tell me, you're the one who contacted *us*," Lucas replied, suddenly curt.

And that was it: with his final word, Lucas Forrester had, in one heart beat, erected any walls that I thought had been wearing thin. *I* was back to being journalist and *he* the subject of my work.

We travelled the remaining distance in silence. Lucas had resurrected the soft-top as we approached Oxford, protecting us from the outside world's prying eyes. The blue Porsche drew attention like a firefly at twilight as we flitted through the countryside.

Lucas expertly wound us through the busy streets of London, crowded with buses, taxis and pedestrians on this fine Saturday morning. The city was surprisingly sunny, causing the light blanket of dew to shimmer on curbs like a mirage in an oasis.

The Carrera slowed as we cruised along Park Lane, which I was keenly aware of as being one of the most prestigious locations in London. I observed the apartments we passed: elegant white sandstone pillars at street level, neat brown brick apartments towering several floors above.

Lucas knew each curb and bump in the road, swerving at the last second like a bumper car driver to avoid each pothole in the road. He transitioned the roadster into a lower gear, and the car purred like a Tabby at tea-time. The Porsche's owner drove mechanically and single-mindedly, clearly enjoying the machine he commandeered, as though he had moulded into its form to become one with its body.

We drew suddenly into a driveway, which took us beneath a series of porcelain sandstone apartments. A grill gate lifted as we approached and closed hastily behind us like an ancient drawbridge against the modern technology. A row of wall lamps bled along a narrow corridor to three double garages. Lucas pressed a remote button hanging from a chain in the car's console and the third door rolled open.

He drove us to a reception entrance, delicately tiled and decorated with luxurious armchairs and wall lamps. Lucas introduced me to his Concierge, Benjamin, who must have been expecting me because he showed no signs of surprise at my sudden appearance.

Benjamin pressed the elevator button after exiting the car and within seconds the doors opened, exposing us to a light dose of classical music and a full-length mirror. Lucas appeared perplexed at the image that greeted him as Benjamin waited to press the level 1 indicator. I watched with interest as Lucas ran his hand sub-consciously through his tousled hair, like he does on film.

Ben waited as Lucas and I stepped into another graceful foyer, which looked out through paned-glass doors onto street level.

Lucas turned to me sternly. "My apartment is on the third floor. Meet me back here in an hour and a half." He paused for a moment, his thick brow creasing slightly. "Don't draw attention to yourself."

"Which apartment on the third floor?" I asked.

"There's only one. Ben will take you to it. The lift will open into the reception area of the apartment. Make yourself at home," he said with an amused lift of his brow, followed by a quirky grin.

"Thanks," I replied. "Do I need to wish you good luck, or break a leg or whatever?"

"No," he laughed, and I lost another part of myself to him unwontedly. "I already have the part, remember? I have another audition here next week in London. Gerry might be able to swindle something for you," he said with a shrug of his broad shoulders.

I was beginning to realise that Gerry may not be the lone assassin dictating my *schedule* after all. Lucas was being overly cautious with me for some reason. Was he trying to dictate my every movement or was he just being touchy?

"Well," I said mustering a brightness that I no longer felt. "Have a good reading and I'll see you later."

I strode over to the landing doors, leaving a troubled-looking Lucas staring motionless after me. I folded my scarf closer to my neck and retrieved my sunglasses from my bag. Without a second glance I walked out into the open British air like a soldier preparing for battle – except that my battle raged internally. I kept walking until the condo was out of view, without turning to acknowledge the low purring engine, which cruised out onto the street behind me moments later, stealing in the opposite direction like a minx after its prey.

My mother had often spoken to me of wanting to stay in this bright and busy part of London. I walked towards the notable and prestigious Oxford Street and Piccadilly Square. I vaguely remembered walking through here years ago, picturing my mother as she had rabbited on about her childhood visits to London city. I had to admit now, though, that Park Lane did provide a glorious vista of the expansive greenery of Hyde Park as well as the famous arch monument on Hyde Park Corner, not far from the London Hilton Hotel.

I also knew I was not far from the shopping and entertainment venues of London's notable West End. I decided to venture in search of a more fitting wardrobe selection for this evening and leave the sightseeing for another day. I did not want to risk losing my way and having to call a reluctant Lucas Forrester to come and save me…for real!

7. The Globe

Satisfied with my shopping expedition I headed back to Lucas' apartment on Park Lane unable to control the awe I felt each time I realised I was living a tabloid dream. I had booked myself in for a hair appointment for later this afternoon, which had been a long shot in this busy location, but had managed to land a cancellation while in the salon. I carried my bags up to the landing and waited as Benjamin pressed the level 3 indicator.

"Did you find everything you needed, Miss Falls?" Benjamin asked.

I quickly absorbed my appearance in the full mirror, shaking my head in dismay at the dark rims beneath my eyes that made me look more akin to an albino kangaroo than a human being. My pale cheeks were further demonstration of my emotional and tiring week. And this was only the start of a busier week.

"Thank you, yes," I mustered.

I held my breath as the doors opened into an enormous double living room. Though I had expected to walk into two stunningly exquisite residences in as many days, the luxury still surprised me. The interior decoration was adorned in pale cream, turn of the century cathedral ceilings and large aspect sash windows parted across wide double French doors overlooking several petit balconies. Half a dozen chandeliers hung from the centre of each open living and dining areas, spanning the breadth of each room like outstretched arms welcoming me into Lucas' world.

"Enjoy your afternoon, Miss Falls," Benjamin said with a dip of his head full of dark hair. "And if there's anything you need just page me on the wall by the lift."

"Oh, thank you so much," I managed, taking in the atmosphere as he disappeared behind the closed metallic doors.

I wandered through the apartment in a stupefied daze, forcing myself to accept that real people actually spent their lives calling this magnificence "*home*" on a daily basis. I wondered if people like Lucas Forrester could actually be called a real person, since most people did not enjoy this level of high-class existence…or fame…or physical perfection. I blinked at the image of perfection that crossed my open mind, an image that now stalked me while out of his presence.

I knew Lucas was from a successful and somewhat wealthy family and I wondered if it had always been this way, living out of the grasps of what most people could only ever dream about. I decided that I would ask him about his family later, and hopefully meet some of them in several hours from now. A lone shiver ran the length of my spine at the thought, despite noticing that the apartment had been serviced and had been heated throughout by a series of double radiators.

The condo was more than inviting for my bone weary body and I halted at the doorway to a bedroom, which I knew was not the master: two double beds graced the pale blue coloured room, also bordered by a frosty white Victorian architrave.

I placed my shopping bags neatly in the accompanying dressing room, and then drew the large quilted curtains, leaving several recessed low burning halogen spotlights to undress in. Leaving my jeans and long grey sweater on, I collapsed on the nearest royal blue bedspread, nestling into the large array of soft bed-cushions. I spoke into my trusty hand-held recorder for several moments, describing in detail everything I saw around me, completely forgetting that I was to publish nothing about the apartment.

When I awoke the room was darker than I had remembered. The dictation device had been placed neatly on the dresser. I sat up defensive, my instincts alerted to the sense of intrusion. I hadn't turned the spotlights off. Nor had I covered myself in a light Cheshire blanket.

I padded across the tiled hallway into the main living quarters like a feline at masquerade, and noted a vibrant fire crackling in the hearth. The apartment was otherwise silent.

A neatly folded note lay on the dining room table, with my name scripted across the cover.

April,

I thought it better to let you catch up on some sleep before tonight.
I have a meet with Gerry for lunch down town. Shouldn't expect to be away for long. Phone for food if you are hungry, there's a list beside the fridge of decent feeds in the area.
Remember that we're going to the season opening of the Globe this afternoon - if you still want to come with me.
Phone if you need.

Lucas

I wasn't at all upset about missing the meeting with Gerry today. With the jet lag still holding onto me like a swarm of angry bees, I probably would have given him a piece of my mind, and ended up throwing the whole honey jar at him as well and ended up back in Australia with no book to write at all and my career smack-bang over before it really began.

I sighed as the kitchen clock chimed one o' clock. I still felt groggy. And speaking of honey, this girl was hungry! I decided that I would have time to race downstairs to grab a bite to eat before Lucas returned. I scribbled him a short note before donning my shoes, scarf and coat from the dressing room. I recalled the sweet aroma that had assaulted my senses when I had passed a small boutique café further along Park Lane earlier today and hurried to the elevator.

Hoeing into my sandwich when I was sure no one could see me, I paced back to Lucas' apartment, entering the foyer and waiting as Benjamin pressed the button for level 3. When the door opened I almost chocked on the bite I had just scoffed, as a familiar and all too attractive face greeted me.

"I see you found yourself some lunch," Lucas indicated to my almost consumed sandwich as the doors closed. "Have you got everything you need for the *Globe*?"

"Yes," I replied, tapping my bag, which held writing implements and the dicta phone, after awkwardly swallowing the remainder of my lunch and wiping self-consciously at my mouth with my sleeve. "I got some lunch, and I'm good to go. Lead on, Macduff!"

He smiled openly at my quote. "A Shakespeare fan, no less."

The doors opened into the stylish reception area underground.

"Who doesn't love *Macbeth*?" I asked with a grin, hoping that I had left behind no traces of the parsley and chive sandwich.

"Correction: who hasn't *studied Macbeth*? I think it's compulsory, world-wide!" he laughed. "But I agree, it's one of the greats."

Benjamin had already retrieved the Carrera for us and even held both of our doors open as we slipped in.

"Gerry was disappointed that he didn't get to meet you," Lucas offered flippantly, a warm smile lighting his features.

Sure he was.

"How was your morning?" Lucas continued either ignoring the sarcastic flicker across my face, or completely ignorant of the fact.

"Fine. I rekindled the memories around Buckingham and the War Memorial; strolled the shops, nothing too exciting."

As we approached the opening grill gate the Porsche came to a sudden stop. Lucas' brows took on a somewhat serious expression that I recalled seeing countless times in his films.

"April, we need to talk."

I swallowed the lump that now filled my throat, though it would have been impossible for him to miss the golf-ball travelling down my windpipe. I turned to face him directly. I held his emerald green eyes as they pored into mine, transfixed by the serious tone in his voice. His chest heaved as he inhaled deeply.

"This is as awkward for me as it is for you. I've never had someone tag me like this before. When Gerry told me of his idea for you to…observe me for a while, I didn't like the idea at all. I like my privacy. I'm not an open person by nature."

No kidding.

His breathing was slow and steady, like the ebb and flow of a predictable tide. He was struggling to say what he needed to. I continued to stare at his face, making no attempt to soften whatever he was going to say.

"The thing is, I'm not sure how you and I are supposed to be. We aren't supposed to be friends exactly; more like business associates, I guess. But we're going to be…together…for a while and I need to be able to trust you. You're going to find out things about me that probably no one else knows. Some of those things are going to remain that way," he said, as a warning, as his green eyes narrowed. "But this can't be one-sided."

I held my breath, looking away. This was exactly what I had been dreading.

"You're going to have to give a bit too. This isn't going to be a one-sided interrogation for a couple of months."

I expelled my breath. He was right. Things had been far too awkward, boundaries and expectations unclear. I felt suddenly relieved; there would be no more pretence. But my heart still sang in expectation: *how much did he want to know?*

I nodded slowly. This wasn't going to be easy. We were still practically strangers.

"April, is there anything I should know about you, that you haven't told me, that might help me…understand you better? Gerry told me about…"

"About what?" I snapped. Something about that man, who I had never even met in person, sapped my patience right up!

"Take it easy!" Lucas mused holding up both palms in surrender. "Gerry always does his homework."

"You mean he went snooping about me?" I demanded.

"You can't be too careful these days," Lucas said in Gerry's defence.

"You condone his behaviour? Or maybe you set him up to it?" I glared at Lucas, expecting him to defend himself and lay the blame at Gerry's door. At least, I was hoping he could.

Lucas remained calmer than I knew he must have been feeling as he continued. And he didn't deny my accusation – supporting evidence that he didn't trust me one bit.

"April, I can't leave anything to chance. I had to know who was going to be following me…I know about your…fiancé."

I inhaled a deep breath and faced him once more, allowing him to see my anguish.

"Lucas, I was engaged to be married two years ago. It's not something I speak about often, and I don't want it bandied across the nation."

He managed to maintain the brief shock that passed across his features as he took in my suffering. "Well, that explains why you still have the ring on your finger."

I looked down in confusion as I realised he was talking about the immovable ring from the attic.

"I'll explain *this* in a minute," I replied pointing to the thin gold band.

"What was his name?" Lucas pressed cautiously.

"Hugh," I breathed.

"And you…were in love with him?"

I took a long time to answer. This was a question I had asked myself over and over again and had come up with no definitive answer. How does one know they are in love? Did I even know what love in this sense was?

"I think so."

"You think so?"

He looked shocked by my response.

"Well, are you still?"

His eyes narrowed, searching mine carefully.

"I think so."

There it was again: the uncertainty.

"Part of me will always love him, Lucas. For who he was. For what he stood for. For loving me." That part I knew had been true. I had felt its loss afterwards, like the shedding of a warm blanket.

Lucas sat motionless, nodding gently to himself.

"Don't freak out when I tell you about this ring, okay?" I volunteered, changing the subject quickly, and deliberately spinning the gold band in frustration. "I'm not exactly thrilled at it being there."

He looked confused. "Okay, I won't freak out."

"This isn't the ring from Hugh. I found a couple of rings in a music box in your attic at Erravilla yesterday. M and I tried them on. And now we can't get them off."

"You met M?" Lucas asked, confusion still lingering upon his upturned face.

"He was at Erravilla for the day. I literally ran into him."

"He told you to call him M?"

"Yes. Why? Is it some kind of sacred name or something?" I joked, and then remembered M's formal allowance to call him such.

Lucas ignored the jest. "So… these rings just magically jumped onto your hands?" He furrowed his brow, reminding me of a provoked wild cat.

"I'm really sorry for snooping. I had no right."

"I don't care about the snooping." He was quiet for a minute and reefed his hand through his thick hair. "Why can't you get the rings off?"

"It's kind of strange. You'd have to see it to believe it. Nothing works. M's trying to figure something out. If all else fails, he'll cut them off," I replied.

Lucas seemed mildly disturbed at the idea, but reached across and took my hand briefly, squeezing it gently before releasing it. He pressed the heating button on then pressed a second one to open the grill gate and transitioned the car into gear, cruising out into the afternoon sun, the dark windows and roof safely and privately wrapping us inside.

"Let me tell you about my family," he offered. "You've no doubt heard and read all sorts of things about them?"

"Only a little," I replied, settling back into the cushioned bucket seat and taking out the recording phone. I had *tried* to find out more, but some of his family were virtually non-existent in the media. I clicked the *record* button. "I know that M is some kind of architectural entrepreneur…"

"He's an international architect and designer," Lucas corrected. He spoke about M's success with an obvious pride and I smiled knowingly at the fondness that was so evident between them. There was something about siblings that held a connection like no other relationship.

"A very successful one in his own right," Lucas continued. "M works hard and his designs are incredible. He travels around the world designing homes for the 'nobles and aristocrats' as he calls them."

"Wow, so the stories are true," I mused. "No wonder he's on Britain's *Most Eligible Bachelor* list."

"You should look them up for yourself sometime," Lucas suggested.

"I have," I admitted, feeling suddenly sneaky for having hidden the fact. "They're unlike any I've ever seen…truly fascinating."

"Yes, and most women are smitten by M," he retorted, the side of his mouth turning up with a sly grin. "He gets some flack about his *at-one-with-nature* views, though. Sometimes he comes across as one of those tree-hugging types, you know?"

I smiled to myself, somewhat surprised, more thinking of myself sitting along in my Do Jo for hours on end, just sitting, meditating until all else fell from my consciousness. I wondered if Lucas would call me one of those *tree-hugging* types too, if he knew. And did I care if he did?

"It's not surprising really. You wait until you meet my parents," Lucas offered, an enormous grin spreading across his face like a candy cane tidal wave. "He's pretty private too, but he doesn't shy away from talking about his political views if asked."

I pressed pause on the dicta phone and slouched back in my seat in thought, pondering this curious side of these Forresters.

"What? You have a problem with it too?" he asked, his brows creasing in consideration.

"No!" I replied too quickly. "I mean, I accept all kinds of views."

"I don't share in my brother's new-found political views, but I do believe in second chances." Lucas paused, raising his dark brows in consideration. "He was a lousy drunk not so long ago."

I waited for Lucas to offer more of this surprising information but he didn't. "And that's *not* for the record."

"Of course!" I snapped, still shocked he had blurted out what was quite obviously a well-kept secret.

I struggled against the strain in my chest as I retreated further into my mind once again, as the remote was pressed and the film began to roll: and there we were, Andy and I, still lying on that sofa laughing. This time Andy lay with his whole body pressed up against mine, and I wondered if he had known more than I had what was coming for us, like a thief in the night…and that the burden would be mine alone to carry?

And defuse…

"April? Are you all right?"

Lucas' voice drifted into my sub conscious, clawing at me to return to the present like an intruder tapping at the door.

"Sorry." I glanced across at his inviting visage and smiled faintly. "I'm glad you told me about M. So where were we?"

I pressed play on the recorder and focussed my attention on my next subject.

"So, tell me about your sister, Agnes. The only thing I could find out about her is that she's a twenty-six-year-old teacher," I offered.

"You've done your homework. I'm surprised you found out even *that* much about Aggie," Lucas said, nodding in approval. "Agnes is more or less the black sheep of the family. She teaches music and maths at a country school in southwest Wiltshire. Aggie's married to a farmer named Leicester. He's nearly ten years older than her, and he's great. Actually, it's Aggie and Leicester who hold the family together sometimes."

Lucas paused, a fond smile weaving its way across his defined jaw line. "When Leicester met Aggie it was like some kind of chemical explosion," he said laughing softly, and I imagined the affectionate memories playing in his mind of a girl and a man I had never met. "She always wanted to settle down and live the simple, private life. She moved away from the city after the release of Max Grey—"

"Your first big film?" I supplied. "She didn't like the attention it created for her?"

"Yeah. She took a teaching position out of the city as soon as she graduated from university and met Leicester shortly after. They had a whirlwind relationship and engagement and then married him when she was just twenty. Sounds crazy to me!" he scoffed. "But she's a smart girl, and one of the happiest people I know, our Aggie."

Ha! I cringed to myself as I thought of Hugh standing on a platform in the tailor shop being measured for his wedding suit. *I would have been nineteen when we married...*

An irrepressible hue lightened Lucas' features as he spoke of his siblings, and my chest tightened again as I pictured Alex and me as children on our hammock porch at home, laughing with all the glee of innocence. Lucas' evident connection with his family surprised me and I felt myself warm to his apparent affection for each of them.

"I can't wait to meet her; she sounds intriguing. Will she be at the *Dungeon* tonight?" I asked.

"I expect so. It's important to Darius that we're all there," he replied. "We'll have to run a few things by her too before you write about her. She's *extremely* private."

"How can she possibly be with a family like yours?" I mused, intrigued.

"That's *why* she's such a private person! She wants some semblance of normalcy in her life and her married life is all she has left of that."

I nodded in appreciation and moved on to discuss the youngest Forrester sibling. "And then there's Darius: the twenty-three-year-old baby of the family. An accomplished musician in his own right, who doesn't shy away from the spotlight – *and women* – created by his older brother and superstar, Lucas Forrester."

Lucas let forth a great ripple of laughter at my commentary. His tousled hair vibrated to their blonde tips with the movement of his shaking head.

"That was good!" he crooned. "Hey, you should consider presenting – seriously!"

"Oh come on, they all sound the same; it's not difficult to mimic. And everyone knows your brother anyway. I'm looking forward to hearing him live, actually," I replied clicking the recorder off.

The ice-blue Porsche cruised over the majestic Thames via the towering London Bridge and headed for South Bank, where the infamous Shakespeare's Globe sprang up beside the riverbank.

We had arrived before the major crowds; however, many tourists had begun to mill within miles of the great white building. Lucas led me inconspicuously through a hidden staff entrance, a sports cap covering his famous mop of tousled blonde hair, and large dark sunglasses shading his eyes. I couldn't help but giggle as we weaved our way through passages around the dome structure until we reached the back of a raised wooden platform, feeling like an undercover government agent.

"You laugh now…but once it was no laughing matter," Lucas returned under his breath, with the hint of a smile on his face. "When *Seasons* was first released I had to wear a hood and a cap. I could only go out at night; and I had to run really fast! During the day I couldn't go anywhere without *three* bodyguards!"

"I remember reading about that. I didn't realise it was so bad! What a life!" I replied with some degree of sympathy for the superstar.

A rush of voices, wooden objects being scraped across floorboards and heavy footprints resounded from the large structure above us.

Lucas took my hand and virtually pulled me up the flight of stairs in front of us. "Stay close. It's going to be a circus up here. Almost literally sometimes!"

At the top of the stairs we collided with a rush of people in all manner of costumes, moving giant set pieces and calling loudly to others who were clearly not within hearing range. The circus atmosphere wasn't a bad description at all of the chaos.

"We're *back stage*…at the *Globe*!" I called incredulously above the commotion, taking in the atmosphere of the charismatic theatre.

Lucas glided undetected as we thrust our way through the mad throng of actors, make-up artists, stage managers and crew. He led us to a door, knocked twice and walked in unannounced.

The room was a small office, decorated with accolades and framed, signed photographs of celebrities, either shaking hands with or embracing a middle-aged robust man.

"Albert!" Lucas exclaimed in an almost show-biz style voice, his arms flying out instantly for a beckoning embrace after removing his disguise.

The animated man from the photographs turned from his desk at the sound of Lucas' voice and crossed the room in a faster time than I thought possible for a man of his carriage. Albert threw his arms around Lucas as though he were a long lost son, completely oblivious to my presence just inside the door.

"The man of the hour!" Albert exclaimed in comical excitement. "Now that you're here, the show can go on!"

Lucas pulled away from Albert's fierce embrace and whacked him amicably across his large shoulders. "Albert, I want you to meet a friend of mine, April Falls."

The two men turned to acknowledge me and I stepped forward to shake the older man's hand. To my surprise Albert by-passed my hand and gathered me into a bear-hold embrace. Lucas laughed heartily beside me – I'm sure at my complete discomfort, and apparently not surprised by Albert's affectionate greeting.

"Well, you're a fine pretty little thing, aren't you?" Albert laughed, releasing me at arm's length to further study me.

"Oh, Albert, don't start!" Lucas joked, still clearly amused at my startled expression. "April's here to *report* on me: Give me some good publicity," he said almost seriously, with a deliberate nod of his head.

Albert continued his possessive hold of me as he nodded in acceptance of Lucas' cryptic message. "Well, you make sure you take care of her real well, Lucas," he warned. "A pretty girl like this will only draw you more… attention."

"She'll be fine, Albert," Lucas said, his tone denoting a brightness that complemented his engaging eyes. He gently unlocked the rotund man's grip from my arms and placed an arm around my waist.

I warmed at his touch, which was a welcome change from Albert's iron hold grip – more like a mother bear protecting his prey, than Albert's squid-like hold. I felt the limp in my shoulders when he released his hold moments later, motioning us towards the door.

"Same as last year, Albert?" Lucas asked with a grin over his shoulder.

"Same as last year, Lucas ol' chap! You go get 'em! Open with a blast! You're the star of the show!" Albert howled.

Lucas shook his head in mock embarrassment before calling over his shoulder, "I'm not even *in* the show!"

I glanced over at his thick spiked hair and giggled.

"What's so funny?" he asked as he donned his hat and sunglasses once more outside Albert's office.

"I was just thinking that your golden locks are so famous that they could have a starring performance all of their own," I laughed.

He grinned at me from beneath the cap and I had to steer him away from a man carrying a large backdrop, which made me chuckle even more.

Most of the *Globe* was exposed to the elements through the round open roof, allowing the bright glow of the sun to light up the corridors. A thatched semi-enclosed covering rimmed the circular roof, providing a measure of protection for viewers in the three-tired stalls.

"Come on, I'll find you a safe place to watch, while I go and find the Stage Manager," Lucas said, taking my hand again and leading me up a narrow wooden flight of stairs which circled around on top of the large stage area. "Where's a stall with a view?"

There were no spectators in the stands yet, allowing Lucas to find me what he believed was the best seat in the house – one level above the floor, directly opposite the grand centre stage.

"Save me one, won't you?" he asked, an energetic flare lighting up his countenance. Then, as swiftly as he had tucked me in, he had gone, leaving me feeling once again that his presence was but an apparition at the best of times, still untouchable for the likes of me.

A while later, amidst a murmuring audience, a loud bell sounded and an actor dressed in Elizabethan attire clamoured onto the stage, shaking a clock tower sized bell. A rush of anticipation flooded my veins, for the intrigue of the audience was enough to signal the forthcoming presence of one considered great amongst his species; and I sensed his aura enough now to know he was nearby.

<u>Winter, 1859, rural Gloucester, England</u>
<u>Sir Walter Finnegan, last Earl of Erravilla Court</u>

The months passed slowly across the cold seasons, though Erravilla never experienced the wind that the great homeland of Ireland could muster during the winter. I had written three letters of correspondence to my beloved Rosie in as many months, and had received naught a word of reply in response to my request that she board a ship and sail to England…to Erravilla, where I waited for her in earnest. Mayhap the postal service took longer here than on the Island…or perhaps the letters had been misplaced in transit.

In truth, I was occupied much of the time with matters of the estate and had barely a moment to connect with matters of the heart. But I was sure that she would come, eventually. During the cold season there was a lull in social activities, due to the bitter winds and rain and occasional snow falls. I had slowly begun to take over the management of the more important financial procedures of the estate, relieving a much-embittered Maisy of many managerial tasks. She spent more and more time on her knees with her head bowed and palms together.

The sight unnerved me greatly and I scoffed at her futile attempts to liaise with a God who surely did not exist.

Christmas provided one of very few occasions to throw a lavish party for those of our social standing, and I took the opportunity to boast our finest tasting imports. We hosted festivities for days on end at my bidding; while my pale-looking wife, who I noticed then, no longer seemed to make a determined effort to appear cheery on all occasions as one should. I would have to have a word with her about keeping up a better appearance as the spouse of a popular and noble standing husband.

On the morning of the 29th of December I remember waking, albeit with a rather dull headache, to the feel of an ice-

cold stone around my finger. The infuriating band was so cold that it burned my finger and those which it touched. I tried in vain to remove the infernal ring from my hand, but my attempts were futile: the ring simply refused to budge! I stormed from my suite, in fear that my finger would surely snap from its very station upon my hand if the blasted thing were not removed post-haste!

I stormed into my wife's quarters; but she was not to be found. The house was bereft of her and no one seemed to know her whereabouts. More alarming still, as I held my hand beneath a scarf in an attempt to relieve some of the frost bite that would surely be threatening the very flesh on my hand, I noticed that the peculiar pendant had tightened somewhat, and was emitting a deep shade of blue from the band. I blinked furiously at the ring as I ran at an unruly speed, down to the pine forest and through to the icy pond. It was the only remaining place I could think of to find Maisy, who I was sure, knew something about this wretched ring that I did not. And I would demand to know the truth!

In hindsight I should have realised that Maisy would be at the pond – it was where she always whiled away her idle time, as I called it, now that she was no longer required to assist with the affairs of the estate. The clearing in the forest was eerily silent as I stood at the edge, surveying the reeds along the banks. She was nowhere to be seen; and my frustration mounted as the ring burned colder still. I had never experienced an ice burn of its equal; and planned to make sure that I never would again.

And then I noticed a small opening directly in the centre of the ice, where, no doubt, the ice was thinnest. Immediately my mind returned to that fateful day when I was a boy of seven, when I had discovered my own mother face-down in the river behind the potato fields where my father worked during the summer months, earning barely enough coin to see us through the fatal winter months. It had been too much for my mother to bear, on top of losing five babes in as many winters.

I scolded myself for hesitating, and pulled myself together as I made my way across the slippery ice. I tried to convince myself that Maisy was different from my mother; that maybe this was a chance accident and naivety on her part. But the more intuitive side of me knew the truth. As I recalled the last six months of her life it was evident that she wasn't happy. I knew that Maisy realised I had no feelings of love for her; but I certainly did not wish her harm either. Surely she hadn't been driven to this...Maisy was a woman of class, of prestige, of social breeding. Her life was comfortable compared to most people – definitely compared to the life my mother had lived...

I reached the break in the ice, slithering like a snake on my belly inch by inch to test the ice. She was face up; her eyes were closed and her face was so pale it looked blue. I couldn't estimate how long she had been in the freezing water as I dragged her heavy limp frame from the ice. I undressed the outer layers from my warm body and wrapped them around her as I ran the half-mile to the big house. There was a faint pulse beneath her icy flesh and her chest moved ever so slightly with fading breath.

I scampered up the porch steps and entered the house through the dining hall, shouting for the maids, who trailed me swiftly in hysterics up the grand staircase and into Maisy's suite.

"Undress her at once!" I ordered. "Boil some water for the hot tub! And for heaven's sakes, call the doctor immediately!"

I began to undress the unconscious child-bride before me, stripping away her soaking garments with haste, forgetting all propriety. I skimmed the room for a blanket and retrieved the quilt from the foot of her bed to cover her.

I was caught off guard by the child-like innocence of the lifeless body before me. She looked so beautiful, so untouched, so undefiled, as she lay there naked. I had seen my fair share of exposed women in the bars and charlatan houses my father had taken me to as a young man after my mother had drowned. I knew every inch of a woman and more. And then of course there had been Rosie...

But Maisy looked different from them now – no bright red rouge or make-up at all; no exposed Chantilly underwear or high shoes. Just white-washed lifeless Maisy, my wife only by legal obligation. I felt strange standing there, admiring her natural feminine splendour; aware that somehow this figure before me caused an uncomfortable physical response deep within me. It was as though I was really beholding an unclothed woman for the first time in my life and I felt exposed.

"You can't do that! It's inappropriate, Mr Finnegan, to see a lady in naught but her skin!" Mrs Connolly, the housekeeper, scolded as she returned from sending for the doctor.

"She is my wife," I reminded her bluntly.

"It is no secret that you have not seen your wife in such before, Mr Finnegan," she replied tersely.

I was not surprised that the household staff knew of our estranged relationship: that we slept in separate quarters, and that I had never frequented her suite. I also knew they despised me for my neglect.

"She will surely die if we don't get her warm, Mrs Connolly," I said in a more amicable voice than I usually spoke to her. "Help me wrap her up."

It was a difficult procedure as Mrs Connolly all but slapped my hands away from her every time I accidentally brushed her cool soft skin in the process. In no time at all Mrs Connolly had her wrapped beneath layers of blankets with warmed towels across her face and hair, glaring at me as she went about her duties as I stood by the door and waited for the doctor to arrive.

"Why would she do such a thing now? And why was she wearing that illustrious white dress?" I whispered.

"T'is her mother's wedding gown. Her mother died on this day…five years ago," the more timidly spoken maid, Miss Hayes, voiced. "She's been at a loss ever since she lost her mother to the influenza."

"Forgive my bluntness, Mr Finnegan, but you'd know that if you had ever bothered to speak to her…even once . . ." Mrs Connolly admonished, staring me directly between the eyes.

Ordinarily I would have dismissed her from the house for such discourtesy.

But I could not think about trivialities when someone who had been placed in my care lay before me with the life slowly slipping from her being. If there is a God, Maisy, he'd better show himself soon and work a miracle for you…

Oh Maisy…why would you do such a thing? And why wasn't I there to stop you?

8. The Actor and Me

April Falls

*When you walk through the waters I will be there, and through
the flame, you shall not burn.* Isaiah 43:2
And yet I find myself constantly on a lake of fire.

"Here ye! Here ye! Take your seats! The show's about to start!"
The man repeated his chant at the top of his Cockney voice until all
spectators were seated and their chatter lowered to a hush. He exited
the stage and was replaced by none other than Lucas Forrester himself.

The crowd roared to their feet, clapping and crowing at the top
of their lungs like a cock signalling daybreak. Women were literally
wiping tears from their cheeks and wildly waving hats and any other
objects they could in the hope it might draw the superstar's attention. I
reached for the hand recorder, hoping to catch some of the ambience
live before Lucas opened the show.

The atmosphere was euphoric and contagious, like waking up
to find yourself at a rock concert and being unable to mimic the
adoration of the fans. I stood to cheer and clap with the rest of the
spectators, overcome with a surprising sense of pride for my newest
acquaintance. Travelling in close proximity with Lucas, I had lost my
perspective of just how popular and famous he really was. I shook my
head in awe of his success and tried to focus my eyes on the lone figure
whose presence filled the entire Globe.

The crowd had to be hushed to hear Lucas as he elegantly and
expertly opened London's season premiere event at the Globe, the
grand monument in memory of Britain's greatest playwright, William
Shakespeare. Lucas introduced himself with a few witty comments
about his own humble beginnings on stage and went on to introduce

some of the better-known cast of the Globe Theatre Company, who would be performing in this afternoon's production. All the while I repeated his every word under my breath, loud enough for the recorder to hear.

"It is without further ado, and with great honour," Lucas concluded, his booming theatrical voice echoing around the *Globe* like a clap of thunder, "that I give to you now, this heart-rending and side-splitting account of William Shakespeare's very own....*A Midsummer Night's Dream.*"

With his arms spread wide like the mighty wedge-tail in flight, Lucas bowed low to the stage floor before exiting, without raising his eyes to the applauding crowd. I stopped the recording and placed my treasured tool back in my bag.

I was so enthralled with the commencing show that I barely noticed him surreptitiously take his seat beside me some minutes later, with the cap and dark sunglasses back in place. I tried not to glance at him for long, fearing it may lure unwanted attention.

I leaned in ever so slightly to his seat, overly aware of his nearness, breathing in the scent that was becoming as familiar to me as my other senses. "That was truly entertaining," I whispered into his shoulder, my breath gently reaching his skin and returning to my lips with a part of him carried in its wake. "You were amazing!"

Lucas rested his cheek briefly on my head and I froze at the response his proximity caused to my skin. He then casually took my hand in his and squeezed it, sending a rhythm of vibration across the smoothness of my palm. Instinctively I shifted my face away from Lucas' and began to unwind my hand from his as well. To my astonishment, Lucas pressed his hand harder into mine, indicating that he was not going to release me.

I inhaled deeply as an image of Hugh cut through my heady flight, staring up at me through blue eyes as he turned in semi-circle to showcase his three-piece black suit. And there it was again: the guilt. The guilt that he wasn't here enjoying life, as a young man should, the guilt that I was enjoying it with another man. And most of all, the guilt that had begun to question whether I had ever been in love with Hugh at all…

And then I pictured his face. He nodded slowly, as though he were giving his consent through time; and I exhaled slowly, expelling with it some of the guilt I had built up since the accident.

Our hands remained linked throughout the performance, even as we clapped, cheered and cried with laughter. I could not release myself from the awareness I had of Lucas either, and the realisation confused me. This intensity of feeling was new to me. Different from what I had ever felt before.

As the cast was beckoned back onstage to take their encore bows and the crowd took to their feet, Lucas whispered that it was time for our departure and led me around the circular theatre and down the stairs leading to the back stage area. We were nearly flattened by cast and crew running madly in and out of the wings as we paced ourselves down the second flight of stairs and along the corridor that led to Lucas' Porsche, a symbol of the world I was not an official member of, but one that I was now fast intruding upon.

I was still laughing with that silly sense of euphoria you get when faced with a surreal moment in time, as we headed back over the Tower Bridge and into London city. I had to concentrate to steady my breathing as I turned to appraise him. "That was brilliant! You have to let me write something on that."

"On the opening?" he mused, his mouth upturned in delight with my enthusiasm. "There'll be lots of press over it already."

The inconspicuous hat had run away with the oversized sunglasses, replaced by a pair of chic Ray Bans that sat as snugly upon Lucas' nose as we were hidden from outsiders' view within the car.

Lucas tilted his head in query and I realised that I was still appraising his alluring profile and I turned my eyes away as the heat crept along my jaw line.

He glanced back to the road and then to me once more. "April?"

"Yes, on the opening," I replied, taking a moment to gather my senses. "But not from the up close and personal point of view that I now have!" I said triumphantly. "I'll email the editor of the *London Times* first thing Monday morning. I'll check with Mary-Anne, of course. And talk your ear off the whole way home to get the info I need."

Lucas nodded in satisfaction. "And Gerry. And me."

I scowled before glancing out the window. "Yes, and I'll check it with Gerry. And you, before it goes to print."

"Sorry, it's protocol," he said with a twist of his full lips. "But I think they'll be wrapped with the idea as well."

I had mellowed so much that we could chatter away, recorder on, observing the interesting landmarks that we cruised by, snaking our way towards Hyde Park like Batman and Robin – two extra-ordinary individuals co-existing within a universe, who had no idea of our very real presence.

"Before I turn this off," I said, motioning to my extended hand piece, "I have a few more questions about your family."

"Shoot," Lucas replied, a lop-sided grin emerging and settling comfortably across his face. "I think I'm getting used to talking to you *and* your dicta-phone now!"

"Why, thank you! Well, the first is about your names: Emerus, Lucas, Agnes and Darius?" I asked curiously. "They're…unusual names."

The grin expanded, sending vines of skin indentations from the corners of his eyes and mouth. "To answer that, I'll have to tell you about my parents."

"They were the subject of my second question," I stated matter-of-factly.

Lucas laughed out loud, apparently amused by my light probing. "Emerus was named after the travelling theatre company my parents worked for when they were young."

He paused and I waited for him to continue, intrigued. "My father had travelled with *Emerus* since he was a boy. No one knows what Dad's real name was, or what happened to his parents; so he took on the name of the ring-master, so to speak: Forrester. Dad's memory of the past isn't great at the best of times, but it seems blank before this time in his life. He doesn't even know where the company found him, busking in the streets of London all those years ago. I don't know if they felt sorry for him, or just knew talent when they saw it, but Dad became part of the travelling show. He grew up acting under the guidance of *Emerus*, drawing large crowds wherever they went. He met my mother, a singer, when they were both seventeen. She was a runaway, who had been badly mistreated by her mother and stepfather.

"They were married a year later and my brother, Emerus, was born a year after that. They'd been so grateful to the travelling show that they felt it an honour to name their firstborn after the company," Lucas offered, feigning a gagging motion before smiling at his own humour. "The group fell apart, going their separate ways for different reasons shortly after I was born, four years after M; then Aggie four years after me; and Darius two years after her. My parents said they liked the names of the 'beautiful magical creatures'" (he creatively mimicked a woman's dreamy high-pitched voice) "in the plays they wrote following *Emerus*, all ending in an 'us'. At least mine's a bit more normal sounding."

"What happened after *Emerus*-the-group ended?" I probed.

"They both found work in little theatres here and there, saved some pounds from their small successes and eventually opened their own company. They struggled for years just to keep it afloat," he replied as a grave, almost sorrowful expression turned down the corners of his mouth. "The four of us kids grew up on the stage, threadbare and all that for most of it. I never understood how my parents were ever content with their lives, and how they allowed it to continue…the way we lived. But they were so happy that it was almost impossible not to feel any other way around them."

"And now?" I ventured cautiously.

"When M was a teenager, he realised that he wanted more from life than what our chaotic lives were ever going to provide. I wanted to be like M, who took himself off to a permanent school, away from where my parents held any kind of reputation, and studied hard, working and paying his way through college. I flatted with him for a while, enrolled into a private, *educational* acting school, taking up modelling shoots to pay my way. It was the only thing I could manage to do; I had no skills outside the theatre."

Lucas inhaled deeply before continuing, pulling into the underground garage on Park Lane mechanically. "I wanted to excel at whatever it was that I did and would have done almost anything to get there. Fortunately, my amateur experience paid off quickly, landing me a small part in a stage production at the West End before gaining a lead shortly after. From there I was handed a couple of supporting roles in small budget films before landing the part of Grenoline in *Saucy Sorcery*, which led to the part of Ethan in *Seasons*…and the rest you know."

I returned the dicta phone to my bag as we were waiting for the lift to open, Benjamin already waiting to escort us upstairs in his fine dark suit.

"That's an interesting story," I said seriously. "There's so much more to your life than anyone could imagine. But I can see why you've chosen to keep some of this private, Lucas," I said, turning to face him when the doors closed. "I'll publish only what you want me to. I promise."

"I know," he replied, taking my hand and lifting it to his cheek. "Somehow, I believe you. And I wouldn't want you losing your pretty head over it if you ever did."

I respected the warning for what it was as he searched my eyes for a few heady moments before the doors opened, and to my surprise in full view of his Concierge, before walking into his warm apartment.

I dragged my hand free from his and hung both our coats up in the guest-cloakroom as Ben descended behind the elevator doors, observing myself in the delicate mirror above the marble basin. A red glow clung to my warm cheeks, and I knew it wasn't just because I had entered a fire-warmed house. My hair lay limply about my shoulder blades.

"Shoot!" I suddenly exclaimed. My hair appointment was in ten minutes!

"Are you okay?" Lucas called from the lounge.

"Fine!" I returned, splashing some water on my face and retrieving my coat and scarf from its hanger.

"I've gotta go to an appointment. I'll be back in an hour or so," I said motioning to the ornate clock above the granite fireplace. "What time are we due at the *Dungeon*?"

"An appointment?" he asked bemused, propping himself up slightly from his comfortable position on the sofa.

I raised a mysterious eyebrow for effect. "Yes, I made an appointment this morning."

"Where?" he asked, clearly intrigued.

The truth was I was embarrassed to tell him, in case he thought I was trying to impress him, when all I wanted was to feel fresh again, rejuvenated.

"Never you mind, Lucas Forrester. You will know in time. It's not far, just down the road."

"Okay, whatever," he replied cautiously, his almond shaped eyes almost squinting into a frown. "I'll order us some dinner when you return. We aren't due at the *Dungeon* until eight, at the earliest! Darius' band, *Shirtless*, won't play till nine."

I pressed the ground floor indicator and watched as Lucas' mystified expression followed me until the lift closed and all I could see was my own wearisome reflection.

I was conscious of the increasingly late hour and hurried back to the apartment, and was greeted with a warm but curious silence. Lucas was not lounging upon the sofa as I had left him, and no note was atop the mahogany dining room table. I considered buzzing Benjamin to ask him…

I returned my coat, shoes and scarf to the guest cloakroom and tiptoed cautiously towards the master suite. Good etiquette forbade intruding into someone's private domain, but I couldn't help myself. The door was ajar, so I craned my neck far enough into the dim room, lit only by low burning wall lamps. And there he was, soundlessly slumbering on his side, with his head and one arm cradling a plush pillow.

Curiosity and fascination drew me further into the creamy coloured room until I stood barely breathing, afraid I might wake him. I knelt down to gaze at the smooth serene looking face just centimetres from mine. I would probably never have another chance like this to observe Lucas' face without him knowing. Instinctively I wanted to reach out and run my fingers along his even cheekbone and jaw line, but fear withheld me and I withdrew my quivering hand.

I knelt there in the silence for moments before he stirred, his full lips mumbling to himself through his subconscious. My good senses finally won, and I left him to sleep peacefully.

I decided to order dinner from a pizza pamphlet tucked into the side of the fridge by a magnet, ordering the two that had been previously circled before getting ready for the night that I now hungrily anticipated, like the moon anticipated sundown as it followed the sun across the universal plains.

The intercom buzzed from the lounge room some time later and I hurried as quietly and gracefully as I could manage from my guest suite so as not to disturb Lucas. As the wide hallway joined the reception lounge I almost collided into my host, who had woken with the buzzer. His cheeks were coloured with the warmth brought by the comfort of sleep and his eyes grew wide as he noticed me suddenly appear beside him in the foyer.

Neither of us spoke with words, taking in the other with the curious intrigue of recent strangers as the intercom sounded again. Lucas repeatedly ran his hand through his tousled hair.

"I ordered dinner; I hope you don't mind," I stammered, feeling self-conscious at his sudden awkwardness, apparently surprised to see me, as though he had forgotten that I existed altogether.

Lucas made his way towards the lift as Benjamin's voice echoed out: "Master Forrester I have two pizzas here…shall I bring them up, sir?"

Lucas made his way to the doors and pressed with his index finger. "Thanks Ben; that would be great."

"I did tell Miss Falls to call if there was anything she needed," Ben replied.

"Thanks, Ben, she will next time," Lucas replied sleepily.

Lucas followed me with his gaze, eyeing me with the same cautious regard a gazelle would have for a lion in the wild as the doors to the lift opened before me.

After Benjamin was safely secured inside the lift, I approached the kitchen as Lucas wiped at the runaway droplets of water from his jaw with the back of his hand and firmly placed an empty drinking glass beside the kitchen sink.

His back seemed rigid to me as I opened the hot boxes on the counter and began searching for plates with wild abandon. My host seemed to grow more rigid with my every movement, overly aware of each and every cupboard door that opened and closed with the fury of a tornado.

I could no more ignore the level of tension created by his overbearing silence than I could have ignored the hands that trembled before me.

"I assumed the ones you circled were your favourites," I said finally, cutting the air like a reaper's blade with the sound of my voice. "How many slices do you want?"

He didn't reply straight away, scraping the glass along the serrated edge of the sink. I followed the movement with my eyes and noticed the whiteness that had appeared on the backs of his knuckles as he clasped the glass like an apparent lifeline.

His entire body sank and then straightened as he inhaled deeply before turning to face me. I felt the blood rush to my face as he allowed his eyes to run the length of my stature, examining me with apparent distaste, shaking his head as his eyes skimmed across my face.

I followed the path that his gaze had burnt into me, feeling more humiliated than I had ever felt in my life. Clearly the alternative dress style I had chosen for this event had failed his approval in some *very big* way.

He seemed to swallow the lump hiding behind his Adam's apple as he met my gaze. "I don't think this is going to work, April."

"I can change…I bought a spare outfit in case this style wasn't quite right," I said glancing to the floor and back to his hypnotic stare, aware that I was chewing on the tip of my tongue as though it was a source of sustenance.

"It's not about what you're wearing," he replied seriously. "Actually, it is…partly. It's about you in general."

My eyes shot up to meet his, a sudden fury whipping up my pulse.

"When Gerry told me of the change of plans, that you would be staying at Erravilla for a few days, I was concerned about this arrangement for many reasons, mostly because I was worried that the media would have a field day if they found out I was living with a stranger, and female no less," he said glancing away.

"That's what I tried to tell Gerry!" I cried apologetically, knowing where this was going and that I understood his sentiments perfectly.

"I know, and I was surprised that Gerry allowed it. He's so…territorial of me," Lucas exhaled loudly. "That's why I agreed to it. Like Gerry said, we didn't want some half crazed fan living under the same roof as me."

I let out a rush of air through my teeth, relieved that at last we were on the same page.

"And then you turned up, just days ago, which feels like weeks already," he continued. "And now I'm even more concerned about how the media will react if they catch on to this…arrangement. I know, I know…I'm the one who asked you to stay on…"

I searched his eyes with more attention, waiting for him to continue. Lucas took a step towards me, his face a frieze of indecision. His hand seemed to tremble as he raked it through his hair. Suddenly I understood where he was going and I howled in my defence.

"I promise I won't get in your way! Gerry told me that I would be invisible!" I retorted.

He laughed with a grim resolve. "Like *you* could be invisible," he choked out the last word with more than a hint of distaste. "Like I said, I don't think this is going to work."

I felt the wind leave my body like sails in a desert sea, defeated and run aground. I was clutching for his earlier lifeline, but I felt the sting of abandonment as he reeled it back in without me.

I placed the pizza back onto the bench and stormed from the kitchen, making no attempt to mask the hurt and the bruises that his words had inflicted.

"April, where are you going?" he called after me.

"To pack," I answered through gritted teeth.

I reached my door at the same time as he did, desperately trying to find the door handle through my clouded eyes. A warm hand touched mine, gently forcing it to stop fumbling as he turned my chin up to meet his face with the other hand. I closed my eyes and tilted my cheek away, trying to hide from exposure as a traitor tear escaped down my cheek and onto his palm.

"April, I think you've gotten the wrong idea here: I'm sorry if I offended you," Lucas crooned, his voice smoothing some of the wreckage caused. "This isn't going to work…because I'm scared to death of the effect you're having on me."

I opened my eyes tentatively and met his troubled expression with one of my own. "Lucas, you really aren't making any sense. Can't I just pack, and we can talk with Gerry and figure out a better…arrangement? Or if you want, we can forget the whole thing and I'll catch the first plane out."

And you never have to see me again.

"Now I really feel as though I'm on set," he laughed wearily. "But I'm not pretending when I say this, April; I don't want you to go."

"Lucas, you're really confusing me now," I offered, avoiding his gaze and trying to ignore the way my heart beat like a trapped bat. "Do you want me to write the story or not?"

"In truth, I don't know."

"Why?"

This time I turned my face up to his, still resting in the palm of his hand, which seemed to be holding the weight of both our anchors at once.

"Because. I…don't know… if I can be purely… *professional*, with you," he replied carefully, each word resounding like the chink of a metal chain as it bound his words on my heart.

He held my gaze, just inches apart, through a battle ensuing on the plains between us.

"Why don't we forget about this for now, eat some dinner, and go and enjoy your brother's band?" I suggested finally, swiping at the band of tears that had managed to escape down my cheeks, landing in the palm of his hand that was no-man's-land.

He nodded slowly, a half grin returning to light up his infallible features, a beacon for my wandering soul as I stumbled home through the darkness.

"Are we still friends?" I asked sounding more like an uncertain teenager than a professional businesswoman, ignoring the voice of reason warning me against this feeling, that was vying for my attention from deep within.

Lucas laughed a deep infectious reverberation and suddenly ensnared me to his chest, a peace offering as he wrapped both his arms around my battered soul. He kissed the top of my head gently, and then released me, inhaling deeply as he held me at arms' length.

"You know, Albert was wrong," he said shaking his head in disagreement. "You aren't a '*fine, pretty little thing*' at all," he mimicked the charismatic man's broad accent. "Those words don't even *begin* to do you justice!"

9. The Dungeon

Emerus Forrester

I checked my watch: eight o' clock. The warm-up band had taken to the stage, tuning guitars, testing mikes and amps, hitting some backbeats on the Fender kit. The *Dungeon* was alive with the droning sound of random instruments, and the crowded talk of two hundred excitedly feverish young people. It was as if they all had totem poles attached to their feet, the way they seemed to spring through the air in small clusters across the room. Why security let these many people into venues like this was beyond me; I could barely move, and I was in my usual place, at the bar. People were drinking, laughing, slapping each other over the back and shaking hands as the groups pulled together above the noise.

I finished the tequila shot and gave the bartender a nod for another as the smooth liquid stoked the engine in my belly for more. *Steady.*

"On second thoughts, I'm finished," I said loudly, and the bar tender poised his arm mid air, holding the tequila upside down like he was about to feed a calf a bottle of milk.

"You sure?" he asked, his brows rising in marked disbelief.

"For now, thanks," I managed, swallowing the thirst that burned the back of my throat as I eyed the tequila.

"Hey, stranger! When did you blow in to town?" An affectionate kiss was planted on my cheek before I had time to respond as gangly female arms were thrown around my shoulders. "Could spot you from a mile away in here!"

I looked over my clothes and shrugged. "I thought this was fine. I got rid of the tie, the scarf and the coat for you, Aggie babe. What? I'm not grunge enough for you now?" I teased my baby sister, ruffling her hair.

"Hey! Cut it out! I actually spent time on this mop this afternoon," she said pretending to pout, pointing to her long dark hair.

"Where's Leicester?" I asked glancing around for her taller half.

"He's gone to see Darius backstage," she replied loudly. "I hope these guys aren't playing for long. They sound woeful!"

"They're just warming up," I said with a grin. I had heard them before though, and they weren't nearly as talented as *Shirtless*. "Do you want a drink?"

"Sure, grab me a girly one!" Aggie shouted. Sometimes I found it hard to believe that she was twenty-six and not still sixteen. "I hope you're behaving yourself," she said lowly, whispering into my ear before giving me the concerned sisterly eyes, which squinted at the ends, causing her mouth to pull up at the ends in mock disapproval.

"Of course, sister. I've had one shot and now I'm on to the soft stuff." I called over to the barman again as Aggie took a seat beside me at the bar. "One *Cruise Control* please."

"You sure?" he returned, eyeing me stranger still.

"For the lady," I explained, flicking my head towards Aggie.

"What have you got me?" Aggie asked moments later, sipping the cocktail I had ordered.

"Oh, just some peach schnapps, some grapefruit, shaken and poured over some champagne," I replied matter-of-factly.

"Hey, how many women do you buy drinks for anyway? I thought you were too busy to have a social life," Aggie retorted.

"I have female associates, you know, not that it's any of your business, Agnes. I'm not always alone," I added, *though most of the female company was unrequited.*

"I gather from your… choice of clothing, that you've just flown in?" she asked smoothing the collar of my shirt.

"From Russia," I replied. "I've been there twice in as many weeks!"

"Sounds interesting…and dangerous," Aggie retorted with a cheeky gleam in her eye. "Speaking of danger, where's the main event?" she asked with an affectionate role of her eyes.

"You just told me he's back stage," I replied, recalling an image of my bronzed baby brother, Darius.

"No, the *other* main event," she drawled. "You know, the reason half of these crazy people are here."

"You mean our *other* talented brother," I corrected. "You can't always hate the mob, Aggie. Lucas brings it on himself, and he revels in it."

"I know. I just wish my brothers were more *normal* sometimes so that we could enjoy the entertainment like normal people do," she complained. "I'm surprised to find *you* alone!"

I placed a sympathetic arm around her and held her to my side for a brief moment before shrieks erupted from the level above us. "I think you just got your answer. Be nice, Agnes. You've chosen your path; he's chosen his."

The room became a deafening roar, and I felt like Daniel in the lions' den as the hungry crowd stalked in wait of their prey. People turned to stare and shriek at the familiar man who made his way slowly through a throng of people desperately trying to reach him as he tried to descend the narrow stairwell, escorted by four security personnel. I recalled the queue of people who had lined up behind a roped off section on the pavement as I had arrived not long ago, and was grateful to have been escorted directly downstairs. The escort had been completely unnecessary for the likes of me, but the geezers on the door had recognised me instantly and taken it upon themselves.

The *Dungeon* was busy on the quietest of winter nights, let alone a Spring Saturday night with *Shirtless* playing. Since Darius' association with Lucas had become known to the public his band had become increasingly popular, and to his credit, not just because of who his brother is. But the association definitely helped; if there was a snicker of hope that Lucas would show up to one of Darius' gigs, people teamed the streets in the hope of a glimpse.

The *Dungeon* entrance was a narrow opening at street level, which led down flights of stairs deep underground, like most of the older London venues from the Middle Ages, consisting of many tiers of dance floors playing various styles of music like a carnival. The largest underground rave lay deep in the rock beds of history, reserved for the more significant bands to play.

Lucas had made his way over to where Aggie, Leicester and I sat, now off to the side of the bar in a booth beside a row of stools. Leicester had joined our click upon hearing the sudden hike in volume, noting Lucas' arrival. The additional security lingered nearby, standing like soldier cabbages ready to pounce against the cave walls.

I stood to greet my brother in the usual manner our family was accustomed to: with a bear hug and a huge slap across his shoulders, which was always returned with enthusiasm, trying to make the other one flinch harder with each whack.

"It's good to see you, Lucas," I said warmly. "What can I get you to drink?"

"Whatever you've just had; it smells good!" Lucas replied. "And another of whatever Aggie's sipping."

"Slow down, boy! One at a time!" Leicester laughed, not a heavy drinker himself.

"Not for me, idiot!" Lucas said affectionately shaking Leicester's hand and slapping him on the back.

Leicester and I glanced around expecting to find a girl waiting nearby, but could see no one out of the raging crowd, who were all gasping and pointing above the noise of the band in our direction.

"She's upstairs. Security are going to escort her down when this lot calm down," Lucas said with a flick of his head.

Moments later I returned from the bar with the two drinks for Lucas and a Coke for myself.

"So, who's the girl?" Agnes asked him, eyeing the cocktail.

"April," he replied simply.

I felt the punch to my gut and realised that I had been hoping for a different answer. I recovered from the loss of breath I'd experienced at the mention of her name; the intriguing Australian girl I had returned home early for, in the hope that she might just run into me again. How could I forget her existence when I now wore a wedding band on my finger, the mate to which she wore on hers?

"Why are you bringing her here?" Agnes asked, her mouth a half moon shaped frown. "I thought she was supposed to be 'strictly business'," she said mimicking Lucas' earlier words.

"Chill, Aggie. She's fine. I asked her to come," Lucas replied defensively. "What's it to you?"

"I don't like snoopy reporters," she shot back. "In case you've forgotten, I happen to like my privacy."

"Oh! How could I forget, Agnes? With you constantly shoving it in my face!" Lucas jeered.

"Take it easy, Lucas," Leicester said, narrowing his eyes ever so slightly and leaning a hefty shoulder in Lucas' direction.

"She's not going to print anything I don't want her to anyway," Lucas offered, downing the shot and shaking his head afterwards to ward off the burning sensation that sent an involuntary burning down my own throat. "I'm making sure of that."

"Fine for you. What about the rest of us? I don't want anything in those papers about me," Aggie persisted.

Leicester took her arm gently, a gesture of reassurance. "Aggie, dearest, Lucas won't let her print anything at all about us."

Lucas rolled his eyes in defiance. "She's not like that anyway. You'll see."

I stood silently as the battle raged, taking Lucas' side involuntarily as I pictured the sea-green shade of her eyes and recalled the balmy spring fruits of her brown hair, relaying the image of her in my arms in the kitchen at Erravilla just days ago. I knew first hand how bewitching this girl was, in roughly the same amount of time it took to blink.

I glanced to the top of the staircase in time to see a heavy-set security patrolman pushing his way down the narrow flight of stairs, parting the crowd like they were particles of the Red Sea.

A sight behind him caused me to double take, imagining that I had caught a glimpse of my dark past. When I glanced back into the crowd, the blonde curls I had imagined were gone. I shook my head with vehemence: maybe I had drunk more than I remembered, for surely that woman wouldn't dare show her face in here now.

Would that wound bleed forever? I wondered.

I felt the pressure of a palm upon my shoulder and I spun, landing face to face with Leicester like toy soldiers. "What is it?"

I shook my head, swallowing down the lump in my throat with the remaining Coke in my glass. "Nothing. I thought I saw someone…"

The security guard had made his way to our private cluster, followed by a line of people taking advantage of the path he was clearing through the dimly lit underground. The burly man turned as if to retrieve a parcel and promptly placed a bewildered looking April in the centre of our curious group, and then stalked his way over to the wall beneath the stairs, where he stayed, arms crossed menacingly against his broad chest with the other cabbages.

I felt my knuckles tighten as I gripped the underside of the bar for support as I stood, inhaling the sight of those haunting blue-green eyes.

I don't want to feel like this again. It's too soon. I'm not ready…

Something about April was different, apart from the fitted black shirt, leggings and boots that hugged her in a way I could only imagine feeling, wrapped around her in the same way…

I turned from her to behold Lucas, whose eyes sought hers and no-one else's as he wrapped his arm around the very waist I had just been admiring, his lips the owner of a possessive smirk.

To say that April was unique yet…exquisite, could have been the understatement of the century, even though we were only a decade in. She looked like she had walked out of a catalogue and into a cave, making all who stood nearby, including Lucas, look as rough around the edges as a shaven 4x2 plank of wood.

I gathered my strength and senses, balling my fits beneath the edge of the bar ledge like two hot potatoes. *How could Lucas humiliate her like this? Couldn't he have one female acquaintance that didn't end up as his latest catastrophic conquest?* After all the angst he had had over *not* wanting April to stay at Erravilla, which, for all intents and purposes, was the Forrester family home, how was he keeping things purely *professional*? Well, he had done it this time. He was going to blow his reputation and *hers* right out of the water!

I can't do this. I don't want to go through this again. Not with Lucas, and not with her.

I swallowed and fought for control of my senses again, feeling the skin wrinkle beside my mouth before evaporating as I pasted a welcoming greeting upon my face.

"April, it's nice to see you again," I said, taking her lightly by the shoulders and placing a chaste kiss on either cheek, inhaling the scent of ripe apples and cinnamon that stalked me as I held her into my chest, just out of Lucas' grip.

She pulled away enough to find my eyes with her own and knitted her brows together in consternation, her eyes darting about wildly as she chewed subconsciously on the tip of her partially revealed tongue. "This ring is burning my finger," she whispered loud enough for me to hear.

I immediately took her left hand, squinting through the dim light to examine the ring out of the sight of our small group. The gold was definitely warm to touch, but seemed to cool by the second. I stood back enough to take in her perplexed expression, noticing the way her eyebrows creased in the centre as her mouth twisted to one side.

"I have no idea why it would do that, April. I'll get these off, if it's the last thing I do," I whispered just loud enough for her to hear and felt the rim of my own corresponding ring: as cool as stone.

"Be careful what you wish for, Emerus Forrester: the inscription says *Til death do us part*," she mused, her face twisting into a light grimace. "It may well end up being the last thing you do."

I held onto her hand for longer than necessary, savouring the feel of her smooth skin in the palm of my hand, resting as comfortably as a clam in a sea-shell.

"Hey, hey, let us meet the Australian girl too," Leicester interrupted from somewhere that seemed as far away as the band, who had faded into the background the moment April had taken my attention.

I took a seat while the introductions continued, allowing me to study April more discreetly. I waited for her head to tilt from side to side as she spoke, watching the brilliance of colour reflect in her eyes as the light hit them from above. I had never seen eyes that colour before and wondered whether I could create any masterpiece that would do justice to their magnificence?

"So, how do you like your stay at Erravilla?" Aggie asked April.

April's face stupefied momentarily as though she had been caught with her hand in the proverbial cookie jar, and she sought out Lucas for consolation.

"It's okay; *they* know where you're staying. Just not this lot," he replied, motioning to the raging crowd around us.

Her entire frame seemed to relax at his response and I watched as she replied: "Well, I admit I haven't stayed long enough to explore thoroughly, although I do plan to spend some time soon. Erravilla is just breathtaking, from what I've seen so far. Lucas has done a wonderful job with the décor. I just love the meeting of antiquity and modernity. It's magnificent."

I grinned into my glass, concealing the small amount of satisfaction I received from her compliment, and marvelled at her obvious appreciation for the arts.

"Actually, it's M's creative genius on display," Aggie said proudly, hugging me with her free arm.

The sea-blue of April's eyes coursed with sheer wonder, spilling over into her cheekbones and the corners of her mouth as she smiled. "Of course! I should have figured that out earlier."

I nodded simply, strangely elated that she seemed genuinely appreciative of my work.

"Anyway, enough chit-chat. Who wants to dance? Darius and the boys are on soon and I want a good spot down the front!" Aggie bellowed above the noise.

"You're on!" Lucas hooted back.

"Not you!" Aggie returned. "You'll just attract more people!"

"Oh shut up, Agnes! Do you want to dance or not?" Lucas returned. "April?"

"You know, I think Agnes is right. I think it'll be safer staying over here for a while," April replied, looking overwhelmed again as she took in the magnitude of the unruly crowd.

"Suit yourself," Lucas said with a hint of disappointment, while his striking green eyes lingered on April's delicate features a moment too long for my liking. "I'll come back for you later."

I watched as Lucas walked away, his shoulders looking decidedly lean beside Aggie's broader farmer husband, despite his appreciative height. A cheer erupted as the populace welcomed their king to the floor, followed by the small army of cabbage soldiers. I shook my head and released the build up of tension I had felt in Lucas' presence.

My brother was a great guy. *Stop*. I almost said 'kid' in my mind, and realised I had to stop trying to be his parent. He made his own bed, and he could sleep in it too. I glanced at April standing alone, her gaze trailing Lucas as he vanished into the folds of the crowd.

April perched herself upon a stool beside the bar two feet from me, sipping her half full cocktail. Within seconds a man in his early twenties approached confidently, eyes gleaming wildly as he sidled up to her, and filling the empty stool between her and I.

The stranger opened his mouth to speak, but I stopped him before he'd even begun. "This seat's taken."

He appraised me from shoulders to ankles before moving to take the vacant stool on the other side of April.

I shook my head, impatient at his persistence.

"That one's taken too," I warned, leaning far enough towards April that he held up his empty palms in a gesture of peace offering.

"Oh, I get it; you're with him, are you darlin'?" he asked April, his eyes pleading with her to say no.

I felt my chest broaden instinctively, preparing for an altercation if he hesitated, expecting April to retreat from his presence.

April remained calmly perched on the stool, her shoulders relaxed, seemingly less threatened by the heavyset stranger than by the boisterous crowd.

"I'm not *with* him, as you say. But nor am I interested in *you*. And both of these seats are taken," she replied coolly, flickering an eyebrow in either directions beside her, indicating the stools. April's admirer smirked at her response, apparently as surprised and impressed with her bravado as I was.

Within seconds her calm demeanour transformed into a glare that could have rivalled any gargoyle I had ever seen, and I had to check myself lest *she* provoke an altercation with the two-hundred pound Brit.

The man stood at once, holding up his hands in mock surrender and fumbled back into the sea of dancing urchins before us.

"Impressive," I admired, motioning to the newly vacated seat beside her. "You can hold your own just fine."

"You have to nowadays," she replied simply, as though ridding the world of all bar-creeps was her secret mission in life.

"I mean, you didn't even flinch," I said incredulous.

"I spar guys bigger than him," she replied modestly, glancing from the fraying crowd to me.

"What do you mean? Like martial arts?" I asked skimming her slight frame, unable to picture this girl sparring anyone who weighed more than my sister's barn mice.

"Well, I guess we won't have to worry about you after all," I said with a pleasantry that overshadowed my darker thoughts on the matter; April might be able to hold her own at a barn, but how well would she go resisting the wily charms of my brother at Erravilla?

She nodded and returned her attention to the untamed dancing that Darius provoked with his electric voice, creating a vision that could have provided scientists with the missing link to our prehistoric primates.

Shirtless played a range of hard and soft pop rock tunes, and like most semi-professional bands, played some originals and some covers. Their unique style evoked an almost ecstatic response from young audiences across the continent, especially since the well-toned all-boy band lived up to their name while on stage: they performed completely shirtless.

"These guys are great!" April called to me above the noise.

I leaned in across the vacant stool to hear her better, or so I told myself as I inhaled the drift of her orchard fresh scent. "They've done very well for themselves," I agreed, catching a glimpse of my bare-chested brother through the fern-like fray of hands swaying between the stage and the bar. "Not my usual style of music, but I always enjoy seeing Darius perform. He's in his element. I guess performing on a stage runs in the blood, for most of our family."

"Lucas told me," she replied as her ocean-coloured eyes swept the crowd from beneath her dark lashes. "But not you?"

I laughed lightly, imagining myself in Darius' place, complete with my usual suit and tie, looking more like an AC/DC copy than a teenage grunge band. "No. I'm not one for the stage."

I examined her gentle profile as she looked away and suddenly wondered what her skin would feel like if I brushed the outside of my hand softly across her high cheekbone and defined, yet feminine jaw. And her mouth…

"This ring's warming up again," April said, agitated as she spun the ring on her left hand.

"I'm at a loss. But I'm going to see a friend of mine in Dubai soon. He supplies all of my raw materials. Maybe he'll have some ideas."

"Dubai?" she cried above the throng. "I would die to visit Dubai!"

I smiled gently, feeling old and worldly despite her intrigue.

"Yeah, it's definitely one of the Seven Wonders of the World," I mused, thinking of the high-rise glass city, nestled mirage-like on the fringes of the middle-eastern desert.

"Maybe someday," she replied with a yearning that I hadn't detected in her before as she scanned the crowd again, and I wondered if the yearning was for Dubai or for Lucas.

"Do you want me to take you to them?" I asked with a nod of my head towards the multitude, resisting singling out Lucas' name.

"I used to be such a party girl," she replied, with a melancholic edge to her voice. "You couldn't keep me off the dance floor!"

The room suddenly grew louder still; people began shrieking hysterically and I stood up on my stool, instinctively on alert. The cabbages began rolling through the crowd.

"What is it?" April asked, concern riddling her voice from below me with the same etching sound as a highly tuned fiddle.

I caught a glimpse of Darius as he threw himself onto a sea of upturned hands and expelled a deep laugh from the pit of my stomach.

"What? What's so funny?"

There was that concerned fiddle again in her voice.

"It's okay. Darius decided to take a stage dive. He's crowd surfing," I replied. "He's going to be sore tomorrow from all those hands!"

I noticed April place her drink upon the counter before I followed her to the back of the soaring crowd. "Do you want to join them now?"

She looked as though she was debating the idea and I couldn't resist taking her hand in preparation to lead her through the horde.

"No. I don't think I could possibly get in there now. It's turned into a mosh-pit of sardines!" she replied, shrinking back from the fringe of the crowd and shaking her hand free of mine.

April retrieved her drink and sipped the remainder in silence.

Darius suddenly appeared over the edge of the crowd as though about to tumble over a waterfall, but landing on his feet steadily, with an exhilarated grin plastered across his face. I had to remember that he did this on a regular basis and that it probably wasn't as dangerous as it looked; Lucas and I had given him far worse in our younger years.

"Hi!" he called, quickly filling the gap between us and throwing his arms around me before whacking me across the back as hard as he could. I almost choked on the final mouthful I had just thrown into my mouth.

"This is April," I said motioning for her to come closer. "This is Darius, as you've probably gathered."

Without further introduction Darius had lifted her off her feet like a child and held her in the traditional Forrester bear hug greeting, thankfully minus the back slap. April's eyes bulged out of her head like a caricature, then softened quickly, and to my surprise, she returned Darius' hug with one of her own. I caught myself in time before I had allowed myself to completely wonder what it would feel like to hold her that close…

"Nice to meet you!" Darius bellowed at April before turning to me. "I have to tell you something later! About Penny!"

He disappeared into the crowd before I could press him further and within a minute his loud voice boomed through the microphone again. Had Darius seen the blonde curls here too?

April's expression was one of utter amusement as her eyes trailed Darius back into the wall of followers. "He's great! What a wonderful family you have."

I nodded slowly, allowing the grin to escape from within. "It's an absolute circus most of the—"

"Oh, I don't feel so well…is it getting dark in here all of a sudden?" April asked, pressing her hand up against my arm as her legs buckled from under her and I stooped to gather her up instinctively. Her eyes were half moons in her head, iridescent and glazed as she lay heavily in my arms. The ring on my left finger grew colder by the second as the skin covering her jaw began to perspire against my chest.

10. Doctor's Orders

Lucas appeared at my side within seconds and flew into a fury at the sight of April in my arms. "What are you doing?" he demanded, looking from me to April. Her eyes were now fully closed and I looked around for a safe passage.

"I think she fainted," I explained, panic quickly chasing away the annoyance that had risen in me at his accusing tone.

"We need to get her out of here," I said, turning for the stairs. "Go and tell Agnes. They can meet us later…at the flat."

Lucas hesitated momentarily, indecision creasing his face.

"Lucas, *you* can't exactly leave this place with April in your arms like this, can you? What do you think will hit the headlines tomorrow?" I said calmly, trying not to draw attention.

Sense finally won and he slipped back into the crowd. I headed up the stairs, praying that it wasn't something worse, as I was flattening my back against the wall. I held April tightly against my chest in an attempt to shield her from the excited and curious crowd, who were making their way downstairs to join in the euphoria that *Shirtless* had created.

The queue on the street by the entrance still stretched into the distance like the overnight cues for a Spice Girls show used to produce, as I ordered the security guard to hail a cab. The security guy looked surprised as he looked over April's limp body and then tried to hide her from onlookers. I hoped that I wouldn't be recognised as I hastily entered the cab and ordered the cabby to Park Lane, getting him to stop a conspicuous distance from the apartment.

I took April directly to the guest room that I usually bunked in, and found it already occupied with shopping bags and make-up trays. April had been here already. I was shocked about it and that Lucas had broken his own house rule: strictly no *outside* visitors. No wonder Benjamin hadn't questioned me about her on the way up.

When I lay April gently on the bed she moaned and clutched her stomach, rolling onto her side facing me. "I'm going to be sick." She still hadn't opened her eyes and seemed delirious.

Expletives came to mind. Lots of them!

I hurried to find the broom closet and rummaged for a bucket.

Within a minute I was back by her bedside, brushing her hair back off her clammy face and holding the bucket up for her.

"April, there's a bucket right here if you need. I'm going to call a doctor," I said, hesitating, not wanting to leave her in case she needed help, but leaving to retrieve Lucas's cordless phone anyway.

There was only one doctor our family trusted with confidentiality. Doc Allan was an old family friend who had never divulged information to the public. He was also as brilliant a physician as London produced and lived not far from the Hyde Park terraces.

Within minutes the lift opened and Lucas and Doc Allan both strode in, heading straight for April's room where I hovered around the doorway.

"I thought she fainted, Doc," I explained, concerned but calm. "But then she started throwing up and hasn't stopped. And she's delirious. Has no idea *who* she is or *where* she is."

The elderly man knelt beside April, talking to us as he examined her eyes with a small torch. "How long was she out for?"

"On and off since she first fainted," I replied.

"What has she eaten?" the Doc asked.

"We ate pizza for dinner, hours ago," Lucas fumbled, his eyes darting back and forth as he recalled information from his memory.

"Anything since then?" the Doctor asked feeling her pulse and watching his wristwatch, counting under his breath.

"No. Nothing that I'm aware of," Lucas replied, his eyes fixed firmly on April's shaded face.

"What about the drink? Where did you say you'd been?" he asked, writing on a note-pad.

"At the *Dungeon*. Darius and his band were playing there tonight," I replied, watching from the doorway. "She had a cocktail. Nothing serious. A bit of fruit juice and champagne."

"Did she put the drink down at all?" the Doctor asked, concern lines indenting the creases below his pale eyes.

Lucas stared at me, accusation in his eyes once more. "Did she, M?"

I shook my head slowly; then remembered April running to the edge of the crowd during Darius' stage diving exploits. "Yes. But it couldn't have been for more than a minute…two at the most."

"Had she been approached by anyone?" the Doctor inquired, peering at both of us over the rim of his spectacles.

Lucas glared at me, daring me admit my mistake.

"Hang on a minute, brother," I said in disbelief. "*You* brought her along, when she shouldn't have been there. *You* left her to go and *dance*!"

"Yes," Lucas replied, barely audible above the anger that seethed from between his teeth. "I left her with *you*!"

"Please, Lucas, Emerus," Doc Allan interrupted. "You must answer my question."

"She was approached just after Lucas and Agnes left to dance," I said regrettably. "I didn't think anything of it: he left when April and I told him to leave. I didn't see him again. April was never out of my sight."

"But the drink was," the Doctor supplied. "Long enough to have been *spiked*; I believe that is the word you young people use. Have you notified the police?"

I shook my head, furiously spinning the cool metal on my finger. "I didn't think it was serious. Doc?"

"Time will tell," he replied. "I will stay for a while and if her condition worsens, then I'm afraid we will be forced not only to call the police, but also an ambulance."

Lucas' face looked as grave as the six-foot hole deepening behind my heart as I took in April's frail form.

More of those expletives.

"I respect that you boys need to maintain a certain level of…privacy. But this may be more sinister than it looks," Doc Allan reported.

I sighed and leaned up against the doorframe. "Lucas, I truly am sorry. I didn't even think about that possibility in such a short space of time," I said glancing from Lucas to Doc Allan, still hunched over his patient. "You don't think this could be connected to those other threats, do you Doc?"

Lucas' eyebrows peaked instantly. "How could it be? They were just threats. No one's actually *tried* anything before. It has to be a coincidence. How could anyone have possibly known April was even with us? She's barely been in the country a week!"

I instantly recalled the frame-by-frame images of April being thrust into our midst at the *Dungeon,* and Lucas' protective arm weaving its protective web around her waist like a vine. Any blind man could have seen the affection Lucas had already developed for April.

April moaned, delirious, muttering in her confusion. "It burns…so hot."

Doc Allan instantly placed a hand on her brow as he continued to question Lucas and me.

"It could be a coincidence. But you have to consider all possibilities, Lucas," the Doctor cautioned. "She doesn't actually have a temperature: she's quite cool. I can't quite make out what it is that she's talking about."

"I'm not going to call the police…not yet," Lucas resolved, still eyeing April warily. "She's not burning up?"

"Not so much. Fever isn't usually one of the side effects," he replied.

"Say, Doc, that there is a link here; that means Lucas' *stalker* was in the same room tonight?" I asked, mortified by the thought.

"Yes, or someone doing his or her bidding," Doc Allan replied, with obvious alarm in his voice.

"Good Lord," I muttered under my breath.

"Well, M, you'd better send up a prayer for her. She's going to need it," Lucas said curtly, eyeing me with utter disdain.

I thought about telling him to send one up of his own, but now wasn't the time – he'd only become frustrated at my "political spiel" as he called it.

Against the Doctor's orders that Lucas and I rest, the three of us took shifts beside April as she continued to drift between sleep and consciousness – our own sleeping beauty in a grim fairytale of our own. I held her clammy hand as Lucas rested in the armchair on her other side.

During the bleakest hours of her plight, when she seemed bound for the hospital and a bed of earth, the ring on my finger cooled so much that it burned like ice against my skin, sure to leave a mark that would never leave – one to match the one she had already burned into my very soul.

After four hours April took a turn for the better: her vomiting stopped and she remained silent for a long period of time, and I breathed a silent prayer of thanksgiving. Her skin was pale and cool to touch, but she slept soundlessly, her breathing light as I watched her chest rise and fall rhythmically.

Doc Allan left, satisfied with her improving condition, promising to return in the morning, and still trying to convince Lucas and me to get some shut-eye ourselves.

On Lucas' watch I eventually gave in to my exhaustion, crashing out on the lounge in front of the fire, clutching at the cool gold metal around my finger, which had begun to thaw as the hours passed.

I was woken by the mantel clock as it struck seven times – the lone tolling of the past bleak hours.

A steady rain beat against the windowpanes, matching the rhythm of my padding feet as I wandered down the wide corridor to where April's door was ajar. All was quiet. Lucas was sound asleep in an armchair opposite her bed. He looked like hell warmed up, which was usually hard for Lucas to pull off. April had been tucked in soundly. Remnants of her outer clothes and shoes lay on the floor. She slept deeply, her skin still a shade lighter than the complexion I remembered when we had first met, and dark rings circled her eyes like the rims of Saturn.

The buzzer sounded and I strode hastily towards the lift, so as not to wake the sleeping beauties down the hall. I smiled to myself; that they looked nothing *like* sleeping beauties was almost amusing.

Benjamin had escorted old faithful Doc Allan to the apartment. The Doctor greeted me a little too cheerfully for someone who had slept only a little more than me.

"I'm surprised you're not out for your seven A.M. run, Mr Emerus."

"Not today, Doc. What about you?"

"I have worked shift work my whole life, you know. Often doing double shifts with no breaks!" he replied with a chuckle as I noticed his bright countenance. "How's our patient today?"

I led him into the kitchen, hitting the kettle switch. *If I could just have a shot of coffee…or three…*

"She's sound asleep. Lucas too. What should we do with her?" I asked bleakly.

"She'll need plenty of rest. She may not wake up properly for a day or two—"

"A day or two! That's some serious doping!" I cried.

"Yes. I would like to take a blood sample while the drug is still in her bloodstream," Doc Allan said, motioning to his medical bag. "I didn't want to take a sample last night in case she reacted to the anaesthetic I'm going to give her."

"Here?" I asked, wincing.

"Well, it's either that, or at the hospital, which I doubt Lucas will be too fond of," he retorted.

"Hmm," I nodded in bleak agreement. "Would a hospital be a better place for her now that she's more stable?"

"No, she's fine here," Doc said thoughtfully. "She's suffering from the effects of an overdose or *hangover* more than anything. She'll need plenty of rest for a few days. And keep her out of London for a while. Lucas too."

I nodded as I poured two cups of coffee.

"Make sure she keeps her fluids up, and get her eating as soon as she's well enough," the Doc instructed. "The poor girl will be very weak and dehydrated after losing so much fluid last night. And for heaven's sake, tell Lucas to keep her away from large crowds."

We stood in the kitchen sipping our shots of caffeine, which did its job within minutes, and I felt the shock sensation that came from shaking myself from the inside out like a child's toy with new batteries.

"I gather from your . . . discussion with Lucas last night that April wasn't meant to be at the club last night?" Doc inquired.

"No, she's meant to be here strictly on business. Writing an article or something on Lucas, to encourage his better public profile. There's been some bad publicity lately. And then this stalker…April's supposed to be saving his hide, not taking one for the team!"

Doc Allan was able to rouse April enough to get her permission to take a blood sample, which she nodded to sleepily and then moaned from the movement. She was mildly aware of where she was when we reminded her and relayed to her briefly the details of her arduous night. With prompting, she could also recall her name, date of birth (which happened to be in late April), and her address back home in Australia, which Doc said was good enough consent for him to take the sample; although he said she wouldn't remember giving the details later. We were his witnesses.

I winced as Doc stuck a decent sized needle into April's arm, expecting her to react with a howl of pain. Instead she rolled over and returned to sleep as soon as the procedure was finished. I stood back in awe, resisting the urge to pinch her to see if she could feel pain at all.

April slept the whole day and following night, drinking the water that Lucas coaxed down her throat. Lucas and I slept on and off; answered concerned phone calls from Aggie and Darius; then mum, who had spoken with Aggie, wanting to know if *Lucas* was okay. I explained that *April* had had a close call to which she asked what "that nosey reporter was doing there anyway?" I then explained that it was *Lucas'* fault that April was at the club, and she seemed momentarily satisfied. I knew she would call again later to speak with Lucas.

April's phone rang on and off continuously, the same two songs playing over and over until both Lucas and I sat side by side on the couch with our fingers in our ears like a couple of kindergartners.

"Next time her phone rings I'll take *Scissor Sisters*; you take *Thriller*," Lucas suggested, eyeballing the incessant phone.

Minutes later *I don't feel like dancing* filled the room and Lucas sighed, reaching for the receiver.

"Hello, Henry speaking," Lucas said in an overly theatrical voice. "Yes, this is April's phone. Who am I speaking with?"

I could hear the shrieks from where I sat as Lucas held the phone away from his ear. A second later the shrieking stopped and Lucas snapped the phone shut.

"Who was that?"

"I don't know. But she's got a good set of vocals on her," Lucas replied with a shake of his head as if it was still vibrating from the effects.

A few seconds later the same tune filled the room and Lucas hesitated before answering again, this time holding the phone out from his ear after pressing the green receiver.

"Hello?...Her sister? Yes, this is Lucas Forrester..."

More shrieking followed as this time Lucas held the phone a good half metre from his ear and we both grimaced.

When the shrieking stopped Lucas tentatively held the phone up against his ear. "Hello?...Yes, this is Lucas Forrester...for real, yes. Please don't make that noise again...that's okay...April?...ah...is still asleep. It's early in the morning here...no . . .she's not with me. She's up the hall, in her room. She left her phone in the lounge room...Yes, I'll get her to call you as soon as she wakes...you too, bye." More shrieks followed until the line clicked out.

"Her sister?" I asked. "Isn't she a kid?"

"That was no kid. She said her name was Alex. And she sounded far too concerned to *not* be her sister," Lucas replied.

"Well, I hope for yours and April's sakes, that it *was* her sister, and not someone out for some gossip," I retorted.

"If it was some random person, why did they have a personalised ring tone?" Lucas retorted. "Think about it: *Scissor Sisters*. It has to be her sister."

"All right, all right, just be cautious."

"That was definitely her sister: she sounded exactly like you do when you get all brotherly and annoying," he jeered.

"I wonder who she's tabbed under *Thriller*?" I pondered aloud. "That can't be good."

Doc called first thing Monday morning confirming that April had been doped with a high level of Rohipnol, a well-known and dangerous drug from the pool of date-rape sedatives available through street suppliers. And another, more venomous drug, that he had yet to identify.

Doc Allan suggested that we inform the police, but Lucas still refused.

"This is becoming serious, Lucas. What if next time it's something more lethal? What if it's your own family, or you?" Doc Allan persisted.

We were sitting by the fire in the reception lounge when April stumbled into the room with the grace of a tipsy teenager. Her brown hair lay wet and sleeked over her shoulder like an eel and she had dressed into fitted jeans and a long sleeve top that hugged her waist enough to reveal the thinness of her physique from her ordeal. When she looked up I felt the muscles in my jaw tighten at the sight of the dark rings beneath her eyes.

April sleepily plonked herself down on the couch beside Lucas, who snaked an arm across her shoulders and pulled her to his side. I shifted my weight uncomfortably, annoyed that I felt like an intruder to their affection. I couldn't shake the inexplicable protective, possessive fountain that had sprung into my being since Saturday night, and how it had escalated into the notion that *I* wanted to be the one to comfort April Falls.

I gathered my wits from the pools of water within me and practically swam into the kitchen across the carpet, watching the natural waterfalls spill down the outside of the windowpanes when I arrived. "What do you feel like eating, April?"

"I don't know. Toast maybe? Some tea?" she requested, sounding unsure. "This ring's been driving me half crazy with heat. And now it's green. Go figure…"

The last thing I wanted to be reminded of was the ring that seemed to cause friction every time I was around.

I began to prepare April breakfast as the phone rang. Lucas answered the receiver and a moment later I listened to his swift footsteps along the floor and the sudden shake of the doorframe as it closed behind him, swallowing him whole. I stared in surprise after my brother, wondering what could have been important enough to tear him from April's grasp.

I handed her the plate and stood across the room from her, returning the smile she waved at me, which, despite her recent ordeal, made her look like she could still have made the cover of *Mode*. I watched silently as she chewed slowly until Lucas returned.

"That was Gerry, freaking out, as usual. He said one of the local papers had a story on page three, speculating that I was involved with an incident on the weekend at a local club. It claimed that a woman, who looked like she had collapsed, was carried into a cab, and that several minutes later I was spotted leaving the scene. It said that the two incidents *might* have been related."

April groaned and cradled her head in her hands as though in pain.

Lucas was beside her so quickly that I thought he had indeed developed super-human powers like his character Ethan had in *Seasons*. "What's wrong? Are you going to be sick again?"

I clicked my hands anxiously and began pacing, fiddling absently with the cool ring on my finger. "She's worried, Lucas."

"You don't need to worry, April. We're going to keep you as far away from these monsters as possible," Lucas assured her protectively.

I huffed under my breath, not convinced that Lucas could in fact come good on that promise while April was anywhere near him.

"I'm not worried about *me*, Lucas. I'm meant to be protecting *your* reputation, not making it *worse!*" she cried weakly.

Incredible! The girl was a martyr, more concerned about my hazardous brother than her own hide.

"Anyway, Gerry decided to reschedule my audition with Rose Byrne," Lucas continued, his brows dipping in frustration. "To L.A. I fly out for a few days, leaving tomorrow. He thinks it's safer this way."

"Oh," April replied, her voice a sigh to my ears, a lop-sided grimace curling upon her full lips.

Did she care that much for my brother's company already?

"So, I take it Gerry won't let me go and *observe* that?" April asked hesitantly.

Lucas sucked in a deep breath before answering, his shoulders spanning their full breadth. "April, *I* don't want you going either under the circumstances. Besides that, the Doc said you need a few days of rest," he replied, running a hand through his rough hair.

"But I'm fine now. I can look after myself, honestly," she debated, a surge of determination appearing across her brow. "At the risk of sounding petulant, I feel like I'm missing all the exciting stuff."

"I think you take the cake where excitement's concerned, April," Lucas mused bleakly.

"Not funny. You know what I mean, Lucas. You didn't let me go to your reading and now I can't go to the audition? You're standing in my way without giving me any options," she said defiantly. "This is *my* story."

"A few days at Erravilla will be good for you, April," I interjected. *And some time away from Lucas.* "You know what they say: the country air is good for you and all that."

"He's right. It may be a bit boring though," Lucas conceded. "Maybe Aggie could come and stay for a while? Just tell her to keep her political rants to a minimum."

"Well thanks, both of you. I feel like a child being baby-sat."

"You're *acting* like a child being baby-sat," Lucas returned, to my surprise.

I winced, feeling the darts as they continued to fly past me, narrowly missing the film of my heart.

"Come on, you two, you're acting like a couple of eighth-graders. Dad and Mum will be back from Inverell in two days, Lucas,"

I pondered aloud. "And I was going to visit them before I flew out again on Thursday. If you'd like, April, you can hitch a ride with me this afternoon? I'll show you around Erravilla properly."

April opened her almond shaped mouth to protest, but I seized the moment to voice the longing in my heart. "You need all the information on Lucas you can get, right? You never know what you'll find out from his family when he's not around."

Lucas threw the final dart, aiming with his mastered precision to hit the mark on my chest.

"Speaking of finding things, M, I notice you haven't figured out how to get that ring off your finger…or hers," he said in a low voice, his lips lifting above his mouth in a snarl.

I returned his glare with a shake of my head. "Grow up and stop being so possessive already," I returned under my breath. "I'll get the rings off when I can."

<u>*Spring, 1860, rural Gloucester, England*</u>
<u>*Sir Walter Finnegan, last Earl of Erravilla Court*</u>

I wandered between the rooms of the great house for weeks, oft times finding myself pacing by the foot of Maisy's bed in angst, trying to make sense of why one thought life so futile to take such extreme measures. If she was so unhappy, why didn't somebody tell me? But would I have listened anyway? I doubted it...

The ring remained cold, as cold as she lay, motionless, and lifeless. Her breath staggered in and out of her weak body for weeks. The doctor said she was gravely ill, and suffering from a severe chill to her chest. Her sunken eyes remained closed, framed by dark rings. She looked older now, as frail as though she was an elderly woman upon her deathbed.

In these times I thought about all of the possibilities that her death would entail. Her property was rightfully mine upon our marriage agreement, although I still needed her knowledge and expertise in certain areas of the estate. Perhaps there was something I could do for her: she had been happier when managing the estate. Not the financial affairs though; there were agendas that were purely my own and I wanted no interference from her in this regard.

And then of course there was the matter of a rightful heir. No illegitimate heir could inherit my significant fortune; thus if she died I would need to take on another wife. Rosie still had not responded to my letters and I was beginning to ponder the notion that her father had simply forbidden any correspondence and possibly even married her off already. While Maisy lived, she was my only source for a legitimate offspring.

And I certainly wished her no harm. The longer I watched her as the weeks passed, the greater the gnawing feeling within me grew, persuading to take but an ounce of responsibility for Maisy's poor state. I couldn't live with myself if she died. I could at least try to compensate for her misery if she lived...the problem was, I didn't know how. Like my father before me, I had never been a man of many words, especially not of the wooing kind. And while I had no intentions of wooing the lass, I was determined to keep her alive. I knew most marriages were not founded upon love of the romantic kind, such as in women's novels and the like.

But Maisy displayed potential for the sort of wife a good man could aspire to have in his keeping. She was diligent with her work, and dedicated to the estate and her family heritage. Indeed the girl had nursed her very grievance of a father to the grave without complaint; and from the insignificant quantity of time that I had held with the late Earl, he was not a man built upon niceties or affection. In fact, Harrison Bishop was not too dissimilar to my own father, despite the great differences in the ways they were fostered and nurtured in as young men...

"What are you doing here?"

The scratchy weak voice caught me momentarily by surprise and I halted on the spot at the end of her bed, sending involuntary thanks upward. I stared into her dull grey eyes for a moment before taking myself awkwardly to kneel beside her bed, taking her frail hand uncomfortably in my own. She withdrew it immediately and turned her face away, her delicate nose poised in the air.

Well of course...she was as uncomfortable with my touch as I was with hers. I swallowed hard, searching for the words of reason I knew she needed to hear.

"Maisy, I...would very much...appreciate it if you would allow me...to help you," I began. There. That wasn't so bad.

"I don't require your help," she replied simply. "Who did this? Who brought me back to this place?" she demanded.

I had never heard her speak with such angst before. I was not used to being spoken to in such a blunt manner. I took in a deep breath.

"I brought you back."

"Why?" She turned on me with such fury in her pale eyes that I automatically retreated from her side.

"Well...well because it's not fitting to end one's life so...so unfittingly!" I stammered, pacing the room again. Her questions were highly inappropriate. One did not speak of such things. A lady of her bearings should be glad to be alive.

She turned her face to me, with the full might of her strength as she could muster. "Unfittingly, Mr Finnegan? Why, you ought to know a thing or two about unfitting!"

I fought against my natural tendencies to lash out at the woman for speaking so poorly to her husband. I clenched my fist and strode from the room. But only momentarily, for I returned soon with a composed front.

"Maisy, dear wife," I began, the words sounding strange upon my tongue. "Again, I beseech thee. Pray, what is it that I can do to make up for my lack of attentiveness to your needs?"

"You can't help me now," she returned, the venom still lacing her soft voice. "And I have nothing to lose. You can't do anything to me now, or for me now, that could make me regret my actions."

I huffed a deep breath, my mind in a quandary as to how to help the woman, who clearly did not want to be helped. Not by me anyway. It would take every ounce of courage and strength to ask her what I was about to. Who knew what the unstable mind would bring forth?

"Maisy," I began, reaching for her hand again. She withdrew it immediately. "I will do anything...within reason...to make your life...happier."

She was silent for a while in contemplation. Every so oft her brow would rise in thought, or her petit nose would crinkle in consideration.

"There's only one thing that I want from you, Mr Finnegan. The only thing I'll ever want from you."

She looked me square in the eyes, her determination evident and her lips slightly raised at the edges. Was that a faint smile of confidence I detected?

"Yes, Maisy?" I probed, since she obviously thought I must know her thoughts.

"Why, Mr Finnegan, what every woman wants: a child, of course."

I sat upright in consideration: I had to admit that it wasn't the furthest possibility of thought in my mind; but nor was it the first.

"A child will make you happy?" I repeated.

"Yes. And I will bother you no longer."

I nodded my head in consent, my eyes wild with contemplation. She certainly wasn't the least favourable of women to the eye; I thought fleetingly of the raw flesh that I had beheld weeks earlier and nodded further to myself. Not unfavourable at all. And I knew without a doubt that she had lain with no other; there would be no need to concern myself with worrying about a true heir, or of contracting any unsavoury diseases as one worried about in public establishments.

"Maisy Finnegan, I will grant you your request."

I returned her stare, meeting her directly in the eye. I could not have been entirely certain, but at that moment in time, her cheekbones rose to meet her eyes, and an ever so faint light of hope shone through them.

"May God grant us a child," she corrected, nodding with a measure of satisfaction I had not seen in a year.

11. Company at Erravilla

<u>*April Falls*</u>

Like birds of a feather we flock together. So how is it that three's a crowd...?

The drive back to Erravilla seemed smoother in M's sporty silver Jaguar, and not just because of the difference in luxury the car provided. I noticed M took far more caution as he drove, and not for the benefit of the car or because the roads were slippery from the rain. He slowed considerably around bends, always glancing at me out of his peripheral vision checking for signs of seasickness. I also had the added advantage of fresh air from the open windows, tasting the cool rain as it landed on my tongue.

M drove mostly in silence, his shoulder length brown hair waving in the breeze like a sail on a steady mast, asking how I was feeling every so often, or if I needed to stop and refresh, or to drink. I couldn't help but admire the way he always wore a pleasant smile upon his defined jaw, radiating a form of contagious serenity from his features. His piercing blue eyes always seemed to be thoughtful, as though he was planning ahead like a sat-nav system; and he hummed tunefully to himself as he drove.

I phoned Alex on the way, who did not seem annoyed that I had woken her up; I hadn't realised the time difference between the two continents. I decided not to tell her about the incident at the *Dungeon* because she would panic like she was expecting an alien invasion to follow. I turned my face as far from M's view as possible when she cracked a few jokes about Lucas answering my phone, fishing for gossip.

Alex guessed I had company when I refused to take her bait, and I held the phone out from my ear as she roared with laughter into the receiver before making me promise to call her back as soon as I could; and to ring Mother, who was going spare because she hadn't spoken to me in almost a week.

We arrived at Erravilla beneath a late afternoon sun-shower, the Jag cruising up the driveway as the white pebbles crunched beneath the shiny tyres. M drove straight around to the side of the house on the sea of pebbles, which led to a smaller sandstone adaptation of Erravilla. He pressed a remote trigger that rolled the furthest door of the six to allow the Jaguar through.

"This is quite a sizeable garage," I said indicating the mostly vacant sandstone hall stretching out before us. The black Rolls Royce occupied the furthest position from us. "Why does Lucas need a garage this size?"

"He doesn't. The previous owners kept boats, bikes, caravans and all manner of other hobby vehicles in here, that Lucas doesn't have time for," M replied. "It was once used for stables I believe."

He used the remote to close the door behind us before opening a large umbrella above us. I felt as if I had entered the set of a Julie Andrews film. As I glanced from the rolling pine forest to the black umbrella above, I didn't know whether to burst into a round of *The Hills are Alive* or *A Spoon Full of Sugar*!

M led me around the back of the house, insisting on carrying the few bags himself, mostly from Saturday's shopping spree. We were standing on the furthest point of Erravilla's west wing as the faint glow of the sun covered the pine forest, casting long shadows through the haze across the stunning rose garden beyond the house and lawns. We passed by a looming glass room, which took up the entire back section of the house; its walls transparent, stretched from floor to ceiling like a cylinder, three stories high.

Double French doors opened out onto the sheltered esplanade that M and I strolled along, spanning a lengthy part of the Court. Dominant white columns stretched up like Roman pylons to support the overhanging balcony from the second floor, reminding me of a famous scene from Venice as the mist rolled in from across the forest.

"This place is mystical." I said and shivered, breathing in the cool country air. I realised then how right M had been about the healthy change from the city. "Not too dissimilar either from a scene out of a Jane Austin novel," I marvelled feeling the release of tension with each breath I took.

M threw his head back momentarily and laughed heartily, the shock of wavy hair dancing upon his shoulders like a string puppet. "Well, you'll just have to find yourself a Mr Darcy."

I laughed along with him at such a fantastic notion. "Do you consider yourself a Darcy?"

"No!" he laughed. "But Lucas—"

"Thinks *he's* Darcy?" I laughed incredulously.

"No, no! Lucas is far too flighty to be Mr Darcy. He's more like Wickham," M replied, his eyes flickering momentarily before returning my comical chuckle. "I'm always Bingley, I guess. Just the quiet guy in the shadows…"

He trailed off in thought and I waited for him to continue, but he didn't. I felt his tension. *Why would he say that Lucas is like Wickham?*

We arrived above a flight of stairs and another set of French doors, and I recognised the room through the glass as the dining room. M folded the umbrella and led us through the open doors, continuing on through to the foyer, and then up the elaborate staircase to my room.

I breathed in deeply when M opened the door, smelling the stoked fireplace, and basking in the beauty of the setting sun through the ghostly haze beyond the glass panes. Admiring the plush four-poster against the far wall, I realised that a part of me had yearned to return to what was fast becoming my British haven, despite the short time we had been acquainted.

I spun on my heel, catching the passing sense again that I was like Alice in her own Wonderland here, expecting to be alone; but finding another instead: one who was barely a friend, staring quietly back at me. A faint smile brushed his somehow familiar lips, a deep fire smouldering in his eyes that lit me involuntarily, and I took a step back.

"You like your room?" he asked softly, his hands placed casually in the pockets of his trousers as he leaned against the doorframe.

"Yes, it's adorable," I replied earnestly. I studied his intense expression and discovered that an emotional connection between himself and my new haven lay hidden between the lines on his face. "M, did you do this?" I whispered, fanning my hands in a sweeping motion before me, taking in every facet of the suite.

The corner of his mouth tilted upwards in a modest grin. He nodded slowly. "This was my favourite room. I spent a lot of time designing it when Lucas first moved in. I'm glad someone can enjoy it at last…"

His voice trailed off and his gentle demeanour fused into one of marred grief. "Well, I'll see you later for dinner. Just call if you need anything."

"Thank you," I murmured, wanting to reach into the cords of his emotions and pluck the pain from their depths. Who had hurt Emerus Forrester? "For everything, M. You have been generously kind, and I am virtually a stranger to you!"

"There's no need to thank me; I would have done the same for anyone. Just as you would have done," he said dismissively. "If you need me I'll be in my room on the second floor, directly below you."

A burning sensation rippled through my ring finger and I clutched at the heated gold band.

"Do you think there's any way to—" I began, lifting my face to plead with him to discover a way to rid us of these exasperating pieces of metal, but he had gone. I held up the burning ring on my quivering finger to examine the incredible sight before me: the golden band flashed a deep shade of orange.

I followed him at once, eager to share with him the bizarre occurrence, but he had disappeared from the landing and the ring gradually returned to its familiar golden tinge.

I soaked in the hot tub until the clock chimed six o' clock, reminding me that dinner would be served downstairs in half an hour. I cleared my mind of any thoughts of the ring, of M, of Lucas, of the *Dungeon*; eventually, of anything at all, as I had taught myself to do since the accident and the months after Andy.

And I waited for the Voice to come, as it always did when I wandered through the desolate desert of my mind, always offering hope to quench the deep thirst for peace and assurance that I had carried with me since the accident.

Dinner seemed morosely quiet without Lucas, whose face I was trying to put out of my mind but finding about as easy to do as chopping ice with a veggie peeler. How strange that his very name and image stirred emotions in me that I thought had been buried years ago… and scarier still, ones I hadn't felt this deeply before at all. I couldn't describe exactly why I felt such a surprisingly close bond with Lucas, other than that he was pleasantly different from the man the media often portrayed him to be. He was caring and considerate, bright and interesting.

And he noticed me. This most of all I could not understand.

I felt safe with Lucas, in a way that I didn't feel with most people. He didn't seem to judge others for what they had done; and this gave me some peace about who I was and what I had done. In Lucas' whirlwind lifestyle, floating from one relationship to another, he couldn't possibly judge me for what Andy and I had done. And this gave me a sense of closure that I hadn't felt before.

"M," I ventured quietly towards the end of our meal, leaning in close to his shoulder some inches from mine. "Does Lucas have a…punching bag?"

I watched as a flicker of intrigue sailed across the oceanic depths of his blue eyes before he pointed me in the direction of the lounge room off the front foyer. "Past the doors off the main lounge area there's a gym, with all sorts of equipment: weights, a heated indoor pool and spa, bags, mitts, etcetera. Help yourself."

"Thanks," I managed, trying not to gawk at the thought of such luxuries at my disposal.

After dinner I decided not to join the others for a drink in the lounge and headed for my room, immediately closing the west curtains and not peering through the high glass windows into the lounge room below. I retrieved my laptop, setting my hand held recorder into its table top cradle before pressing send and waiting for the information to transfer via Bluetooth across to my laptop. I then spent an hour typing the outline of an article for the *London Times* about the *Globe's* charismatic premiere on Saturday, writing as positively and enthusiastically as I was capable of about Lucas' lively display.

If I sent the email to the editor now, it just might make the deadline for tomorrow's paper, I pondered, looking up at my reflection in the glass. It was self-edited well enough already, and a basic, uncontroversial piece about a play. What harm would there be in emailing the article tonight? Lucas wasn't back for days and the information was newsworthy *now*. If I left it too much longer it would be old news…besides, I was doing Lucas a favour, wasn't I?

I hit the send button without another thought. Lucas would see that it was a good idea once he read the story; and Gerry would just have to get over *protocol*.

I glanced out into the rear gardens, which had been lit up like a fairy dwelling after dark. I went to bed early for the night, feeling comfortable in my niche at Erravilla.

I woke to the tuneful sound of Geraldine again the next morning, humming to herself as she opened my curtains and stoked the fire.

"Am I late again?" I asked, sitting up hastily.

"Noo, noo. I's ten-t'-eigh'," she replied with an amused grin upon her features. "Father and I have already eaten, and I'm about to wake Master Emerus. I heard wha' happened in London. Frightful times these are…very unlike 'im to be sleepin' in. 'e's missed his morning run an' all."

I nodded, stealing myself to the shower, shedding my guilt along the way. It really was unnecessary on the part of Lucas and M to have stayed up all night on my account. It was my own silly fault to have left my drink alone at a crowded bar! I should have known better.

"You're quite the buzz of the house this mornin'," Geraldine called after me.

I ground to a halt and groaned.

"Not in a bad way. Actually, the consensus is a pleasing one from those who are at home," she replied, closing the door after her.

From those who are at home? Did that mean I was in for it from Lucas when he returned? I grabbed the recorder before heading down to breakfast. You never know what you'll need it for!

Sitting mid way up the table, M looked impeccable, which I quickly noted described him perfectly. He was always in trousers, a button-up shirt and fitted jumper, with his hair combed until it looked soft, never one out of place. He had placed the *London Times* upon the table as I entered the dining room, greeting me with a warm smile as I took my seat opposite him.

"Turns out you are in fact quite the saviour after all," M said maintaining his broad grin.

"What are you talking about?" I asked.

He motioned to the *Times* with a wave of his pale brows. It took me a moment to grasp what he was indicating and I reached across the table in a hasty manner to retrieve the paper, thumbing through to the entertainment section.

My article was the main feature of the section, accompanied by a photograph of Lucas, probably downloaded from their old files, and undersigned *A. Falls*. I felt overwhelmed, not expecting my article to generate this level of interest. *I am in London*, I reminded myself. *This is Lucas' hometown; of course the masses are interested!*

"So it seems you can write quite well, even hung-over," M teased good-naturedly. "What did Lucas and Gerry have to say about it?"

I winced through clenched teeth, looking into my cereal bowl as though it were the most profound historical discovery known to man.

"April? You didn't send this without *Gerry's* permission, did you?" he asked. "He'll have you for breakfast!"

I looked up and to my surprise found M sporting a large and incredulous smile. "Good on you! Gerry's a wolf at the best of times. I don't know how Lucas puts up with him."

I have an ally, I pondered in amusement. *So, I'm not the only one who thinks Gerry's the Big Bad Wolf!*

I hoped the small success was enough to counter any bad publicity regarding Lucas that had circulated from the local rag about the incident at the *Dungeon*.

"Well done, April Falls. It seems you are worth every bit and more, than that prat-of-a-man who calls himself Lucas' manager, was hoping for," M said matter-of-factly. "Sorry, that was rude of me."

"So long as it does its job," I replied, not wanting to blow my own trumpet too soon.

"Don't get me wrong," M added, his face becoming more elongated as he took on a more serious tone. "I'm not saying I agree with the whole…" He waved a charismatic hand through the air as he pondered… "You *following-Lucas'-every-move* thing. Quite frankly, I think it's going to be nothing but trouble for both of you: the other night proved that already."

I stared at him warily before broaching a lighter subject.

"So, are you visiting your parents today?"

"No, they return from Inverell tomorrow. Didn't Lucas tell you where they live?" he asked with a hint of amusement playing upon his features.

"No, in London somewhere I assumed," I replied with a shrug.

"They live here," he replied simply.

"Wait!" I interrupted, placing the dicta phone in the centre of the table. "If you don't mind? This is information I need."

"Sure," he replied with a shrug of his own. "My parents, Rick and Olivia Forrester, live in the further west corner on the second floor of Erravilla, beside the ballroom we saw yesterday. Lucas is gone so much of the time, especially when he's filming. They thought it a great waste of space to leave Erravilla unattended so much of the year, and decided to move out of the city, to Erravilla. We had the flat built for them and they live here as sort of caretakers, with the Chisholms. Erravilla is sort of viewed as the family home now I guess."

"That makes sense," I said nodding thoughtfully. "So, where do the Chisholms fit in?"

"Urland and his late wife—"

Late? Why did everybody speak of the dead as "late"? It made no sense to me. *Late* is what Hugh *had* been the night I had waited for him, *before* I knew he had died. How could somebody be "late" when they were already dead?

I avoided M's eyes for fear he would read me like the book I was with those all-knowing eyes of his, feigning sudden interest in the volume button on the dicta phone.

". . . were the caretakers at Erravilla for the previous owners, who were childless, and left the estate to the local parsonage. Lucas accepted Urland's request to stay on, as they knew the estate so well."

I glanced up at M and shied away from his gaze – one that had the opposite effect on me at times from Lucas'. I felt paralysed by his intensity, as though he could see everything I'd ever done and was waiting for the explanation behind my actions. And I wasn't ready to answer even one of them. Justice would have to wait.

I glanced across the table to the empty seat that was usually occupied by Urland Chisholm and imagined the ghost of an elderly woman I had never met standing behind him, resting her frail hand upon his shoulder. "And what of Geraldine? Doesn't she want to have a family of her own?"

M's lips twisted into a curl of hesitancy and he narrowed his eyes into half moons, as though trying to decipher my reaction before he replied, treading carefully upon the trail of eggshells that had been laid before my heart after the accident.

"Merrie Chisholm died some years back, after Geraldine had moved far north near the Scottish border. She had Geraldine in her forties, more than a decade after their only son was born. Geraldine had married young, barely eighteen; but lost her husband in a farming accident within a year. Geraldine moved back down to Erravilla to be with her father. For all of her grief, she's a surprisingly content woman. Her father and her dote on one another."

I swallowed the scales in my throat and leapt into the pond of tragedy fully clothed; if there was any more grief in this world that could touch me, I wanted to know it all. "And what of the son?"

"Geraldine's brother lectures at Aston University in Birmingham. He lives in Birmingham with his wife and two children," M offered.

I waited for more of the story to unravel, peeking through the wall of surf to steady myself against the blow that never came.

"Well," I said, stopping the recording phone, and released the tension slowly through the whistle between my O-shaped lips. I had not been expecting *that* kind of information about the residents of Erravilla.

The conversation left me feeling windswept. I still didn't cope well with too much bad news in one hit, which was why I stuck to entertainment reporting.

I decided to hit the gym to expel the unsavoury friction coursing through my veins. I took clothes to change into, closing the curtains and doors once I was inside the large gymnasium. M had been right: the gym was a wonderland of equipment just waiting to be explored.

I stretched, and then jogged laps to warm myself up, listening to the high-tech stereo unit to increase the adrenaline. Then I slid the punching bag across its runners until it was in the centre of the room and threw punch after hook until I could barely stand up. My limbs were aching from lack of use and I was dripping with the aftermath of a tidal wave. I returned the bag to the wall, dragging it along its runners in the ceiling.

It was time to clear my mind, now that I had beaten the adrenaline out of my system. I threw myself into the warm pool to neutralise my temperature and then I sat in the middle of the room upon a cushion of gym mats. I skipped the ipod track to one of my more tranquil melodies, and closed my eyes, crossing my legs yoga style in front of me. But for my melancholic mood, I would have giggled at the sight of myself upon those mats with my hair up in a blue towel, looking like Marge Simpson.

I spent a long time banishing the thoughts from my mind that still threatened to overtake me, fusing forlorn images of the past with pleasant ones of the present. I wrestled with the reflections and the emotions they provoked, until my mind was completely bereft of anything at all, except for the light rain pressing against the windowpanes outside. I remained this way for what seemed like a short eternity, determined to linger in my small chamber of solace.

The Voice always found me here too; here in the peace and comfort of my own mind it would wander, beckoning me to sit down by the cool waters of its embrace and drink of the life-giving sustenance I had once tasted. I wanted it so badly every time I stared at the outstretched hand before me, the hand that had fed me.

But I couldn't take it. Who was I that I deserved such love? Not after what I had done.

When I awoke from the slumber-like state, I felt rested but still displaced, breathing deeply, slowly becoming aware of my surroundings once again. My eyes popped open as I heard a creak; I turned my face to the door, which was now ajar.

M entered the room and knelt down a few feet from me. I did not feel self-conscious, as I would have ordinarily if I had been disturbed. I met his gaze serenely, his sky blue eyes an ocean of concern.

He swallowed steadily. "April, I'm sorry to interrupt you. It was quiet for so long…I get overly…apprehensive. I thought maybe you needed help or something," he said gazing around at the orderly gym. "I realised that I may have upset you earlier. And then this ring…changed colour…it's really weird."

I shook my head and smiled at his brotherly concern for me. "You didn't upset me, M. I guess I just needed to get the last few days out of my system."

"Is there anything you want to talk about?" he asked, the apprehension still fervent in his alluring blue eyes.

"You are very sweet, M, to be troubled for me. But really, I'm fine," I replied, touched by his sincerity. "What colour did it turn?"

"You don't sound as surprised as I was when it happened," he replied, his blue eyes searching mine. "It went orange for a while, and then back to gold."

"I went to find you yesterday, but you left my room too fast, before I had a chance to tell you. As you left, the band turned orange. And it was green at the *Dungeon* too. Why would it do that?" I probed.

M shook his head, looking as baffled as I felt. "I wish I knew. I wish I knew how to get it off for you. Are you sure you're okay?"

"Positive. Why?"

"April, your face is soaking wet," he replied gently, reaching out to trace the riverbed of a runaway tear along my jaw line.

I put my hands to my face in alarm. *It couldn't be*. But it was. My face was damp with the aftermath of a flood. I wiped at them furiously with the overhanging ends of the droopy towel still on top of my head. *When had I started crying?* I felt ashamed as heat surged onto my face; yet again, a private moment had been shared. I glanced away, wanting to cover myself beneath the giant bath towel.

"Would you prefer I left you alone?" he asked.

"M, you don't need to do anything for me." My shrill voice resounded harshly off the stone walls, sounding more like a rebuke than I had intended.

I heard a squeak as he stood and then the padding of shoes as he walked away. Too late I turned to ask him to stay. The door closed firmly behind him, but not before I saw the ring on his left hand glow a deep shade of orange.

M never showed for lunch, even though I lingered overly long eating the club sandwiches that Geraldine had made. I spent the afternoon typing in my room, occasionally glimpsing out into the rain soaked gardens. Intermittently I pulled aside the western curtains and glanced into the vacant lounge room below.

The guilt assaulted me as I chastised myself for my bluntness. He was only trying to be a brotherly shoulder to lean on, after all, and I couldn't even trust another person enough to do that.

Would I have told Lucas the truth if he had found me instead of M?

I didn't know the answer to that yet. But I promised myself that I would find M before he flew out for…wherever he was flying to this time…and ask for his forgiveness.

Alex had been right: I had become far too accustomed at isolating everyone for the past two years; and it had to stop. I was living a new chapter now – one where the wild ones of prey that constantly stalked me weren't going to catch up with me anymore.

12. Ghost Stories

When M didn't show for dinner I broached the subject with the Chisholms.

"Do you know where M is?" I asked between mouthfuls.

"'e didna' tell you?" Geraldine asked, her eyes wide. "Mr and Mrs Forrester called some hours ago: they flew in a day early, due to a bad weather forecast for tomorrow. Sco'ish weather is always precarious."

"When did he leave?" I asked, relieved to think that his disappearance had nothing to do with my earlier disregard.

"He left before lunch," Geraldine replied. "He said he was on his way to find you, and tell you where he was going. He mustna' found you."

I nodded and continued eating, conscious of the shame still wedged in my throat after swallowing my food. *He had found me all right.*

"Shouldn't he be back by now?" I pressed.

"Oh, he called to say they were goin' to visit with Agnes and Leicester for the afternoon and return after dinner," Geraldine replied.

"Is there something we can help you with, Miss Falls?" Urland asked, eyeing me steadily above his spectacles.

"Uh, no. I just…wondered where he'd gotten to, that's all," I answered. "Well, if the Forresters would like to, I'd be happy to meet them when they return."

"I'll le' them know," Geraldine said curtly, her cheeks stuffed full of food like a bullfrog. She could have been playing a final round of chubby-bunnies. And won.

I spent the evening lounging on the sofa in my warmed suite, listening to music above the drumming of the rain upon the tiled roof. I had borrowed Lucas' CD of the current *Shirtless* album from the downstairs player, seeing I missed the majority of the performance on Saturday. It wasn't bad: kind of a Green Day meets Kings of Leon…

A knock sounded on my door at nine o' clock and I leapt a mile off the sofa, fumbling for the remote to turn off the music.

"I didna' mean to startle you," Geraldine's singsong voice said as she snuck her head around the open doors. "The Forresters have returned and would like to meet you."

I followed the knot at the nape of Geraldine's neck all the way into the grand reception lounge where she left me to the company of the Forresters. I hazarded a guess that it was not too dissimilar a feeling a field mouse had in an open paddock of swooping vultures…

"April, these are my parents, Rick and Olivia," M said steadily with a sweep of his arm, his ice-blue eyes never leaving mine as he indicated towards the middle-aged couple opposite him. "Dad, Mother, this is April Falls."

I instantly covered my left hand with my right as the gold band turned a striking shade of red. M eyed me curiously, following the motion of my hands as I glanced at his parents to confirm that they had not noticed the ring. How would we explain the situation without me sounding like the snoop they probably already thought I was: a journalist lodging at Erravilla House?

"Hello, April, it's a pleasure to meet you, after hearing all about you from the children," Rick Forrester said amiably, reaching his hand out to take mine as he approached. I shouldn't have been surprised when he removed his hand at the last instance and took me into his arms for a chesty embrace, while I maintained a cover for the ring with one free arm.

Rick Forrester didn't look as I had expected him to, although I shouldn't have been surprised, from what Lucas had told me of his charismatic parents. He was not a tall man and I wondered where his sons had inherited their height… He had white-blonde hair that was streaked with grey through his temples and a neatly trimmed beard. I lifted my chin to embrace a familiar pair of startling blue eyes, lined with the bemused creases of age and abundance, as though they were constantly laughing.

Rick was built like a backhoe: strong and broad as a henchman. He was attractive for his age, though not as striking like his children. He was dressed eccentrically, from the green and yellow tweed coat, the sky blue knitted top and black shirt that hugged him closely, down to the bottle green bowtie and brown slacks. *Theatrical indeed*, I mused to myself.

Over Rick's shoulder I beheld his wife and son share a grin as I took in the entirety that was Rick Forrester.

"It's a pleasure to meet you too, Mr Forrester," I replied, trying to breathe beneath his crushing embrace.

He roared with laughter, finally releasing me from his grip. "Rick, please. I'm no gentleman!"

"Now Ricardo, let me see this *reporter* I've heard so much about," Mrs Forrester interrupted, sashaying her way towards me with her elegant limbs, and holding me at arms' length.

"I'm not a reporter," I began, at the same moment that Justice suddenly jumped to my defence with one of his own: "She's *not* a reporter."

 Mrs Forrester observed me from head to foot, with an interested gleam in her eye as they tracked every inch of me like a drill sergeant, eventually resting upon the gleaming ring on my left hand. Her eyebrows rose in curiosity, and I opened my mouth to explain. But she brushed me aside with a smile, taking herself to the liquor cabinet and pouring herself a glass of Sherry.

Olivia Forrester's appearance was a stark contrast to her husband's. She was quite tall for a woman; slender, with long dark brown hair, making her look far too young to have a thirty-something-year-old son. Her skin was an exotic olive complexion, the same as Aggie and Darius. The similarities between herself and her youngest three children were mystifyingly evident, right down to the pair of mesmerising emerald green eyes.

Olivia turned with her glass full, steadying her hand in salute and eyeing me with guarded interest. "Welcome, April," she said and then she drank, even though no one else had a drink. Her eyes never left me as she drank.

I was intrigued with this woman, whose powerful aura bewitched most people, I was certain. Not even Lucas oozed the control and confidence that his mother did; and I stood rooted to the floor as I took in the overpowering resemblance between mother and son.

"Let's all have a seat, shall we?" M suggested, motioning to the lounge suite. "We'll all have a *light* drink before bed."

"Emerus, should you be having—"

"He's fine, Ricardo," Olivia interjected, the glaze of a warning coating her tone. "It is just a *light* refreshment before bed."

Feigning indifference to his father's insinuation, though noting Lucas' earlier sentiments of M's past drinking habits, I immediately positioned myself beside M, feeling safer having created a clearway between Olivia and myself. I also knew that this was the safest way to avoid eye contact with M, afraid that my resurging guilt from this morning would be revealed for all to see if he caught my eye.

The Forrester family's dynamic pulled on every facet of my yearnings for the relationship with my own family which I had never had. I imagined a time when my mother and father had shared the buoyancy of life's ebbs and flows as Rick, Olivia and M now shared before me, embracing one another in conversation that centred around the core of who these people really were: desperately sharing in the lives of their children and one another in a way that astounded me, and one that I had never encountered.

I marvelled at the fact that Lucas Forrester really did have everything a human being could ever want.

Not everything, I heard the voice cry from deep within me, and I closed the door to it, lest I be swallowed by my shame.

My life seemed sheltered and mundane compared to the flare and worldly knowledge exhibited by the Forresters. Rick and Olivia did not need prompting to direct conversation, rapidly volunteering information about their trip north. M chatted to his parents warmly, asking details about friends and landmarks along the way – as an equal, not a child, as I often felt when with my own parents.

At ten o' clock Rick and Olivia headed upstairs and I was surprised by the light brush of their lips upon the crown of my head before they left, leaving the sensation of their warmth in their wake as I stared after them.

I heard the light clink of glass as M began clearing the empty flutes off the table behind me, and I turned as he took them to the kitchen through the dining room.

I drifted across the slate floor to stand by the fire, waiting for my chance to confront M about my ungracious behaviour this morning, still wrapped up in the simple gift of acceptance that the Forresters had bestowed upon me moments earlier.

<u>M</u>

I closed the doors to seal in the heat before looking up to see that April had her back to me as she warmed herself in front of the fireplace, watching the way her shoulders sank as she thawed. I could only see her profile as she stared into the flames, and I stopped to gaze at the perfectly smooth skin around her petit nose and bright eyes. I allowed my eyes to linger on the base of her neck where her skin met with the fitted long sleeve top and dark jeans she wore. Her straight brown hair cascaded down over her shoulder blades, resting on the woollen fabric covering her chest.

Lord, she's so beautiful…

I sucked in my breath in disbelief at the response of my heart's cry. It couldn't possibly be this way already. I had been down this path before, many times before, and it always ended in anarchy.

"It's purple now. It was blue before," April said simply, acknowledging my presence and dragging me into hers.

I caught my thoughts before they ran away completely, and approached her, stopping beside her and gazing into the flames. "April, I want to apologise—"

"*You* want to apologise?" she interrupted, her eyes wide with astonishment.

"Let me finish, please," I pleaded. "April, I had no right to intrude on you this morning. I should have left when I saw how upset you were. The thing is, I'm used to being the big brother around here, and I treated you as if you were one of the others, and I shouldn't have. I hope you can forgive me, and we can carry on as if it never happened," I pleaded hastily.

I caught the glance she dared throw my way, trying to measure her response.

Her chin lifted thoughtfully and she met my gaze with those startling opal coloured eyes. "M, I meant what I said earlier this morning, about you being sweet to be concerned about me. You're one of the kindest people I've ever met, and I barely know you. If I could have an older brother, I would want him to be just like you."

So that's how she thought of me: a brother? Pain lanced through my chest at the confirmation I was not ready to hear. I needed to distance myself and fast. Tomorrow couldn't come fast enough.

"Look, it's turning orange again," she said, holding the ring up against the fire light.

I held my hand up a safe distance from hers: it was the same gold colour it had been when we had first tried on the rings. "Yours seems to change colour an awful lot more than mine does. I've truly never seen anything like it…" I pondered, aware of the all-encompassing rhetoric in my words.

"I'm so sorry I was rude to you. You caught me off guard this morning…but that's no excuse. *You* don't need to apologise to me, but I'll accept it anyway, if it makes you feel better. I would love for us to be friends, M," April said, a bright smile lighting up her features. "It sounds a bit fifth-grade, doesn't it? And perhaps a bit *un*-professional on my part…I get the gist that you aren't happy with me following your brother around and reporting on him and your family, though. I know it must feel like a huge intrusion."

"And I still stand by my belief that I think what you're doing – seeking to write this book about Lucas – is dangerous for both of you and possibly for others." *And the idea that you're spending so much time around him…*"But as for the intrusion, I apologise for first thinking you might have been someone you're quite obviously not, from what I've seen so far. You just never can be too trusting with people these days…" *Especially the ones you think you're closest to…*

Without warning, April turned and nestled herself into my chest, her arms wrapping around me tightly. I hesitated a brief moment before my arms cradled her to me, aware of the instant effect her proximity held over me. I hoped to God that she didn't feel the racing beat of my heart within my chest, or notice the way my breathing almost stopped as the scent of her hair assaulted me without warning.

She stayed there for some time with her eyes closed; and I felt the tension drain from her as her body relaxed into mine. I rested my chin atop of her soft head, cherishing the feel of her silky hair against my coarse skin. I resisted the urge to kiss the top of her head, although I thought about how easily I could have, and reined in my senses before she would feel the awakening she caused through my *entire* body when she was this close to me.

I didn't want to disturb the comfort I found in holding her the way I was and decided instead to examine the ring on her left hand, which, as I watched in wonderment, turned a bright shade of red, and then faded to a deep purple.

"I'm sorry," April said in time, a rueful smile twisting her lips as she pulled herself away. "I used to be such an affectionate person. I miss it every now and then."

"That's what brothers are for," I returned, cringing inside and placing my hands in my trouser pockets, to prevent myself from taking her in my arms again and following through on my desire to kiss her in the most *un*brotherly of fashions.

"April, I don't want to be nosey, but if there's any way that I can help you…anytime at all…I want you to know that you can ask," I said, searching her eyes once more. "Oh, and in case Lucas forgets to forewarn you, we're hosting a sort of birthday bash thing here next weekend."

"Whose birthday is it?" she inquired, her eyes dancing already.

"Mine," I replied. "It's no big deal really, but Lucas and Darius look for any excuse to throw a party."

"Will you be…32?" she asked curiously.

"Yes. Well done. I wasn't home for the last two, so this is their way of getting me back, so to speak."

"Well, that's a huge reason to celebrate!" she laughed as a curl of cheekiness was added to her tone, while her perfect face suddenly became alive. "I mean, I'm only *twenty*-two..."

I laughed out loud in disbelief at the decade and lifetime between us. "You're just a baby!" I teased, alarmed that April was the same age as Darius: she probably thought I was over the hill!

"So what date is your birthday?" she said, glancing away into the fire as though the answer might materialise through the leaping flames.

"April second," I replied.

I felt the tremble of her frame as she leant up against me, an involuntary movement to stabilise herself. What was this dam she had so obviously built up with steel reinforcement over time, that occasionally spilt when the rains were too much to hold it back...?

An aching seized me as I recalled the image of her nestled in amongst the mats in the gym like a broken bird bound to her nest, tracing the water mark left by her earlier tears with my thumb. What on earth had happened to this incredible girl to bring her to such a place of burden?

I hesitated before placing an arm around her shoulders and pulling her gently to my side. This time I did kiss the top of her head, yearning to know what caused this vulnerable woman such pain, wishing that I had the power to heal, but knowing it was not my place. *Not yet...?* I wondered.

I hoped.

I balled my hand into a fist as it shook, and my finger burned hot beneath the bright orange band.

"It's burning you, isn't it?" she asked, wiping furiously at her runaway tears. "Why does it do that, so randomly?"

Her face tilted to inquire after mine, and I lifted my chin off her hair. "Oh, M," she sighed, exhaling deeply as though she could regather and soldier on through the battle alone. "I'm sorry you have to see me this way."

"It seems I have that effect on you," I mused quietly, gathering a strand of hair and easing it behind her ear.

"No, it's not your fault you share the same birthday as Hugh, my fiancé."

I dropped my hand like a loaded grenade as the searing pain returned, shooting through my arm like a hot spike. I waited for her to tear me wide open with more of her words, knowing I should have been more concerned for her troubles.

Why do I feel this way about a woman I cannot have?

"I told Lucas some things the other day, and I felt relieved after I'd told him. The thing is, I only told him part of the story: the easier part. I couldn't tell him the rest. I was afraid that I'd fall to pieces…" she laughed softly to herself. "Like I'm doing now."

I tightened my hold on her as she continued, aware that the burning sensation on my finger was not smouldering in intensity.

"I was engaged to be married a couple of years back. My fiancé's name was Hugh," she said, avoiding my gaze. "Lucas asked me if I still love him. Part of me does…and always will."

I flinched at her admission, willing myself to listen to her angst.

"I'm trying so desperately hard to move on, I really am. I've had such a wonderful week here, it's been easy to forget…what I feel when I'm at home in Australia…in the house that Hugh and I were going to live in for the rest of our lives."

I stole a glance at her and felt the battle rage as she spoke. Why did she need to pretend she could fight all by herself, whatever the risk?

"Now it's just me, and my two Border Collies, and occasionally my sister, Alex." She finished with a ghost of a smile upon her face, which fell short of her exquisite eyes.

Scissor Sisters.

"Go on," I coaxed, chastising myself for wishing I could borrow her armour to defend myself as she revealed more.

"A month before we were to get married, I was waiting for Hugh to come home from work; he always stopped by Audenlea to check in for the day. A knock sounded on the door and I went to answer it. But instead of Hugh standing on my doorstep, it was his parents. His mother was beside herself, hysterical, and his Dad looked like hell warmed up. They didn't need to tell me what I already knew."

I held my breath as April paused, waiting for confirmation of the blow that had shaken her world. Had Hugh left April by choice or circumstance?

"He had been involved in a motorbike accident. A truckie was driving home from a late finish and fell asleep at the wheel…"

April's voice trailed off into the ravine before us as I tried to sift through the wreckage her words had left behind.

"…as Hugh was on his way home from work. They said it was all over in seconds."

I focussed on the flames as they came into view again and glanced at April, astounded by the breadth of the chasm she had been walking through alone for two years. Suddenly the valley I had been walking through seemed somehow lighter compared to her plight.

I brushed my thumbs along the crevices below her eyes, wiping away the dampness left by her tears and then led her over to the lounge to sit down. She curled up instantly beside me, laying her head upon my thundering chest, her legs curled up on the lounge beneath her like a weary kitten.

I closed my eyes to the longing that beat against the cage in my chest, like a wild animal that yearned to be set free, feeling the warmth that covered my skin as the awareness of her proximity registered.

The rain continued to drum against the glass panes outside, reminding me of the many safe havens I had been given. I gathered the strand of hair between my fingers that had broken free from behind her ear and eased it back from her face; a small measure of what I felt for this hurting girl.

As the grandfather clock chimed eleven, I realised that April's breathing had become deep and even against my core, lulled into the confines of sleep. I savoured the gentle pressure of her hand resting upon my stomach, and I brushed the top of her ring, relieved that both of the rings were cool, and golden. I smiled, grateful for this measure of peace given to her through sleep, feeling the rise and fall of her chest against mine, but unsure if I should disturb her after her exhausting disclosure.

I wondered how well she would take my own disclosure if she ever found out, the one my father had so nearly disclosed this evening.

I held my breath momentarily, staring back down at her innocence before me. That was one side of me April didn't ever need to know about: Emerus, the whimpering drunkard. And that was the least of it…

I made one attempt to take her up to her room, but she mumbled in her wariness, her words rendering me powerless to take her anywhere.

"Please don't leave me," she had asked, her voice quivering like the aftermath of a mandolin string after being plucked.

April Falls

I don't know at what point I woke and at what point I still dreamt. I could smell the alluring scent of old spice, a pleasant aroma to my senses; and I heard a faint background rhythm, a steady methodical *thump-thump-thump*. The noise wasn't overbearing; rather, it was calming. I was warm and comfortable for the first time in a long time and I didn't want the dream to end. My hand ran absently along a smooth warm surface, up and back, feeling the contours along the surface as it moved, lingering every now and then on shallow grooves. At some point I heard steady breathing nearby, again a soothing sound, and the surface moved lightly with every breath.

I realised suddenly that the steady rhythm was a heartbeat, and the warm surface was bare skin. I sat up with a start, also startling the body beside me, who raised himself up on his elbows to gaze at me. A sleepy and welcoming grin lifted the corners of his mouth and he ran his fingers ever so gingerly through my hair. It took me a moment to realise who belonged to the lazy blue eyes and handsome face, and I exhaled with some kind of a relief, remembering where I was.

Laying my head back down momentarily, I startled again when I realised how closely I lay against *Emerus* Forrester.

Had I passed out drunk on the sofa last night? What had happened after that? What was Lucas going to say?

I cleared my throat and attempted to keep my morning breath away from his face, motioning with my hands as I spoke. "M, what happened here? Did we—?"

I glared wide-eyed at his bare torso, his shirt completely unbuttoned. I tried not to be distracted by the impressive lean flesh revealed beneath his clothes. I quickly examined myself and noted that at least *I* was fully clothed.

M laughed in apparent amusement at my sudden discomfort, lying back down and running his hands through his own dishevelled hair. Again I tried not to notice as each intake of breath caused his defined abdominal area to stretch and contract, right where my hand had been lying.

"Oh, April, don't you remember anything? I hadn't noticed you drinking more than a glass or two of wine, but maybe that did your pretty head in," he teased, before turning serious. "You don't need to worry about me, April. I would never take advantage of you. I was simply a shoulder to cry on, and then you fell asleep."

A rush of memories flooded my mind and I felt the heat rush to my face. "Oh, M! I'm so sorry! You seem to cause a spout of waterworks to erupt whenever I talk to you! And of course I trust you," I said quickly, though hopping off the lounge as I spoke. "I'm really sorry."

"Stop apologising," M returned, buttoning up his shirt, while an amused grin played upon his handsome features. A dark shade of stubble now lined his usually smooth jaw-line, and he ran his fingers along it as though it itched him slightly.

As we went our separate ways on the landing I heard a tuneful whistling escort M through his bedroom door, while the ring on my finger turned a pleasant shade of red. I chuckled to myself, no longer feeling strange that the warmth still lingered within me from M's body, and I recalled with an odd but inexplicable contentment, the feeling of being locked in his arms.

M and I were both late for breakfast, and I apologised to Urland and Geraldine, who were finishing breakfast with the Forresters. Through the French doors the rain still drizzled down, blanketing the estate in a thick cloud of fog.

"You two look like you've been visited by the tooth fairy overnight," Olivia said, a strange grin threatening to take her entire face hostage.

I had no idea what she meant and smiled politely, taking my seat opposite M. I glanced at M, who returned his mother's banter with raised eyebrows and a glare from his piercing blue eyes.

"I think someone had too much to drink last night!" Rick exclaimed, a throaty chuckle bursting from his lungs.

I stared dumbfounded at the Forresters as I realised what they were insinuating. They must have seen us curled up on the lounge together. My face coloured instantly, and I feigned sudden interest in my muesli.

"No-one had too much to drink, Dad. It's a long story," M returned. "And a private one! Now don't go thinking things that didn't happen. You know what will happen if word gets around."

Rick and Olivia said no more, taking heed of his warning, but Rick continued to grin with amusement between each spoonful of cereal nevertheless.

"Sorry, April. Some people are nosey and have not learnt appropriate etiquette," M apologised, ignoring his parents at the far end of the dining hall. "I thought maybe later, if you wanted to, we could go for another walk through the pine forest?"

I glanced hesitantly at his parents, noting that they had quietened somewhat as M lowered his voice to speak with me. I wondered what I was scared of exactly about their reaction. Was it my fear of Lucas' reaction if he misinterpreted their banter?

"Thanks, but I think I'm just going to lie low today, do some typing, exploring indoors, that sort of thing," I replied sheepishly, not quite meeting his gaze.

M nodded, although I knew I hadn't fooled him. He accepted my decline graciously. "Another time then." He left me to my privacy then, chatting lightly with the Chisholms and his parents, occasionally glancing in my direction as though he were gauging my temperament.

I was thinking of how best to excuse myself, when Urland Chisholm did so first. To my own surprise I took his arm as he passed by my chair, exiting the lavish dining room, where he said goodbye as he started his rounds for the day.

13. The Surprise Assailant

On Thursday morning M left for Heathrow Airport, destined for Sri Lanka. He never spoke much about his work, but the décor of Erravilla and the quantity of time he was away for work indicated that he was obviously devoted to his architectural world with a keen passion. I was beginning to realise that M spent as much time away from home as Lucas did, though in shorter bursts.

I hadn't known at what time Lucas was due in from L.A. and so I decided to spend my morning swimming laps in the indoor heated pool in the gym. True to the Australian culture, I had grown up loving the water and spending as much time as possible over the long hot summer months leisurely swimming in pools, rivers and of course, the many picturesque Sydney beaches.

I spent some time lapping before allowing my body to float around the sizeable mass of water like a snow angel, staring at the beautiful dome ceiling, painted with Roman-style mosaics.

I hadn't noticed that I had company until I felt the ripples of water ascend upon me, rocking the boat that was my body in small waves upon the surface. Before I had time to right myself, lunar style in the water, I was ensnared by two rather large hands around my waist and pulled below the surface. Instinctively I tried to fight the assailant off, fearing I would not make the surface again from the depth that I had been dragged to. The assailant did not release me: instead I felt my body being launched to the surface in a firm embrace from the floor of the pool.

I gasped for air when my mouth finally broke the surface, still trying to wriggle my way free. I was immediately spun around and found myself an inch from a very familiar and pleasant looking face, whose blazing green eyes blinked through droplets of chlorinated water. A large grin spread across Lucas' face as his warm breath reached my face and he ran a dripping hand through his spiky hair.

"You're quite the cat in water, aren't you?" his rasping breath seemed to cry, echoing off the plastered walls around us. The sound of his low crooning voice sent a flood of warmth through my body and I realised how much I had missed his company, however brief the interlude had been before he had left for the U.S.

I wanted to reach out and take his oval face between my hands, just to make sure I wasn't dreaming, or too involved in a film I was watching.

"You scared me half to death!" was all I could manage through my flighty breathing and water treading, while his dancing green eyes were still just centimetres from mine.

"That was quite an article you wrote," Lucas said tentatively, his hands still firmly around my waist.

I cringed, waiting for the onslaught. He studied my face for an instant before answering my silent question. "Mary-Anne called Gerry while we were in L.A."

"Are you mad?" I asked timidly.

"No. And neither is Mary-Anne; although she sends a light rap over the knuckles for not checking with her first."

I nodded, feeling like a misbehaved schoolgirl, while accepting that Lucas was perhaps right. "And Gerry?"

"He took a while to calm down. It took Mary-Anne *and* me to stop him from calling you. It wouldn't have been pretty…and I don't like being put in that position, between Gerry and you. He's my manager; I have to do what he wants sometimes. Luckily Mary-Anne sees potential in you."

Potential? Was that a backhanded compliment?

"Come and sit in the spa for a while," he suggested, changing his tone to a more light-hearted one. I looked across to the hot tub, centred in the middle of one corner of the room, which had been shaped into a glass sunroom, and where the sun now bounced brightly through the transparent windowpanes in prism showers.

I did as Lucas suggested, shrugging into one of the corners of the roomy spa, instantly grateful for his suggestion as the hot water thawed my mind. Lucas lingered in the corner beside me, my feet gently resting upon his in the centre like a silent pact of our mutual affection.

Lucas positioned himself with his arms arranged along the edges of the spa, one hand resting inches from my shoulder like a low-lying reptile. I was overly aware of his lean body, half exposed above the bubbling water and I tried to look at his face, or anywhere else, lest my emotions – which were fast galloping out of my control – overpower any dignity of reason that had been left in Andy's wake.

"How was L.A.?" I asked too quickly.

He didn't seem to notice. "Great, I think. Gerry's positive I'll get the part. It's going to be a huge film by the sounds. They've already cast Rose, Russell, and Naomi." A childish confidence spread across his adult features. "An almost all-star Aussie cast."

The pride I had felt for my newest acquaintance at the *Globe* resurfaced, and I smiled broadly at him. "You're a great entertainer. You'll never fade into the background like many actors eventually do." I was making a fool of myself. Lucas Forrester did not need another annoying half-crazed female fan at his doorstep. Or worse, *inside* his doorstep.

"I think I'll go and type for a while, leaving you to unwind," I said, rising to my feet like a shooting vine in spring.

I allowed my eyes to linger upon the furrowed brow that sheltered Lucas' sea-green eyes like a sandstone cave and sensed his dissatisfaction.

"What's the hurry?" he asked, as the unfamiliar tone of confusion in his voice reached me. I hesitated, channelling my hands together in a ball of indecision, lowering my eyes to settle upon his, pondering exactly what is was that he wanted of me.

Lucas stood slowly, standing until he had to tilt his face down to look into mine. Then he gently reached out and took my hand, raising it to his warm cheek and nestling his face into the soft contours of my palm.

My chest tightened at his touch, but I was unable to release myself from the bout of enchantment he had poured over me. My feet could not have moved even if I had willed them to and my mind raced at a tremendous speed, fear and ecstasy fusing together like the marring of colour within a kaleidoscope.

I watched the movement of Lucas' bare chest, heaving in and out as he breathed, and felt the gentle release of pressure in my hand as he lowered his face slowly towards mine. I instantly snaked my empty palm around his shoulder, running my fingers through Lucas' wet hair and pulling his lips to mine, taking hold of the lifeline that he willingly gave.

I folded myself into his hold freely, returning the need I sensed in Lucas with a fierce desperation of my own, giving reign to the source of warmth and thrill that had been unearthed in me through his affection.

I felt the incessant weight of life's inflictions begin to lift from me beneath his stronghold and I held firmer to his frame, trembling as I sought to rid myself of every last tendril of despair.

Too soon our seal was broken; the sudden detachment left me feeling stranded on one shore and he on another, amidst a lonely gulf of memories.

"You're shaking," he murmured, gently pulling me to him and cradling me to his chest like the shipwrecked vessel I was.

I felt the warmth of his frame as I rested my weary head in the crevice of his neck, his lips brushing the tip of my forehead.

"I've missed you, April Falls," Lucas breathed, and I seized the comfort of his words, wanting desperately to believe in the hope that each one gave.

As I tilted my chin to search for the path of truth behind Lucas' words, I knew that I was already lost in the current of emotions that he stirred in me. I didn't know how I was ever going to navigate my way out of the ocean I had leapt into, but I didn't care as I drifted there in the confines of his safe harbour.

Periodically I felt the surge of heat on my finger, as if the ring were reminding me that it too had a fast-hold over me and I fidgeted with the metal as I watched the hue of colour appear and disappear curiously.

Lucas steadied my hand suddenly, holding up the ring to examine. His brow creased and a tight line drew his lips together like a zip lock.

"You don't like the rings, do you?" I asked quietly, chewing on the tip of my tongue as I watched his expression darken.

"It's not *the rings* that bother me. It's that you're wearing a ring on your finger, that someone else has the other half too…my own brother at that," he replied curtly, applying a hint of pressure to the flesh around the band.

I winced at his apparent possessiveness, surprised by the intensity of emotion that had captured his being.

"Hey, M's been great these last few days," I offered as a sanctuary to his discontent.

"That's what worries me."

"He's just playing host," I assured him, despite the hint of unease and guilt that crept into my mind as I recalled the utter contentment upon M's face the morning I had woken in his arms.

"He doesn't seem to be in any hurry to get that ring off your finger…even though it hurts you." He held my hand in his and brushed the tops of my fingers with his thumb.

"Let's get out of here and get changed for lunch," I suggested lightly, brushing the unsettling thoughts of M from my mind and standing to leave.

Lucas was by my side in an instant, like a fertile vine reaching for its sun. In an instant I felt the warmth of his hand as it wrapped around my waist; and the sensation of buoyancy returned as he nestled his lips into the recesses of my neck, rekindling the flame that had momentarily began to cool.

"Lucas, I'm going to collapse and drown," I said euphorically, even as I pushed lightly against his abdomen.

But I did not push him away when he claimed my mouth for his own once again, returning his affection with a renewed thirst, allowing myself to be swept away in a tide of rapture.

An image forced its way through the torrent of my mind, weaving itself into the shape of two human forms, and I could not banish it away as they moved together in a steady rhythm, the methodical hum driving them closer together until they were one.

I inhaled deeply as the horror reel played through my mind, at how quickly and easily Andy and I had succumbed to our desire without any forethought at all, and I tore myself away from Lucas, gasping for air, refusing to allow the shame to bury me for a second time. I'd never be so careless again.

"April?" Lucas called after me, his voice barely audible amidst the aftermath of explosion in my mind.

I didn't answer him, grabbing my towel from the empty locker I had claimed for myself and wrapping it around my torso, taking my bag of clothes and shuffling into my shoes. His masculine form was beside me in an instant, resting his hands firmly upon my wrists, forcing me to look at him.

When I finally did, his beautiful features were twisted so that my chest felt as if it had been ripped open from the guilt and shame written across my heart. No matter how much I wanted what he offered, I could not live with the shame of a second cross to bear. Actions are always followed by consequences.

"I have so much more to tell you, Lucas," I said reluctantly, biding my time until I was forced to drive the wedge deeper between us. Lucas Forrester would not take kindly to being refused and I knew there would be no place in his world for the understanding I needed. "There's so much you don't know about me."

"When can we talk?" he persisted.

"I'll see you at lunch," I replied grimly, turning my mouth up at the ends in a premature farewell.

"Are we still…okay?" he asked with the uncertainty of a cautious teenager.

"Of course," I replied bitter-sweetly, wrapping my arms around Lucas' warm body and resting my head momentarily upon the rhythm of his bare chest. His arms wrapped themselves around mine slowly, his lips pressing lightly into my hair. He inhaled deeply, as though he were capturing my entire essence in that one breath.

His hand lingered on mine and his translucent eyes narrowed in on mine as I turned to leave.

"You're a complete surprise, April Falls," he said with mock disapproval, his mouth lifting at the edges as though indecisive.

I returned his gaze with a tentative grimace of my own, hoping that he would one day understand the ghosts who insisted on stalking my every move, rearing their disapproving heads at every opportunity.

After supper Lucas sought me from my room, coaxing me from my laptop and led me along the corridor off the kitchen, pausing halfway along the narrow passage before opening a door. He guided me into an enormous arcade style room, complete with a pool table, an air hockey machine, foosball and table-tennis tables, a large darts board, and a duke-box.

"This, is my indoor garage," he said proudly, his arms spread wide to indicate the enormity of the room. "Just like your…what do you call it in karate?...Do Jo? This is *my* Do Jo."

"This is your meditation room?" I asked, sweeping my eyes across the array of boy's toys. "How can this possibly be soothing?"

"Ah. You should see me with those darts. I'm mighty good when I'm in a bad mood," he laughed.

"So you mean, if I ever piss you off, to look for you here?" I enquired.

"Yep. I'll be here."

"I like it. It's very…you."

"Up for a game?" he challenged.

"Of what? How do you ever decide?"

"Your choice."

"Hmmm. Foosball. I kick arse at foosball."

"I'd like to see that," he said with an impish grin.

And as we played into the night, I told him all about Hugh.

Summer, 1860, rural Gloucester, England
Sir Walter Finnegan, last Earl of Erravilla Court

It took many more weeks before Maisy was able to take to her feet steadily and walk unassisted around the house but her strength seemed to be restored more by the day. And her confidence. She appeared as she said: as though she had nothing to lose. Her head was tilted high as she entered a room; she took her place as head of the table at the opposite end of the dining hall to myself; and she began to take it upon herself to run the household with the dignity of a Lady of her station should. She insisted on Grace before every meal and to my own astonishment, unlike before the accident, I allowed her even this; such was her determination.

I had to admit that this new Maisy, who did not care to take caution or timidity as she previously had, had the staff and the affairs of the house and indeed the estate in ranking order in no time at all. Her frankness startled me; her proficiency astonished me; and her utmost respectability I could not help but admire. Maisy insisted on throwing a delicate celebration to toast to her health and indeed outshone her own husband as the host of Erravilla Court.

Maisy and I had not discussed our private agreement since that day but I held no doubts that the anticipated child was the renewed reason for her will to live. Her new nature baffled the household staff, who eyed me wearily from the corners of their eyes when they thought I was ignorant of their stark perusals.

The evening of her health festivities was the night I remember seeing Maisy for the first time. Really seeing her.

She wore a tailor-made dress from the latest European imported silk, consisting of layers of the soft blue material. No doubt she had taken great care to prepare herself for the occasion, illuminating her best features, which had previously been forfeited in her attempts to remain modestly unnoticed.

However, Erravilla Court's hostess was anything but obscured, I noticed, as the eyes of every gentleman in the room failed to leave her form as she swanned about the house like royalty. I smiled to myself at the notion – a befitting wife indeed I had managed to ensnare...without any concerted effort on my behalf at all.

The affair did not linger late into the night, as most of the guests were keenly aware that Maisy was not quite one hundred percent recovered from her illness and excused themselves accordingly. I came to stand at the foot of the grand staircase as she bid farewell to the last of our guests in the foyer, the sound of coach hooves sounding along the gravel driveway as she closed the large oak door. She turned to face me, as though she knew I had been standing there all along, with a pleasant grimace upon her face, which reached the entire way to her eyes. This new Maisy had found a new element for herself and was much pleased with her efforts.

"Well done, Mrs Finnegan," I acknowledged with a tilt of my head. "A splendid occasion, no less."

"Thank you, Mr Finnegan. I am much obliged that you have enjoyed the festivities."

We stood there facing one another for moments in silence, each one taking in the other with an explicably strange examination. I realised I had been staring for longer time than was appropriate and cleared my throat awkwardly to signify my impending departure.

"Well...goodnight, Mrs Finnegan," I said, tipping my head to her in polite salute before turning up the stairs for the night.

I lay in my suite staring at the architraves for a long while, my eyelids refusing to close over. Sleep refused to assail me, no matter how I tossed and turned upon the grand bed. I was overly aware of the young woman in the suite next door and it unnerved me greatly. I had given her my word. But that had been before...before I had begun to feel this strange and inexplicable desire for the woman. I could not wipe her naked *form from my mind, no matter how urgently I scolded myself for such indecencies.*

She is your wife, I reminded myself. It was natural; nay, a given right that a man should be able to lie with his wife when he wanted, no matter what the nature of the otherwise affected relationship could be. It did not matter that I did not love the woman; it was enough that my affections lay purely in a physical plane. This should be an easy, even possibly pleasurable, task to undertake. And she was willing. Even if for the sole purposes of producing a child, which was the way of it with women of her standing, I reasoned.

Blast! But it was she who had asked – no, demanded – it of me! I silently raged as I strode across the floor and quietly stepped from my suite into hers. It was dark in her suite, but I had remembered the layout of her furniture as I hedged towards her bed. The oil lamps had been extinguished for the night, but a pale ribbon of moonlight revealed a strip of wall-paper above where the wooden bed head was.

She had heard my muffled entrance and sat quietly staring at me as I approached, her hauntingly pale face illuminated by the ribbons of moonlight. Her face was expressionless as I stopped beside the bed, her eyes searching mine fervently, not because she wanted me as a woman in love with a man but because I had the means to give her the only gift that she yearned for.

She did not appear afraid but rather held that fixed look upon her features that she had worn since our discussion, that she had nothing to lose, and cared nought for anything else.

"Are you ready for me, Maisy?" I asked in a hushed voice, barely able to contain the immense tension I felt at the impending activities.

She nodded slowly and methodically. She was bracing herself.

I undressed myself in the shadows, aware that she would not have seen a grown man naked before, and might find the sight intimidating. I slipped beneath the sheets and sat beside her, covering myself appropriately to the waist, before turning towards her and guiding her gently onto her back beneath the covers. She stiffened at my touch, but she did not pull away, willing herself to the task ahead. She did not undress, as I guessed she would not. This was not about pleasure for her – simply a means to an end.

When the moment had come to pass, I retreated hastily back to my quarters, leaving her to her privacy and her stifled prayers interspersed with jagged sobs.

I remembered later that it was her nineteenth birthday that day. And we had been married almost a year. But I knew they were not the only reason for her tears...

14. Question Time

April Falls

On Friday our schedule indicated that Lucas had a live interview on a popular British television talk show to preview the release of his latest film, due for release in early May.

I had to beg Lucas to let me go. He eventually gave in, with conditions. We were to travel and arrive separately at the studio, at least half an hour apart, and I wasn't to speak with him at all during the filming.

"That includes *question time*!" he forbade, his brows knitting in frustration with my persistency.

"How am I meant to write my article if I can't *observe* you?" I had argued. "All right, I won't ask any questions, I'll just have to hope someone in the audience has half a brain and asks you the right questions."

"You know you can ask me anything *off*-air?"

"Yes. But it's not the same as a *live* interview. What if I want to question you about another question?" I challenged, standing with my hands on my hips in the hallway below my bedroom. I had the slight urge to bobble my head from side to side to emphasise the attitude like those African-American women did so well.

He had rolled those unforgettable emerald eyes and huffed across the landing. "No live questions! It's too dangerous. I don't want someone to put two and two together about us."

"How would anyone possibly know that?" I called after him.

"You should *see* the way you look at me sometimes! And I'm so protective of you at the moment…I wouldn't be able to hide how I feel about you, even *with* some acting skill."

Mary-Anne had reserved me a stellar seat in the audience, close to the front, near centre stage. I was humming with anticipation, perched amongst ninety-nine other ecstatic mostly female fans. They were buzzing with chatter like a hive of ladybugs, and bursting at the seams with expectation about today's guest star. I couldn't believe the small fleets of women who made multiple trips to relieve themselves for a "nervous wee" before the filming began, refusing to miss a second of the program once it began. I hoped that aliens would abduct me and crown me their leader before Lucas ever saw me behave like that.

Cindy Rolland spent the first few minutes of the show building up Lucas' career, playing snippets of his most successful screen rolls, before playing a sneak preview of his newest feature film.

Lucas always seemed to satisfy his fans, who still reacted to the very sight of him with cheers of hysteria, whistling, and often tears. Sometimes I felt as if the aliens had already abducted me, for I could not make out a word of English from these women as they twittered uncontrollably. I peered around nervously, waiting for the alien coronation to begin. There I was, in my own little world, surrounded by these hysterical women, trying to contain my own anticipation, calmly waiting for the hype to settle and for Cindy to begin her interview.

Lucas was a superb professional interviewee after seven years and countless films in the industry. I was amazed with the stability, confidence and maturity that he was able to produce in front of a live studio audience. As Lucas had predicted, *question time* was a favourite for the audience, who were allowed to ask anything they wanted.

The questions began simply, asking about Lucas' career to date, his favourite films, directors, scripts and co-actors, his future films and contracts, some humorous personal questions, as well as the controversy surrounding the latest media hype. Lucas answered all the questions with the appropriate degree of wit and humour, flashing that astoundingly attractive grin at every opportunity.

"Well, everyone knows I love my music. Of course if acting hadn't taken off I would have pursued a music career. But I've always had a keen interest in politics," Lucas replied, astonishing me as well as many of the ladybugs around me into nervous chatter. "Not like my brother," he added with a jibe-infused laugh.

And then I saw why this program was so popular. I wondered why Lucas would have chosen to air on a program like this as a fresh round of questions were fired, and it was obvious that Lucas had been prepared.

"Is it true that you haven't been in a serious relationship for years now?"

Lucas answered with his hypnotic grin and a chuckle. "Yes. I'm quite happy this way."

"I read somewhere that you're still in love with your *Seasons* co-star, Susan Cahill?"

"Absolutely not. We have remained great friends, nothing more."

"There's been speculation for years that you're actually gay. Is that true?"

Lucas laughed spontaneously at this question. "You're asking if I'm gay, just because I'm *single*?"

"Yes, I guess so. Are you?"

"No. But time will tell," he replied, a dark humour passing across his features.

"An article in *The Times* recently said that you were involved in a drink-spiking incident at a London club with an unknown woman. How do you respond to this accusation?"

The melodic ring of a broad Scottish accent rippled through the studio and I snapped my head up in the direction of the voice with curiosity. It belonged to one of the most beautiful women I had ever seen. She was dressed in a simple fitted red dress, which complemented her honey-blonde hair and deep green eyes to perfection.

The question seemed to catch Lucas off guard, and I held my heart with my hands, as though I could prevent it from leaping straight out of its cage. I endured a painful few seconds, deliberately shielding my face from his view, petrified that a camera might pan to me in that instant and reveal the strength of my affection.

"No, I was not. It was a coincidence that I was there that night."

It was the first lie I had heard run off Lucas' lips and a bittersweet anguish crept through me at the admonition. He was protecting me, I knew it, but it didn't chase away the guilt the lie had left in its wake.

An unnatural expression slithered its way up through the tendons in the Scotswoman's neck as her eyes narrowed into half moons. Her beautiful face constricted into scales of anguish, thrown at Lucas with the force of a rattlesnake poised to strike.

"Who was the girl?" she hissed, all the haunting beauty of her highland accent drained with the poison that laced her tongue.

"Like I said, it was a coincidence that the incident happened while I was there," Lucas repeated, and I noticed the fervour with which he returned her gaze, like a bug under a microscope.

"But you were seen leaving the club shortly after she was," the woman persisted, wrapping her coil around Lucas with every word, squeezing as though she could drain the fluid of information from him that she sought.

In my heart I knew it was me she sought; probably one of the many obsessed fans upset by the possibility of Lucas having a private relationship.

"Is she your new love interest?"

"I have given my answer, and I don't wish to comment further on the matter," Lucas said, far too calm to mirror the turbulence that careened itself through my body as I watched the two like participants in a tennis match in progress, hoping that he would lob her an ace and send her flying back to her seat in defeat.

The session was cut to an ad break and the Scotswoman unwound herself enough to sit back on her scales, despite the venom still fresh in her eyes.

I couldn't leave the studio quickly enough when the filming was over. I caught a taxi to Park Lane and waited for Lucas in his apartment, pacing the reception lounge until he arrived, flanked by two people who I could only assume were his publicist, Mary-Anne, and his obnoxious manager, Gerry.

The three of them sat around the resin dining table, discussing this morning's *frenzy*, like a board meeting at a bank during a Wall Street crisis. I couldn't fathom how they eventually all calmly agreed that the interview had been a success and watched as they prepared Lucas for the live-to-air radio segment he was co-hosting this afternoon in town.

Lucas disappeared into his master suite to phone M before we left for the studio, his velvet voice lowered, perplexed. "M, she was there, in the studio…I know it was her…I just thought you should know…she was where?...why didn't you tell me?...why would she suddenly be showing up to these things?...you don't think it's a coincidence?...all right…I'll see you when you get home…yeah…bye."

The radio program was far more informal and relaxed, hosted by a couple of juvenile upstarts, while the listeners were mostly young people and laid-back Londoners. Any calls that were even mildly harassing were upturned on the callers, who were told in no uncertain terms by the larrikin DJs not to phone again. Lucas and his co-hosts found these calls hysterical, joking about the deranged callers for the entire show.

Hysterical? I was sitting on my nerves like a roosting hen in the next booth!

Then she phoned. My senses were so attuned to Lucas' safety net that I couldn't have missed the toxin any less than a bite to my own face. I watched as Lucas' brows dipped again, the same cautious irritation that he had worn in the television studio.

"Hi, Lucas," her melodic highland voice chimed. "I was just wondering how your little *Joey's* going after her drinking binge at the *Dungeon* last Saturday night?"

Lucas reacted the second that the caller spat the word *Joey*, snapping his emerald green eyes up to meet mine, a grim expression upturning his handsome mouth into an arc.

The DJs did not notice her Australiana jibe, despite the cautious exchange between the guarded Gerry and sombre Mary-Anne beside me, both avoiding my eyes. Lucas dragged his forefinger across his taught throat, indicating to the producer to cut the caller immediately.

"I'll ring M later tonight," Lucas said to Gerry as they emerged from behind the closed doors of Lucas' room at Park Lane. "He'll be home on the weekend. It's his birthday on Sunday."

"You throwing him a do?" Gerry asked, his tone taking on a lighter pitch to disguise the darker tones his voice had projected from the room.

"Yeah, the family's coming over Sunday," Lucas replied, running a hand through his hair, distracted.

"When are you leaving London?" Gerry sighed, eyeing me speculatively. I sensed that he found me as safe for Lucas to be around as a trapdoor in a mine.

"I plan to leave at dusk," Lucas said, looking out into the overcast afternoon as the steel doors clambered together, ensconcing Gerry and Mary-Anne within their robotic clutches.

"Okay, so what's with all the cloak and dagger?" I demanded, spinning on my heel to glare at Lucas, which was difficult to do while my heart spun on its own axis, rendering me powerless to feel frustrated for long with him.

"I can't tell you yet," Lucas replied, pausing with his hand halfway through his tousled hair as though someone had interrupted him during a photo shoot. "It's kind of complicated. I need to speak to M first. There are things that you need to hear from both of us before you..."

"Before I what?" I whispered, wondering if I could reach him from the other side of the room with mere words, the way he could hold me with his.

He crossed the room to where I stood and gently lifted my chin to look into his face. "I wish for all the world that you didn't have to be involved in this. If I had thought for one minute that you could have been hurt in any way by the things in my life…I would never have agreed for you to come to London. We didn't think it was serious."

I knew he was speaking of the fanged Scotswoman, whose involvement in Lucas' life now intrigued me. And what did M have to do with all of this?

We left London as Lucas had intended, at dusk.

"For stealth reasons," he said as a grin turned up the sides of his mouth while we purred along Park Lane at a pace that left my solemn mood behind.

I rolled my eyes in his direction as if he needed an excuse to test the capabilities of the lean machine beneath his fingertips.

Lucas and I spent Saturday in various parts of the old estate, lounging from one part of the house to another as I typed, while Lucas read over his lines for an up-coming film shoot.

After dinner I ran myself a bath, running the hot water until it reached my chin and I had to blow wind tunnels through the bubbles just to see my feet perched against the far end, my toes gripping the porcelain to feel the cool against my hot skin.

And then I submerged myself into the world that only I had access to, waiting for the battle to start anew as the colours began to fade from darkness to light; separated by the hand of peace through the centre that still waited for me to accept its invitation…

From within the abyss of my mind I became aware of a being not of the spiritual realm and he called to me from a far off place. An image of the two human beings broke through into the abyss like a creature of the darklands, and I hurled the grotesque carving from my mind, revolted by the sounds of their cries…and then the sound of a third, far more innocent cry…the one that I had abandoned. And I was their only hope…

And still the voice called to me, familiar and welcoming, and I extended my hand in desperation, longing to reach across the endless black expanse that had swallowed me. *Please! Please, I want to see you again! Bring them back, please! I'm sorry!*

"Hugh!"

"April! Stop struggling or you're going to drown!"

My eyes sprang open and I gasped for air as though I had been under the pressure of a thousand litres of water.

A warm hand touched my shoulder where the skin had cooled and I winced. "Take it easy; I don't want you to inhale any more of these soap suds!"

"Lucas!" I gasped again, alarmed by his proximity. "What are you doing here?"

"I was about to ask you the same thing. You've been gone for over an hour. I thought you'd been sucked down the pipes!" he said with a grimace, his mouth dipped into a frown.

"Well, you can let go; I'm not going to drown."

He nodded slowly before releasing me, as though he were testing the stronghold of my word.

"It's kind of cold in here now. Can you get me my towel?" I asked, pointing to the heated towel rack beside the door.

Lucas returned swiftly, holding up the large open towel above the woollen bath mat. I eyed him precariously, far too shaken by the experience I had just had to play Russian Roulette with Lucas' hormones.

"I promise I won't look," he said, with the look of an audacious schoolboy dancing across his lips as he pinched his eyes closed so hard his dark brows became a furrowed line.

"I'm beginning to believe those play-boy rumours I read about you," I said with a hint of a grin, my eyes locked onto his face as I stepped out onto the warm oval carpet. His arms were around me in an instant, the warm towel swallowing me whole.

"Oh, you scorn my test of honour," he drawled in mock offence.

"You call this a test of honour?" I asked, amused.

"Are you decent?" he asked, his eyes still closed, while an enormous grin streaked across his face.

"Yes, thanks to you," I said, trying to remain calm in his close embrace.

I was still gazing into his face, just millimetres from mine, when his eyes opened and searched mine for a short eternity, my pulse threatening to crush my weak heart. His hands didn't move an inch as his lips slowly parted and embraced my own welcoming pair. Despite the warning that ran as clear as the water I had just emerged from, I wanted to throw my arms around him and pull his body closer to mine, but they were fortunately still trapped in the straight-jacket of a towel that Lucas held me in.

He seemed to enjoy the complete power he held over me as he kissed me urgently, knowing that I could not escape, even if I wanted to; knowing that my lips were currently being held hostage to his and powerless to order him to stop.

15. Penny McClellan

Erravilla Court

M

The trip to Sri Lanka was a success: details of the project were sealed within 24 hours – a whole day earlier than expected – and I returned to London immediately.

I hummed as I scaled the steps of the grand staircase, admiring the European modern art talents that lined the walls of Erravilla. I glanced up the steps to the landing above as I reached the second floor, a fusion of emotions coursing through me as I paused to study the slightly ajar door on the top floor.

Thoughts warred in my mind; part of me curious to visit the guest who was staying in that room, the one who I discovered with a sharp twang that I had missed while I had been away. I was beginning to give in to the side of me that wanted to befriend April in more than a sisterly way, but much too aware of the connection I sensed that she shared with Lucas. I wasn't sure how deep their affiliation ran, and I found that I tormented myself with the thoughts that occupied my mind in that regard. And though I knew it was best for me to put her out of my mind altogether, the task was proving more than impossible now that she was so close.

I glanced one final time at the door off the landing above before dismissing the urge to scale the remaining steps to pay her a welcoming visit. I felt the hum of the ring upon my finger and paused to startle at the deep shades of purple and red.

A shriek rang out from April's room as I stood nearby, my body reacting instinctively. I scaled the stairs in an instant, bursting through the double doors to save April from the terror that had caused her outburst.

I stood breathless, transfixed upon the sight before my eyes, pausing only momentarily to assess the situation before reacting to my intuition. I covered the length of the floor in seconds, striding with the fury of a jealous lover towards the bed where she lay, clad only in a bathrobe, with her wet, but neatly combed hair, partially concealed by the towelled hood of her robe; and covered by the larger body of my brother, whose lips moved at an eager pace down the face of April's neck, his hand above her exposed knee and slowly moving towards her torso.

I felt the anger fuel as I gathered a force of all that I thought was holy within me, reaching the large four-poster and hurling my brother onto the floor in one swift movement; my breathing tearing from my chest with the rage that surged through my scorching hot veins.

My concern was only for April as I hovered close to her still form, skimming every facet of her that I could take in for evidence of her mistreatment.

I felt the swift thump against my back and turned with enough sound defence to catch Lucas' fist before it landed its mark against my jaw. His eyes were filled with a wild fury and his mouth lifted at one side as though he were baring his teeth for a kill.

"What in the hell do you think you're doing?" Lucas demanded, shoving me with his ensnared fist.

"I was about to ask you the same thing," I returned, the hint of a wolf growling out between my teeth.

"You're the one who barged on in here!" Lucas howled, his torso squaring up before mine. "I've had enough of your controlling and meddling, Emerus!"

I winced at the use of my full name, a name that Lucas had not called me since we were children.

"And I've had enough of your Hollywood power games, using your fame and fortune to throw yourself at anyone you choose," I retorted, outraged by his pompous arrogance.

I measured my stance, retreating to a slightly more civilised bearing, while still holding out cautiously.

Lucas' fists fell to his side as he took measure of my submission and stepped past me towards April, eyeballing me as he danced by with the ferocity of a Spanish Matadore.

"You think I was *throwing* myself upon April? That I would actually take something from her against her will?" Lucas demanded, placing himself between April and me.

"Stop it! Both of you!"

I started at April's shrill cry, daring to peer around Lucas. April had sat up, hugging her gown to her body, the ashes from the fire now scattered across her face.

"M, I'm sorry, but I think there's been a misunderstanding," she offered, her opal coloured eyes widening in a gesture of admission. "Lucas wasn't taking advantage of me."

She looked away as a becoming shade of red crept along her cheekbones, and I realised too late the blunder I had made. I felt the weight of my sensitive instincts rest heavily upon me like a shroud of responsibility as I stared at her raw indecency.

"Well, it wouldn't have been the first time," I said levelly, my pride taking a swing for the ledge on the side of decency, but missing and landing deeply in the crevice below.

"What do you mean?" April asked, ascending discreetly from the bed and positioning herself away from both of us.

Lucas shook his head and I caught the passing ghost of guilt in his eyes as he glanced away. "I knew I should have been the one to tell you, April. M has a…distorted view of things."

"I'm not surprised he hasn't told you about Penny," I said, my bruised ego still scratching at the edges of the crevice.

"I've told you it's not what you think," Lucas sighed, flaring his angst in my direction.

"April," I began, looking to her but only seeing the image of another woman through my pain. "Six months ago I discovered Lucas," I paused, surprised by the renewed strength of betrayal that threatened to seize me after all this time, "in bed with my girlfriend, Penny."

"Is this true, Lucas?" April asked, her sea-blue eyes slowly taking form as I reigned in the vision and focussed on the present.

Lucas took a deep breath. "In the literal sense that he says, yes. But it wasn't what it looked like. I've explained many times to you, Emerus," he retorted, grounding out my name.

"Then what *was* it like?" April asked, her voice an octave higher than I had ever heard her before.

"I'd had too much to drink the night before: we hosted an after-party here for some of the London celebs after the release of the final *Seasons* film. I went to bed – *alone* – and woke up with Emerus in my face – kind of like *this* . . ." he hissed. "And Penny was beside me. I don't know when she got there; or how she even got into my room – it's always locked! She says we…" he gestured absently with his arm, looking me directly between the eyes as he continued. "But I swear, I don't remember a thing, and *that's* not something you're likely to forget."

"That doesn't mean nothing happened," I said running my hand through my hair. We had been over this six months ago until we were blue in the face, but I still didn't believe Lucas. "How do I know you two weren't seeing each other behind my back?"

"M, come on! I'm your brother! Why is it so easy to believe *her* over *me?*" he cried.

"Because it's not like Penny to do something like that unless she were…seduced or taken advantage of! She was a perfectly fine woman up until then."

"She's not the girl you thought she was, M. Admit it. I mean, look what she's done recently; for all we know, she could be that stalker from the paper! She could have spiked April's drink!" Lucas bellowed.

"Penny McClellan is not a dangerous person," I said, emphasising each word. "I think you're blowing your own trumpet there Lucas, to think she's so obsessed with you. We haven't had anything to do with her for six months!"

"Maybe we have. Maybe seeing April that night at the *Dungeon* set her off," Lucas said, quite resolved.

"Can someone please fill me in?" April asked, taking a step towards the centre of the room and hugging her gown tighter still.

"This is what I couldn't tell you yesterday, April," Lucas began. "I called M to tell him that Penny was at the talk show yesterday—"

"She was?" April gasped.

"Yes, the Scottish woman," Lucas replied through his teeth.

The mist of dawning seemed to roll in across her face and she placed an absent fist against her open mouth. "The beautiful blonde woman in the red dress…"

"Yes," Lucas replied and then glanced at me, shifting his weight to a defensive stance. "Not that I think she's beautiful like I once did. I think she's dangerous and downright potty! She phoned up the radio station while I was there yesterday too."

"Of course," April whispered, her eyes scanning the sea of carpet before her as though it were the jaws of life. "She knew details that weren't published, details that would insinuate I was here for more than just on a *professional* visit," April choked. "She knew that I was an Aussie, knew about my apparent *hangover*, and she mentioned the *Dungeon*. M, he's telling the truth."

"I don't believe that the woman I was going to marry would harm another human being, let alone a stranger, who's done nothing to her," I said, throwing the rope of disbelief up towards the ledge I was swinging beneath. "And I still don't believe that you did *nothing* to encourage her six months ago," I added, glaring at Lucas, before turning to April. My heart was about to rip wide open as I let go of the final rope of desperation, taking a giant leap off the edge and looking back. "And I thought *you* were smarter than to fall for Hollywood boy here, with all his charms and fast cars, risking your own decency and safety to write a *book*. I thought you were different from all the others. You barely know him…and Penny's right: he's made you his not-so-*professional* hussy."

"Get out of my house, you drunken bastard!" Lucas breathed. "Before I give you a taste of your own medicine and throw you out by your pathetic limbs!"

I blinked at Lucas feeling as though every layering of my protective shell had just been stripped bare, not quite believing what he'd just labelled me; after all I had been through…after all that *we* as a family had been through.

As I gazed at Lucas I felt myself slip further into the chasm, daring him to come good on his promise and have it out with me once and for all.

I glanced fleetingly at April, wishing I could have prevented her from being privy to the encounter, and hoping she wasn't piecing the ugly pieces of my life together, knowing full well I would fall far beneath her gaze if she knew how bad it had gotten. Her chest heaved in and out heavily, her eyes an endless well of lost hope as I strode from the room, the ring on her finger glowing the same burnt orange tinge as mine, and I knew that she felt the same sting from it as I did.

April Falls

Thy rod and Thy staff they comfort me. Psalm 23
And yet I refuse to shed this fleece of shame…

I stood bereft, fidgeting with the burning metal upon my finger, afraid to look at Lucas lest he should see my turmoil.

"April—" Lucas began, his crimson voice threatening to melt my resolve. "Lucas, I don't want to talk to him, or to you right now. I just need time to think things over. I shouldn't be involved in this mess between you and him," I seethed, pacing the room, utter humiliation coursing through me like a shaken bottle of pop. "And now this between you and me. I feel sick."

I looked at the bed where Lucas and I had been fooling around minutes earlier, so close to something so shameful, and I saw the body of Lucas with the face of Andy and I felt my body begin to shake uncontrollably.

What had I been thinking? This kind of harmless fooling around was what had gotten me into trouble with Andy in the first place. It was the reason that I had wanted to have a short engagement with Hugh and no fooling around in the meantime. It was one relationship I counted as having begun to balance the scales of righteousness against what Andy and I had done. No one was going to commit to me long term if they knew the truth: that I *was* the hussy Justice had spoken of: and far worse. And that I was unlovable, as Andy had so pointedly made me aware of.

At least Hugh had never found out.

And although M was right, my anger surfaced, raw and ferocious at myself, at Andy, and at M for flaring the shame and humiliation so blatantly.

How dare he call me a hussy! How could he think so lowly of me without even knowing me? And to question my professionalism!

Who was he anyway, the moral beacon of the world? What makes him think he's so perfect?

What stung the most was the way he had so blatantly minimalized my one true passion: writing this book. This "*book*!" Justice had said with such distaste for the very idea… the one thing I so desperately wanted to achieve. And I had wanted his support to do it. I needed it. He was one ally I was counting on to get this book done.

Had been counting on.

I stared at Lucas, who leaned up against the bedpost with the weight of too many burdens dipping his broad shoulders.

"For what it's worth, I'm really sorry you landed in the middle of all this. If I could do anything to make it better for you, I would. But I can't change the way my brother behaves and thinks. I was never involved with Penny. I didn't even know she had feelings for me until I woke up that morning and she was there. I was as surprised as M," Lucas offered, lowering his gaze to mine from across the sea of despair that had been created. "I would never cheat with somebody's girl, especially not my brother's. And especially not after what Susan had done to me a year earlier."

I remembered reading about the affair.

Every sense in my body wanted to believe him; to cling to the lifeline he had proven to be so far. But I couldn't swim through the mash of images fusing in my mind…Andy and I; Lucas and I; the needle-sharp words of M's fury…*Hussy! Book!* And the one that rang the loudest and truest: *Murderer!*

I knew how easiy it was to get carried away, even without forethought. Lucas' reputation with women didn't serve him in good stead for one with self-control. He had practically thrown himself at me and I was a no-body! I had seen Penny McClellan's beauty firsthand. What if he couldn't come to terms with what he'd done, even unintentionally?

"And if you can believe me, I wasn't taking advantage of you. I wouldn't do that to you either," Lucas added, his parting words an offering of peace, an offering I didn't know if I could accept.

A week passed with Lucas and M both away, both avoiding Erravilla and leaving shadows of themselves in their silence. And I was drowning in it. I searched through every photo album I could find, every certificate, trophy, and sporting and artistic memorabilia packed away in storage or on display; examined every ornament and artefact that could give me more clues on who Lucas Forrester was before stardom had taken its reformation on him; taking verbal notes into my handheld recorder. I wanted to find anything and everything to discover what had shaped Lucas into the private and public person he was today. To prove to myself, and one day I hoped – to others – that he *was* a noble cause to write about, and that I was the one who could do him justice.

I took notes on names of his senior year colleagues from the elite boys' College he had attended to complete his O Levels, intending to contact them to better my research. I made a mental note to speak with Albert at the Globe regarding Lucas' earlier career performances, and spoke the words that had been haunting me for a week now very cautiously into the steady recorder, afraid to wake the ghost and all that she might further bring in her wake...*Penny McClellan.*

I sought out Geraldine, the one who held the keys to all the locks and bolts of Erravilla, and the one who knew exactly where each and every member of the Forrester family was at any given moment in time. The scent of polish reached me as I descended the stairwell, leading me on a short journey through the parlour where I found the pot of knowledge waiting beneath a rainbow arc of the dining room.

"Geraldine, I must find Lucas," I began, ready to pry for information from the book of knowledge she potentially carried in her memory. "I thought he might be home today but he's not in his room."

The housekeeper narrowed her eyes as though she could glean the reason for my inquiry like she could the furniture with her polish. "Noo, he lef' this morn'n' for France," Geraldine replied, matter-of-factly.

"France!?" I cried. "Without me?"

She stood back to appraise me, resting the polish rag upon her hip. "Wha' Lucas does is no' my concern unless he tells me otherwise."

"Well, did he say why he left without me?" I asked, petrified that I had upset him so much he could no longer stand my very presence.

"He has to work, I suppose. Interviews, publicity…'e's a busy man is Lucas," Geraldine said, a hint of reproach in her lathered voice. "He canna' wait for all things t' come t' him, my dear – he has to press on with life."

I needed no further encouragement: I would pack my things, return the music box to the attic, and leave immediately.

I wrote Lucas a simple note of my thanks for his hospitality, and that I would be in contact with Mary-Anne for correspondence regarding future press releases.

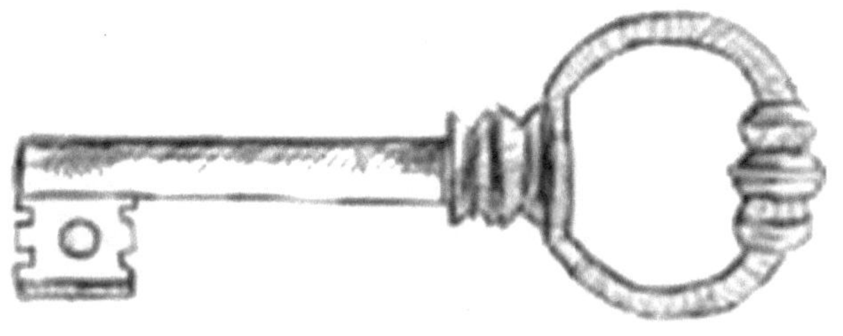

Part 2

The Road Not Taken

A Poem by Robert Frost

16. The Crown & Stag

Almost a month passed without them as I travelled the south of England, interviewing the links I had managed to contact with the help of Mary-Anne, writing constantly of all that I possessed of him to keep me company. I wrote of Lucas, creating a draft of all that I had gleaned of him in the short time I had spent at Erravilla, and desperately trying to ignore the temperature surges of the gold ring against my flesh, an ever-constant reminder of M and his final words, desperate to prove him wrong. And maybe even quash my own fears that he was right. Could I really make this happen?

I spent another week lodging in London in cheap hostels from day to day, listing myself under a different alias as I travelled. I needed to feel the pain that only solitude could provide, and used it to fuel the pouring out of my work onto the pages. I also needed to prove that I could write this book *without* placing anyone in any more danger, as Justice had so vividly pointed out.

Maintaining my own identity and privacy, however, did not shield me from the news of the Forresters, who graced the covers of practically every genre of media publication in London. Lucas loomed around the gossip columns while Darius hit the music mags regularly and M featured throughout the business and art reviews almost weekly.

Towards the end of April posters began to appear on bulletin boards and street poles on the outskirts of London for an up-coming gig at a well-known pub. I smiled to myself, twisting my lips in satisfaction that I could at least revel in the company of Darius and his band, *Shirtless*, without causing a scene, and without putting anyone in danger.

The large corner pub was at full capacity when I arrived, and I managed to find a stool close to the bar to perch myself on. I had forgotten how frequently single women were preyed upon in crowded venues, even when they were trying to be invisible. After the incident at the *Dungeon* I avoided drinking any of the drinks bought for me, keeping to myself.

Well into the evening I had relaxed enough to sing along to the words being belted out by Darius, enjoying the thrill of the crowd as my energy lifted with their vigour, all the while scolding myself for allowing my attention to drift towards the well-toned bare torso of Darius Forrester and his band.

I cheered as Darius lunged himself into the screaming throng of fans milling near the stage, his body riding the current of hands that passed him above their heads. The band stopped playing as Darius landed on his stable feet not far from my niche by the bar, signalling intermission.

I winced as applauding fans inundated him, congratulating him on the release of the new album as he signed his autograph on t-shirts, CD covers and exposed human flesh.

Deciding on an enigmatic whim that I wanted to reach Darius, I swam my way to the bar through the crowd where dozens of people ordered drinks for the band, who had joined Darius at the bench. I didn't quite make the island bench as the band was escorted by security towards the back-stage area for a break. I took my chance and squished my way through the crowded venue until my body was shoved up against a burly patrol guard, who thrust me back into the crowd.

I lost my footing and found myself sandwiched between the throng of eager fans, who were packed in to the venue like sardines; and I thought for one breathless moment that I was about to be trampled to death in the stampede. I felt the strength of a steady arm as it wrapped itself tightly around my waist, lifting me to my feet and ushering me through the crowd. I was unable to turn to see who had intercepted my fall in amongst the sardines, but felt the waves of relief as I was shielded from the quicksand.

I wondered why he persisted in following the band the entire way to the restricted zone that had swallowed the band and security whole; and was even more surprised when security allowed us through. I was ushered into a back lounge area, where the band and stage crew sat laughing and drinking to fuel their adrenaline.

I had felt the change in temperature and observed the array of colours of the ring throughout the ordeal, surprising me with its intensity – one that I had not felt for some time.

"April!" Darius cried, leaping from his chair like Jack-be-nimble, the drink in one hand raised above his head like a salute. "Hey, girl! I didn't know you were still local!"

His powerful frame filled the space between us in three strides and lifted me high off the ground in a winding embrace as though he'd known me for years. Placing me back on the ground with a light thud he turned and rested his arm around my shoulders as though he were parading me like a prized possession to his buddies.

"Where did you find this one, Darius?" one crooned between gulps.

"Does she have a sister?" another crowed.

"How come *you* always score ones like that? What've you got that I don't?" one asked in mock defeat, staring at his chest as he flexed the chiselled pectoral muscles, laughing as his fellow musos launched empty beer cans at him.

"This is April, my brother's new *reporter* friend," Darius said, his tone mock cloak-and-dagger as he squeezed me affectionately.

I winced, and then turned to glare at him, pulling myself free of his close embrace.

"Why does M need a reporter?" one of the boys asked, at the same time as another asked, "What do you mean by 'friend'?"

"*M* doesn't need a reporter," Darius replied, leaning over to slap his compatriot over the head playfully. "She's Lucas' girl."

"Lucas?!" a chorus of voices cried in disbelief.

"Then what's she doing here with *him*?" one of them asked, nodding beyond Darius and me.

I spun on my heel and released steam at the rate of a freight train as I came face to face with *Emerus* Forrester. I dug my hands into my hips, dragging my eyes away from his tight fitting grey top and blue jeans, and the now *short* tousled brown hair, which curled affectionately across his forehead.

<u>M</u>

I had arrived late at the *Crown & Stag*, deciding at the last minute to attend Darius' gig, having not been to one since the *Dungeon* and knowing that he got a kick out of his family instilling some pride in their youngest member.

I had taken my seat at the bar beside a chatty brunette, who had immediately run her spider-long fingers over my bare forearms and pressed her blood-red lips up against my ear as she purred above the noise of the band.

Darius had landed metres from the bar at intermission and I took the opportunity to run, leaving the fiery woman a five pounder on the ledge of the bar before she could protest, beside the two empty shot glasses we had downed.

I trailed the band at a safe distance from the main throng of the mob, knowing that the geezers on the door would recognise me.

I felt the drop in temperature on my ring finger at the same moment that I noticed a woman throw herself in amongst the rowdy fans and the band's security, watching as though in slow motion as she was thrown roughly into a group of fans trying to get a last minute autograph from the band. I had reached the girl before she hit the floor, my senses suddenly assaulted by the familiar Autumn scent as her fine hair brushed my face, and I curled an arm around her waist instantly, folding her frame into my chest.

I remembered instantly the feeling of her against me, curled up on the sofa one morning at Erravilla as her hand ran gingerly along the crevices of my bare torso…

And now we stood, chin to crown. I was the object of her wrath and scorn, as evidenced by her full pouting lips and flared opal-blue eyes.

I huffed at the whistles and banter that erupted from the excitable band members, channelling my energies away from the bitter feud she was determined to have so publicly.

"Hello to you too, April," I drawled, aware of the engrossed crowd behind her and ran a hand across my hedged scalp.

"Hey, this looks like a lovers' quarrel to me! Are you sure she's Lucas' girl?"

The call pushed my fragile patience over the edge and I moved April aside to confront the overgrown boy, still slouching on the couch beside my brother.

I glanced from my trembling fists to the young lout as he downed the last of his pint, delirium circumnavigating his face like an eager drunken sailor, and I thought of how close to the edge I had been again lately.

But he was just an oversized kid.

I lowered my fists.

Darius had already wedged himself between my fists and the couch.

"Whoa, M! He didn't mean anything by that; he's just joking around!" Darius cried, one hand resting on my shoulder to steady me.

The joker stood, a menacing smile upon his face, daring me to take the first swing. Darius turned to glare at the boy, shoving him back to the couch like a rag-doll.

"And you shut up! Or next time I'll let him deck you!" Darius warned.

I removed Darius' hand from my shoulder and turned to leave, reigning in the fists that wanted blood. "Sorry, brother."

"Why do you always have to interfere?" April said under her breath, glaring at me with as much malevolence as Darius' crony.

"Happy birthday," I muttered, brushing past her. "I hope it was a good one."

Her mouth gaped open as though starved for oxygen as I passed, my hand quivering as it passed hers as the rings tried to reach for each other across a forbidden cavern.

And just as though the rings were aware of the absence of the other, I was reminded again of how much I'd missed life without her being around however infuriating the situation now was.

Autumn, 1860, rural Gloucester, England
Sir Walter Finnegan, last Earl of Erravilla Court

We spent weeks in this manner, where I would frequent her room each eve, and then leave immediately afterwards. Her desperate prayers and sobs would reach me before I reached her door. I did not understand this behaviour of Maisy's: I thought I was giving her what she had asked of me. I felt a strange sense of fulfilment after leaving her each night as though a great and unbeknown weight was released from my burdens as I lay with her. I could not understand how her body did not react in the same way. It was as though she wanted more...but more of what I did not know.

During the days I would smile pleasantly at her should I come across her in my ventures about the house and estate. She returned my greeting with a blushful scorn and a glare on each occasion, turning about on her heel post-haste and again I wondered why. Was I not fulfilling my oath as she had asked?

For three weeks we behaved in such a manner. And then on the night beginning the fourth week I entered her room to find that the fretful sobs had already begun. I approached her bedside as usual, this time kneeling beside her pillow.

"Maisy? Is there something the matter?" I asked, disturbed by this pre-emptive outburst.

"Please leave. Just go," she ordered through her sobs.

"But, I...don't understand. I thought this was what you wanted?" I probed cautiously, not comfortable with the distresses prone to women.

"Not tonight. Come back in a week," she replied, her face still concealed in the shadows.

"As you wish," I conceded, turning on my heel and taking my leave.

I did not understand the nature of her misery for some time.

Maisy spent the entire week erupting in sporadic tears all about the house. I could not remember Rosie being prone to such outbursts, although my father had said such things of my mother, when she had lived, and her wee bairns had not.

And then I realised: it seemed her God had not answered her prayers after all. But I dared not say it out loud. We would have to go through the entire course again. Surprisingly, this notion did not bother me, as it appeared to inconvenience Maisy.

I began my nightly vigil once again, a week later, as she had directed. The following three weeks leant itself to a similar pattern as the previous month. So did the fourth week, where her spells of involuntary sobs echoed through the entire household once again. Her God had still not answered her prayers as Maisy had hoped.

The nature of our relationship toiled on in this manner for some months...

And every day the ring quivered with a silent humming as it emitted interchangeable hues of orange and blue; at times it burned hot like an inferno and at other times it cooled to a more pleasant temperature, but always temperate.

17. Twenty-Three and Shirtless

April Falls

"So, ah, April, you're cool right?" Darius hedged, coming to stand beside me as I stared after M as though a freight train had ripped through me.

I sighed and put an arm around the younger Forrester. I wasn't going to take my anger out on Darius because of his brother's pig-headedness. "Yeah, Darius, I'm cool."

"That's my girl!" he cried, suddenly lifting me off my feet in his firm arms and spinning me around to face the crew. "Hey, listen up, you all gonna be nice to my girl April here, okay?"

They replied haphazardly:

"Sure thing, boss."

"Hey, can I have a hold when you're done?"

"She can join us for our after-party tonight!"

"Actually, that's not a bad idea, Baz," Darius chirped up. "Say, April, is it really your birthday today? We always go out after a gig, to celebrate, you know. You should stick around and come with. It'll be like a mini birthday bash."

"I don't know," I said, my voice sounding more as if I was preparing for a wake than celebrating a momentous occasion.

Darius' misplaced green eyes pleaded with mine, and his hands clasped at his chest, feigning heartache. I laughed at his dramatics and punched him playfully in the arm. Maybe a good cheering-up was what I needed.

I woke the next day as the sunlight streamed in through a set of white French doors with the curtains pulled wide framing a picturesque sight of a park below. The familiar scenery played upon my hazy mind as I took in the creamy white décor within the room, and the faint scent of Armani lingered in the air, stirring memories of haunting sea-green eyes and a breath-taking smile.

I froze instantly, afraid to breathe for all of the bats flying around in my lungs and stomach. I closed my eyes, desperately trying to remember how I had come to be in Park Lane, in Lucas Forrester's very bed! I looked around for any sign of his presence and found none.

What had happened to me last night? I wondered, feeling the rise of my pulse as my head swam in a whirlpool of memories that I could not make any sense of. I had gone with Darius from the *Crown & Stag* to an apartment outside of London with the rest of the band. Had Lucas been there too?

I caught sight of the clock above the mantel and groaned: midday. I hurried into the bathroom to check myself over, knowing that I was wearing the stale clothes from yesterday and had no clean clothes to change into. Nor could I brush my teeth to eliminate my horrid breath, brush my hair or cover the tired creases below my eyes.

And then I spied a series of bundles along the dresser: a complete set of female clothes, with the price tags still attached; a towel, hairbrush, toothbrush and other essentials.

I wandered out of the en-suite still dazed and ventured into the kitchen, where I halted at the sight of Darius and Lucas chatting over a cup of tea like two old English buddies.

"Morning, Sunshine!" Darius greeted, a little too cheerfully for my crackling ears. "Cup of tea?"

"I, I…guess so," I stammered, still rooted in my tracks. "Thanks for the…stuff."

"Oh, that was Lucas' doing," he replied with a nod of his head. "I wasn't expecting big bro here to be in town right now, so I figured we'd crash here. Hope you don't mind, April."

I was mortified about the thought of Lucas having to purchase me personal items and I looked to the floor as heat surged into my face. "I'll pay you back for the clothes. Thanks," I mumbled, forcing a smile as I glanced at him quickly. "I hope *you* don't mind me being here."

"Of course not," Lucas answered quickly. "You're welcome here any time you like. I didn't get the clothes and other stuff for you: I organised the service lady downstairs to get them for you. I hope they're okay." He examined me for approval and I nodded slowly. "Sorry for the intrusion."

"Don't be ridiculous!" I cried, an edge of hysteria lacing my voice as I glanced at him again. "This is *your* home. *I'm* the one who shouldn't be here."

"Now *you're* being ridiculous." Lucas' resonating voice held a serious edge to it as he gazed at me directly; his green eyes remained a mystery to me. "I thought you had left the country, until Mary-Anne told me you had called her."

"Business," I replied simply, afraid to look at his face lest the dive my pride had taken be splattered across my face.

"Oh. Well I'm glad you're still around. I'd like to talk to you about more publicity."

"Mary-Anne and Gerry seem to be handling it just fine," I said steadily. "Actually, I'd like to write a feature on *Shirtless* while I'm still in the country, if that's okay with you, Darius? At least *that* one won't have to go through Gerry first, and it shouldn't *endanger* anyone," I drawled.

"Hey, you can write whatever you like about the band! I'm not into all that privacy and stuff," Darius replied casually. "And my manager's not a tight-lipped arse-hole like his is. Anyway, I'm glad you had fun last night."

I glanced away, chewing absently on the tip of my tongue as I fought desperately to remember, afraid of what distaste I might discover hidden beneath the fresh paste.

"You should try your hand at some real karaoke some time: you can surely wail after a few glasses of red!" Darius crowed. "Lucas, did you know that it was April's birthday yesterday?"

"No, I didn't," Lucas replied, his brilliant eyes narrowing as his jaw tightened. "Sounds like you had a ball with Darius."

"April joined the band for a little after-party!" Darius crooned, oblivious to Lucas' apparent disapproval.

"Anyway," I said, sipping my tea and covering my forehead with my free arm as though the shame would also be hidden beneath the visor. "I'm going to have to get back to the hostel I'm staying in to collect my stuff. They're going to wonder why I haven't checked in today."

Lucas' brows shot up like "n"-shaped caterpillars. "You're staying in a *hostel*?"

"Of course," I replied, sailing straight past his frustration in the dark.

"Why on earth for?" he demanded, as though I had just announced that I had moved into the local Nazi Supremacist camp.

"Well, where else was I to go?" I asked, baffled by his apparent irritation.

"Here!" he cried.

"But *you* live here," I replied, unsure why he would think I should also stay here after he had abandoned ship to head for France on a solo journey a month ago.

"April, you were – are – my guest, while you're in this country. Anyone at Erravilla could have given you a key. All you had to do was ask Urland or Geraldine and they would have arranged it."

"But, how would I have known that I was welcome here, Lucas?" I reasoned, surprised by the intensity of his fury.

"Because you were living under my roof!" he said, sounding like a tyrannical father.

"Yes, and *you* left," I reasoned, my voice weakening through a resurging of the memory.

"To go to France…on business," he returned, his voice softening beneath the sweet lullaby it promised.

"Without me," I reminded him, refusing to meet his magnetic gaze. "Geraldine said you needed to move on with your work."

"I left without you because *you* said you needed space."

"You didn't even ask me, Lucas!" I returned. "What else was I supposed to think?"

"Whoa!" Darius interrupted, his voice crashing through the waves that threatened to drag both Lucas and me under. "Don't kill me for saying so, but *this* sounds more like a lovers' quarrel."

"What is that supposed to mean?" Lucas said, turning on Darius, his eyes a cauldron of heat.

I groaned and covered my face with my hands.

"M showed up at the *Crown & Stag* last night and these two sort of had a run-in," Darius replied, realising too late what he had unleashed.

"*M*?" Lucas spat. "You saw *M* last night, April?"

"Yes, he helped me back stage," I said, regretfully. "We argued. Someone said we sounded like we were having a "lovers' quarrel". M nearly ended up in fisty-cuffs with one of the band."

"He has a nerve," Lucas muttered.

"Darius sorted him out, said he'd unleash M on him if he said any more about it," I volunteered.

"I meant M: *M* has a nerve!" Lucas fumed.

"Did I miss something big?" Darius asked cautiously. "Is this why M's birthday bash was canned?"

"I really do need to go," I heaved. "Thanks for everything…both of you. I'll catch you round."

"April!"

The sound of my name echoed and splintered into a million pieces as though it had been thrown like china cups against the walls as Darius and Lucas called after me, their voices drowning in the well I left behind me.

"What about the story?" Darius called.

"Look for it this week in the *Times*," I replied over my shoulder.

"And what about *my* story? When will I see you again?" Lucas asked, a surprising urgency in his voice.

"I'll call Mary-Anne," I replied, not looking back, afraid of being hit and wounded by the flying fragments.

18. Breathless

The *Shirtless* article was warmly received and I was asked by the editor of *The London Times* to trail The Forresters and submit my work as a freelance writer for *The Times Entertainment Review*.

Within a fortnight I received an invitation to attend the London premiere of the film *Breathless* as a press VIP on behalf of the *Times*. *Breathless* was tipped to win several Oscars, and I would be personally interviewing the stars of the film after the premiere.

I thought my heart would give out when I realised that this would entail interviewing Lucas and his rumoured new romantic interest and lead co-star of the film, Alicia Morrissey.

In order not to look desperate and dateless, I asked a colleague at *The Times* to escort me to the premiere. Rob picked me up early without saying much and held my waist stiffly at the appropriate times during the evening, as though he were afraid I would break.

Too queasy to endure the red carpet chivalry, which I would have ordinarily given my right eye to be a part of, Rob and I snuck into the lavishly furnished lobby where we were served Champaign and houres de orves, before being seated inside the enormous studio cinema.

Lucas would be here, nearby, with someone else, I reminded myself, trying desperately to untangle the knotted web I had spun my hands and heart into.

A hush fell over the cinema as the lamps dimmed. I didn't dare to glance around, fearful of laying my eyes upon the person who I knew was somewhere close, adorned with the beautiful brunette who I had seen on screen many times before.

The film's director opened the screening with an introduction about the film and the script, before being loudly applauded and taking a sweeping bow. I felt the moisture on my palms as I gripped the edge of my recliner.

Could I really endure seeing the romantic and intimate scenes that I knew were coming? The ones that he shared with someone else, that I would have to discuss with him afterwards?

I bit my lip to pull myself from my reverie, remembering that I was here strictly on business, that I would have to write openly and objectively, and that I needed to remember every detail of this film! There would be no closing my eyes through those impossible scenes, and no crocodile tears as I watched.

For the most part I was transfixed by the giant images on the screen. I considered slamming the film in the hope that no one would go to the cinemas and see Alicia draped all over Lucas. But I had to admit that the actors and the film lived up to its name: Lucas Forrester definitely left me *Breathless*. I memorised his every movement, his well-delivered and humorous one-liners, his endearing, commanding voice, and most of all, every inch of his insatiable face.

I laughed when I had to, shed more tears at the appropriate moments than was strictly necessary and sighed during the heart-wrenching and intimate moments, inhaling for longer than was healthy, and exhaling until my ribs ached.

As the credits rolled up and the lights brightened, cheers and applause rang through the cinema as though I had suddenly landed in a stampede of summer crickets. I wiped along the rims of my eyes to make sure that my mascara hadn't transformed me into some resemblance of a small furry animal during the outbursts of water-works.

Breathless' director returned to the stage, to another round of applause and cheers, before introducing the panel of cast and crew who would answer questions about the film. The breath in my body caught in the wind-tunnel of my throat when Lucas' name was called, even though I had been expecting it. I had not been prepared when he stood, just four seats along and one row in front of where I sat, staring directly into the winded sails I had become.

I met those crystalline eyes head-on, rooted to the spot and waiting for the onslaught of emotion to steam roll me as I took him in. His stylish all black three-piece suit accentuated the green of his eyes, and I took the force of their gaze with pleasure, basking in the aftermath of the collision from a cloud somewhere far above the cinema.

I watched as Alicia Morrissey joined him and other film associates on stage, and I floated towards the front when the director called the media VIPs to fill the chairs closest to the front of the stage, before he opened the floor to an eager media forage. It took every ounce of concentration I had to scrawl notes between the questions and answering that took place for the next few minutes, even though the hand-held was on and recording as well.

"Aren't you going to ask any questions, April?" Rob whispered.

"I'm saving them for the one-on-ones," I replied, knowing that I couldn't trust my emotions right now. The last thing I wanted to do was draw attention to myself.

When the Director asked for last questions, I rushed from the room, desperate to get some fresh air, and some distance from Lucas, before I completely lost my nerve.

I waited outside the deserted lobby, pacing back and forth and chewing on my tongue like a piece of pink bubble gum. How was I going to interview him? *Maybe Rob could do that one...*

In time the lobby filled with talkative media VIP's, discussing their opinions of Lucas' latest box office success. I tried to filter out their voices in the funnel of my mind, not wanting to be influenced by their views.

An arm rested lightly upon my shoulders and I turned surprised, looking up into Rob's furrowed expression.

A commotion erupted in the lobby and I glanced up across the room to see the VIP's gathered in a semi-circle like it was feeding time in the chook pen.

"We should probably go and see what the kafuffle's about," I suggested, still wrapped lightly in Rob's concern, barely registering the heightened clucking of the VIPs as they approached the patio in a bee-like fashion around their honeycomb centre.

Too late I heard the glass doors open as the noise filtered out onto the patio and then faded as the doors closed, and I glanced up to find Lucas standing a sterile distance from Rob and me, shifting his weight from one foot to the other in time with his wincing jaw line.

Rob stared at Lucas, his mouth opening and closing like a faulty trap-door.

"Lucas Forrester, to what do we owe the pleasure?" Rob finally asked, seeming to find his voice from somewhere beneath the hatch.

"April, are you okay?" Lucas asked, ignoring Rob, a battle raging across his features, his body swaying as though he were going to move in between Rob and I, but refraining.

I swallowed, wanting to reach into the same hatch as Rob in the hope of also finding my voice there.

"You two know each other?" Rob asked, unable to hide his astonishment. "April, you didn't tell me you knew Forrester. I mean, I know you *trail* the family, but…"

"We've worked together," I explained, aware of the proximity between myself and Lucas and trying to swallow the dryness in my throat.

"Can you give us a minute?" Lucas asked, glancing from Rob to me.

I nodded and watched as Rob headed back into the foyer, aware of the interest our encounter had stirred amongst the VIPs watching on from within the hourglass behind us.

Lucas hesitated only briefly before placing a firm arm around my shoulders and ushering me down a flight of back steps, which led around to the back of the studio. He seemed to know where he was going as he led us through a door, snaking us through a series of corridors until we reached a chamber with his name plastered across it, and I followed him in to the potential lion's den.

The room was set up for the promotional interviews, with giant posters and life-size cut outs of Lucas with the cast of *Breathless*, cameras on tripods, microphones on stands and recording equipment.

"Oh man, I forgot they were filming the interviews," I said, finally breathing deeply and eyeing the equipment with disdain.

Lucas placed his hands firmly over my arms, holding me away from his chest. His Adam's apple bobbed as he swallowed and I heard the steady sound of his breathing.

"April, I'm sorry about what happened out there. I thought you were in trouble. I saw you leave the studio and I followed you…And then I saw how upset you looked, and then his arm was around you. I thought he was…accosting you or something."

I stared at him incredulously, watching as a vision of Lucas being ripped from above me at Erravilla shrouded my mind, and I opened my mouth to lecture Lucas for behaving the same way M had that day.

But the shame washed over me anew and I looked away, aware that both M and Lucas had behaved in the same manner out of pure concern.

"April, are you okay?"

"I didn't expect you to notice me."

"How could I not notice you? Look at you: you're the most beautiful woman in the room to me."

I ran my hand self-consciously over the skirt of the fitted silver satin gown, which lightly kissed the floor behind me. Lucas gently reached down and retrieved my hand, turning it over to press his warm lips onto the ridge of my wrist.

"I had hoped that you would be here tonight," he whispered. "You have no idea how much I've missed you…Cinderella."

I closed my eyes to the feel of his skin, carried away with the torrent of my pulse.

"The film was great," I managed, listening as my heart tripped again and again.

"I had hoped that you were here for more than just the film."

"I don't understand," I breathed, daring to hope…

"I wish we weren't here, like this. With the press breathing down my neck," Lucas murmured.

"I am the press," I replied with a half smile.

"So I've heard," Lucas replied, returning my grin.

"Thanks…for your thanks. Darius called…" I mumbled.

"I should have called you myself. But I was chicken."

"*You* were afraid…to call *me*?"

"M-hm."

"Why?" I breathed, my eyes the size of Valentine's Day harts.

"Because you left. I thought you didn't want to speak to me again."

"Why?"

"Because you had said, after the…incident, with M, that you needed some space. I thought you wanted to do your own thing now. So I told Gerry not to pester you to go to France with us." He took a deep breath. "I should have asked you what you wanted, instead of assuming. I'm sorry. It really does make an "ass of u and me"."

I laughed lightly at his joke, which I had heard a hundred times before. His apology was endearing, certainly enough to forgive him for leaving me behind. Now *I* felt like the ass.

"I thought you had left because you didn't want me hanging around anymore," I admitted, feeling a sheepish grin breaking through the lines of my mouth.

"We really did bollocks this up," he said, shaking his spiky head, bridging the gap between us with his broad chest and holding me tightly to him. "I feel bloody terrible about the way things turned out there for a while. I really thought I'd lost you."

19. The Wild Ones

"Lost me?" I repeated.

"I thought you'd skipped the country," he replied brushing his lips into my neck as he spoke.

"You *did* skip the country," I reminded him. "Lucas, I read a lot of things about France…that confused me. About," I swallowed nervously, "your other co-stars. Girls…who you were with."

He brushed a curl back from my forehead with his hand before tracing the curve of my cheek with his fingertips.

"You of all people should know not to trust everything you read. I went out to dinner with the entire cast, which some stupid journo failed to disclose when he only mentioned Alicia. I was hoping you hadn't read it. And she isn't my date, either. I came alone. I had hoped you would be my date. But I was too scared to ask you, and I know you like your privacy, just like my sister." He laughed softly for a moment, before his face clouded over. "And it's the one thing I can't give you with this life."

A knock sounded at the door and the handle wriggled. "Lucas?" a familiar voice called. "Are you in there? Where's April?"

"Gerry," we said together, despair resounding in both our voices. Our time was up.

"Maybe you should get *Rob* to interview me and Alicia," Lucas suggested, running a hand through his sun-streaked hair.

I smiled at the tone lacing his voice as he said my colleague's name. "Rob's a pretend date," I supplied. "I was scared to come alone."

Lucas laughed in disbelief. "And here you are with your Karate brown belt and all."

"Not *physically* scared, silly. I was afraid to see you, in case you didn't want to speak to me, or I lost my nerve to interview you. I know it was stupid," I confessed, wincing. "How did you know about the belt?"

"You left it in the wardrobe at Erravilla. I was kinda hoping you'd return to get it."

"I hadn't even noticed! That's how out-of-it I've been lately."

"Lucas? I can hear you talking!" Gerry raged from outside. "Open this door! You've got press to meet!"

He gently brushed my hand with his, the warmth covering mine as he pressed tenderly before going to meet Gerry.

"Lucas," I called as he opened the door. "I want to do the interview. I can do it."

"How can he stand to be around people like that all the time?" I mused aloud to Rob after we had finished interviewing Alicia Morrissey.

"I should think quite easily," Rob answered too quickly and then shot me a sheepish smirk when he noticed my thunderous expression. "I meant to say: he would be around so many people who look like her—"

"Not helping, Rob."

"I'm sure they all start to blend in together after a while, is all I'm saying."

"April Falls? You're up!" a man with a clipboard said, shuffling over to me. "Keep it short; he's had a big night. No personal questions. And keep your hands to yourself."

"Do people try and…touch Lucas…Lucas Forrester?"

"People try all sorts of things…on celebs much further down the food chain than the likes of Lucas Forrester," he replied, his eyes wide and eyebrows raised in warning. "And much less attractive than the likes of you."

"I'm not planning on touching him," I replied, hands raised in surrender, ignoring his last comment. *At least not while anyone's watching!*

I held my breath as we walked in. Lucas stood immediately and the crew looked about nervously.

"It's all right, guys. I know these two," he said, motioning to the crew to stand down. He walked straight up to me and wrapped his arms around me in a firm embrace, kissing both of my warm cheeks before turning to shake hands with Rob.

"Hey! I said no touching!" the man with the clipboard hollered from the doorway.

I raised my hands in defeat once again. "I'm not the one doing the touching!"

He eyed Lucas suspiciously before closing the door, muttering as he left and using two fingers at eye level to signal back and forth that he would be keeping a close eye on us.

"Who's he? Your mother?" I balked.

"I hope not. He's focking ugly for a woman," Lucas chuckled, turning to Rob, his arm still draped around my shoulders. "I'm Lucas Forrester. And you're April's colleague, Rob. It's good to meet you properly. Sorry about before."

"Absolutely fine, so long as April's okay," Rob replied.

"You've got 10 minutes," the cameraman announced, clicking the timer on his watch.

I decided that a casual approach was the best, asking Lucas the questions that I had wanted to know about the film from a less personal point of view. For the majority of our whirl-wind interview the conversation was light and amusing, and I was satisfied with the information that I had gained, both from a professional and personal point of view.

When the cameraman called time, Lucas stood and shook our hands while the camera still rolled, walking us to the door. "April, we're having the usual premiere after-party tonight, back at Erravilla, for some of the cast and crew. It's not official, so there's no media invited."

"But you're inviting us?" Rob asked, incredulous.

"No, I'm inviting April," Lucas replied shortly. "Strictly no media. My family is private."

"Look, I'll give you the inside scoop at work," I offered to Rob, whose face had taken on a hue similar to that of a thunder cloud. "And you can put your name on it."

"Okay. But I want to hear all about this little thing going on here," Rob retorted, gesturing with his pointer finger between Lucas and me.

I felt the heat rise and flood my cheeks. "There's no *thing,* and if you so much as *suggest* it to anyone, I'll dig up dirt on you so bad, you'll be forced to change your name and leave the country," I warned. Then smiled sweetly.

"Let's get out of here," Lucas said, scanning the emptying hallway and taking my hand. "I have to leave with the cast, back out through the rest of the media haulage and screaming fans." He looked agitated, but resolved, and I understood that this was an obligatory part of his work. "Not that I usually mind. But I'd rather hitch a ride with you and Dario. Much more entertaining."

Lucas called Darius and arranged for me to catch a ride to Erravilla with him and the *Shirtless* gang, while Lucas would travel via Limousine with the other *Breathless* stars.

I was ready for a late night again after the ride with Darius and his wild companions, who sang English ditties the entire way to Erravilla, with the windows down no less. Erravilla Court looked as alive as a fairy garden when we arrived, with lights flooding the driveway, the entranceway, and the front façade of the great House. Darius led us through the kitchen and down the dimly lit hallway that led to a flight of descending stairs, which guided us directly into the grand ballroom.

The great hall had been converted into a comfortable celebration room, with spot lights, disco balls and DJ, and lined with clusters of lounges, chairs and food tables. A modest bar, complete with two bar tenders, spanned one entire corner of the room. From the raging throng of bodies on the dance floor I guessed that there would have been over one hundred people in the room, all in some way connected to *Breathless.*

By three-thirty most of the guests had taken taxis home; some lingered on the lounges with Darius and his party boys, half of whom were passed out on couches. I nestled up against Lucas as he chatted with the gang, feeling the hum of his voice through his chest, as warm and comfortable as a glass of his mother's finest Sherry.

"April?" Lucas whispered, and I smiled at the tickle of his lips brushing my forehead.

"She has a habit of falling asleep about now," Darius jibed from somewhere nearby. "She's quite the cosy kitten."

"Oh, and you'd know?" Lucas laughed. "You're not her type, Dario boy."

"Don't I know it?" Darius hooted.

"Well, I'm going to get this *cosy kitten* to her basket," Lucas said stifling a yawn with the back of his hand.

"No!" I cried.

"No?"

I'm not ready to leave you yet!

"You should keep talking," I offered, staring up into his silhouetted face. "I don't want you to leave your own party on my account."

"April, I think the party's mostly over. I'm not going to miss anything if I leave now," Lucas replied, his voice ringing with the merriment of a drunken sailor.

But that means not being with you, and I don't want to leave your side...ever again!

"But we haven't even had karaoke yet!" I fumbled, my voice as drunk on fatigue as Lucas' sounded.

A roar of laughter erupted from Darius' boys.

"She's delirious! What did you spike her drink with, Lucas?"

I felt the jostling of movement as Lucas laughed affectionately along with the gang and the subsequent heat of embarrassment travel along the ridge of my cheeks.

"Come on, April, time for bed for you," Lucas said gently, turning easily and lifting me up against his chest, the train of my cocktail dress cascading over his arm with my legs.

I cradled myself into his neck for dear life, afraid for the moment to end, and breathing in his familiar Armani scent, which sent my senses spinning. The fear of his imminent departure increased with every step he took towards my room, and then I was gently placed atop of the quilt in my usual suite on the third floor.

I groaned and felt the pressure upon the mattress as Lucas lay beside me, leaning in to brush my forehead with his warm mouth. "April? Are you okay?"

"No," I replied. "This dress is itching me, and I want you to tuck me in."

I felt the pinch of movement against my side as he chuckled and brushed a strand of stray curls from my eyes. "You are very tired."

"No, I'm not. Help me up."

He did as I asked, supporting me to my feet in the dark room like an invalid. "What do you need?"

"Unbutton me," I requested, delirious with fatigue.

"I don't know if I want to do that," he replied cautiously. "You just look too damn good in this dress."

"Where are my shoes?"

"Downstairs, we'll get them tomorrow."

"Good. They cost me almost a week's wage."

Did I say that out loud?

Lucas chuckled again, louder than before. "Are you sure you want me to do this?"

"It's either you, or one of the *Shirtless* guys downstairs. No one else is awake."

Lucas immediately began unhitching the stream of satin buttons along the spine of the dress as I held the bust-line in place, the touch of his fingertips imprinting upon my flesh like frost on window-panes.

"Have you got it from here?" he asked in a low voice as I felt the release of the final button slip through its eyelet just below my waistline.

I felt the warmth of his breath on the nape of my neck and relaxed into the mould of his chest. "Don't go. I want you next to me," I pleaded.

"You want me to stay with you?" he asked, the sentiment catching in his throat.

"Yes. Stay with me till morning. I can't bear the thought of being without you for even a minute now that you're back…or I'm back."

"I hope you know what you're asking, April. Just don't wake up tomorrow and regret it," he whispered against the flesh of my shoulder.

"I don't expect anything from you," I breathed, turning to face him. "Just being here with you is enough."

"April, I meant what I said the last time we were here: I won't use you. I feel terrible about what happened before, with M." I could feel his breath on my face through the dimness, even though his features were caught in shadow before me. "I'm going to go and get changed, and bring you back something else to wear."

He switched on the lamps as he left, which provided a dim ribbon of light, enough to be grateful that the western curtain was still closed. I hobbled over to the southern window and managed to draw the heavy curtain while still holding up the corset of my dress.

Lucas returned within minutes, and even in my groggy state I was struck by his masculine physique, now adorned in a pair of Peter Alexander pyjama pants and fitted singlet. He handed me a large button down shirt. "This was the best I could do, sorry."

I shook myself out of the cocktail dress and slinked into the shirt, soaking up the scent that was all him as I loosely buttoned it and rolled up the sleeves. Then I removed all my jewellery, except for the bloody golden ring upon my left hand, before slipping beneath the blankets. Lucas glanced at me from across the room as he flicked off the lamps.

I listened to the swift press of his feet against the floorboards and relaxed as his body sank into the mattress beside me. I rolled into his embrace and closed my eyes, wrapping myself pretzel-like into the providence of his promising arms.

Fulham, London

M

I returned from a morning jog with the usual three papers to read over breakfast, including *The London Times*, which I thumbed through to read the *Business*, *Arts*, *Entertainment* and *Sports* sections, sometimes just to keep up to date with my family, who seemed to frequent the tabloids more often than not. Occasionally I still read the *Personals*, even though I had not seen any messages, encrypted or otherwise, for Lucas in weeks – for as long as I hadn't spoken to him. I thought this a strange coincidence until Mother informed me that April had disappeared the day Lucas had flown to France, a week after the incident at Erravilla.

Of course, I had known for some time now that April wrote on a regular basis for *The Times Entertainment* section. Her articles were always well researched and well written. If only she would drop this book and stick to journalism, a much safer option. I was baffled that she could be so naïve when it came to Lucas, while she seemed to have such a steady head and brains on her shoulders the rest of the time.

I often wondered why some people were so easy to love, for no apparent reason at all, while others, people who I should love unconditionally, were sometimes the hardest…

As I sat in the sunshine on the terrace balcony of my apartment, reading the paper over breakfast and watching the morning traffic ferry up the Thames River, I noticed the surge of headlines and photo snaps of Lucas and April…together. I knew full well that headlines and even photos were deceptive, but I couldn't help the rising astonishment I felt at seeing the two of them, publicly liaising, and by the looks of things, openly embracing.

A vein pulsed on the side of my head as I balled my free hand into a fist. Did Lucas realise what this would do to April's career? Or how it might place her in further danger when his stalker-fan saw these pages?

I couldn't see how things could possibly work out well for April when she was so consumed with Lucas and his bollocks ways.

My instinct was to phone Lucas immediately, to warn him, to make sure April was okay. *But no*, my selfish mind argued: he was the one who had gotten her into this fix; he could sort it out himself. If April wanted Lucas so badly, then she would find out, the hard way, that life with my brother was not going to be easy: Pursuing Lucas and this *book* would cost her far more than what she bargained for.

Erravilla

April Falls

I awoke in the morning to the gentle chiming of the clock above the mantel and was startled when I counted the slow rhythm to ten. Then I remembered it was the weekend. I was so used to sleeping by myself that the familiar Armani scent, which tapped me lightly on the nose, was enough to persuade me into thinking I was still dreaming. I rolled over and found myself pinned against a warm fleshy wall. My forehead tickled as it brushed against a spiky peak, which moved when the jaw attached to it spoke.

"You're finally awake?" he murmured.

I had missed that voice in the short eternity that we had been apart.

My arms were against his chest in an instant, cupping his oval face with my hands. "Why didn't you wake me?"

"Well, you were purring like a *kitten*, as Darius affectionately calls you nowadays. You went straight to sleep last night, and then rolled to the other side of this enormous bed for the rest of the night," he chuckled softly. "How could I wake a sleeping beauty? I was enjoying being able to see you at all."

I groaned. *Incredible!* "I really rolled away? All night?"

"Mm-hm."

<u>Winter, 1861, rural Gloucester, England</u>
<u>Sir Walter Finnegan, last Earl of Erravilla Court</u>

Christmas was not the joyous occasion it had been the previous year. Six months had lapsed and still Maisy was not with child. She did not speak of it, but her tears had subsided, all spent from the months of down-pouring. Concern began to etch itself back into my forethoughts when Maisy began to spiral into her miserable state again: neglecting her household obligations. Any traces of hope had vanished and she started to take long walks unaccompanied along the fringes of the estate. It had been a year since her frightful incident at the pond, and I feared she might consider the option once more.

I was not concerned by her apparent inability to conceive a child as yet, for there was still time a plenty. However, my desire to fulfil Maisy's request was growing with each day that she worsened. If a child would truly save her from her wretchedness, then I was more than willing for a child to come of our union. Perhaps there was a better way forward...

I decided one morning, against my better judgments of etiquette, to visit her in her suite, which I had never done before during daylight hours. Quietly I stole into her quarters and was alarmed to find her already absent at this early hour. I searched the house, but to no avail – she was nowhere to be found. I raised the maids and had them search the estate while I hurried myself down to the pond, fearing that I would be too late this time, praying that I was not.

All the while the blessed ring upon my left hand burned with a fiery heat: radiating between a burnt orange and a deep ocean blue. And still I did not have the answers from her that I sought. Why must I be stalked like prey from my own lowly piece of metal?

I slithered my way out onto the slippery ice, but she was not in sight and there were no detectable breaks in the ice. I clamoured back off the ice and retreated back to the house, where a fretful Mrs Connolly awaited me, empty-handed.

"Begging your pardon, sir, but Lady Finnegan is nowhere to be found," the dottery woman confessed. "We've searched in all her usual places."

"Well, have you tried searching in some other perhaps unusual places?" I prompted, frustrated by the woman's incompetence.

"No, sir. I haven't a clue as to where to look," she replied, dumbfounded.

"Are there any hidden rooms, stairwells, attics, anywhere that she might be, Mrs Connolly?" I pressed, rubbing my hand across the stubble on my chin.

"Actually, sir, now that you mention it...when Maisy...Mrs Finnegan...was a child, she would oft spend an innumerable amount of time in the attic on the third floor. But she hasn't been there since her mother died. There's too much up there that reminds her of her."

"Show me to this attic," I demanded, sweeping my hand across my body in a gesture to implore the woman to move post-haste.

I followed her along the corridor behind the servants' quarters and kitchen, past the dining hall and various other entertaining rooms. At the end of the corridor Mrs Connolly indicated to a narrow flight of stairs leading up to several stories above. The stairs looked like a safety hazard to say the least. It was amazing that Maisy had survived childhood at all after frequenting these rickety stairs so often.

"I will take it from here, Mrs Connolly, thank you," I said curtly, examining the unsteady flight as I began to ascend. Mrs Connolly watched me wearily as I climbed; the fury in her eyes evident as I shooed her away. I did not want an audience as I approached my wife. "That will be all."

The grand house was silent, except for the clip-clop of Mrs Connolly's shoes as she marched herself back down the *corridor. If Maisy was up here, then she certainly knew of my presence as I placed one foot in front of the other on the squeaky wrought-iron steps. I reached the first landing and found myself in a stagnant, dark room, bereft of light and warmth…and Maisy.*

Three walls were lined to the ceiling with shelves of unused volumes. A desk sat in front of a neglected fireplace, accompanied by an antique chair and dormant wall lamp.

Above me the hazardous stairwell ascended through the ceiling into the floor above. I glanced out of the sole window as I climbed still, gazing out onto the perimeter of the front garden. I turned upon the landing, noticing that I had reached the structural beams of the house overhead. The room was comparably lighter than the room below, thanks to the candles that sat upon the shelves of the forgotten furnishings lining the long narrow room.

I passed my eyes across a series of keepsakes along one side of the room, blanketed in dust and cobwebs. The lids to the boxes had been removed on some and I could see that they mostly consisted of miscellaneous keepsakes, along with a cradle pram, crocheted infant clothing and blankets, and some wooden toys, including a rocking horse and a dolls house. At the end of the uninviting room stood an oil lamp, which could have been attractive had it not been trimmed with cobwebs and a thick layer of brown dust. The lamp had been lit and cast light on the items immediately nearby.

And there she sat, beneath a white vanity unit, upon a blanket on the floor, staring vacantly at an open photo album. Ordinarily I would have thought it strange for a lady of her position to be seated upon the floor but due to Maisy's current disposition, I found that I could be surprised by little at all.

I approached her timidly, afraid to startle her, although I was fairly certain that she must have been aware of my presence. I swallowed dryly. "Maisy? May I sit with you?"

She was silent as I hedged closer, a haunting look possessing her eyes as she gazed at the pages before her. Eventually she spoke, motioning to the keepsakes lining the wall nearby.

"These were my things, from childhood. Mother stored them here in the anticipation that I would use them for my own babes one day," she said calmly, although there was nothing calm about the way she stared through the items she indicated, as if they weren't there at all.

"And you will, Maisy. There is still time...you are young yet."

She shook her head vehemently and swallowed the lump in her throat. "It's over for me. It has come to pass that I shall not have a child. I know it."

"Come now, Maisy. Such talk is fool-hardy. No one can know what the future beholds," I said calmly, wondering how such notions could enter a person's mind. Certainly not someone of sound mind. "We can work something out...to make you happy again."

"You can't make me happy," she replied instantly, glancing at me with a foreboding expression.

"I can try."

"The time for that has passed as well."

"Come now, Maisy. Be reasonable. We have our whole lives before us. Mayhap we need to be more familiar with each other?" I pondered.

"Familiar?" she said as though the very word itself was cursed, closing the album with a fierce thud, sending pockets of dust particles into the air. "Are we not already familiar, Mr Finnegan? It doesn't appear to be helping the situation at all! There's no other way I am presently aware of that could lead to the begetting of a child!"

I was stunned by her abrupt indecency although I was nought offended by her forthrightness. "Mayhap we can be more cordial...more amicable...talk perhaps?"

"More amicable?" she said furiously, standing to her feet and balling her soft hands into small fists by her side. "Mr Finnegan, I tried for months to be amicable to you. And you refused me the courtesy! What, pray thee, do you expect me to do now?"

"Perhaps you could call me by my name on occasion, Walter. And I could endeavour to speak with you at an appropriate time that suited you," I suggested, mildly flustered by her outburst.

"Mr Finnegan, I will not call you Walter. T'is highly inappropriate!" she cried indignantly.

"Mayhap when we are alone, then?"

"You wish to speak to me alone?"

"Yes. Perhaps in the evenings...or at night."

"At night?" she pondered with a mystified expression on her face.

"Yes. That is...if you'll still have me?" I asked cautiously, afraid that I would cause her yet another outburst of rage.

She was silent for several moments while her breathing slowed and returned to its usual pace. Maisy stared at me fleetingly, between moments of apparent thought and consternation, while she surveyed the rustic attic walls, as though they might hold the answer.

"And to what purpose would this talking lead?" she inquired eventually.

I had not realised that I had been holding my breath in such earnest and expelled it with sudden volume. I felt strangely relieved that she was considering my suggestion: almost hopeful. If I was going to live with her for the remainder of my life, then we may as well live in peace.

"Perhaps we could be friends, as other spouses are sometimes?" I offered.

I thought of my own mother and father, and remembered the nights I had lain awake listening to them in the tent, when she had been of a happier disposition. Her laughter was *endearing to my ears as my father spoke in a low voice to her after the oil lamps were blown out. They had been happy together then. Friends even. It was possible...*

"Mr Finnegan, forgive me, but I find it difficult to believe that you wish to befriend me. You did not care for me at all a year ago, or six months ago, and certainly not when we were wed. Why would you wish for such a relationship now?" she asked stubbornly, her lower lip pouting in defiance, despite the faint hue in her eyes that had become familiar to me six months previously: a ray of hope...

"Because, Maisy, you are my wife. I will not demand it of you, but if it is a family you wish to raise, then we have no other option. There must be peace. I want you to be happy again, Maisy."

She stared at me for an indeterminable amount of time, distrust and defiance framing her every feature. The walls she had built were so very high. Almost unassailable.

"I will consider your request, Mr Finnegan," she said simply, striding past me and making her way surprisingly swiftly down the precarious spiral staircase. "If it is God's will."

I stared after the extraordinary woman that was my wife, and I found myself wishing that it would be God's will.

20. Rumours

April Falls

The fool says in his heart, "There is no God." Psalm 14

"Can we stay here all day?" I asked with the crescendo of a love-sick teenager.

A gentle laugh escaped from Lucas' throat like the release of a thousand butterflies to my ears, and he wriggled down to look me in the eye. "If you don't mind the rumours that are going to fly like hot-cakes; then I definitely don't mind staying here with you, for as long as you like."

I thought about the possibilities of those rumours as I ran my fingers along the stubble of Lucas' jaw and weighed up my current priorities. "To hell with the rumours. We may as well give them something to really talk about," I replied, pinning my lips to his, my hands gently folding their way through his brown-blonde hair as he accepted my embrace.

A knock sounded at the door, followed by Darius' hesitant voice. "Lucas? Gerry's on the phone. Says it's urgent. He sounds pissed! Angry – not drunk that is. Not that he doesn't always sound pissed…I'm *really* sorry for the interruption!"

Lucas groaned and I heard the faint grinding of his back teeth as he seethed, continuing to kiss me with the force of a summer storm. I heard Darius retreat from the door and I gasped for breath. "You have to be kidding!"

Lucas hovered above me, his hands holding his weight against the pillow as I gazed up into his tortured eyes, just a few inches from mine. Another battle raged within him; his breathing ragged and chest tight.

"Go," I said simply, alleviating his indecision. "I'll be right here."

He kissed me fervently for one long minute before extricating his body from mine, and jogging to the door. It felt like an eternity to wait for Lucas to return. By the time he did, I had visited the bathroom and cleaned my teeth with the spare toothbrush and paste, and was pacing in front of the southern glass window, admiring the almost summery morning.

I hurried across the room, throwing my arms around him and resting my head against his chest. He was quiet, his breathing soulful. I unwrapped myself from his waist and searched his stony face.

"Is it her?" I asked.

"Worse. It's you. And me. All over the front of every paper you can imagine. Even the *Times*."

"Rob?" I gasped, horrified that he could have betrayed me like this.

"I don't think so. No single person could have done this so quickly."

"What are you saying?"

"The pictures were taken when we were out on the patio yesterday, and the rest is speculation," he held me at arms' length. "April, they named you. All of them."

"You mean the VIP's took *photos* of us?" I breathed.

"Some are of us looking very intense, labelled the "lovers' quarrel". Then there's a picture of me with my arm around you escorting you off the patio steps, which they've called "the make-up". It's a mess. Mary-Anne's beside herself, and Gerry too…well, I probably don't need to tell you what *he* thinks. He's also worried that this might set off the stalker again…Bloody Penny!"

I thought about that for a second. The stalker was the least of my concerns. How stupid to have thought that I could stay invisible! So much for my fleeting "To hell with the rumours!" I was no longer anonymous, and the wings of my career had just been clipped before they had even been given proper flight.

I sighed, walking slowly to the bed and flopping onto it. "I need clothes…more than a shirt."

"I brought you some back. Mum had these clothes of Aggie's in her wardrobe," Lucas replied, leaving a folded bundle beside me. "You should eat something."

"Where are you going?" I asked, as he turned to leave.

"To have a shower. And then have breakfast with you. Or brunch," he said, motioning to the clock. "I hope they fit."

I sat down at my laptop knowing I was now too baffled to type the story I knew I needed to from the Premiere. How bizarre it was going to be to write an article about an event that I had now become a party in of my own.

I decided to email Rob with all of my notes on the event, wishing him luck with the article that I suggested he alone should write.

A day later the messages began.

The morning papers were flooded with fans wanting to know more about the "journalist friend" of Lucas Forrester's. I began to realise just how many angry-obsessed fans Lucas had. I was at least grateful that I seemed to be the main target of their wrath, not Lucas. I received several emails from Vivienne demanding I explain myself though she seemed altogether excited about the extra attention the paper was now receiving once word had spread which paper I worked for. Lucas was beside himself, blaming his "stupid" behaviour at the Premiere for ruining my career and my life.

I thought he should have been more concerned about the menacing letters he and I were receiving through the *Personals* column of *The Times*. The stalker had returned with a vengeance.

"She's harmless," Lucas scoffed. "What can she do to me? And she won't touch you unless you're out of my sight, which I'm not going to let happen."

"Actually, I think she's more annoyed when I'm *in* your sight," I sighed. "Maybe I should head back to Oz until this blows over." However, leaving Lucas seemed as conducive for the survival of my heart as the desert was for a fish.

"The Australian premiere of *Breathless* is in a few days," he said thoughtfully. "I've never been to Australia. Might not be a bad idea."

I sighed. It could be the answer to both of our problems for the moment.

"I have the French and Italian premiers this week as well. I could do the Oceanic circuit at the end of the week, starting with Australia, then New Zealand and Asia. I'll call Mary-Anne."

I emailed Vivienne and told her that I was temporarily abandoning London for some travel pieces Down Under, and that I would email her stories regularly from my travels.

My phone rang so constantly that I ended up switching it off. If my family didn't believe that I was safe and alive, they could continue to read the papers, which they seemed to believe over me anyway.

Lucas flew out for Paris on Monday while Gerry, Mary-Anne and I planned the upcoming "promotional tour", as Mary-Anne so promptly named it. I spent the first part of the week maintaining a low profile, packing up my apartment and moving back to Erravilla, typing notes at a furious rate, and spending copious amounts of time on the gym mats, sometimes kitted up in Ghi, belt, mitts and pads for a complete martial arts work-out.

Lucas returned from Italy on Wednesday and we left Heathrow for Australia immediately, escorted by his personal entourage in the Forresters' private jet.

We did our best to disguise Lucas at Sydney International, flagged by Gerry and Mary-Anne, wearing sunglasses and a hat as we headed through customs and luggage, and then into the Limousine waiting for us.

I declined a dozen times before Lucas accepted that I was not going to accompany him to the Australian Premiere at Fox Studios with the two other cast members who had flown out for the event. It was simply too dangerous at the moment to bring unwanted attention to our precarious relationship. I promised him that I would watch the event live from my very comfortable lounge room at Audenlea, with Alex, Tobi and Ginger.

Our plan seemed to be working…

Except for the dozens of messages on my answering machine and emails from relatives and acquaintances – including a few from Andy, which nearly boiled my blood – it was incredible for me to confirm whether it was me in the photos with Lucas Forrester in London, and whether I had accompanied him home to Australia. I didn't answer any except my Dad…

"Are you sure you're all right, Apes?" he pressed.

"Please don't call me that! I'm not a Neanderthal," I whined.

"I'm sorry, April, baby, but some of my associates told me about this new boyfriend of yours…" he replied with a sigh. "They said he's dangerous and high-profile, and in some kind of trouble."

"Seriously, Dad, people would believe that I'm dating Jack the Ripper's grandson if the tabloids said so."

"You're not, are you?"

I sighed in frustration. "Dad, I'm not *officially* dating *anyone*!"

And then there was cousin Joel, who had teed me up with Gerry Ottoman in the first place.

"Does that mean you won't be accompanying me to the AFI Awards this week in Melbourne?" he hedged.

"The AFI's?" I shrieked. "You've been nominated?"

"Yeah, in the Short *and* Feature film categories," he said proudly. "I want you to come with me."

"Oh, that's so great! I would love to!" I cried.

"But you have to bring that boy of yours. It'll be huge."

"You want me to bring Lucas? I don't know…he might go anyway…on his own. I don't want to be seen as his date, you know?"

"Then we can all go…together. It'll be a group thing," Joel laughed.

"You want us to go as a trio? Isn't that a little weird? A little boy-band-ish?" I asked cringing.

"Can't be a boy-band with you in it, sweetness. Besides, think of the high profile he'll give the awards."

"And you, no doubt," I said with a grin.

"Of course, there's that too," he said with cheek. "And the after-party!"

<u>Melbourne, Victoria</u>

"I am beyond nervous! How do you people do these high profile gigs all the time?" I asked Joel, staring at the reflection of the bracelet on my wrist in the mirror and trying to pin the clasp together.

Joel laughed, rearing his dark head back before straightening his suit jacket, which was shoved on over a t-shirt and dress trousers. "My dear cousin, why on earth are you nervous? You look a million bucks!"

"Because I think I'm *wearing* a million bucks!" I huffed, running a finger over the smooth surface of the sapphires on the platinum white gold bracelet.

"Those rocks suit you. You look like Grace Kelly," he marvelled, doing up the clasp of the necklace behind my neck, which supported a sizeable blue sapphire shaped as a teardrop. "See, these are the benefits of going to these gigs. Jewellers will throw these sorts of beauties your way, even if it is only on loan."

I admired the matching sapphire earrings, which swung from my earlobes like legs swinging over the ledge of a park bench. "Well, he did wonders matching the stones to this dress; they're almost an exact match," I replied thoughtfully, eyeing the jewels in the reflection. "You know I think you're right, there is a part of this lifestyle I could get used to. It's just the rest of it I couldn't stand. No privacy. Crazy fans! Stalkers! I'd rather be little old me: someone who ends up writing feature articles and corny romance novels for the rest of my life."

"Well, that could be a problem," a familiar voice interrupted.

Joel and I jumped around at the sound of Lucas' smooth tone. We looked like a pair of court jesters as I tripped on my heels and Joel fumbled to catch me.

"You two are quite the pair," Lucas continued, perusing Joel and me with a charred-grin.

I marvelled at the sight of Lucas, hands in his pockets leaning against the doorframe, as though he was posed for the next *Marie Claire* spread, still wearing fitted jeans and a casual shirt.

"Are you going to introduce me to your cousin?" Lucas asked, not moving from his post.

I found my voice and untangled my feet to stand without Joel's help, suddenly nervous about Lucas and Joel meeting, as though I were introducing a boyfriend to an older, protective brother.

"Joel Falls, Lucas Forrester," I managed, unable to tear my eyes from Lucas' guarded stare.

Joel approached Lucas with his arm extended, which Lucas took firmly. "It's nice to finally meet you," Lucas said genuinely. "I've seen some of your work. You've got a real talent."

"The honour is mine, Lucas. You've achieved great things for someone so young; you're a credit to the industry," Joel replied. "Not to mention the help you've been for my dear cousin here."

The two turned to acknowledge me, and I felt a shot of heat surge up my neckline beneath their open gaze.

"Well, I don't know about "help". I seem to have caused her a bit of trouble back home," Lucas replied, his eyes darkening with each word as though in retreat.

I brushed off the comment and started towards the door. "Come on, Lucas, you need to get ready."

"Hey, did you guys elope?" Joel asked curiously, eyeing the gold band on my finger.

"Don't believe everything you read," Lucas replied curtly.

I shook my head, glaring at Joel and motioning with my head for him to leave.

Lucas grabbed my hand as I walked past him, stalling me before him. "Can you excuse us, Joel? I need a word with April."

"Of course," Joel replied, eyeing us openly. He had caught the perplexed tone in Lucas' voice – the one that seemed to be a preamble for something more sinister.

Once we were safely alone, Lucas dropped my hand and shifted to rest against the arm of a sofa lounge. "April, is it true what you just said? That you couldn't get used to this lifestyle?"

His tone unsettled me, my mind leaping in a dozen different directions like a sprawled octopus. What was his concern? I didn't know how to answer him; did not know what he really wanted to discover.

"You know I don't like the spotlight. If it weren't for Joel, I wouldn't be going tonight," I replied slowly, measuring his response.

"So, you won't go anywhere with me, but you'll attend events like this with someone else?"

My pulse quickened. I had not expected a confrontation about this. Not now. Not this soon.

"It's not that exactly," I replied, cautiously.

"Then tell me what it is. You sure keep your distance from me when anyone's around, April. Are you going to live in the closet forever?"

"The closet? I don't like creating a mess, Lucas. And that's exactly what I've done for you. I don't want to be your burden."

"April, anyone I'm seen with will create a media frenzy. You saw the pictures of Alicia and me supposedly out to dinner. They'll bite at anything."

"That's exactly what I don't want," I replied too quickly, as the words *"professional hussy"* forced themselves into my mind.

"So, you're worried about your reputation?" Lucas glanced at the floor, but not before I caught a glimpse of the thin line his lips had flattened into and the shake of his honey-blonde head.

I took a step towards him, debating whether I was going to refute him, or admit that he was right.

"Lucas, I don't know what you want to know," I pressed, keeping my breath steady under the pressure of my ribs, which were squeezed into the blue silk dress and supporting corset.

His eyes flickered, the flames smouldering within, and burning with an intensity that only he could manifest. "The papers are asking whether I've bought my 'Australian girlfriend' Down Under with me."

"Brought," I corrected automatically. "Sorry. Habit."

Lucas rolled his eyes and huffed.

"Well, that's none of their business anyway," I hurried on.

"Are you going to hide forever April, or acknowledge your relationship with me?"

"I'm going with you tonight, aren't I?" I knew I was hiding, avoiding.

"Not exactly. Not as my *date*," he replied, taking a few steps towards me and lifting my chin towards his face, dancing the same steps to a different tune and meeting me at my game.

"That's a bit official," I whispered, not wanting to meet his gaze.

"And you don't want that?" he murmured.

I swallowed painfully, desperately not wanting to answer him. Not wanting to decide. Could I live in both worlds? Could I have Lucas to myself, and still live my quiet, private life?

I knew the anguished truth before I answered him. "How could it possibly work, Lucas?"

"So what's this, then?" he asked gesturing his open palm back and forth through the gulf between his torso and mine.

"I don't know," I said, exhaling. "Please don't ask this of me now. It's too soon."

He searched my eyes fleetingly and then gently released my chin. "I think it's too late for too soon, April."

He walked over to the wardrobe and produced a bundle of garments in a suit bag. I watched him silently, frustrated at my stupidity. He was right, of course. I had created the biggest mess to date. I had not considered that his feelings were headed, astonishingly, in the same direction as mine, and not this quickly.

I was furious with myself that I had caused him distress and heart-wrenchingly disappointed that I hadn't caught myself sooner before plunging off the face of sensibility, for having allowed my emotions to sweep me away without a second thought for the future.

I left him to dress, blinking the tears back from my eyes before they had a chance to cascade down the escarpment of my face.

Europe

M

I watched the miles of green acreage pass thousands of feet below me, always enjoying the scenic flights between Britain and the

European Continent. Shorter flights were always the best, leaving enough time for me to put my feet up in Business or First Class, have a bevvy or two, and catch up on some reading.

I flicked on to the movie channel, shaking my head as my brother's face flashed before my eyes, entwined with a busty blonde, who I thought looked far too much like high maintenance, then flicked to cable. Alicia Morrissey did not look good as a blonde.

It seemed that I was being haunted by Lucas, for there he was again on the screen, this time with his arm around April, who was sandwiched between Lucas and another bloke who I had never seen before. The Red Carpet special of the Australian Film Industry Awards, the presenter announced.

Since when did the Australian Film Industry Awards feature on an international flight? I supposed since my famous brother was presenting an award there. Were all Brits so obsessed with him that I couldn't even escape my own brother for a few hours?

I sighed, resigning myself to switch off the tele, when the camera panned full length to April, who smiled hesitantly, her brilliant opal eyes illuminating straight down the barrel of the lens and reeling me in. Oh, Lord, but she was beautiful! She stood tall, assisted by the height of those tremendous heels she wore, strapped elegantly around her slender ankles. Her hair was folded up delicately, revealing two brilliant sapphire jewels about her dainty ears, and the third adorning her slender neck.

And then there was the ring on her finger.

I hated to admit that I had given up on trying to remove the piece of metal from my hand, the one that joined her and me by some unknown, yet somewhat significant, power. It was my one connection with her, and I wasn't ready to give it up.

April managed to conceal the ring at all the right moments, but not before I noticed the flush of a becoming shade of violet catch in the lens. I followed her gaze and came face to face with Lucas. My hand balled instantly and I shut off the screen.

I hated admitting that I was jealous of Lucas, and for the second time in my life, over a girl. This was proving more and more difficult with regard to my brother and April. It was more frustrating that I sincerely didn't want to covet April, but I could no more prevent these feelings than I could prevent the sun from rising each day.

I flicked the tele back on and watched as Lucas whispered into her ear, bringing a shy smile to her lips. Every look, every brush of his arm against hers, sent a cursory wave of protest through my chest. I finished the last mouthful of whiskey from the glass in front of me and poured another solo round.

I listened to their live interview for a little while longer, torturing myself as I allowed her confident, feminine voice to willow itself into the depths of my mind. I hoped that Lucas wasn't about to let April make the biggest mistake of her life by throwing herself out into the open waters of Lucas' life, with herself as bait, and a life-raft that was at best unstable. I drank the rest of the glass in full.

"She's the most wonderful woman in my life..." Lucas proclaimed, his voice trailing off with the pan of the camera lenses.

I flicked off the tele for the second time in as many minutes. I had heard enough. And he was wrong: she was far more than merely wonderful; April Falls was the most captivating woman I had *ever* met. There was so much more to her than meets the eye.

I pushed the empty shot glass away in frustration, watching carelessly as it soared off the palate before me, remarkably not smashing as it free-fell onto the carpeted isle below, and then spinning momentarily before it rolled for its life out of sight.

How could this be happening again?

21. Crossroads

Melbourne

April Falls

Two roads diverged in a yellow wood, and sorry I could not travel both...

The stretch limo finally pulled to a stop at the beginning of the Red Carpet, after waiting our turn behind the other prestige hire cars, watched by streams of excited onlookers and cameras. Joel stepped from the car first, waving to the crowds and cameras as though he had walked the prestigious red carpet a thousand times before. I smiled proudly at my cousin as he opened my door and gently helped me from the leather seat opposite where he had sat.

I would normally have felt silly waving to a crowd who had no idea who I was amongst these celebrities, but I felt alive with the thrill of the atmosphere, and waved along with Joel, who linked my arm in his.

"April! April Falls!"

I was shocked to hear my name being called from all different directions as we stepped away from the car, building the tempo for the prime guest star of the evening. I tried to locate who was calling my name, but I was blinded by the hundreds of camera flashes and deafened by the screams of anticipation. I stared at Joel incredulously, trying to smile as naturally as I could manage. His face was alive with a truly genuine grin, still waving at the cameras and eager spectators.

A lull blanketed the crowd fleetingly as the door to our limousine was opened once again, the fans hushed by their curiosity, until Lucas casually stepped from the car, raising an arm above his head in salute, and flashing the most glamorous smile I had ever beheld. I was almost deafened by the sudden volume of the Melbourne crowd, and placed my arm around Joel for support, whose smile could have lit up the entire Red Carpet.

"You're in your element, aren't you?" I whispered between the teeth caught in my smile.

"Sure am, sweetheart," he replied, still waving regally.

Lucas signed autographs for the fans closest to the roped off section of the carpet and continued to salute the multitude as he walked. He stopped when he reached Joel and me, pausing to pose for the cameras, one arm around me as I stood between both my escorts, beaming in bewilderment. I subtly hid my left hand between my escorts as the ever-present ring burned mildly against my skin, and I was sure that it blazed a brilliant colour against my complexion, as though it were forcing me to remember that it yearned for its absent mate.

We were stopped a dozen times before we reached the tail end of the carpet, interviewed by reporters and posed by cameramen. It was strange being on this side of the carpet before having experienced the media side. Most of the questions were directed at Lucas, occasionally at me; and were answered humorously and wittily by Lucas, who flowered in his element. I beamed with pride like a prized Poppy standing between these two talented men in my life.

Only once did his beautiful face turn serious, a line etched across his lovely lips, as a reporter questioned him about the rumours flying like saucers around us.

"Do you really have to ask what I think?" He had leaned in closer to the reporter, who had a wide barrel-lens positioned behind her shoulder. "She's the most wonderful woman in my life."

By two-thirty I was past ready to leave the official after-party in one of Melbourne's prestigious hotels, knowing that Joel would stay until the sun came up, and I whispered to Lucas that I was calling it a night.

Lucas followed me to the lobby where he called for his shiny grey Audi that he'd hired (with driver!) to be brought up outside for us.

"You beat too?" I asked as he slipped into the back seat beside me, surprised that he was turning in when the party still raged on inside.

He directed the driver to take us directly to his hotel, which was closer to the venue than mine, before answering me. "There's only so many of these you can do in one week," he joked, resting his head against the seat rest.

"Yeah, and there's only so long one can be expected to stand in these heels!" I returned, leaning over to loosen the straps around my ankles. I caught Lucas' light perusal of my bare legs as I straightened, suddenly conscious of the short length of my silk dress. "It's not too short, is it?"

He seemed to chew on his lip as he ran a hand through his tousled hair, glancing out of the window as he answered. "Not to me. You should show those legs off more often."

"Ha!" I cried, punching him lightly in the arm and feigning shock at his comment, even though I was a little unsure if he was mocking me or not.

"You know, I could get very used to you prancing around in outfits like that," he teased, reaching over and lightly laying his hand upon mine.

"I don't prance," I said, playing offence, but snuggling into his side nevertheless. "And it is fun, every now and then. But you're right; I couldn't do these gigs all the time."

"But I don't. Most of my time is taken up filming, learning lines and promotions."

"Which means you're away an awful lot. Like my Dad."

I felt the indent in Lucas' spine as he exhaled slowly. "And you don't like to travel?"

"Of course. But it's not exactly a holiday with you working long hours day after day; and I'd never get to see you. That's what my Mum hated about my Dad's job. And what am I going to do for three months in one place and then another? I would only have you to report on. And that could get a bit stalker-ish."

Lucas was silent for a moment, and I felt his body stiffen as he digested my aversions.

"What I mean is: I'd lose who I am. I'd become known as 'Lucas Forrester's reporter girlfriend'," I said as softly as I could. "Who's going to take me seriously as a writer?"

"So you can see why I haven't had a long-term girlfriend for years," he jested, a weak smile upon his dim features.

"I'm sure it's not because you don't have a thousand women who aren't willing to travel the world with you and wait while you shoot a film or two," I replied, stooping to sarcasm in my fatigue.

"It never works because they always want more, and I can't give it in this line of work. I'm not ready to give it up."

"There must be some way around it. I mean, lots of Hollywood actors are together for years. Look at Kyra Sedgwick and Kevin Bacon. And Mark Harmon's been married almost 30 years! And there are loads more I'm sure," I said optimistically, more for his comfort than mine.

"What about marriage one day?" Lucas asked with a grin, his eyebrows piqued in curiosity.

"I didn't take you for the marrying type, yet," I replied, surprised he would bring up the other dreaded 'M' word. "I'm not really a big believer in marriage…it just…doesn't seem to last whichever way you go into it…" I explained, thinking firstly of my parents, and then of Hugh…

I looked down at the ring on my finger and smiled at the irony of a ring that had been placed on my finger *very* lightly, but now it was part of me whether I liked it or not. For now.

Lucas and I alighted in front of the doors of the Radisson Hotel, taking my hand as the driver left to park the Audi.

"Come with me, please? I'm not . . ." he paused to make sure we were out of earshot, "I'm not finished with what I have to say to you."

I started debating about the no-good it would do to go with him, but gave up, knowing I wouldn't refuse an excuse to spend more time with him.

Up in his twenty-fifth floor suite I flopped onto the couch in the dimly lit lounge room. "How come I always end up the one with no clothes to change into?" I huffed as Lucas removed his jacket and shoes.

He laughed spontaneously, his eyebrows raised in amusement. "We'll just have to order you some more clothes in the morning. We can't have all those chins wagging when you leave here in the morning still wearing that dress."

I glared at Lucas wearily. "Not helpful."

"Sorry. I'll find you something. They usually have robes and overnight wear in these places," he mumbled walking into his suite, and returning moments later with a lopsided grin on his face, carrying two plush items over one arm. "I don't know why everything is always white in these places…"

I staggered in my fatigue and curled up beside Lucas on the sofa after I had changed into the nightgown and silk-light dressing gown. "Now, what were you saying in the car? Something about your anti-*marriage* sentiments?"

I groaned. "Do we really need to talk about this now?"

"Yes. I'm sick of goin' roun' and roun' with you. I want to know what you want," he said through a suddenly thick English accent, resting his cheek gently on top of my head. "I promise I won' laugh…or get mad."

I sighed, feeling the air of my argument deflate within me. If he wanted the truth, he would get it. "Lucas, it's not about what I want from you, it's about what *you* want from *me*."

"You know what I wan'."

"Actually, no, I don't."

I felt the pressure against his chest as he sank further into the couch beside me.

"I wan' us to be together…for as long as it works out."

"For as long as it works out?" I repeated, incredulous. "And then what? You just turf me out?"

He sat up rigidly, holding me at arms' length. "No. That's no' wha' I meant."

"Then what?" I demanded, blinking as though in a stupor.

"I meant until the day comes *when* it doesn' work anymore, for both of us, or for you," he explained, his brows furrowed in agitation.

"You don't understand. I'm not looking for something that will just end like that. I'm not like that. It's not an option."

I recalled the image of Hugh kneeling down on one knee on the dusty porch of Audenlea, gazing up into my face with his eager brown eyes and wavy blonde hair. "Forever?" he had asked, without a doubt in his mind that it was going to be.

"Forever," I had replied, rubber-stamping the best solution to all of my quandaries, past and present.

"What are you getting so upset about?" Lucas asked, his strangely familiar voice interrupting my reverie.

I pushed against him and lay aligned with his side so that I wasn't looking at his face, afraid to see whose ghost was really looking at me through his translucent eyes. "I don't want a *Hollywood* relationship! I don't want something that's good for now and then thrown away at the drop of a hat! I can't risk going through something like that again."

"Neither do I!" Lucas objected. "Do you think so little of me? Haven' I proven anything to you?"

I rolled back over and hugged him tightly, nestling my head into his chest. "Lucas, I *hope* that you aren't like all the others. But the stats aren't in your favour."

"Wha' have I ever done tha' was truly questionable?"

I thought for a moment. "Nothing, I guess. But you just said you haven't been able to make a relationship work."

"I thought I had once, remember? And she's the one who cheated on *me* – no' the other way round…"

It was the second time I had heard Lucas mention his once long-time girlfriend of three years, Susan Cahill. The first was *that* day at Erravilla after Justice had accused Lucas of cheating with Penny. According to the tabloids at the time, Lucas' very public break-up with Susan had been a very bitter one. I had never asked him about it, and wasn't about to now. I knew I would have to at some point. I'd save *that* particular topic for a sunny day.

"Don't you think that's also because I haven' found the right person? Someone who I know I can trust."

I desperately wanted to believe him, wanted to be that person, wanted to have him all to myself, for the rest of our lives. But I also didn't want to make that decision so soon. I had done that once before and ended up losing him prematurely. "We've only known each other for a couple of months. It seems a bit ludicrous to be talking about this now."

"But you want your cake and to eat it, and you won' take a risk. It's you with the commitment issues, April, no' me," he offered, tilting my chin with his firm hand so that I had to meet his gaze.

"Well, can you blame me? Look what happened with my parents; and then Hugh. Long term relationships don't seem to be my life's forte."

"I thought you said you weren't averse to a long term relationship?" he pressed.

"I'm not…I'm averse to marriage and divorce! And death!"

"So let me get this right: if you had a crystal ball and you could see the future, and it said that we would live a long and happy life together, then you'd commit to a relationship with me, right now?"

"When you put it that way, yes."

"April, that's impossible…so plan B: you can take a chance; or walk away and wonder what could have happened if you'd stayed."

"Or plan C: we carry on like we are now, in this casual comfort and no-one's the worse off if we fall apart," I suggested, glancing away.

"That's also not going to happen," Lucas replied dropping my chin from his hold. "I can't live like this and neither can you. April, this is limbo. This is nothing, with a little something every now and then. Do you really wan' that?"

I huffed, too weary to keep my eyes open any longer. "I don't know."

"Yes you do."

"I just want us to be this way forever. Peaceful, uninterrupted, private."

"And I would love that too. But it's not going to happen. Even if I stopped filming, I would still get hounded for the rest of my days, and you along with me. You're sort of a celebrity in your own right, you know. 'The Aussie journo, who stole the heart of a British Screen Prince,'" he said mimicking an *E* reporter.

"You've been watching too many movies," I scoffed, running the tips of my fingers along the smooth skin beneath his shirt.

"And you haven' been watching enough," he breathed, turning my face to his before lowering his mouth to mine, lightly kissing the rim of my bottom lip.

I felt the ebb of the rise and fall within me and allowed myself to be swept away by the torrent, returning his kiss with an urgency of my own. I wound my hands around his neck as he rolled swiftly onto me, his hand trailing my bare leg and hitching it up around his waist, tracing the smooth of my skin with his fingertips up to my hip. My fingers found his shirt and fumbled as I hurriedly slipped each button through its eyelet, throwing the garment to the floor.

I ignored the voice that came with its warning, allowing the exhilaration of longing to course through my frame as I contracted against the promises in each kiss that dissolved into my flesh. Lucas' adoration became the epitome of an ecstasy that I had denied myself so many times before, and one that I had not experienced with Hugh. I could have blamed the fatigue for my frenzy, or the fear of abandonment that I knew had chewed its way through to my core since my father had moved out when I was five, or the rejection of Andy after I had given myself to him at seventeen, and the murder that followed, or yet still the unexpected loss of Hugh…

But as my mind walked down that bustling road of excuses for why I chose to lose control over my senses at this moment and detoured straight for the cliff at the end, I knew the ugly truth with each thrust of my stride; selfishly, I did not want to lose this opportunity to create a bittersweet memory with Lucas Forrester, who I knew I would hold forever in my heart, but feared that I would be only one of many in his.

And at the realisation that I would never truly be his because he had already shared his heart and flesh with who knew how many women before me, I also knew that one day, this lifestyle of chasing our dreams wouldn't work for him, or for me; and we would go our separate ways. I knew that I wanted him; but not the life that he would bring.

In that moment I heard the voice again and knew it was right; I had been at this fork before – the one I had thought there was no return from. But here it was, given to me again, and this time I heard it loud and clear.

And yet I did not tear my lips away from Lucas', or push him off of me when my awareness of him burrowed deeper into the recesses of my consciousness.

I want it! I want it all! My desire called out from a selfish and yet broken place within.

And then as though barraging through the door of my conscience, that all-too familiar burning sensation upon my hand interjected my experience of Lucas, in exactly the same way that M had interrupted at Erravilla. Suddenly and without want my eyes blurred to a vision of a hand outstretched through the tumult and the crowds surrounding me, reaching through the throng and steadying me with a strong and assured arm, not walking beside me through the mire, but carrying me through it Himself, bearing the load that should have been mine when I would have been lost and trampled by the stampede running in the opposite direction.

I tried desperately to catch a glimpse of the being bearing my weight as he walked straight through the crowd, but he did not look down. All I could see was the gentle bob of his shoulder-length brown hair as he walked on.

And yet there was something timeless and familiar about him, a sensation of Hope that reverberated with each step he took, and thundered back to the beginning of time…

"Wait!" I cried, holding Lucas' head flat against my nightshirt, my body screaming against the injunction I had just administered.

"*Wait what?*" Lucas' trill voice asked, his broad chest heaving against mine.

"I can't do this!" I gasped, my chest heaving from lack of oxygen.

"April, this is not a good time for a bloke to stop," Lucas gasped. "But just say the word, and I will."

"Ohhh!" I groaned, shaking my head in utter dismay at the untimely interruption. "Tomorrow, I'm having this ring cut off, even if it means I lose a finger in the process!"

"You can't do this…with me…can you?" Lucas asked, tearing himself away from my convulsing frame. "There's something else."

He sat up with the grace of a mountain lion denied his kill, covering me up with the nightgown and blinking through his long lashes.

"It's so late. I can't think straight," I breathed headily.

I sat up, tucking my knees to my chest and pulling the nightgown over them. "You must think I'm the lousiest person alive… that I do this deliberately."

"I shouldn't have started this tonight. It's too soon for you. You haven't moved on yet," Lucas breathed, folding my huddled frame into his side.

"It's not that. I'm ready to move on from Hugh. Like I said, I'll always love him in some way, but I am ready to move on. It's more than that."

22. The Road Less Travelled

"You don't have to tell me, if you don't want to," Lucas offered, raking an absent hand through his tousled hair. "But I'd be more than happy to have that ring removed from your finger. It's kind of creepy. And sometimes, I feel it burn against you. It makes me angry."

I smiled faintly at his possessiveness. It was more of a protective defence than the selfish type Andy projected. I supposed it must be weird for Lucas that I shared a wedding band with his brother, even though it wasn't an official symbol.

"You need to understand something." I took his face between my hands, feeling the bristles of stubble against my palms like an old welcome friend. "I want this…you…more than anything right now. But I made a promise to myself a long time ago, when I was just seventeen. Before I had met Hugh. It's going to sound like a soppy, childish story...

"In high school I had a friend: his name was Andy. We were best friends like a couple of girls, or boys, the same age were. We never got together during school; we just hung out. He looked out for me, that sort of thing, but he had girlfriends, and I dated a couple of guys too. It never bothered us; we were just friends. Then in our senior year of school I noticed that our feelings had gotten, well…beyond friendship. I started getting jealous of a girlfriend he had, and so I went out with this other guy, just to make him jealous. Which worked."

"Go on," Lucas encouraged as I paused to gauge his interest.

"The night before our final exams began, we were hanging out, just the two of us, in his bedroom. His parents were out for the night…"

As I told Lucas the story I knew I couldn't close my eyes to the surreal images that regurgitated themselves up from my memory, blinking through the prints of that night like a cartoon reel. I remembered the headiness of exhilaration, the electricity and heat of Andy's naked flesh against mine, and the clammy breathlessness that followed as we rolled apart, staring up at a ceiling that no longer seemed familiar. I groped for the blankets and reached across the bed to Andy.

I felt the retraction of his hand as though I were reaching for it still, and the sting of confusion that follows a slap of rejection.

"Andy?" I voiced, the wonder and awe that had slipped from my tongue only moments before now replaced with bewilderment and uncertainty. "Andy! Talk to me. Please!"

"There's nothing to talk about!" he returned, rolling onto the edge of his mattress to shield his face from my view.

"I'm your best friend!" I begged. "I love you, Andy."

"Yeah? Then why don't you prove it?" he said, biting with a venom I had never sensed in him before as he turned over to face me.

"I did…I just showed you how much…"

"Show me again," he demanded. "Right now. Do it again!"

I swallowed, trying to gulp down the confusion and hostility of Andy's reaction. *I thought this was supposed to turn out happily ever after…*

"No. Not like this…" I replied, feeling the nip in my skin as I chewed on my tongue, tasting the blood of bitter disappointment. "What was wrong with the first time?"

"Everything! Everything was wrong!"

"I left in tears. He called me the next day, and the next. I refused to return his calls. Not only did I regret what happened, but I had also lost my closest friend. I couldn't bear to see him or speak to him for the shame of what we had done…and all that I had lost as a result. I left school after the exams were over and I moved an hour away to live with my Dad. I made a vow to myself after that: that I would never again do that with somebody who wasn't prepared to love me for the rest of my life, and who was willing to testify to that by putting a ring on my finger first. Stupid, huh?"

I glanced up at Lucas and he traced the line of a stray tear with his thumb, tasting the salt as though he alone could soothe the memory.

"It sounds pretty childish, doesn't it? A great hoo-ha over nothing…"

But then again, I hadn't told Lucas all of it. I never would. That was my cross to bear…the one Andy should have carried with me.

"Not at all," Lucas replied, filing a shock of hair behind my ear.

"I didn't see Andy for two years," I continued. "Then one day he just showed up at my house, after Hugh and I had gotten engaged. I was nearly twenty. He was angry, yelling at me for not waiting for him and said that I had ruined his life, that I owed him, and that he was coming back for me. He was surprised that I would 'do a stupid thing like get engaged.' He had become so angry and bitter. It was as if he blamed me for something. Blamed *me!*

"I was so hurt, so confused. I told him to leave, that Hugh would be around soon. He threatened that he'd have his way with Hugh, and that he wasn't good enough for me, even though he'd never met Hugh. I convinced him to leave and eventually he did, after I threatened to call the cops. He's never left me alone since: phone calls, notes in the post, he visits my family…the last I heard he was a Security Guard up the coast somewhere.

"The thing is, I still felt such a connection with him, even after all those years. It's something I've tried to get rid of and just can't. I don't love him; I haven't for a long time. But he's taken a part of me, forever. And I'll never get it back. I told Hugh that Andy and I had had a falling out in high school, leaving out the exact details, and he was furious with Andy for coming back and threatening me.

"We were one month and one day off getting married when Hugh was killed. Can you imagine the anguish I felt, never knowing what it would have been like to have been with Hugh? Never telling him the truth of Andy and me…and yet, part of me knows it was the right thing to have done…to wait . . . that Hugh wasn't meant to be the one anyway. Part of me was even relieved that he never had the chance."

"The chance to what, April?" Lucas queried, with softness in his tone.

Visions of shrouded cloths dancing with my heartbreaks filled my mind, of the tortuous months that had followed the incident with

Andy at seventeen, and then again during the aftermath of Hugh's death nearly three years later.

I glanced at Lucas to gauge his full response, wondering what on earth he thought of me now and feeling the continents between our worlds as though for the first time. Did I sound as pathetic as I felt? One thing was for sure; I wasn't about to admit to him my greatest fear, that I was glad Hugh hadn't had a chance to find out about me being the ultimate monster that I was.

"To see me this way: still so messed up sometimes. You know, it felt so right, you and me, a minute ago," I confessed, deterring him from the train of thought he was seeking, searching his sea-blue eyes. "It felt so right that I got confused. I didn't think I was meant to feel this intense about someone I haven't known for very long."

"And that's why I think you're perfect, April Falls."

I blinked robotically, wondering if I was so tired that I had misheard him.

"I know, with one hundred percent certainty, that you want to be with me, for all the right reasons," he said with a lopsided grin, and I traced the fatigued crop circles beneath his eyes.

"You don't think I'm ridiculous?" I asked, squinting into his eyes as though I would find the right answer if I searched hard enough.

"Definitely not. Sexually frustrating: yes," he mused. "But with reason. Do you know how hard it is to find someone who isn't obsessed with me for what I am, and what I have to offer them, with a price tag attached?"

"We are a strange pair, aren't we?" I mused, leaning into him again.

I felt the warmth of Lucas' mouth planted firmly against my forehead, and sunk into his hold. "We need sleep. Luckily, there's nothing on tomorrow except flying back to Sydney in the afternoon. Where do you want to sleep?"

I expected to hear the ring of alarm bells as I considered the options, but knew instantly where I would sleep best, and it occurred to me for the first time that I actually *trusted* Lucas: at least not to take advantage of me after what I had just told him.

I nodded toward the master suite. "In there with you."

He grinned steadily, with a slight shake of his head, steering me to the master bedroom. "You know, you might just be your own worst enemy."

"I'm happiest when I'm near you."

"Except that you actually sleep far away from me."

"Then I'm not my own worst enemy, after all. And you can sleep in peace."

London

M

I hadn't slept well for many nights. The ring woke me constantly, burning my flesh like a fire spoke, or waking up after having a nightmare about April, to find the ring illuminating the room in a vivid shade of colour. I ran an extra few miles each day, just to clear my head for the day.

I considered changing my name for the shame as I read the morning papers. My international clients were beginning to link me to Lucas, since we both shared the same last name, and we were the only two English men some of them knew. The pretentious, selfish side of me didn't want Lucas' antics influencing my career probabilities or discouraging potential clients. I had built my architectural and design firm single-handedly and was not prepared to lose my credibility due to media hype surrounding my brother's latest affairs with either Alicia or April, who was now rumoured to be his 'Aussie Journalist Girlfriend'.

The British papers were going mad over the accusation, fans either outraged or eager for more information to confirm the rumours. The *Personals* segment was running like wildfire since April had been confirmed on tour with Lucas. Darius phoned me continuously, outraged that Lucas and April were receiving threats for "going public".

I placated him as best as I could, just managing to suppress my own irritation in the process. Lucas and April were adults, and would deal with whatever came their way. And, I pointed out, they had not "gone public" with anything, other than that April was now officially touring with Lucas as he promoted his latest film, writing for the *London Times*.

I refused to enter into discussion with either Darius or Mother the morning they had both phoned to hear my views on the most recent scandal, which had eye-witnesses state they had seen both Lucas and April leaving Lucas' Melbourne hotel together, the afternoon following the AFI's.

Lucas and April were their own worst enemies. It was their problem, not mine, I told myself over and over again, as I began throwing out half empty bottles of Bourbon and Russian Whiskey. This wasn't my concern.

And it was all I could do to stop myself from teetering over the edge…

April Falls

And be one traveler, long I stood, and looked down one as far as I could…

Dad phoned on the way home.

"Apes, darling, are you sure you're okay? I…I saw the papers this morning…is that boy looking after you properly?"

"*Lucas* isn't a boy: he's thirty. And yes, he's looking after me just fine. I can't believe I'm about to say this: stop reading the papers until I'm back in England! They're always going to assume the worst," I replied, rolling my eyes.

"So long as you're safe."

"Yes Dad, alive and kicking. And *happy*."

Thriller erupted from my phone shortly after I had hung up from Dad. *Here we go again!*

"April!" came her shrill voice.

"Mother," I replied flatly.

"I've seen you on the television! And I've had half the country ringing me for details!"

"Mum . . ."

"I didn't even know you were back in the country! So how could I tell them anything?" she said without pausing for breath.

"I didn't tell you because I knew you'd go berzerk! I just needed some distance from everybody," I said more calmly than I felt.

"You've seen an awful lot of that *boy* while you're here."

"That's because I'm touring with him! We practically live together! I'm writing about him, Mother."

"You didn't tell me you were *living* with him," my somewhat conservative and appalled mother returned.

"Not like that! Anyway, I'm twenty-three! What's it to you?"

"Hugh was such a nice boy..."

"Grrrrrrrr!" I growled in frustration. *Let sleeping dogs lie!* "I will see you before I leave. And don't say that to anyone, or you'll have a media circus on your front lawn!"

Dad visited the day I arrived in Sydney, greeting me with a bear hug to rival Darius' as I opened Audenlea's heavy oak door. "You're okay! You're okay!" he chanted, strangely out of character for my Dad to have physical contact. He must have really heard some bad information.

"Of course I'm okay," I assured him, squirming free from his embrace. "Look, Dad, this is Lucas."

"Say, aren't you the bloke from that movie?" Dad asked, scratching his head with one hand and shaking Lucas' with the other one.

I rolled my eyes.

"Dad, it would do you well to actually flip to the *Entertainment* section, maybe once a decade!" Alex offered.

"Yep, I'm the guy from that movie," Lucas laughed in reply, shaking my Dad's hand firmly. I thought he was going to turn around and slap my Dad on the back like he did with his brothers, but thankfully, he refrained. That would have pushed the physical limitations of my Dad's affections.

"Is this the fella you showed me on the flight on the way over?" Dad asked, still scratching his head.

"Yes, Dad, that was Lucas' film, the fourth of a sequel. Don't worry," I replied, waiting for him to stop interrogating Lucas.

"And stop scratching your scalp, or you'll be bald before your next birthday!" Alex warned.

I attended each of the New Zealand, Tokyo and Malaysian premieres with Lucas, as his date, but he didn't push the relationship. On the contrary, he was more protective of me than ever, placing an arm around me only when necessary, and answering all the controversial questions that were thrown our way.

We arrived at Heathrow to complete chaos at the airport: someone on board our flight had tipped off the media, who were waiting to steal a shot of Lucas for their latest feed. It wasn't long before we discovered the reason for their latest frenzy: headlines flooded the covers of every British paper and magazine, accompanied by pictures of Lucas and Alicia Morrissey, that had been taken at recent premieres for *Breathless*. According to the media, Alicia was pregnant with Lucas' child.

My stomach spiralled into my feet: so this was what round two of *an eye for an eye* was going to feel like…

Winter, 1861, rural Gloucester, England
Sir Walter Finnegan, last Earl of Erravilla Court

I crept into her room that night as per usual, although I knew this was the start of the week when she did not require my obligations. Maisy was sitting up in her bed with the oil lamp still burning beside her dresser, reading a leather-bound volume of some sort. I had often observed Maisy reading in solitude when she had not been aware of my presence, or she was choosing to ignore me completely. I had been in a state of shock at first, for none of the men I knew back home in the working class ranks of society could read, and certainly not the women. But her father had schooled her in many fields of service as was proper for a lady of her standing, not just the financial, I realised.

She glanced up at me with a surprised expression upon her face. "Why, Mr Finnegan, I thought it would be quite obvious to you that I am not in want of your..." she glanced away from me, her cheeks turning a becoming shade of rouge in her discomfort.

"I thought we might better get acquainted tonight, Maisy, after our discussion this morning," I stumbled, equally as uncomfortable under the circumstances.

"Mr Finnegan, I have not yet given you a response to your request," she began, glancing back at me awkwardly.

The fact that she had not verbally ripped me to pieces gave me a brief moment of comfort; she was not completely against the idea. I cautiously made my way across the room and took the liberty of seating myself across from her on one of the sofa lounges in the suite. She made no effort to join me on the other arm chair, simply pulling the blankets up a little higher than her waist. Fine, if she insisted on conversing with me while still beneath her bedclothes, then so be it. There were few of the usual mannerisms of decorum left between us anyway.

She turned the Volume upon its spine and stared at me in expectation, tight lipped and with a slight tilt of her head to the side. "Yes, Mr Finnegan?"

"Maisy, I was wondering whether you would be kind enough to shed some light upon these...fascinating wedding bands of ours?" I ventured, with greater restraint upon my urgent desire to know about the strange rings than I felt.

The corners of her mouth lifted lightly, despite the passing sorrow that crossed her eyes. "The rings are unique. There isn't another pair of them in existence that my father knew of. He said that they had come via the east, from a large continent down south, past the Americas. His father had brought them back with him as a young man on one of the many sea-faring mission voyages he undertook, before he married my grandmother. The story tells of a frightful adventure that befell my grandfather when his ship ran aground in unknown waters during a freak storm. My grandfather survived, along with only a handful of other young men.

"They spent many months repairing the ship before setting sail once again, this time successfully crossing the Atlantic to reach Continental Europe. During my grandfather's stay on the island, the crew hoped to befriend a tribe of natives, who spoke some kind of rare dialect of the Latin Spanish descent, from what they could decipher. My grandfather and his men learnt the language and were eventually able to communicate to the natives, helping them build shelters and schooling them in the mother language."

I smiled lightly at this, and wondered if she was aware that she very much resembled the man she spoke of.

"When it was time for the crew to set sail, my grandfather was handed this pair of tribal rings, that were said to have been washed up in trunks from other boat people who had drowned before reaching shore. The natives had no use for the gold but warned my grandfather that they thought the *rings possessed unusual qualities. They said that these sorts of mystical objects were not unheard of in other tribal villages."*

I had listened in silence and intrigue as Maisy spoke, not solely because it was a fascinating story, but also because it was the longest amount of time I had ever heard Maisy speak. She possessed a strong rich voice, the kind one could listen to for hours at a reading. I was quite lost for words, despite the plethora of questions I still had.

"Is there anything else, Mr Finnegan?" she asked, seemingly more relaxed after having captivated my attention for an unusually lengthy amount of time.

"Well, yes...actually, Maisy," I stumbled. "How is it that I cannot remove the band?"

She seemed affronted by the inquiry, narrowing her eyes to examine me closely. "Why would you need to remove the band, Mr Finnegan?"

"Because on occasion, quite frequently, actually...I know this may sound unbalanced...but I am oft scorched by the 'mystical' ring, as you call it," I replied, trying to calm her outburst.

"Once the new bearers have accepted the rings, the rings forge a pledge between themselves and the bearers, and cannot be removed," she said matter-of-factly.

"Ever?" I exclaimed. "But that's absurd!"

"I'm not sure why it would be absurd, Mr Finnegan. A pledged oath cannot be broken and you have pledged yourself to me, and therefore accepted responsibility for your actions, which you willingly undertook."

"My actions?"

"When you freely married me and accepted the ring."

"The ring cannot be removed...ever?" I repeated, thinking momentarily of Rosie, should she ever decide to accept my offer. How could I be wed to Rosie if I could never take this ring off?

"Well, of course in death, Mr Finnegan, had you read the inscription on the inside of the ring before it was placed upon your finger?" she scoffed.

"But I didn't lay eyes upon the ring until it was placed upon my finger," I replied.

So that was the reason for her father's snide grin on the day…he knew I could never desert his daughter, until death do us part…

"Your father…he tricked me into this," I whispered.

"You would have married me anyway, Mr Finnegan."

"Why would you be so sure of that, Maisy?"

"Because you married me only for my prospects, like any man in your position would have done," she replied curtly.

I was about to refute her angrily for her rude insubordination but I thought better of it, given her frail nature of late, and the fact that she had spoken the truth…

I steadied my breathing before continuing on. She looked strangely pleased with herself for having caused me such angst. The ring was the only power she held over me.

"What does it mean when the ring changes colour, and burns frightfully hot or icy cold?" I asked, unsure if I really wanted to hear the truth now. How much worse could it be?

A wary smile surfaced and then passed across her soft lips, and she looked away from my gaze, unable to meet my eye with her response.

"My father said that the rings tell of the unspoken feelings emitted by one person to the other. So, Mr Finnegan, when the ring on your finger changes colour, that is an indication of how I am feeling." She looked up at me then, with a challenge in her eyes. "And I will know what passes across your heart when you feel it."

"What do the colours indicate?" I asked hesitantly. What had she already learnt about me?

"Father said that there were innumerable colours on the spectrum, and that there are possibly colours that he or his

father had not encountered; so I cannot tell you the answer for every colour."

"I have seen orange and blue mostly. And I noticed a shade of red only once: on the day we were wed," I offered.

"And I have experienced only blue and purple, Mr Finnegan," she replied glancing away. "The red you saw indicates some level of happiness or joy – pleasant emotions. The orange is when I am perplexed, or sad, or hurt. The shade of blue that we have both experienced indicates a display of anxiety, or fear, or great distress, Mr Finnegan."

That sounded correct to me, given the circumstances. "And purple?"

"Such things are not spoken of, Mr Finnegan. T'is inappropriate," she replied curtly, glancing between the bed-sheets and myself, but not quite meeting me in the eye.

I stared at her in consternation. Whatever was she referring to? There had been nothing inappropriate or untoward in my thoughts... "Maisy, please, I beseech you woman: T'is inappropriate only in as much as you know something about me that I do not!"

"The only time the ring has turned purple, Mr Finnegan, has been in the past six months," she supplied, staring at the closed book in front of her.

"The past six months?" I pondered.

"At night, Mr Finnegan. And that will be all," she said dismissively.

"At night...in your company..." I supplied. I smiled pleasantly, surprised by the knowledge that I was glad Maisy knew this one detail of me, that should have made her feel happy. Clearly it did not.

"I said that will be all," she repeated. "Please leave now. You have your answers."

"Thank you, Maisy. This was truly an enlightening discussion. I hope you consider the option for more conversation?" I said hopefully, taking my leave, and then

hesitating. "You failed to answer my earlier question: why does the ring burn and freeze?"

"My father said the ring froze his hand when my mother was near death. It happened three times in their married lives; the last being upon her actual death…the heat indicates the extreme intensity of emotion felt by the other bearer."

I was stunned by the implications and nodded simply before closing the door behind me. What a strange set of circumstances that had landed upon my life. Could these two small bands alter the course of one's relationship or one's very life?

23. A Fork in the Road and a Delivery

April Falls

To where it bent in the undergrowth; Then took the other, as just as fair,

Lucas smirked and shook his head.

Unbelievable! I bet he's fuming on the inside while keeping that professional face he's so good at on the outside. I, however, was not so casual, inside or out. I, of all people, knew not to believe most things I read in gossip mags. I also desperately wanted to believe in Lucas, and *not* believe the headlines. But could I stand to be seen as the cuckolded girlfriend, even if we weren't officially an item? Could I manage being made the fool for years on end, like other celebrities, even if the rumours were not proven true every time?

And a baby…?

Mary-Anne managed the Media as we left the airport, not so incognito, as we had expected. Although, I should have been used to the unexpected by now. For example, I shouldn't have been surprised that the annoying piece of metal upon my finger chose to burn my skin at that very moment, turning a bright shade of orange in the process. I couldn't even look at Lucas in the car, hiding my hand in my jacket pocket from his view.

Maybe the ring was like a mood ring…a *burning* mood ring that reflected my extreme emotions! Today I was going to visit a jeweller or the local blacksmith; either way, it was going to be removed. The antique ring was going to have to find someone else to scorch, *till death do them part!*

Against Mary-Anne and Gerry's insistence, Lucas decided that he and I lodge at Park Lane for a few days. Lucas had copious amounts of lines to learn; and I had several stories to follow up on from the tour.

"You shouldn't laugh at a person's weaknesses, you know," I mused, once we were alone.

"I'm laughing with shock, is all," Lucas admitted, his emerald eyes dancing as they bore in to mine.

"You thought I would be strong enough to resist you?" I asked smoothly, wrapping my arms around him like a sprawling vine.

"I had hoped that you would be in the beginning. Until I met you that night in the kitchen at Erravilla," he said soothingly, and I felt the bob of his Adam's apple as I leant my forehead against his chin. "Do you know that I felt intimidated by you?"

"Why?" I demanded, incredulous.

"Because I knew the moment that you spoke, from the way that you looked me directly in the eye and spoke to me as a person. You didn't look up to me, like the fans do. And you didn't look down on me either, as most other people do, especially journos. You wanted to know about *me*. After you left, I thought about you all night," he confessed, a glimpse of vulnerability shadowing his lovely features.

I pulled him to the lounge, cradling his head against my hammering chest. "Do you know how absurd that sounds to me?"

Thriller suddenly filled the room. I groaned as I reached for my phone. "It's my Mother."

"You should answer it," Lucas said, despite the dip of disappointment edging his tone.

"April! Have you read what that boy's been up to while he was away in France last month? I told you he would break your heart!" my mother cried frantically.

I stood up and walked down the hallway, out of earshot of Lucas.

"Mother, how many times have I told you *not to believe everything you read*?" I retorted.

"Well, what does he have to say for himself?" my mother demanded.

"The same thing I just told you," I replied, my voice shrill.

"So, this *girl* who's claiming to be pregnant with *his* child, is lying? She just…made it up, did she?" my Mother continued.

"I don't know. He hasn't even spoken to her yet. Not that it's any of your business!" I half growled under my breath, my own fears mirroring hers; I could not deal with a baby. With *his* baby.

"Well, I hope you don't go making the same mistake with him as she did! You're better than that, April Falls!"

Of all the things she could possibly say!

"This conversation is finished," I returned, hanging up the receiver, my hand shaking as I threw the phone on the floor.

"April…"

Lucas' calm voice interrupted my raging thoughts.

"Alicia and I—"

"You don't need to explain yourself, Lucas. I'm not your girlfriend. You can go and have your *baby*."

The sound of my own words sliced through my heart, ripping open the floodgate of doubt.

And he said nothing.

For ages.

And ages.

"No," he finally said.

"No?"

"I want you to know the truth. You have a right to know."

"I think I've heard enough about your 'truths', Lucas."

"Please just listen…Last year, during the filming of *Breathless*, Alicia and I had a sort of on-set 'romance' I guess you would call it. It's one of those things that happen when you're working so closely with someone for months at a time."

He paused, and my mind tracked instantly back to the intimate images of Lucas and Alicia on screen during the premiere viewing of *Breathless*. Hand upon hand, flesh upon flesh…

"I was still single. She had a boyfriend, who she was broken up with at the time; but has since gotten back together with," he continued, his voice uneven. "At the time it seemed there was no harm done; nothing was confirmed in the papers, just speculation. You probably read about it."

I nodded, slowly chewing over the lump of doubt caught in my throat.

"We've just been friends ever since. She got back with her boyfriend; and I was still sulking over Susan. You probably read about that too."

I nodded again.

"The thing is, as difficult as she made my time in France, I knew I wasn't interested in her, or anyone else, including Susan, anymore. All I could think about was you. Alicia made her intentions for me very clear when we were in France, practically all over me the whole time." He paused, running his long fingers through his tousled hair. "She asked me why I was no longer interested in her and I told her about you. She wasn't mad. She couldn't really understand my interest in a "reporter", as she put it, but she was fine about it and left me alone after that."

"So why has she come out and said about the…*baby*…being yours?"

"I have no idea. I swear to you: I did not sleep with her in France. If she really is pregnant, it's not mine," Lucas said heavily, looking me directly in the eye. "It kind of sucks balls when this sort of thing makes the gossip columns."

"Or the front page!" I said cringing.

"It happens from time to time: all sorts of false claims like this. They're not even worth commenting on. The truth will come out eventually – it always does," he said sounding far more confident than I felt. "I guess you learn the hard way sometimes, not to fool around with work colleagues."

Though he stood relaxed against the frame of the doorway, the strain was evident in his half moon eyes and dipped mouth. I did not envy his life one iota, even with all the fame, glamour, riches and talent. I did not want the baggage that travelled with it.

The following day the online news sites were teaming with hate mail for Alicia Morrissey. Lucas surely had some die-hard fans, who apparently thought it was *their* right to have Lucas' baby, not hers, or anyone else's. I was glad that Lucas and *I* weren't the object of public outrage this time. Mary-Anne phoned Lucas, informing her that Alicia Morrissey's publicist had contacted her regarding the allegations.

Lucas shook his head in irritation. "I don't know whether to feel sorry for the girl, or wring her neck for her stupidity! Apparently Alicia got a "friend" of hers to go to a chemist and get a pregnancy test for her. The "friend" jumped to conclusions, having read the papers about our supposed "dinner date" in France, and told someone, who posted something on *Twitter* that the baby is mine! Alicia doesn't even know if she's pregnant or not! But she's as angry as hell with her "friend"; and really sorry that I got caught up in all this."

"Well, that's good news for you, I guess…once the truth gets around," I said encouragingly, though still feeling queasy with the after-taste of doubt. "So, does she know who the real father might be?"

"I'd say it's her on-again off-again Spanish boyfriend," Lucas mused. "It's just bloody well not *me!*"

"Well, I have to say that I'm more than relieved as well. That just wouldn't have been a happy start for us," I reflected sardonically.

Lucas' eyebrows peaked in sudden amusement. "Start?"

"To our friendship," I replied hesitantly, though feeling the illumination in my eyes as I met his. "I'm still not sure whether I want to be part of this crazy world of yours. I don't know how many false pregnancies I can handle."

Lucas laughed softly at my bleak humour. "No more. That's a promise! When I start shooting this new film next week, I'll stay far away from any co-star who may look my way…and any who don't as well."

"Do you really have to go so soon?"

"Afraid so. Back to the U.S. for three months."

We stood there by the lounge, staring silently at one another, Lucas' beautiful downcast face mirroring the cloud of emotions that stormed about in my chest.

So this is how it's going to be with Lucas: one catastrophe after another; then he'll leave for months on end. Could I bear to be away from him for so long? Could I trust him while he was gone?

"Do you have time for me this week?" I asked.

"I have only a couple of days that I can spare," he replied thoughtfully. "That's why you're going to stay here with me before I leave."

"Then we'd better make it memorable," I teased, sauntering over to the arch he leant against and relaxed into his fold. Heat lanced through my veins like a hot current and I suddenly desperately wanted to know Lucas intimately before he left, unsure what lay ahead for us beyond the British Summer. His tell-tale eyes grew wide as I nudged myself between his thighs, raising one knee to his hip and guiding his willing mouth to my own within the curves of my hands.

"April, do you know what you're doing?" he murmured.

"I hope so," I replied mischievously.

"Just a word of encouragement: if you're going to start something, please finish it," he pleaded. "The interruptions kill me."

A loud buzz pierced the air, causing us both to pause, his lips lingering softly upon mine.

Lucas rolled his eyes and huffed melodramatically. "Hold that pose."

He unhitched my leg from around his own, gently weaving his way past me to the intercom. "Yes, Ben?"

A familiar voice echoed back. "I have a male here with a post-pack delivery for a Mister Henry Wallace. Says it needs to be signed in person. What would you have me do, Master Wallace?"

He pressed again with his right index finger. "I'll be right down, Ben."

Lucas released the button before huffing again, his irritation apparent. He grabbed the apartment key for the elevator, quickly kissed me on the forehead, and then headed for the lift. "April, hold that thought for a few more seconds."

I relaxed down onto the sofa, still high from the scent and warmth that lingered in his absence and waited in a surreal euphoria for his return, absently wrapping my arms around my waist in the mould of Lucas' last hold.

It was only later – much later – that I remembered Ben would have never allowed anyone inside the building without checking with Lucas first.

24. Bound

After five minutes I began fiddling with a strand of hair that had settled across my eyes and then began picking the random pieces of lint off my shirt as I lay on the couch.

The clock chimed six and I walked over to turn the lights on, noticing how dark it had suddenly become outside as I returned to the couch.

The silence began to wear on my patience and I considered following Lucas' strides into the eerie lift that appeared to have swallowed Lucas.

How big was this package?

I decided to take the lift down to the entrance lobby on street level. The petit parlour was empty; the doors were closed and locked, and all appeared in order. Except that there was no Lucas. Or Benjamin.

Odd.

I decided to take the lift down to the underground garage. An unnatural silence greeted me; and there was no sign of Lucas. Or Ben. Again.

I ventured into the car park and noticed that Lucas' garage door was closed, as it had been left previously. I called out his name, receiving only an echo for a reply. There was not a soul in sight. All grates were closed: nothing out of the ordinary.

I headed back upstairs and called his mobile immediately. *Good, it's ringing.* No answer. Then a sharp dial tone: the phone had been hung up. I dialled again. This time the phone went to message bank. Not wanting to sound paranoid, I left a light-hearted message, asking him to call when he got the memo. *Of course he'll call. He can't be far. Maybe he had to go to the post-office to collect…?* Aren't there people who would do that on his behalf?

After half an hour, an unsettling sensation had developed in the pit of my stomach and I debated with myself whether I would sound like an over-paranoid girlfriend if I called Mary-Anne. I checked the lobby again and still no sign of Lucas. Or Ben.

An hour later Lucas had not returned and the sky outside decided to pour with rain, thrashing against the windowpanes like an abandoned shrieking woman. I picked up the phone and dialled Lucas' publicist.

"Hi, Mary-Anne, it's April Falls here. I'm just wondering if Lucas has called you recently…say, in the last hour or so?"

"No, April. Does he need something?"

"I'm not sure. I can't get hold of him. I was wondering if you could call Gerry and ask him…if he's heard from him…or seen him."

"April, is everything okay?"

"I'm not sure. I can't find him, and he's not answering his phone."

"What do you mean you can't find him? Wasn't he there with you this afternoon?" Her voice heightened a notch.

"He was." I paused, wondering whether I should tell her my premature fears. "He went to collect something from downstairs…and hasn't returned."

"Collect something?" Mary-Anne sounded suspicious already. "From who? Doesn't Benjamin usually collect everything on Lucas' behalf?"

"Ben phoned an hour ago to inform Lucas that 'Henry Wallace' needed to sign for a package. Lucas hasn't returned. And there's no sign of *anyone* in the lobby. Not even Ben."

"Stay where you are. Don't go outside. I'll call Gerry and we'll be there soon," Mary-Anne replied hastily.

So much for not getting her panicked prematurely!

I paced along the tiles like an impatient black panther as I waited, still expecting Lucas to walk through the doors any second. Instead, a rambling Gerry and heightened Mary-Anne clicked their way into the lounge room.

"No one gets in or out of this building without a security pass," Gerry greeted, waving a small rectangle card through the air – "or through Benjamin! What was he thinking?"

And then I remembered that he hadn't been…at least not with his head.

"It had been Benjamin on the phone," I offered instead.

"Then Ben's just made a huge mistake: he must have let someone in first," Gerry fumed.

"So where is he then?" Mary-Anne demanded.

I winced as the mantel clock chimed seven.

"April, Mary-Anne and I agree that it's time to involve others. Maybe his family have heard from him? Maybe Lucas jogged over to Emerus'?" Gerry suggested; his eyebrows arched as though he really believed Lucas would just do that without telling me first.

"I doubt that," I half-scoffed, partially at Gerry's stupidity and partially at the notion that Lucas and M were chums at the moment.

"Who should we call first?" Mary-Anne pondered, clucking her tongue as she thought aloud.

I knew without a doubt who would know best what to do: Justice.

Lucas was still M's younger brother, and the Forresters would band together in a potential crisis: "M. He won't freak out like the rest of his family will."

"Should I call the police first?" Mary-Anne queried, now tapping her toe like it was a hot-shoe.

"Wait till M gets here," I replied, glancing at the silent ring as I dialled his number, and then frowned as his message bank picked up. "I hope he's not out of the country…"

Mary-Anne and I were still pacing up and back along the tiles, our shoes clicking away and occasionally bumping elbows in our absent concern, when the lift sounded outside the condo and the three of us froze like mice at the sound of an owl's screech.

Whoever was about to walk through that door was going to bear the load of grief that was threatening to break through the sandbags I had laid in my tear ducts, pushing aside the voice that told me I was going to go through the roller-coaster of loss for the third time in as many years. I couldn't do it again.

I imagined the faces of Mr and Mrs Grady, the former bearers of grief's hideous misfortunes…and wondered who had filled their shoes this time.

In two seconds I saw his face, and then felt the sting on my finger, glancing from the violet ring to M, who looked as though he had swum from Fulham to Park Lane, wearing a navy blue jogging ensemble and white runners, his hair spiked and his face dripping from the rain.

Whether from disappointment or pure relief I ran straight into his frame, colliding with a well of reassurance as he slowly enfolded two damp, strong holds around my trembling form. "You came, you came!" I sobbed.

"I got your message. It'll be all right, April. We'll find him," M breathed, resting his chin atop my head and cradling me into his chest. "I'm sure there's an explanation."

"She's been great, up until now," Mary-Anne said quietly from behind me. "We think that it's time the authorities were informed."

M

I nodded in thought, trying to pin my mind to reality, trying to find a logical explanation for Lucas' whereabouts. I chased away the voice of destruction that said my brother would deliberately do something to cause his loved ones angst.

April trembled so violently against my chest that I had to extricate her arms from around my centre to remove my soaking jumper which, I worried, would give her a fever. I never wanted to see her in the state she had last been in at Park Lane after *the Dungeon*…

I gazed, irritated at the burning shackle on my finger as it changed from a bright blue to a burnt orange, before folding April back into my chest, and leading her over to stand before the flickering fireplace, her breath a warm sensation against my skin.

As the police arrived I propped April up against a load of cushions on the lounge, her eyes red and glazed despite the forced grimace plastered upon her face. I would have chuckled at her bravado under different circumstances, as April recalled the precise events of the past few months in detail to the two young officers, who held onto her every word, scribbling furiously.

Due to Lucas' high social profile the police agreed to retain his identity, for a maximum of twenty-four hours. After that, the officers recommended that for Lucas' own safety, his disappearance be publicised in the hope that someone had information on his whereabouts.

"The first thing we're going to do is locate Miss Penny McClellan," Detective Wolf stressed, scratching his thick moustache with the up-end of his biro.

I winced, shaking my head in disagreement. "I really think you're putting too much emphasis on Penny. She couldn't possibly be behind a—"

Kidnapping? The idea was ludicrous!

"With all due respect, Mr Forrester, your judgment is clouded due to the personal nature of your former relationship with Miss McClellan," Detective Sergeant West returned, her hazel eyes boring into mine with caution.

I strode over to the window, raking a hand through my hair in angst: *they were wrong.* "It's Emerus," I corrected her. "And I knew her better than anyone."

"We'll be the judge of that, Mr Forrester...Emerus," West objected.

Detective Wolf phoned at seven the following morning, indicating that Penny McClellan was absent from her current known address, and that a search was underway for her whereabouts.

I still wasn't convinced that this indicted Penny: she could have been on a holiday for all anyone knew!

I convinced Mary-Anne and Gerry to return to their homes after a restless night for all of us at Park Lane. I watched through the curtains as they drove off along Hyde Park, nodding to the unmarked surveillance car parked across the road before pulling the blinds shut. And I couldn't help but think that April and her *shadowing* and writing of Lucas wasn't yet again to blame for provoking the attack. They were as dangerous for one another, and in more ways than one, as an open saloon was for me! I needed to get her to stop ghosting Lucas and *Stop. Writing. That. Book*!

Two more days passed with no new information on Lucas' whereabouts. The Press had gone into frenzy, as though Wall Street had crashed for the second time in as many decades. Mary-Anne delivered a press statement, keeping details to a minimum, assuring the outraged community that the police were doing everything within their powers to follow any leads, and called upon the public to come forward with any fresh information.

Despite advice to the contrary, April refused to leave the Park Lane condo, insisting that this is where Lucas would return to soon. My family also refused to stay away, eager to be here as new information filtered through, but their hysteria unsettled me more than April's silence and I managed to convince them to return to Erravilla for some respite.

"Would you like to get some fresh air, April?" I asked her quietly, as she stood facing out the French doors off the reception lounge.

"Thanks, M, but I'd rather stay here…for when he returns," she replied, gazing out the glass panes, a perplexed expression marring her pretty features, as if she were living in a different time altogether. "I can't take this…not knowing."

I had my back to the doors, leaning up against the wooden frame beside her, her hand resting against the frame for support. Instinctively I reached out to her, placing my hand over hers, before realising the consequences of my actions. The alluring rings found each other instantly, binding our hands together in a fierce embrace.

April puffed at the force of the attraction while I struggled to free her hand from beneath mine, laughing with a bittersweet irony at my hand that also seemed to keep reaching out for hers.

"April, I'm so sorry…I didn't think."

I chastised myself at the more ironic truth: that April was almost all that I did think of.

"Just hold still…this might hurt a little," I said wincing as I wedged my free hand between the bands and pulled with all my strength to separate the magnetic force.

April sighed, the totality of the past few days weighing heavily upon her. "Are we going to be stuck with these things forever?"

I laughed bleakly as I remembered the inscription engraved into the underside of the gold: *Till death do us part.*

April tilted her head towards mine as the inquiry passed through her blue-green eyes.

"There are a whole lot of strange things in that house," I pondered aloud. "Urland Chisholm once said something about an old journal that he found at Erravilla when he worked for the previous owners. Maybe that might have the answers!"

April's mobile phone buzzed with vibration upon the glass coffee table. She stared at the phone as though it were a grenade, gripping the windowpane with a force that turned her knuckles white. The gold band upon my finger burned in turn and I flinched until it passed.

"It's blue," I muttered, completely baffled by the maddening rings. "And it hurts like hell!"

I retrieved the phone and brought it to April. "Do you want to read the message?"

"No. You do it," she replied, her eyes transfixed upon the small black object in my hands.

The forwarding number was blocked. The message was brief:

April Falls: arrive at Fleet Street midnight tonight. Do not inform police or you will never see Lucas again. Bring M with you. Wear the dress in the black box in the attic at Erravilla. We will be watching.

"Someone abducted Lucas?" she breathed. "Right here…"

"April, I think we should contact the Police immediately. These people are dangerous, abducting Lucas from his own home in broad daylight…"

"No. If they're as dangerous as you say, we should do as they say," she returned, her eyes pleading as they searched mine. I felt the strength drain from me as I realised the complete confidence that she placed in me. She placed her own life, as well as Lucas', *in my hands.* The wrong hands.

"April…I can't risk your . . . Lucas would never forgive me if anything happened to you," I uttered, my mind swimming against the tide of reason as I watched the hope drain from her face.

"Then you'll have to hold me hostage yourself; I'm going whether you come with me or not."

I stared at her, incredulous. "You love my brother enough to die for him?"

She glanced away silently but not before I saw the lines of doubt being thrown from the depths of her frown. I chastised myself as my own hope swelled in the light of her secret revelation.

"April, are you willing to risk harm to yourself for a friend who you've only known for a couple of months?" I rephrased, forcing the hand of reason before I would comply with her wishes.

"I would risk my life to see him again," she replied with deliberation, lifting her chin, along with the sail of doubt, and running into the wind.

"Ok. We leave for Erravilla and find this box in the attic," I replied. "And we talk to Urland Chisholm about this diary."

"M…"

"Yes?"

"What if…what if Penny is involved?" she asked hesitantly.

I held her gaze as she forced me to consider, drawing my hand as I had hers a moment before.

"Then pray I have mercy upon her."

26. Props

April Falls

And having perhaps the better claim, because it was grassy and wanted wear.,

M drove with less caution than before; the fiery Jaguar took the narrow roads at greater speed than was legally permitted and I had to grip the glove box more than once. He drove with his brow furrowed, his features set hard with determination, as though he could see the end of the road through this catastrophe.

"M, do you think Penny sent me that message?" I asked cautiously.

He sighed, a sorrowful resignation marring his handsome features. "I'm considering the idea."

"What's changed?"

M shook his head, his short hair recoiling across his forehead before he raked a hand through it.

"Because she called me 'M', and she knows Erravilla, and Park Lane. Who else could know those details? She spent loads of time at Erravilla when we were together. She also knew Lucas' alias. She's part of the reason Lucas won't allow any *guests* at the apartment. You can see why it took us all by surprise when he turned up with you that night at *The Dungeon*."

"M, I'm so sorry," I said meekly, unable to find the words to soothe the chasm of pain that I could see burrowed into his brilliant blue eyes. "You don't deserve to be hurt like that."

"Well, the damage was done months ago. This might just confirm how incredibly wrong my judgment was about her." He shook his head in disbelief. "How could I have been so damn blind?"

M and I hadn't even reached the back steps of Erravilla when the glass doors swung open. I was greeted by Alex, who threw her arms around my neck, her breathing erratic.

"What are you doing here?" I demanded, furious that she would willingly place herself in such a dangerous situation.

"Well, I haven't heard from you in days…and then your *boyfriend* gets abducted! Do you think mum isn't going completely spare?" she returned, standing back to confront me face to face.

I didn't bother to correct her about Lucas being my boyfriend; I wasn't sure any more that he *wasn't* my boyfriend. "I'm sorry, okay? But this is the worst idea you could have had. You could be in danger here, Alex."

She huffed and pushed a lock of thick dark hair from her face. "Well, now that I'm here, I'm not leaving until I know that you're okay."

"I'm fine," I assured her curtly, waving a facetious arm down the length of my body to indicate that I was whole.

"Hi, I'm Alex, April's sister," she supplied, ignoring me and instead extending her arm for M to take.

"Welcome to Erravilla, even if it's not quite as welcoming as usual," M returned, taking her hand and giving it a gentle squeeze, as I remembered him doing with me months ago. "I'm M, Lucas' brother."

"I know who you are, Emerus Forrester," Alex replied with ardent fascination. "I'm familiar with your work…I'm a big fan."

"Thank you," M replied, clearly taken aback by Alex's familiarity.

"Alex is a photographer," I supplied, leading us into the grand dining hall.

"A photographic artist," she corrected.

"Now's not the time for semantics, Alex," I returned.

M cleared his throat and I paused to glare at his back, amazed that he found the situation amusing, and knowing that I was far too precious right now to appreciate any kind of humour.

"So, what can I do?" Alex mused, overly cheerful compared to the mood I was in.

"You mean apart from hopping the next plane out of here?" I asked. "Keep low. And, for heaven's sake, don't let anyone find out who you are."

Alex huffed behind me. I knew she would be rolling her eyes at the back of my head too.

"M and I are going to locate some items in the attic. You can help us find them," I said finally, leading Alex and M through to the hallway, which led to the narrow spiral of stairs to the attic.

"Phew, the dust up here is rank!" Alex complained when we reached the long antique room.

"I don't think it gets dusted on a regular basis," I replied sarcastically. "Maybe once a century."

M chuckled lowly, following me through the dimly lit loft. "This is where I found the music box," I explained, pointing to the antique vanity set.

"What are we looking for exactly?" Alex probed, turning her nose up at some of the less fortunate looking boxes of storage. "Some of this stuff could do with some restoration. I bet some of it's worth a dime or two."

"A black box," M and I chorused, gazing around the room.

"That thing?" Alex queried, hunched beside a dust covered old-fashioned storage trunk, adorned with the same hand-sculpted ornaments as the jewellery box that I had found.

"That's got to be it!" I cried, almost pirouetting across the room to her side.

A low hissing sound reverberated from M's throat behind me and I turned to question his irritation. He simply shook his head and held up the brightly coloured red band, which I knew was causing him the same discomfort that it caused me on a regular basis.

"Look on the bright side, maybe we're one step closer to having these things removed," I mused bleakly.

"I assume you aren't referring to the *"Till death do us part"* insignia?" M said, his breathing returning to normal as the ring faded back to its regular golden tone.

"Hey, that was neat. Show it to me again," Alex requested, stalking over to M and taking his hand at liberty to examine the ring. "It's warm. Where did you get this?"

"From right over there," he replied, pointing to the vanity, while seeming suddenly accustomed to Alex's familiarity.

"What an interesting design," Alex observed, squinting to make out the particulars in the dim light. "Does it glow like that often?"

"Um, maybe only when your sister gets into a mood," Justice mused, holding my gaze boldly.

I tilted my head to meet his piercing stare, an affectionate smile dancing upon his lips. My heart flip-flopped within my chest and I looked away quickly, astonished at the sudden rush the moment had caused.

M joined us, pulling the arduous box from its resting place and towing it to the stairwell. "We'll have to carry it into better light."

I took one end of the trunk as M led the way back around the rickety spirals, hauling the majority of the weight with his hands. For some reason I avoided his eyes where possible, staring at the large box instead as we walked through the magnificent old house and up to the suite on the third floor, pausing occasionally for a breather. Thankfully, only the Chisholms were home, busying themselves with household chores and out of our sight. We would find Urland later to ask about the journal.

Finally we reached the landing, where M and I halted for another break, although I was quite sure that M paused for my benefit alone; he looked neither breathless nor fatigued from the expedition. Alex went in ahead into my bedroom, sending out sighs of wonderment and exclamations over the "neatness" of the suite.

"I can't believe that this is really your room," she crooned in amazement as we joined her for the final leg of the journey, hefting the weighty box into the dressing room.

I threw myself down on the bed and closed my eyes, remembering the bittersweet memories of waking up beside Lucas for the first time…breathing in his alluring scent…listening to his hypnotic voice.

"Wow, if that's a mood ring, your pulse must be racing right now," Alex teased, startling me from my daydream.

She was directing her chiding at M, whose golden band had turned a mesmerising shade of purple. He returned her jibe with a mock surrender, a humoured grin across his full lips. "Hey, I'm not thinking anything untoward at the moment."

I felt the heat rush to my face as thoughts of Lucas danced through my imagination as though a carousel and I looked away from my two companions.

"April? Are you okay?" Alex asked, striding towards me. "Your face is flushed."

"Just feeling a little faint, that's all. I'm quite all right," I replied, rolling onto my side and burying into a pillow. "It's been a long few days."

I heard the *pop* of the lock on release as M flipped it open on the antique box and the air growing thicker with dancing dust particles.

Alex gasped over his shoulder and I joined the duo on my knees beside the keepsake, staring at the treasures before us. "It's a glory box. What a beautiful gown," she crooned gently fingering the white lace embroidery. "Look, matching shoes. And what's that lacy thing?"

"A veil," M replied, and I met his anxious gaze above Alex's head.

"It doesn't make any sense," I muttered.

"She wants you to wear it?" Justice whispered, his brilliant blue eyes a mask as they narrowed in thought.

I swallowed hard, eyeing the veil. "The *whole* thing?"

"Are you going to a masquerade?" Alex piped up, a thrill sounding through her pitch. "What about Lucas?"

"I'm going to have to tell her, you know, M. Or she'll never give it up."

"She's right," Alex replied. "I want in."

M's full lips zipped into a line and his brow-line furrowed.

"It's no use: Alex is more persistent than your standard family K9 could ever dream of being. Anyway, it's probably an idea to tell *someone* where we're going, M."

"Okay, at the risk of sounding like Mum, you're really freaking me out right now! You have to tell the cops!" Alex insisted after we filled her in.

"No. You can only tell the cops if you don't hear from us within the hour. Got it?" I warned.

Alex didn't look convinced, but settled for the compromise. "One hour. From the stroke of midnight. You better come back, or I'm going after you myself!"

I shook my head in frustration, knowing full well that Alex would follow through on any threat she made. "I'll rock up in your Karate belt – that should scare them!"

"I don't know why you're finding this amusing, Alex," I scolded. "Lucas' life is at stake here."

"I wasn't joking. I've been looking for an excuse to wear that Gee-thingy for ages."

I lowered my head in utter embarrassment, flattening my eyebrows with my thumb and forefinger. "Ghi, Alex! Ghi!"

M and I set off in search of Urland Chisholm, hoping to find a clue to the missing journal, hopeful that it held the keys to Lucas' freedom, as well as our own, and left Alex to muse over my Cinderella gown.

We found Urland in the rear gardens, tending to the summer roses beneath a light blanket of rain. The elements didn't seem to bother Urland as he toiled away, whistling sweet tunes of old to himself as he pruned, and welcoming us as we approached. He motioned for us to take a seat upon a nearby wicket bench while he continued to work, his stooped frame suddenly looking every bit of his eighty-something years.

"We won't take up too much of your time," M began. "We're looking for a journal that you may have come across here at Erravilla."

Urland Chisholm paused momentarily, searching M's eyes with his wizened grey pair and nodded. "Years ago. I found an old journal in the attic while I was looking for something of historical interest. I read the first page and brought it down to the previous Lord of Erravilla. I thought it might have been of interest to him."

Urland kneeled to continue his work, concentrating on the thorny vines between his fingers.

"And was it?" I asked.

Mr Chisholm took a while to respond, the ghosts of another time hovering in between the lines on his face and clouding his eyes. "Nope. He threw it back at me saying: "the old bastard was no relation of mine, so why would I care?" That was the type of fellow Lord Hoffman was. Not overly interested in anybody but himself."

"I guess that explains why he died alone, and had nobody to leave the estate to," I pondered, remembering back to the day M had told me of how Lucas had come into possession of Erravilla.

"Urland, what happened to the journal?" M persisted gently, laying a spider-sized hand on the older man's lowered shoulder.

Urland inhaled deeply, a whistle accompanying the sigh that rushed from his lungs. "I gave it to Geraldine to read. She seemed interested in the old stories."

"Thank you, Mr Chisholm," I said graciously, feeling a sudden empathy for this gentle old man who had lived with great sorrows, but who still toiled with his entire soul while he lived.

"One more thing, Mr Chisholm, before we leave you in peace," M said pausing in time. "You don't by any chance happen to remember what was written on that page that you read?"

The old man closed his eyes for a moment, craning his face up into the light summer rain. "Something about a man laying to rest his old wife. And a couple of rings that went with her, God rest her soul."

My heart hammered within my chest as I stared at the elderly man, possessed by the hosts of another place, and the loves lost with time. And I wondered if I too was destined to bury the loves of my youth, instead of the love of my life...

M placed an arm around my waist, gently guiding me back towards the house, breaking the trance that had flared from the mere words of an old man's memory.

"Lucas is going to make it, April," M whispered when we reached the porch, his firm grip still circling my waist.

"We have to find Geraldine and that journal," I replied, feeling the weight of more than just my short lifetime.

I felt the heat of M's ring through my shirt and followed his gaze to the fiery blue upon his finger before he placed it inside his pocket.

"How about I find Geraldine and you try to sleep for a few hours? We can't leave until eleven," M suggested, still resting his free hand upon my hip.

I groaned, resting into M's shoulder. "I won't sleep. I'll just lie there awake, stressing over what's to come. I'm better off meditating for an hour."

"Then go. Do what you need to do. It's going to be another long night," M said.

"How come you're not tired?" I demanded, annoyed that I seemed so weak compared to him all the time.

"I am tired!" he laughed softly. "I didn't say I wasn't going to rest after finding Geraldine."

"All right. I'll be in the gym if Alex is looking for me. She knows not to disturb me when I'm in one of my *states*."

It was an easier task than I thought to lull myself into another dimension, replacing the negative energies surging through my veins, with brighter, more uplifting forces until the only thing that remained in my mind was a soothing silhouette of a man walking through a crowded marketplace, with his hand extended out to mine like an old friend…

I reached for the hand as I faded into oblivion, pleasantly aware that I was being welcomed into the realms of R.E.M.

Winter, 1861, rural Gloucester, England
Sir Walter Finnegan, last Earl of Erravilla Court

The following morning I met with the three maids in the kitchen, preparing them for a plan I had concocted for Erravilla to host a winter function for the coming weekend.

"The winter has been far too bleak this year. I think we could all do with some cheering up," I said thoughtfully, ignoring their surprised expressions. I was quite capable of considering the entire household, especially if the party would provide Maisy with some much needed cheer.

The door to the kitchen opened then and my wife made as if to enter, but upon noticing my presence, attempted to leave without a word.

"Please, Maisy, I would rather you stayed," I pleaded. "We are planning a party, you see. I would dearly like to know your suggestions for the dinner menu."

She hesitated, her discomfort evident. She and I had never spoken in front of the staff. I also thought in hindsight that my familiar use of her Christian name may have embarrassed her as well. Nevertheless, she conceded awkwardly.

"Very well, Mr Finnegan. A party? But what of the snow?"

"It has not snowed in days now. The snow will not be so thick as to be a hindrance," I replied.

She nodded, the idea setting a hint of a glow in her golden brown eyes. "Mrs Connolly, what suggestions have we already? And what of the guests?"

After the arrangements were made I smiled in pleasant satisfaction; Maisy's spirits had been lifted indeed and it was the first accomplishment that we had achieved together.

The week progressed more pleasantly than the preceding weeks, in anticipation and preparation for the occasion. I had given Maisy full reign of the preparations and she seemed to flutter between the rooms as she finalised her plans with Mrs Connolly and Miss Hayes. She still refused to linger in a room that I occupied but she did not immediately leave a room that she occupied when I intruded upon her. She would not acknowledge me until I acknowledged her first, and she allowed me the occasional chance to listen to her stroke the keys of her father's piano, or adorn pieces of cloth with stitching needles, as she sat upon her armchair by the fire.

Even after our acknowledgments we would not speak but I would simply observe her artistry, and she would look content with the arrangement. She seemed to concentrate, giving all of her energy into the task at hand, her brow creasing slightly and her mouth quivering gently in consternation. Her diligent expressions would have been humorous, had they not been so captivating to behold.

The party fell on the eve of the night that I should have been permitted back into her quarters, and I felt surprisingly hopeful at the idea. I looked out into the bleak afternoon and saw the heavy clouds overhead. If it snowed this evening, we would have guests. It would be inappropriate for me to frequent her quarters with guests in close quarters...

"Mrs Connolly," I called, knowing that the woman was always close by. "Have the guest chambers made up please."

"Do you expect that our guests will stay, Mr Finnegan?"

I turned at the sudden sound of Maisy's commanding voice. I had not been aware of her presence. I turned to her at once and beckoned her over to the window in the central living room by the great fireplace.

"Come and see, Maisy, it appears your prediction might have been correct after all," I said, insisting vehemently with my hand that she join me beside the large panes of glass. She made her way towards me slowly and cautiously, pulling aside the drafts to peep around the window edge furthest from where I stood. Her stilted distances perplexed me: was I such a threat to her?

"Well, I don't think it will snow before the party. Perhaps during. You are right; we should have the guest quarters made up in case." She left the room swiftly to attend to the new requirements.

Maisy simply shone as hostess of Erravilla again. I reclined easily in the knowledge that she had everything completely in order throughout the festivities. And for all of her misery across the winter, Mrs Walter Finnegan looked surprisingly magnificent in a new gown and all. It pleased me once again that my young wife caught the attention of every one of our guests, as the women complimented her forthrightly on her appearance; while the gentlemen perused her at will, complimenting me on the accomplishment of having a fine wife to host the evening. I knew they were further referring to her outward accomplishments, not simply her managerial skills.

I had only one cause for concern on my wife's behalf, and that was the somewhat overt attention of one gentleman, who was the cousin of a local Earl in London, who was staying with his cousin for business purposes. I noticed the bachelor linger about her presence far longer than necessary, as he leisurely observed the obvious and infrequent contact between my wife and myself. The young bachelor observed Maisy's every angle at every turn of her heel.

That this bothered me was no surprise; for she was my wife, my obligation, my property and safekeeping. The depth of discomfort unnerved me mildly. The young man was harmless to be sure and perhaps Maisy needed greater attention than I was giving her. Perhaps she welcomed the attention. This notion burned even more deeply and uncontrollably within me; my lips thinned and my jaw locked at the idea that she welcomed other company.

She looked up sharply at that moment, her large eyes imploring mine from across the lounge room where she reclined with the women before the fire. Her head was tilted on an angle with inquiry, her brows knitted together in curiosity. It was only then that I noticed the unsightly green colour emitting from the discernible band upon her finger.

I tightened the reigns upon my emotions hastily, glancing away from her perplexed expression. Thereafter I did not leave her sight as far as possible, refusing to make eye contact with her at all, but maintaining a view of her nonetheless.

The snow fell with a fierce intensity throughout the evening, rendering all of our dozen guests at the mercy of Erravilla for the evening. I was uncomfortable and irritated by the idea. I knew that the ring on Maisy's hand must have been stinging her frequently during the evening, but I could not dispel the strange and uncomfortable feelings I felt when I looked at her...and him.

I made sure our guests were all in their quarters before I bid Maisy a curt goodnight at her room. She seemed confused by my manner, and I wondered if she had been completely ignorant of Mr Shillingworth's behaviour towards her.

I lay awake for a while, my senses overly alert. I was deeply frustrated. I should be in the room next door with my wife as was customary now. Blast! But I had waited long enough. And she had looked so very appealing tonight. I knew I did not love my wife as a husband should; but my affections and desire for her were definitely increasing at an alarming rate and I could not bind them.

I thought perhaps at first my senses had run right away from me as a nearby door closed in the dark of night. I sat up sharply and listened. A low rhythmic sound came from the chamber next door and I knew without a doubt that it was the vibrations of a gentlemanly voice. I pricked my ears up to listen more attentively. The barely audible sound of her voice reached my ears; it came at a low pitch. What was she saying? I was more desperate now as I crept from my bed and leaned up against my wall that adjoined hers. I could not believe my ears, the two voices conversed, increasing with volume and pace by the second.

And then the shrill cry of her voice reached me and I instantly gazed at the burning blue ring upon my finger. I remembered instantly that the colour denoted fear or distress and I needed no coaxing to proceed from my room and enter Maisy's quarters without invitation.

The brute Mr Shillingworth was atop of her as she clawed at him with all her might and had her face turned away from his seeking mouth. In several strides I had reached her bedside and placed two hands around his lithe torso, tearing him from her body and throwing him up against the wall, my elbow against his throat. My father had taught me to fight as a young man and I had never turned out the worst off after the frequent saloon brawls I had rolled into.

"What do you think you're doing with my wife?" I demanded, the anger seething from me now.

"She looked a bit lonely, Mr Finnegan," Shillingsworth hissed between his teeth. I almost chocked in shock; the young rat actually thought he was doing her a favour!

The rough and brazen lad I had once been, returned to me with full fury. "If you ever LOOK at my wife again, Mr Shillingsworth, you won't be walking away on two legs I can promise you that! I could have you thrown into prison and flogged for this!" I growled. "Now get out of my house!"

"But you cannot do that, Mr Finnegan. It's snowing, and I am a guest," he said stubbornly, attempting to lift his chin from my hold.

I shoved him towards the door and without letting go of his arm, opened the door and threw him into the corridor. "You had better be gone by morning!" I hissed, locking the door behind him. I waited until his footsteps retreated down the hall before I turned to Maisy, raking a quivering hand through my thick hair.

She sat up against the wall in a tight bundle, covered to her chin with her blankets and shivering. I approached her immediately, kneeling beside her pillow and placing an outstretched arm upon her hand. She flinched and removed the hand automatically.

"Don't touch me!" she cried, the terror in her eyes giving her the look of a frightened stray animal.

"Okay, okay, Maisy, I won't touch you," I said withdrawing my arm to my side. "I won't hurt you, Maisy. I promise."

She eyed me wearily for several minutes and I retreated to the lounge at the foot of her bed, examining her as my eyes adjusted to the light. She did not appear to be physically harmed, and I exhaled with relief. I felt a gnawing guilt that I had considered her intentions towards Mr Shillingworth as anything other than completely innocent.

"Maisy, I'm not going to leave you. I want you to feel safe. Please...sleep. He won't come near you again, I swear."

She gazed at me for a lengthy amount of time before she surrendered to her fatigue. I dozed intermittently upon the chair, stirring at the slightest of sounds within the old house. Maisy slept fitfully but did not wake until first light.

When she opened her eyes and beheld me with a start, I smiled at her reassuringly. Her alarm faded and she returned my gaze with a perplexed one of her own.

"Is he gone?" she asked weakly.

"I hope so. I will go and make absolutely certain," I replied, standing to leave. I was startled in my tracks when her voice reached me again.

"Please don't leave...Walter. I'm afraid to be alone."

27. Masquerade

_M_

Geraldine jumped as I approached her in the kitchen, chopping away in a frenzy at the line of carrots for dinner. She was absorbed in her work, existing in a parallel world of outlived memories, a world I could not imagine, nor wanted to. Geraldine kept to herself most of the time in this way without offering much by way of conversation. I liked this trait of Geraldine's for the most part: she maintained the privacy of our home and its inhabitants, as well as her own.

"Oh my! Master Emerus, you scared me half t' death!" she cried, waving the chopping knife around in the air absently.

"Take it easy with that knife, Geraldine, or someone will lose an eye!" I joked, but adjusting my stance just a little farther away in precaution.

"Wha' can I do for you?" she asked, returning to the row of carrots lined up across the board in front of her like soldiers waiting for their death sentence to be carried out. Very rarely did Geraldine ever look me in the eye, and always called me "Master Emerus". It was as though she sought to be subservient in an old fashioned way, even though no member of my family treated her this way. I had noticed on many occasions, however, that Geraldine managed to meet Lucas' eye, despite him being the true 'Lord' of the Manor.

"April and I were just having a word with your father," I broached. "We were looking for an old journal that he found in this house years ago."

She adjusted her shoulders stiffly as she continued to chop, reminding me of one of the sentenced carrots before her, though the pace at which she executed the spiky green toughs of carrot hair had slowed considerably. I didn't mean to give off the impression that she might be in trouble in some way, so I continued in a lighter tone. "It's no big deal really. He thought you might have taken an interest in the old book, that's all."

"An interest?" she asked. "Wha's so impor'an' abou' the book?"

"Your father said he gave it to you. It was probably fifteen years ago. Do you remember reading it?"

Geraldine took a while to answer, her eyes never leaving the chopping pallet as though gathering her thoughts, along with the bite sized pieces of orange. She shook her head slowly, wiping the damp hair from her neck with the back of her hand. "I remember my father showin' me an old diary when I was a young girl. I don' remember wha' i' was abou'. I havena' seen i' for many years. I suppose i' wen' back t' the attic."

I exhaled heavily, disappointed that the lead had turned cold so quickly. April was desperate to find the journal in the hope that she could rid herself of the ring that united her and me in a peculiar way…in a way that I had not yet completely figured out.

"Thanks anyway, Geraldine. If you remember anything, or find the old book, let me know, okay?" I said with a false cheerfulness, leaving her to her chores.

I found Alex in the central lounge room, lying on the sofa with her feet propped up on Lucas' ottoman, listening to her ipod. I stood in front of her to catch her attention and waited for her to pause the music.

"Hey, Alex, when you see April, can you let her know that I'm going to my suite for a few hours if she needs me? I'll be down at ten-thirty otherwise."

"Will do. She hasn't come out of the gym yet. I suspect she'll be there for a couple of hours. Sometimes she falls asleep when she meditates," Alex mused. "I just don't get the whole…*at one with the world* thing."

I smiled ruefully at her confused expression, looking oddly like her sister as she screwed up her nose. "Maybe because you don't need to *feel* at one with the world, like April does. It's not an easy road that she's walked lately."

"Yeah, I know," she sighed, her similarly pretty face now etched with concern for her sister. "I hope it ends soon. April deserves to be happy for once."

"I hope so too…more than anything," I replied solemnly, nodding along with my sentiment before heading upstairs.

I lay down across the large sea of quilt that covered my bed, staring at the ornate cornices of the ceiling. I set my alarm in case I managed to drift off, but I hadn't fallen asleep before midnight for weeks, too caught up in the rip of confusion to grab hold of the driftwood of sleep that floated nearby on occasion.

A great loneliness engulfed me, as it tended to do at this time every evening, being greeted by an empty apartment in London, eating alone after travelling for days on end, and then turning down the covers at night and occupying a giant empty shell by myself. The worst part of my day was waking up alone.

Except for that one glorious morning a couple of months back…I closed my eyes and inhaled as though the scent of her still lingered in my nostrils, as though the touch of her warm skin still penetrated through my icy exterior, as though I could wake up again and have her voice as the very first sound to chime through my ears each day. What I wouldn't give to open my eyes and stare straight into those opal-coloured ones!

It pained me more than a physical burn to have her within my grasp, but completely out of my reach. She was not mine to hold, but she was only a stone's throw away…

And then there was Lucas. His safety meant more to me than who he was in a relationship with, even if the consequences meant that I lost her to him after all.

I woke up several hours later, feeling as if a truck had ripped through me. Sleep had come eventually, but the dreams were eerie and distant, a tide of endless ocean, many passing ships in the night, but no life raft within my reach.

The mantle clock read ten o' clock. I took myself off for a shower to clear my weary mind and then headed downstairs for a quick supper, hoping with grim resolve that it wouldn't be my last.

I peered through the great oak doors leading into the central lounge room and heard deep breathing coming from the sofa. Alex was exactly where she had been hours ago, except that she had fallen asleep. What was it with these girls that they always fell asleep on lounge chairs? Didn't people sleep in beds in Australia?

The old house was quiet; my parents and the Chisholms must have gone to bed early tonight. I wondered if April had in fact fallen asleep in the gym and I couldn't resist the urge to look. The room was dark except for the beam of light ribboning through the partially open doorway, which lit up the centre of the gym mats, and the sleeping beauty thereon. Her face was partially covered by a shock of long brown hair and she was curled up upon the mats in an almost feline manner. And yet, even from where I stood, the serene expression upon her sleeping face was every inch a beautiful woman. And I ached for her.

I wondered whether I should wake her already, or give her every moment of sleep she could get. April stirred, stretching absently and blinking in the spotlight, covering her eyes with her arm as they adjusted. I was unsure whether to approach her or not, knowing how much she coveted her privacy, thinking about the last time I had approached her in here.

"M? Is that you? Have they found him yet?" came her drowsy voice.

"No, April. I just came to tell you that it's after ten o' clock. You should try and eat something before we go," I replied gently.

"Ten o' clock? I can't believe I fell asleep!" she cried, swearing as she leapt to her feet, a little less like the graceful feline she had been a moment ago, and rubbing her eyes to chase away the drowsiness.

April refused to eat, saying that she felt anxious as it was, and that food might make her sick. "I'll just go up and get dressed in that…frilly dress thing up there. Hey, did you find the journal?"

I shook my head. "It was too long ago. Geraldine hasn't a clue where it is."

"Bummer. Oh well, a journal's not going to save Lucas' life anyway. We can always hunt for it later," she said in a stronger voice than I had expected. "I'll see you soon."

I felt nervous as I dressed, my unsteady fingers taking longer to secure my tie than usual. I shoved the pair of shiny black shoes on my feet before standing to examine myself in the full-length mirror within my dressing closet. The man in the mirror frowned in disapproval, looking like a complete fool dressed to the nine's in a three-piece black pin-striped suit. I reminded myself that it was for April's benefit alone, to ease any discomfort that she might have wearing that turn-of-the-century lacy dress.

I sighed wearily, and watched as the man opposite me shook his head in disbelief; this was definitely the strangest night of my life. I didn't know whether to laugh or cry at the thought that someone might be burying me in this penguin suit tonight.

I headed outside to bring the Rolls around front before returning to the foyer to wait for April, pacing apprehensively at the foot of the giant staircase. Within minutes I heard the rustling of fabric and looked up to the mount of the stairwell, after having just taken a large breath, which was then knocked clean out of me.

I couldn't turn my gaze from her, watching her every step as she descended the stairs, swallowing hard with each intake of breath that I managed to take. She held the train of the silvery-white dress in one hand to steady herself, avoiding my gaze as she floated down the stairs, the antique veil folded neatly over one arm.

I could not tear my eyes from her, and I didn't care that my undeniable affection for this woman standing before me was so evident to anyone who might have been observing the moment.

As April came to rest before me her eyes flickered to my gaze and I searched her depths with open fascination and desperation, wanting to find a reflection of the emotions I had discovered within me lately, a treasure chest of surprises washed clean to the surface of my very being. April looked away, seemingly uncomfortable with my blatant perusal, fingering the metallic ring upon her finger absently.

"It's burning you," I offered, taking her hand gently in mine, unable to dismiss the admiration I held for the exotic rich burgundy that illuminated from the band. "I've never seen it turn that colour before. If it didn't hurt so much, I'd say it complemented your skin tone perfectly."

"Actually, it doesn't burn at all," she replied, staring at the crimson ring in astonishment.

"And where do you think you're off t' in this terrible weather, dressed for a celebration no less, Master Emerus?"

April and I turned in unison to encounter the unrecognisably shrill voice that had interrupted my fantasy. Geraldine stood with her arms around her body, hugging her nightdress to herself self-consciously.

April looked to me for an answer.

"We've been invited into London for a late night meeting of sorts," I offered, forcing a light-heartedness to my voice, which chased away the better part of my longing for the other woman who stood just centimetres from me.

"And you're goin' t' attend? Under the circumstances?" Geraldine inquired.

I had never heard her question my decisions before, and was concerned as to how I could best approach her without her getting suspicious.

"We will be very safe, Geraldine. The police have been informed and are going to escort us to the function from Park Lane," I lied, not quite meeting her unsettling stare. "The police said to continue on as usual, for Lucas' sake."

Geraldine met my gaze with an almost contemptuous one of her own. I knew that she was fond of Lucas and probably felt that we were betraying him in some way by attending a celebration.

"We'll see you in the morning. You don't need to worry, Geraldine," I assured her.

Geraldine didn't look convinced, and I hoped she wouldn't brew anything with her bubbling concern...

April Falls

Though as for that the passing there, had worn them really about the same

I couldn't leave Erravilla fast enough, following M out the front door as though I was late for the Mad Hatter's birthday party, practically tripping down the stone steps through the heavy rain and into the awaiting black Rolls Royce. I knew that Geraldine didn't trust me; she didn't trust anyone where the Forresters were concerned. I wondered if she had always been so protective of her employers, or if her resolve had worsened since Penny McClellan's disturbance nine months ago?

The further we were from Erravilla, the closer we were to Lucas, and unlike the White Rabbit, this was one date I would not be late for! We drove mostly in anxious silence, Justice with his thinking brows creasing above his blue eyes while I pressed the radio button on and off as if it were a faulty vending machine. Lucas parked the Rolls on a deserted part of Fleet Street, between the illuminating street lamps, hiding in the darkness.

We waited fifteen minutes before my phone buzzed with a new message.

Walk two blocks. Turn right.
Walk towards Cheapside.
Wait.

Wait for what? I wondered.

We walked in the pouring London rain for a mile or so before M decided to pause beneath an old canopy hanging from the side of a building. I had a vague idea of where we were, and wondered where we would be instructed to venture to next, assuming that Lucas wasn't suddenly going to appear in the centre of London town.

I shivered in the night air and huffed, stomping my foot like an impatient draft horse.

M removed his jacket and held it out to me but I refused, shaking my head with vehemence. "I'm not cold, just anxious."

He replaced the jacket without a word, nodding as he rotated the everlasting ring on his finger.

Minutes passed before we received further instruction.

Wait by the rear gates to St Paul's Cathedral.
Switch off phones. Discard.

"So we can't be traced?" I presumed aloud, wiping the streams of rain from my eyes.

M took both handsets and discarded them in a dumpster as we walked down the esplanade leading to the great cathedral, lingering in the shadows of the mighty churchyard.

"At least the rain's letting up a little," I said bleakly, glad that my long hair was tucked up in pins and not soaking my clothes further. I was suddenly grateful that the many layers of the dress were thick enough to prevent the dampness from reaching my skin.

"April…if things get…complicated tonight, I want you to get out of there in any way you can. These people are clearly potty, to say the least. I know you're trained well, but it won't do anyone any good if none of us makes it out…you know what I mean," M said in a low voice, peering at me through the shock of wet hair against his brows.

I didn't like his suggestion; I didn't want to be the one to ducktail and run at the first sign of danger. Not that I had ever dreamt of being faced with a situation like this; and I didn't know what lay ahead for us. I had already decided though, that I wasn't leaving without Lucas. I also knew that M wouldn't take no for an answer.

"You wouldn't leave without Lucas or me, M."

"Just play it safe. Promise me."

I nodded in agreement, despite the waterfalls of uncertainty running off the ledge of my resolve.

A low whine sounded nearby and a silhouette appeared against the black sky, stooping through a low-rise rear access to the building. We were shuffled roughly through the gate and into the lion's den via a side access to St Paul's Cathedral. I heard the low utterings of M's heart upon his lips, and my heart sang out instantly, as though it had been in communication with its Maker all along: *do not forsake us now…*

28. And when the Penny finally dropped...

M grabbed my hand as he followed our silhouetted guide through a series of low passageways, snaking our way down two flights of stairs before reaching the bowels of the church. The large tiled room was dimly lit by wall lamps, which cast shadows across the silent stone floor. Our well-built escort turned to face us, motioning with his hand for us to wait beside a lonely lectern in the centre of the old rectory.

"Where's Lucas?" I demanded as I walked cautiously past him, sounding more confident than I felt. "We've played by your rules...now you give us what we came for."

"So, the reporter has a temper after all," came a sleek feminine voice, echoing off the chamber walls like screeching bats in the night.

I turned to see the beautiful Penny McClellan appear from the shadows of a blackened entranceway. I felt the immediate tension spike through M's fingertips as his hand gripped mine, the other balling into a fist at his side as a blue shade illuminated from the ring. I winced at the sudden pain of the ring against my flesh, awed that my ring illuminated the same colour.

A feral smile tipped the edges of Penny's features as the serpent returned to roost atop of her beauty. "Well, well. I'll be."

"What's so amusing, Penny?" I demanded, spitting out the syllables of her name.

"So, you know who I am? Well of course...I'm sure Lucas has told you all about me," she mused, her eyebrow arched in pride.

"Actually, Lucas has never mentioned you," I returned, not giving her the satisfaction she clearly sought.

Her smile faded instantly and I felt the black clouds appear like the evaporation of a rainbow. "Don't tell me that you're still pining after me, Emerus? I was hoping that you'd have moved on by now, as I have."

I flinched at the low rumble of thunder that escaped from M's chest beside me, sensing the pain that stormed within. "I can't believe he ever gave you the time of day. What a waste of breath you are," I returned.

"I'd watch what you say, Joey. I have precious cargo that I don't think you want harmed," she warned shrilly.

I went to move towards her but felt the restraint upon my wrist. "What do you want, Penny?" M asked, his voice low, haunting.

"Hmmm…it's tempting to take the easy way out with you, Joey," Penny replied, ignoring M completely. "But I have *specific* instructions. We continue with plan A. Bring Lucas out."

And as though awaiting the thrill of the Second Act, Penny clapped her hands three times as Lucas was brought into the middle of the room. His hands were bound and his mouth gagged with thick rope, and I strained against M's hold.

"If you promise not to do anything stupid, I'll cut the ropes. If you attempt to touch her, Lucas, I'll shoot her," Penny warned simply, her strawberry-blonde curls bobbing as she motioned towards me.

The second accomplice retrieved a large knife from his jacket and strode towards Lucas, placing the knife between his head and the rope. "Don't move, boy."

"Hugo, if you leave so much as a mark on Lucas, I'll shoot you too," Penny said simply.

"It's all fine, Penny. Relax," he said sliding the blade through the rope around Lucas' head and then doing the same with his wrists.

Lucas rubbed at the rope marks etched into his skin around his hands, swallowing hard and eyeing me with a curious intensity. "Are you okay?"

"Yes, we're fine," I replied, reaching for him with my free arm. "Are you?"

He nodded, and I watched the heavy rise and fall of his chest. "The company was the worst of it."

Hugo made as if to hit Lucas about the head but was interrupted by Penny's shrill command. "Don't! I said he's not to be harmed. Any more comments like that, Lucas, and Joey will receive your punishment."

Justice flexed beside me, his breathing staggered in short huffs.

"I think it's time to begin the ceremony," Penny announced, sounding suddenly festive, eyeing the clock on the wall above.

Quarter-to-one. I thought of Alex at Erravilla. Was she awake and waiting for our call? I wasn't sure if I wanted her to phone the authorities or not. What was the greatest danger? It was clear that Lucas wasn't going to fare badly from all of this, and I was about to discover what lay ahead for M and I.

"Hugo is a certified celebrant," Penny began cheerfully, as though she were instructing us how to bake raspberry muffins with pink frosting.

I winced as she continued, trying not to draw any conclusions in my mind between her announcement and the Chantilly dress I wore.

"Where's the veil?" Penny demanded, turning on me. I motioned to my arm reluctantly. "Put it on."

I hesitated, wondering if she was joking.

From beside me, her second accomplice suddenly lifted his pistol to my head, with a menacing gleam in his eyes. I slowly lifted the light but lengthy adornment to my head, fixing it in place with hair pins.

Hugo came to stand before us, lifting a wad of papers from his jacket and waving them jovially in the air. "Face one another please."

"Us?" I asked, motioning to M and me.

"Of course. Lucas, you will be their witness. Come and stand beside your brother, please."

"You can't be serious," he replied, a black cloud misting his lovely features.

"Stand where he says, or the bride won't look so pretty," Penny threatened, her dainty palms pressed into her hips.

Lucas dragged his feet over to the far side of M, who stood beside me.

"This is a joke, right? You can't force people to get married against their will," I laughed, as words flowed through my mind like *duress, involuntary, null-and-void...*

"But you *are* getting married willingly," she replied matter-of-factly. "You're willingly getting married so that Emerus here can see his brother again. I can make him disappear very easily, you know."

"So, we get married, or Lucas gets it?" I stammered. "It makes no sense."

"Penny lost her senses the day she chose to forego all human feeling," M retorted.

A loud crack echoed off the walls as Penny's henchman whacked M across the head with the rear end of his pistol and I howled in protest.

"You have turned my world upside down, April Falls, ever since you stepped foot into Erravilla. That was *my* home. *My* family. *My* boyfriend. *Our rings!*" she cried while tenderly gazing at Lucas. "And now, you go tramping off around the world with him, ruining all my plans for *our* future! The others were easy to get rid of…but you…you just won't go away!"

I stared at her incredulously.

"So you think you can marry me off, to keep me from Lucas?" I demanded. "That's not going to work."

"Oh, but it will. Because when this is over, you're going to hop on the first flight back to Australia, and never return here. And if Lucas tries to follow you, Dominic Falls will never see the light of day again. He's currently in Glasgow on business. I would hate for him to miss his flight back home."

I felt my skin crawl at her threat as the blood rushed from my head. "Do you really think that Lucas will have anything to do with you after this?"

"He would have, if you didn't steal those rings from me. They were going to be for Lucas and me, sealing our union forever: the true Hosts of Erravilla. But now, *you* two have them. So I thought I'd make it official, since you haven't broken the bond between you and Emerus and given them back. I've waited long enough and now I can see that it's already too late. I could have had you both killed of course, but it seems someone else has plans for you…I was even prepared to forego Lucas' body to you on one occasion, but you failed to seal the deal in *that* department, so it seems. Apparently you don't feel as strongly for him as he does for you. What a peculiar girl you are after all."

"What are you talking about?" I demanded.

"Those rings can never be taken off once they're on. Except in death. Or infidelity. But you and Lucas haven't…" she shook her head in amusement.

I felt the pressure lift from my arm instantly and I tilted my face to M's, feeling the warmth from his spotlight of awe and…hope.

<u>M</u>

A grating sound came from above like a drainage lid being lifted in haste beside a street curb, and I turned instinctively towards the noise.

"Not a sound!" Penny growled lowly and then indicated to the boxer-dog behind us. "Patrick, go and see."

I exchanged a glance with Lucas, trying to placate him with a pressing motion of my hand, despite the unsettling feeling forming deep in my core. This is not how I wanted April to be mine; I had hoped that her feelings for me might develop on their own one day. But I didn't like that her arm was forced into a relationship with me…for the second time in as many months.

The ring burned with a blue hue as though in response to my anguish.

Yet, I reasoned, if this was the worst outcome of the night, and no lives were lost, then that was as much as I could hope for. The rest would sort itself out later. I recalled with regret, but necessity, the name of a client who was one of London's most successful Barristers.

I glanced at April's shadowed face, blackened by more than the darkness of night, haunted by her ghosts in a vaulted crypt. Was it true about the rings…that they could never be taken off? That whether she liked it or not, April was bound to me till death do us part? Maybe I should do her the favour and wait for my opportunity to arise…and break the bond in the other way that Penny had suggested.

Footsteps resounded above, one set heavy and one light, travelling down the narrow flight of stairs behind us. April gasped as Patrick shoved a bewildered Alex into the room.

"I've checked her," he informed Penny. "She's clear."

"Alex! What are you doing here?" April demanded, and I knew that her burden had just increased ten-fold: another person to be used as barter against her.

"Well this just gets better and better!" Penny snapped, glaring at Patrick.

"I followed you," she replied apologetically.

"I thought you said they weren't followed?" Penny hissed at her henchmen in turn.

"No one followed that I saw," Hugo replied hastily.

"You better not have called the police," Penny warned the wide-eyed Alex. "Or this won't go well for your sister."

"I didn't tell anybody! I swear!" Alex replied holding up her arms in surrender.

At least she didn't wear the Ghi.

"Well, we'll see. While you're here, you can be your sister's witness," Penny said getting back to business. "This should make for a pleasant family chapter in your book, April."

"What do you know of my book?" April demanded, grounding out her words with incredulity.

"I know *everything*, Joey," Penny replied, the other-worldly feral delight in her face transforming her features so that she was barely recognisable to me as the girl I once thought I would marry.

"Witness?" Alex chimed in, swallowing hard. "What's the occasion?"

"Your sister's getting married today," Hugo replied with a crescendo of false cheerfulness.

"Married? To M?" Alex gasped. "I think you have the wrong guy."

"Any more comments like that, and your sister will earn herself a bullet in the leg," Penny warned. "Begin the ceremony."

"Now, I've downloaded the quickest and easiest set of wedding vows that *Google* had to offer," Hugo began.

April huffed; Lucas winced; Alex still looked aghast, as though she still expected someone to suddenly spread their arms wide and announce the entire scenario was an April Fool's gag.

"You first, Emerus. Repeat after me: I, Emerus Alistair Forrester, take you, April Abigail Falls, to be my lawfully wedded wife," Hugo prompted, nodding his head so buoyantly that my hands instinctively fisted in irritation.

I paused, taking in a full breath and rubbing my head, which ached from the recent assault it had taken. I had been thinking about possibilities that might save April from having to go through this farce, but could find none that wouldn't result in more violence against her from Penny.

I held April's deep set eyes with a silent apology of my own, shaking my head in disbelief that she had to go through yet another traumatic event, and a mock wedding no less. She certainly seemed to be haunted by the ghosts of her past more than the average person.

"What happens after we say the…vows?" I asked. "Will you let them go?"

I had every intention of staying if it meant the others could return to safety instead.

"After the vows, ring exchange and signing of the register, you are free to go at first light," Penny replied with false cheer. "No contact between these two; and no legal voiding this marriage within twelve months. Now, get on with it."

"But by that time…the marriage will stand…" April whispered.

"You're a quick learner," Penny replied with a click of her tongue. "Emerus, if you will…I know you'll have no objections."

"I, Emerus Alistair Forrester, take you, April Abigail Falls, to be my lawfully wedded wife," I repeated, exhaling slowly, still holding April's simmering gaze, watching as her upper lip stiffened at the sound of Hugo's insistence.

"Before these witnesses," I repeated slowly, hoping that by some miracle the authorities would appear at any moment and put an end to the proceedings. "I vow to love you from this day forward, until death do us part."

"Now, April, repeat after me: I, April—"

"I know what to say, you imbecile!" April retorted. Before my hazy reflexes could defend the blow, April received a steady strike to her face from Penny, leaving a vivid red mark. I moved to grab at Penny, but Lucas' strong grip held me back.

"You'll just earn her another one," Lucas hissed into my ear.

"Say it!" Penny demanded.

"You can't make me," April growled, her lips curling up to reveal her perfectly straight white teeth.

"No, but I can shoot you…or your sister," Penny replied, eyeing Alex with open curiosity as though the idea had fantastic merit. "I'm only following orders, after all."

April took a deep breath, her glare never leaving Penny's curt face as she ground out the words. "I, April Abigail Falls, take you, Emerus Alistair Forrester, to be my lawfully wedded husband."

"Before these witnesses…" Hugo coaxed.

"Before these witnesses, I vow to love you from this day forward, until death do us part," she choked out.

"Excellent. Now, take her left hand, Emerus, and repeat after me," Hugo proceeded.

I took April's cold hand apprehensively, wishing for all the world that she would look at me so that she would know that I did not wish this for her. Her hand shook as I raised it up between us, a bridge from my heart to hers, and yet I knew that the gesture would instead feed the chasm that had been widening since the dispute at Erravilla. April's gaze never left Penny's smug face, an expression of great distress and loathing fused upon April's face.

"How interesting, that both of the rings should be the same colour. It's quite fitting to have something blue at the wedding ceremony, you know," Penny said matter-of-factly, leaning over to examine the radiant pair of rings. "Feeling a little anxious, are we?"

I could feel the heat radiating from April's ring, as it did from mine as well. The intensity of the burning had a smouldering effect upon my skin, and I wondered how it never left a burn mark in my flesh.

"What are you talking about?" April demanded, her voice low.

"I have a little wedding gift for you when this is all over. I'll let you read all about your mystical rings," Penny returned with false amicability.

"You have the journal?" April asked incredulously. "Where did you get it from?"

"Enough questions. Continue, Hugo," Penny commanded.

"I give you this ring to wear with love and joy. As a ring has no end, neither shall my love for you," Hugo resumed. "I choose you to be my wife this day and forevermore."

I repeated his words, meeting April's beseeching gaze with every word, encouraging her with my imploring eyes and faint smile, that it would be over soon, and Lucas would be safe. How desperately I wanted to reach over and cradle her as I had done before, to free her from the burdens that weighed so heavily upon her.

As I pulled my eyes away from hers, the gold band on April's hand transformed into a flaming shade of burgundy. Beneath my fingers I could feel her hand stop shaking and the heat fade quickly. I met April's gaze once more, the amazement in her eyes mirroring mine.

"I misjudged you after all, Emerus," the musical tones that I had once known and treasured, came resonating through Penny's voice. "You *have* moved on. What a strange turn of events!"

"April: hold Emerus' hand and repeat after me," Hugo instructed. "I give you this ring to wear—"

"I heard you the first time," April ground out through her teeth.

"Just say it then," Penny ordered, her voice snapping back to the foreign one that I still struggled to grasp the sound of. This harsh new tone of Penny's had me wondering how I could possibly have thought I knew her at all. The lullaby of her once soothing voice now sounded like a rusted farm wheel being forcibly moved against its will.

"Why don't you tell us about the rings first?" April challenged.

"I told you, you can read all about them later," Penny returned, her patience fading.

"I want you to tell us now," April demanded, glaring at Penny afresh. "It's the least you owe us."

"I don't owe you anything! You stole from me!" Penny cried, lashing out at April with the back of her hand.

April was ready this time, catching Penny's fist firmly in her open palm and swinging her around until Penny's arm was locked in solidly behind her back. "Let's get something straight: you're the bad one, not me. Tell me about the rings or I'll break your arm; *then* I'll finish with this farce of a ceremony."

"Shoot her!" Penny ordered, wild hysteria capturing her features.

"If they shoot, I'll use you as a shield," April warned, tightening Penny's arm enough that she released a shriek, and April moved the Scot in front of her own body.

"All right, all right! I don't remember what all the colours mean! I know that . . . that blue colour means that you're anxious, or distressed, or afraid. And that burgundy colour means true love."

"You're lying! I'm not in love with M! I'm in love with Lucas!" April cried, sending a sharp pain coursing through my head and chest. I hadn't expected the truth to sound so ugly to my ears.

"And that orange shade on your ring means sad, or hurt, or unhappy," Penny groaned under the pressure of her captivity.

"You lie! I'm angry; not sad!" April bellowed.

"Not you: *him*," Penny replied, pointing at me with her free arm. "The ring tells you what the *other* person is feeling," Penny finished quietly. "Those rings are priceless."

And when Penny finally dropped from April's hands, it all began to fall into place…

29. Till Death Do Us Part

April looked up into my eyes imploringly, a powerful sympathy registering in her opal-coloured eyes. "M, I'm so sorry," she whispered, as she dropped her hold on Penny as if she had been scorched.

"Are we ready to continue now?" Hugo asked.

A bottomless sorrow registered upon April's beautiful face. "I'll do what you want." She took her place silently beside me, her apologetic gaze never leaving mine as she held my hand, her fingers resting on the orange band upon my hand.

"Don't. It's hot," I said, shaking her fingers off the smouldering ring.

"I give you this ring…" Hugo coaxed.

"I give you this ring to wear with love and joy. As a ring has no end, neither shall my love for you. I choose you to be my husband this day…and forevermore."

April Falls

And both that morning equally lay, in leaves no step had trodden black.

No words could express the guilt I felt and for the pain that I had caused M, my dear friend and comfort. Hoping that a gesture might better convey my gratitude, I leaned over and placed my arms around his neck, burying my face into his damp vest and holding him firmly. "I'm so sorry, M. I do love you for all that you've done for me. You're a true friend."

"Before the honeymoon begins, you two need to sign the register," Hugo smirked, presenting us with three documents to sign. I sighed, grabbing the pen from him and signing on the lines that indicated "wife", before giving the pen to M, to sign under "husband". "Anyone want to take a photo?"

I scowled at the wretch named Hugo. "I'm going to make it my business to hunt you down and have more than just your marriage license taken from you!"

"Bind her," Penny ordered.

"Hey, you didn't say that was part of it. We've done what you wanted. Take your papers and leave," M ordered, stepping towards me at the same time as Hugo.

"It's all right, M, they aren't going to hurt me," I insisted, glaring at Penny and her mutts.

I stiffened as Hugo bound my hands and feet with thick rope, feeling the strain and knowing I couldn't free myself if I tried. I caught Alex's furrowed brow and smiled at her ruefully, a false assurance of my wellbeing. My companions were ordered across the cold basement floor and then turned to face the stone wall on the other side of the rectory like POW's lined up for the firing squad.

"No one is to leave until sunrise," Penny called, her footsteps pausing on the stone steps. "Joey will be on the first plane for Australia. Mark my words, you will be watched very closely in the next twenty-four hours. All of you. And Lucas, NO CONTACT with your brother's new wife. I *will* know. And *she* will pay. Emerus, You make sure you don't legally void this marriage either…or she gets the same. I suggest you make better use of your time and legalise your union before Joey gets any ideas along the lines of infidelity with your brother."

I heard Lucas and M both mutter something unholy under their breaths: one as a curse, the other I think a cry for help, and I wondered who it was that *my* heart cried out to now, as the silhouettes of Penny and Hugo recoiled up the narrow stairs, leaving a faded brown leather binding on the bottom step.

"Oh, and Joey, this is for almost breaking my arm," Penny's voice cried, carrying through the stone basement.

They were the last words I heard before a searing pain assaulted my head and my knees gave way to the ground.

The first sensation was pain, followed by a bleak memory, and then anger. I groaned, feeling the bandages around my head, and the grogginess of concussion.

I felt the warmth of my free hand enveloped in the confines of another and I groped to feel the strong forearm of a man's hold. "Lucas? M?"

"April, it's Lucas. You're okay. How do you feel?" came his soothing voice.

"Oh, like I'm on the spinning Gravatron at one of those theme parks," I moaned. "Where's Alex?"

"I'm right here. So's Dad," came her gentle reply.

"Dad? You're okay?" I asked, although my voice sounded slurred and unfamiliar.

"Yes, sweetheart, I'm absolutely fine. Thank God you and Alex are okay – that's the main thing. And as soon as you're able, the three of us are all flying home together." His familiar voice lulled and rolled across me like a calm breeze and I blinked at the sudden tears as they came silently.

"Where am I?" I asked, opening my eyes gently and feeling the giddy sensation of the earth moving around me, with faces whose features didn't quite match up like they should.

"You're at Erravilla," Lucas replied, running his thumb softly along the back of my hand. "In your room."

"Where's M? Is he okay?" I asked meekly, leaning back into the pillow and closing my eyes.

"I'm fine, April. Doc Allan has been taking good care of us all, but you still need to rest some more," he replied softly, and I sensed his guard, which unwillingly brought more tears to my eyes.

"Always thinking of everybody else," I mused, choking on the sorrow I knew he felt.

"I never should have let you go to St Paul's, April. It could have gotten a whole lot uglier," he sighed heavily. "And now…"

"Stop blaming yourself, M. No one could have guessed what she was capable of," I said, resigned. "So long as you're all okay."

"I would have thought the dress and veil might have given it away," Alex muttered under her breath, and I heard her sympathy cloaked in the jibe.

"Alex—"

"It's okay, Dad. She didn't want to be there any more than the rest of us," I said. "So what happened to you the other day in the lobby, Lucas?"

"I stepped out of the lift and was greeted by a pistol," Lucas drawled. "I've always feared that sort of thing, but I never actually thought it would happen to me. I mean, there is security and all in the building. Poor Ben…they tricked their way past him with Penny as a diversion and knocked him out before he knew what had happened. The poor guy woke up in a closet in St Paul's basement."

"What did she do to you?" I pressed.

"Nothing, really. She was insistent that I wasn't to be harmed. She kept me in a basement somewhere in London. I was blindfolded and still have no idea where they took me. They moved me on the third night and the next thing I know, I was in the basement of St Paul's with Ben."

I doubted he had given me all of the details, but it was enough for me that he was here, and safe.

"I'm going downstairs for a spell. I'll catch you before you leave," M offered, grimacing as his blue eyes swept across me before he left the room.

"M said you weren't good there for a while, April," Dad said gravely.

"Thank you, really, but you can all stop worrying; I'm not dying yet," I said, deflecting my father's words of consolation. I considered what he had offered about M, who seemed to have yet again felt my malady as though it were his own. "What did M say?"

"He said that his…wedding ring…turned so cold that it burned his skin. He said it did that the night you were drugged at that club. You were touch-and-go for a while," Dad replied slowly. "A great ally you have there, Apes."

"Hmmm," I agreed painfully.

You have no idea what I've put him through since finding those rings.

"So he told you about the *Dungeon*, huh?" I asked meekly.

"I was here when the police interviewed him. They seem awfully interested in your rings, amongst other things," Dad said, his brow dipping in concern.

"How did M know that I was so unwell?" I asked, peering out at my father, who turned his chin as though he were avoiding my gaze.

"There's plenty of time for all that later," he said patting my hand with deliberation, like I was five years old again.

I removed my hand swiftly from beneath his and did my best Queen of Hearts glare. "Time for what?"

"Do you remember that…Penny…left the journal?"

"Yes."

"Well, M stayed up all night reading it, learning as much about the rings as he could," Lucas reported from my other side. "Seems Penny was telling the truth after all. M wouldn't share much of it. He said he'd wait till you were ready to hear it."

I huffed impatiently. "Do the police know where Penny is yet?"

"Still looking," Lucas replied, his soothing voice coating the irritation I detected.

"Say, it's a nice group of friends you've got here, April," Dad voiced, changing the subject. "I've met all the Forresters now, and the Chisholms. They've invited me back to stay whenever I'm in town."

"Oh, Dad, please don't inflict yourself on the Forresters. They've got enough problems to deal with," I whined.

Lucas chuckled softly beside me. "Your Dad will fit in just fine here, April."

I thought about Lucas' eccentric parents and I realised he was probably right.

"Besides, we're officially family now…in a strange kind of way," Dad said, blinking as though he had an eyelash caught in his tear duct. I recognised the mannerism as one of Dad's many social shortcomings that occurred when he was overwhelmed by a situation.

There was a wrap on the door and I smiled at the familiar voice of Dr. Allan. "How's our patient going? Mind if I take a quick look at you?"

Doc Allan was pleased with my condition, but insisted on rest and no hyper-activity. He said I could fly home in a few days.

"A few days?" I gawked. "But Penny said—"

"She can't touch you here, there's a heavy police presence," Doc Allan replied. "You can't fly in this condition."

"Honestly, Doc, I'll be fine. I wouldn't put anything past that crazed Scotswoman," I muttered. "It's not me I'm worried about. She can get to me in other ways."

"Your Mother and Stephen are under surveillance as we speak," Dad assured me. "You must listen to the Doctor here."

"I don't like it. What do the police say?"

"They say we should comply with her requests," Lucas drawled, irritation lacing his melodic voice.

"And you will have to, I'm afraid," the ageing Doctor ordered. "As soon as I give you the all clear to fly."

My head pounded with another rhythmic wrap on the door.

"April Falls? I'm Detective Sergeant Hills, and this is Tactical Operations Commander Booth. Do you mind if we have a word with you now that you're awake?"

"I'm sorry, Lucas, but we need to speak with April alone," the dark haired officer said, flicking his head towards the door. "Doc, Sir."

Lucas squeezed my hand before slowly leaving the room with Doc Allan in tow.

"Miss Falls, I have to tell you that we think it's in everybody's best interest that you do as Miss McClellan requests and return to Australia," Hills offered. "Just until we apprehend her and any known accomplices. We aren't sure exactly how many people are involved, and we understand that she and her accomplices are armed and dangerous."

"I understand. But what if you don't find her for months…or years?" I inquired, as a wave of nausea surfed down through my body.

The officers passed a dubious expression between themselves.

"It's highly unlikely that it will take that long," Booth replied. "But we do recommend that you stay out of the country for as long as it takes."

"She can't get away with this. She's practically running our lives now!" I cried in disbelief. "Why should we give in to her?"

"Miss Falls, we understand how complicated your life seems right now, but this will all blow over very quickly, you'll see," Detective Hills assured me.

"You don't know that," I replied dismissively. "That means Lucas has to stay here for as long as I'm gone."

"Yes," Booth replied. "I'm sorry. He's too much of a risk, having such a high profile an' all."

I sighed deeply, unimpressed that we had to give in so easily. "You know I have to figure out what's happening with this…this farce of a marriage before I go!"

"Emerus is looking into it," Hills replied.

"I need to caution you, that your behaviour last night was dangerous and frankly, stupid, Miss Falls. I understand why you felt the need to follow Miss McClellan's instructions, but you really should have left it up to the experts," Booth chastised. "Such as myself and the Senior Sergeant here."

"Well, I'm not sorry. Who knows what she would have done if the authorities had turned up," I said bitterly. "No offence."

The officers took my information quickly, exchanging weary glances occasionally and I knew they didn't believe all I had told them.

"Thank you, Miss Falls. The story confirms the others. You're free to leave when the Doctor says. We'll be in touch," Hills affirmed.

"Of course it confirms the others," I responded. "Who would think up such a ludicrous story?"

"We're just doing our job, Miss Falls," Booth replied. "We never said we didn't believe anyone. Now you get some rest."

"Please let me know whenever you hear anything," I pleaded. "And I'm going to write about this one myself; I want everyone on the planet looking for that *hairy-coo*."

Immediately after the officers had left, a light tap sounded at the door. I didn't look across to see who it was, but beckoned them in with a wave of my hand anyway.

"April?" a familiar voice chimed.

"Geraldine?" I asked, turning to meet her. I was surprised at the swelling around the edges of her brown eyes, and the dark set rings cradling beneath.

"Are you okay?" I asked, concerned that she should be so disturbed by the recent events. And then I remembered her overly concerned behaviour last night in the foyer, and felt sympathetic for her apparent fondness of Lucas.

"I see tha' you got your book, after all," Geraldine sniffed, eyeing the leather bound volume beside the bed.

"Oh, yes. I haven't had a chance to look over it yet," I said, surprised that she had remembered our search for the journal.

"Is i' true tha' you and…Master Emerus, are married?" she asked, glancing away briefly.

"I don't know. M's looking into it. Her threats are quite menacing," I said gravely. "The police advise we go along with her requests for now."

"I hope he finds a solution soon. For both your sakes," Geraldine replied lowly.

"I'm touched by your concern, Geraldine, but M will work something out. He always does."

The housekeeper nodded vehemently. "I hope they find tha' girl, Penny McClellan. I have a few words to say to her, I do."

I hid the faint smile that wavered beneath my shared disdain. "Your concern is very touching, Geraldine."

"She was supposed to be my friend, Penny was. I trusted her. She has betrayed us all."

A light knock resounded on the door again, followed by a far too polished M, and I ran a hand up to the bandage that circumnavigated my head like a lop-sided halo. M stood motionless, hands in pockets, his expression unreadable.

"Sorry to interrupt. Can I have a word with you, April? Thanks Geraldine," he said dismissively.

The housekeeper nodded curtly, looking to the floor as she passed M, a private expression flickering across her features as she ghosted away.

"The poor woman, she cares a lot for your family," I noted once we were alone.

M closed the door behind him and came to sit beside me on the bed. "This isn't going to be easy, April. We've been told to follow Penny's requests until she's taken into custody, assuming that she will be apprehended in the next twelve months."

"The next twelve months?" I interrupted, incredulous.

"The good news is that you can apply for Citizenship now that you're legally married to an Englishman," he mused darkly.

"I could already apply; my mother was born here," I replied, not quite so humoured.

"I know. I was trying to lighten the situation a little." M paused as if he didn't know where to begin.

"And if she's not apprehended in the next twelve months?" I asked bleakly, wincing as I braced myself for the blow.

"Then we can go against Penny and begin proceedings to annul the marriage before the twelve months are up, and risk the ramifications."

"Or?"

"Or we stay married until she is captured and then undertake divorce proceedings," M said, wincing to himself as he almost mouthed the word *divorce* as though he was speaking a heinous profanity. "It should still be a fairly simple process unless something drastic were to happen in the meantime."

"Such as..?"

"Buy a house together…have a child. That sort of thing."

My mouth hung open like a circus clown in side show alley. "You have to be kidding. We were *forced* into getting married and everybody just wants us to go along with it like it is perfectly *fine*!"

"I'm afraid Penny had it all worked out in her crazy little mind, after all; we willingly signed those papers to save Lucas' life. It was a decision we both made as individuals. There was no deception or fraudulence between you and me, the consenting parties, despite the circumstances, which, taken on their own, do amount to duress. But, if we leave the marriage as it is for twelve months, the law assumes we accept the terms of a legally binding marriage undertaken *without* duress. It turns out that Hugo *is* a licensed celebrant as well; and we had two witnesses to verify the occasion. Therefore, the marriage stands for now," Justice announced, his hands suspended in the air as though juggling invisible tennis balls.

"Oh, M. I don't want to get divorced! I mean, I don't want to be married for a year, *or* get divorced. That goes down on all official documents; you have to tick the "divorced" status whenever you fill out a survey or sign a document! I don't even like the idea of marriage anymore, let alone divorce!"

Justice sat silently, staring at the blue ring on his finger.

"I'm sorry. I'm being selfish. You have to put up with it too. What are we going to do?" I asked almost rhetorically, knowing full well that we had little choice.

He whistled out a puff of air from his lungs and shrugged absently. "Hope they catch the bastards and make 'em pay? Marry Penny off to an over-sized Scottish cave man and hope he mops the floor with her?"

I grinned at his grim humour, taking his hand gently. "Who would have thought it was possible in this day and age?"

"At least I know why this ring burns me now. You'll just have to try and keep that temper of yours under wraps," he teased. "And I'll try not to think about you, so that yours doesn't burn either. You know, April," M said quietly, his blue eyes wincing as though he were in pain. "I want you to know that…you're free to do whatever you want…with whomever you want…to get this ring off your finger. To hell with Penny."

I stared at him in utter disbelief, my mind running in a thousand different directions. I didn't know how to reply.

"All I'm saying is that just because you're legally married to me, doesn't mean I'm holding you to any level of commitment. I want you to be happy, and to continue to live as you otherwise would, as if none of this had happened. If we don't…fulfil *all* of the legal requirements for a marriage, who's going to know either way, unless…"

"M…I…"

"You don't need to say anything to me. I just wanted you to know."

Justice stood to leave, a grimace settling upon his face for my benefit, but I could not look past the depth of sadness that washed up from a deeper recess beneath, coming to rest in the blue irises of his tell-tale eyes.

"Goodbye, April Falls."

Winter, 1861, rural Gloucester, England
Sir Walter Finnegan, last Earl of Erravilla Court

"The ring turned blue...that's why I came in," I offered, not knowing what else to say to her.

"I was hoping for such...and that you would," she said swallowing and unable to meet my eye. She was ashamed by what had transpired last eve, even though it had been of no fault of her own. Women were oft blamed to be the cause of unwanted advances. My father believed so but I had not always agreed with him. Maisy could not be blamed for being as pretty as she was. Most times she hid this fact, so I acknowledged deep down that she was not one for such advances.

"Maisy, what did it mean last evening when the ring turned green upon your hand?" I asked, pursuing the conversation while I had the opportunity.

She looked at me then, her expression a curious mystery: "Why, Walter, it is an expression of...envy, or jealousy."

I made to refute her; but found I could not, for she had aptly explained to me the reason for my peculiar feelings last night.

"Though my father did not often display feelings of affection for my mother, who doted upon him in a way that I never understood as a child, he was a very jealous man, Mr Finn- Walter. If any man ever looked at my mother, they were henceforth removed from my father's circle of acquaintance. My mother told me before she died that she hoped I would marry a man who would protect me at all costs, like she said my father did. I could not see it at the time. I am grateful for your interference. I am sorry to have caused—p"

"Maisy, Maisy," I interrupted, striding to her side and kneeling once more beside her bed. "You have caused naught. We will not speak of this again. That you are unharmed is my only concern," I said frankly, reaching out to cover her hand

again. This time she did not refuse my touch, but looked steadily up into my welcoming gaze, an expression of awe upon her face.

"Thank you, Walter," she returned simply.

A heavy rapping sounded at the door. Mrs Connolly's voice sounded her presence and she entered the room without further instruction. Her eyes took me in automatically and she did not conceal the look of disbelief and abhorrence upon her face as her eyes travelled from me to Maisy, via our covered hands.

"Good morning to you sir...Mrs Finnegan," she stammered, as Maisy withdrew her hand from mine curtly. "Shall I return then, to attend to you, Mrs Finnegan?"

"Yes, Mrs Connolly, thank you. Walter – Mr Finnegan – and I were just discussing business," Maisy replied, unable to meet my gaze or that of the older woman.

"I shall finish up shortly, Mrs Connolly. You can wait outside," I said. The matron scowled at me before taking her leave. I smiled humorously at Maisy, whose mouth tilted up in a grin. "She doesn't like me much, does she? She thinks she's your mother."

"Actually, Mr Finnegan...Walter...Mrs Connolly is my aunt," Maisy offered, to my surprise. "It is never spoken of...you see. There is one thing I have not told you yet about these rings. It is not only in death that the bond can be broken." She stared solemnly into my face, just inches from hers. "My grandmother had an...indiscretion...while she was married to my grandfather. He was gone for many months at a time across the seas. The rings were broken immediately, and sealed back together just as quickly, but never to be worn again by my grandparents...they simply would not fit. You can imagine how distraught he was when the ring broke off, miles away from his wife, fearing her dead. Only to return home and find her pregnant with another man's child...

Nine months after her imprudence, my grandmother gave birth to a son. The boy survived, but she did not. My father was ten at the time, and was the only person who ever loved that baby. He pleaded for his father to keep the boy, and rear him as his own. My grandfather kept the boy, and reared him as a stable hand, written out of any inheritance. His birth father never knew; and my grandfather gave him the name Connolly. Jared Connolly."

I looked at her in astonishment. "You mean to tell me, Maisy, that had Mr...Shillingworth...had his way last evening...we would no longer be bound to one another?"

"Yes, Mr Finnegan."

"Good Lord!"

And I found I had yet another thing to be grateful for with my increasing regard for Maisy.

"Thank the Good Lord, indeed, that he did not," she whispered.

30. Exile

April Falls

Oh, I marked the first for another day! Yet knowing how way leads on to way…

M left before breakfast, and before I could say my goodbye. A gloomy blanket covered the household. The rain paltered down beyond the paned glass, bringing with it a heavy coverlet of mist.

I refused to say the words of farewell to Lucas out loud, fearing that they too would haunt me during our separation, or finalise our parting forever. I clung to him in the foyer as though he were the bread to my butter, without a care who shared in our embrace, knowing that it would be the last chance I had to saturate my senses with his being. I touched every surface on his face; breathed in his hypnotic scent until it replaced the very air in my lungs; and listened with meditative ears until I had memorised the sound of his alluring voice deep within my mind. I would not forget an ounce of him to take with me for the potentially long separation ahead.

"I love you, April Falls," he whispered at an audible level for only me to hear, his mouth lingering at the base of my jaw-line. "I'll think of you every second."

He held me to his chest, and I was afraid to say a single word. I did love Lucas; I had announced it for all to hear in the Cathedral. But admitting to such a commitment of my soul tore me to pieces whenever I thought about it. I could not say it again without thinking of the anguish I had caused since arriving at Erravilla, adding myself to the ghosts that already haunted her hosts.

"I'm going to buy every one of your films and watch them over and over again," I said sadly.

"Sounds a bit obsessive," Lucas mused, a grim humour in his reply.

"Yeah, well, I think I joined the fan club a while ago. Maybe I'll make president one day," I returned, chewing on my tongue in disdain. "Email me when you get to L.A.?"

"I'll email you *before* I get to L.A.! I think it's going to be a gruelling three months," Lucas uttered.

Our parting was interrupted by Urland Chisholm, who entered hastily, handing me an envelope with an outstretched arm. "Begging your pardon, Miss Falls, but this just arrived for you by overnight express. Would you like me to inform the officers outside?"

"I suppose we should wait for them," I sighed, remembering that we had been instructed to notify the police of any correspondence.

"I'm Sergeant Whyte, and this is Special Operations Director Booth, who I believe you've already met," one of the officers announced, motioning first to herself and then to her colleague. "Would you like me to open it, Miss Falls?"

"No, thank you. I can open it myself," I replied, noting the postmark from the coastal county of Cleveland in northern England.

The hit must have left a good mark on you.
Consider us even.
Make sure you catch that plane as soon as the good Dr gives you clearance. I'll be watching.

"Consider us *even!*?" I cried in outrage. "I'd like to see what happens to her pretty head when she says that to my face! Or your face, Lucas. Or your brother's! Maybe then we'll be even!"

"Well, don't hold your breath for that," Alex retorted. "She's a coward."

"And we'd rather you didn't approach her, even if she *did* say that to your face," Booth warned. "We understand that you're trained in martial arts, Miss Falls. But you really should leave this to the police. You don't want to wind up on assault charges."

"Yes, leave this one alone, Apes, sweetheart," Dad coaxed, with an anxious gleam in his eyes.

"All right. But I'm going to be spending a lot of time in the Do Jo when I get home," I hissed. "With her face on the punching bag!"

"That'a girl," Dad encouraged, extending an arm to my shoulder but replacing it awkwardly by his side when he noticed that Lucas' arm still rested there. "Now, we really ought to get going, before this Farthing woman changes her mind."

"Penny, Dad," Alex winced. "And not helpful….What's a Farthing?"

I returned Lucas' final squeeze and brief kiss before heading out into the steady rain and the awaiting police escort with Alex and Dad, our luggage already loaded into the cars. I stared after Lucas for as long as my eyes could strain into the distance, channelling all of my remaining energy into savouring his face, locked on his final grief-filled expression.

Audenlea Mance, Blue Mountains, Sydney, Australia

I found the engagement ring that had disturbed me for three years now, sliding it along my finger to rest beside the cool, smooth band that now occupied its place. I felt like a prisoner, ensnared by the two pieces of gold and their worlds. By letting go of one, I had ambushed myself into another, preventing myself from being with the one I really wanted…Lucas. And yet, as Justice had suggested, being with Lucas also held the key to my freedom, and his, if I followed through with it.

I spent three months maintaining a quiet existence. I resumed writing on a regular basis for _The Sydney Herald_ in July, reporting on local entertainment gigs. The reappearance of regular articles in the paper caused a commotion, my name now all too familiar with the regular entertainment readers, bringing with it a spectrum of reactionary letters to the editor, Maggie Wilson.

"It seems we have a problem, Miss Falls…now that your reputation precedes you," she said poker-faced, closing the door to her office once I was inside.

Great. Now I was going to lose my job as well.

"I don't think it would be appropriate for you to take any kind of permanent role in a department here at *The Herald*," Maggie issued. "I don't think that would go down too well with the other staff."

"I really didn't think my being here would cause such a disturbance. Are people worried about their safety with me being here?" I inquired, maintaining a level approach.

"No. It's more to do with the fact that you might seem a little…high-and-mighty now."

"*High and mighty?* I'm not—"

"Actually, I'm quite receptive to the new attention you've brought back with you," Maggie said wistfully, holding up one arm to silence me. "I'd like to give you your own column."

"My own *column?*" I cried, sounding rather mouse like in pitch. "On what?"

"Whatever you choose. But I want it to be controversial. Feed that buzz that seems to be out there after you."

She's feeding me to the wasp's nest?

"Human rights; legal issues; relationships; gossip. Current affairs. You're going to feed our readers a topic; and they're going to respond. Be prepared. And be careful how you respond. G-e-n-e-r-a-t-e readership. Don't lose any!"

And that was it. I was being given my life-vest; then ordered to swim through shark-infested waters. *Should I laugh or cry?*

The only line I refused to cross was my own; Lucas' privacy, and therefore my personal life, was not for public examination or scrutiny.

I spent my free hours researching and developing the form my passion would take as I approached the manuscript that would formally introduce Lucas Ricardo Forrester to the world. Even though my contact with him was non-existent, I was able to build a replica of his life and persona through communication with his business associates, his friends, family, and my own memories.

Communication lay dormant between Penny McClellan and the Forresters, presumably satisfied with the oceans that now lay between Lucas and me. Her location remained a mystery to the authorities, with the occasional lead turning cold quickly. She appeared invisible; indeed, as though she had never even begun her forage on the Forresters.

The greatest pain was M. I knew that at some stage, I would need to contact him for the book. Even four months later, I could not bring myself to phone him, terrified to hear his voice because of the guilt I clung to. I could not remove the image from my mind or his voice – strung like a thousand quivering bows – as he had said his final farewell at Erravilla. I wouldn't cause him that pain again.

I read about the successful entrepreneur online, able to keep up with his latest client list, or which continent he was frequenting the most, or the latest language he had mastered. I grinned fondly to myself as I read articles that placed him on Britain's most eligible bachelor list yet again, knowing that M would find the attention terribly fickle, and suffocatingly annoying.

Occasionally I would brace myself as I felt the heat begin to penetrate through the permanent fixture on my left hand, perplexed that the frequency had become less and less; yet surprised that the intensity had magnified, scorching my flesh until the heat was unbearable.

I stared at the unopened leather binding beside my bed, desperate to understand more about the peculiar ring that I wore, but apprehensive at what I might unearth in its pages: the more I knew about the ring, the more I would be bound to the ring; and I wanted to forget what it symbolised. The choice had not been mine.

As the Australian winter bloomed into spring, *Shirtless* reached cult status as they had in Britain – their music inspiring a large-=scale following and financial support in the Capital cities.

At the risk of being identified, I had decided to greet Darius and the gang at the arrivals terminal of Sydney International; my stomach swam with anxiety as I paced off the customs ramp like a restless panther.

Alex didn't understand my brooding, and I couldn't explain the turbulence I felt at the prospect of live contact with Darius, the safest physical connection to Lucas I could hope for besides the man himself…

"Stop pacing, you remind me of Dad," Alex scolded, seated comfortably, though I noticed her cursory frequent glances towards the deserted ramp. "And stop biting your nails!"

"Look! People!" I cried, grabbing hold of Alex's shoulder and pointing towards the one lone man walking the gangway.

"How profound! *People*. Take your hands off me, they're hurting my shoulders!" Alex demanded, wincing at the pressure of my hands.

"First class should be cleared first, right?" I asked, skimming the individual faces as they began strolling through the automatic doors, wheeling cabin luggage and an array of hand-held artefacts from their travels.

"Yes. Now, don't go hysterical, and I've only seen Darius in print…but, I think that's him," Alex announced, standing to her feet and thrusting herself to the front of the gathering onslaught, who erupted like a cage of chimps at the sight of the band members.

"April, baby! Is that really you?" a voice thundered above the noise from nearby. I had missed his approach entirely looking at the guy Alex had *thought* was Darius and before I knew it I was swept from my feet and sailed through the air in a circular motion.

"Put me down, you git!" I laughed as my head began to swim, and tried not to blink like an epileptic as bright colour flashes erupted from everywhere like strobe lighting.

Darius granted my wish, momentarily, but then drew me to his bear-size chest and crushed me to him for an excessively lengthy embrace. "Oh, I've missed you!"

"I've missed you too," I replied, though terribly conscious of our audience. "But I'm about to lose oxygen."

"Oh, right!" he said releasing me instantly, but placing an affectionate arm about my shoulders, a colossal grin spreading across his olive-toned face. "This is a great surprise, April. I wasn't expecting you here."

"I thought I'd surprise you," I said, following airport security and trying to lead him away from the hasty throng.

"Are you being followed, or is this fine looking woman with you as well?" Darius asked, raising an eyebrow as he examined Alex, who flushed an unbecoming shade of scarlet.

"Darius, this is my sister, Alex," I said, stifling my amusement. "Alex, this is the one, the only…Darius Forrester."

"I'm so happy to meet you, at last," Alex said warmly, taking a hint of a step closer to Darius, though looking surprisingly overwhelmed by his presence.

"Do you think she'd mind if I gave her the same welcome I gave you?" Darius asked with a mischievous grin.

"I think she'd love it," I replied simply, eyeing Alex with amusement, as her deep blue eyes were swallowed up by Darius' form.

Darius eyed her with enthusiasm before closing the ground between them, lifting her with far more delicacy than I had ever seen him display. He held her gently with his arms before setting her on her feet and placing a deliberate kiss upon her crimson cheeks, sending the crowd of onlooking fans into a feral frenzy.

"Alex, the pleasure is all mine," Darius said simply, releasing his overly gentle hold on her.

"Well, I'll be," I mused quietly when he returned to my side, winding his free arm through mine as we walked, following his crew and manager. "Darius the gentleman."

He chuckled good-naturedly. "You didn't tell me she was as gorgeous as you."

I elbowed him in the ribs with force. "Don't think I won't be watching you. There are already enough Forrester men involved with the Falls family for my liking."

"Aw, don't be like that, April. We mean no harm," Darius whined in amusement. "I didn't say I was going to marry her."

"Not even funny, Darius," I replied, raising an eyebrow in mock reproach.

"Sorry, I keep forgetting about you and…M. I still think of you as Lucas' girl."

"I don't think I'm anyone's girl at the moment!" I sighed. "How's he doing? I haven't spoken to Lucas in forever."

Darius shrugged with a hint of heaviness about his shoulders and I knew he missed his big brother. "I haven't seen him in about as long. He went from one film to the next. No one's seen him…except in the papers and magazines."

"And M?" I asked hesitantly.

Darius grinned with satisfaction at the mention of M. "M's doing so well. He's busy as hell; but that's what keeps him happy, you know. I see him every now and then when he shows up to a gig…always the supportive big brother."

"I'm glad he's okay," I replied, unable to meet Darius' eye. My chest tightened as he spoke of M, whom I had missed more than I had dared to admit. I had worried about him for months and now felt a sense of peace about him. Part of me longed to see him almost as much as I longed to see Lucas again, just to assure myself that M was really fine. "I've been keeping up to date with his business adventures. He's a sought after man."

"Yep. You're married to one of England's most eligible bachelors. Which is strange really, because he's not technically a bachelor anymore," Darius mused, oblivious to my earlier sentiments.

"But she's not truly married to him anyway," Alex muttered beside me. "Only legally…which *is* quite significant; come to think of it…"

"I think M kind of likes wearing that ring around," Darius reflected.

"Oh?" I stammered, torn between curiosity and unbearable discomfort.

"It keeps the random women away when he's travelling," Darius laughed. "They don't pester him as much if they think he's hitched."

I grinned at Darius' humour, agreeing every inch with Darius as I imagined M being swarmed by a flock of unrequited women. "Whatever works, I guess."

"She tells everybody that it's a family keepsake, stuck on her finger," Alex offered humorously, jabbing me in the ribs with her elbow.

"The three of you disappeared so quickly out of London, that the papers are still speculating which one of them you eloped with," Darius chuckled.

"People are so pathetic," I sighed. "Why don't they get lives of their own?"

"Because then you'd be out of a job," Alex retorted. "You're one of the mob who writes this stuff, remember? You just don't like it when you become the focus of it."

31. Ghosts of the Recent Past

I felt almost at home with Darius around. Strange that I no longer felt complete without the Forresters. I was confused about where home was exactly. *If home is where the heart is, then where was mine?* Even at Audenlea, the house I had basically been given when Hugh's parents signed over his inheritance to me, felt out of place now somehow.

Darius and the insanely lively gang spent just one week in Sydney before continuing on with the tour in Melbourne, Adelaide and then Brisbane. *Shirtless* performed at one of Sydney's most prominent entertainment venues for three nights only; which Alex and I attended, of course, hanging back stage between segments with the irrepressible and sweaty band members. Darius insisted that we attend all three evenings, spending only one of them in the crowd, and the other between the stage wings for a more personal perspective.

Alex begged Darius if she could unofficially film the backstage action and photograph the gang from the wings. *Shirtless'* manager gave in to the relentless pleadings of Alex, but warned that they were not to be sold as official merchandise.

I was given unrestrained access and licence to write and further promote the band at my discretion: creating an energetic and approachable profile of the young band members, which fuelled their support across Australia.

"How come you're the Pet Poodle?" Alex winged sourly.

"Because, its common knowledge that I only *positively* promote the Foresters. You have to earn your keep, little sister," I replied.

Alex and I socialised with the band after each concert until the early hours of the following morning, crashing either at Alex's rented city apartment, or at Darius' hotel suite. With the energy and vibrancy that had returned, I felt as youthful as I had at sixteen, without a care in the world. I had forgotten during the long months what it was to truly feel alive again, and Darius always seemed to know how to remind me. I laughed until I cried, feeling like one of them, unable to bear the thought of having to let go again.

I didn't even care that Alex and I were labelled *"groupie sisters"* by one of the rival big Sydney papers, after we emerged from the *Radisson* late into the day after *Shirtless'* final performance.

Darius spent his final two nights in Sydney at Audenlea without the gang, insisting on needing some quiet time without the wild band members. I doubted very much that Darius was ever in need of *quiet* time. From my observations, the term "quiet" did not even enter his vocabulary.

I spent more time near Darius than actually with him at Audenlea, listening to the familiar banter of his voice as it carried through the old house as I worked on my laptop, resurrecting memories of Erravilla and soothing my soul, or taking in the sight of him outdoors, laughing and chatting away with Alex, while I worked away in the gardens. He was as close to me then as I could have gotten to Erravilla, or to Lucas.

When the time came to say goodbye I stood on the sandstone steps of Audenlea, holding Darius with a ferocious intensity that rivalled his own. We stood there for minutes, my head resting against his broad chest, listening to the soothing rhythm of his heart: the same blood that pumped through his brothers' veins.

"Okay, we have to go now," Alex announced awkwardly, picking her luggage up from the front stoop after having placed it down while she waited for me to say goodbye to Darius.

I breathed in heavily as I released him at arms' length. "Look after her…she's a wild one," I said indicating to Alex.

"I'm only going for a couple of weeks. Stop being so over protective…you're worse than Mum," Alex replied in exasperation.

"Just stay close to Darius, then I'll know you'll be safe," I retorted. "Call me when you reach Melbourne."

"Yes, Mum," Alex chimed sarcastically, gripping me firmly before taking her belongings to the awaiting taxi.

"Hey, I know you've got talent, Alex. Click away!" I called. "You never know who'll see your work on tour."

Darius climbed in the back seat after Alex, waving fondly out the window as they drove off down the dusty road. I wiped the tears from my eyes with the back of my hand, watching until the dust settled on the rocky driveway, knowing that my tears were the over-kept longing for what lay across the seas and out of my reach.

Mum phoned that evening, rabbiting on about the unavoidable chaos in her life that I had caused, and demanding to know whether or not I would be attending the wedding of "that sweet friend of yours from school? You know, I saw her parents just the other day, and they said…"

She suggested that I take an old flame as my date, for old times' sakes, since the bride was from school. My fingers clenched around the receiver as she suggested Andy Roberts.

"He was around here the other day, asking about you, April. He's such a sweet boy, Andy."

There was that foul metallic taste again. I leant up against the dining room wall feeling light headed.

For someone who was so panic-stricken over small things, my mother surely was a terrible judge of character when it came to people.

"What did you tell him?" I breathed.

"Oh, nothing much; just this and that. He knew more about you than I did anyway, thanks to the internet," she huffed.

"Okay, just don't encourage him. I have my own life now. I barely know him anymore, Mum."

"I just thought it would be nice for you to date a nice boy again, is all," she replied.

"He isn't nice!" I spat. "And don't ever mention his name to me again!"

"Oh, April, honestly…"

The festive or silly season, as Dad liked to call it, approached rapidly. Alex returned from her tour in true groupie fashion, carrying on at a rapid pace for days after returning home, leaving no stone unturned in her flamboyant recounts of the gang and their escapades, speaking Darius' name with a familiarity and fondness that I had both expected and feared.

An uncontrollable agony gripped me when she spoke of flying over to London for New Year. I tried to reason and fight with the notion that I was jealous of Alex, that she was free to fly, while I remained grounded and locked in a cage, held to ransom by an elusive nightmare from the past. I couldn't bear the image of Alex supping with Lucas, M and Darius over Christmas, while I remained alone.

I went to fetch the leather cased journal for the first time, finally feeling that it was time to digest the missing pieces of the phenomenal ring that bound and defined my very future and freedom. But the journal was nowhere to be found. What had Alex done with it?

Somewhere over the Indian Ocean

_M_

The Indian Ocean was more vast and unending than I had imagined. I silently chastised myself for having booked a day flight from Heathrow, flying into the sun, enduring an everlasting daylight. _I should have brought some Valium._ I wouldn't get any sleep while the cabin was so bright. Even First class couldn't turn the sun.

I knew the program for the in-flight entertainment guide, and had either already seen the films several times on other flights, or could be guaranteed to be greeted with my brother's face again. Since the ordeal at St Paul's I had forgiven my brother for much, including his indiscretion with Penny, although I was not entirely convinced now that Lucas and Penny had actually gotten together that night; at the very least, I was convinced that Lucas had been too intoxicated to know what he was doing.

Thus, I didn't mind watching my brother's admittedly handsome mug flash across the small cabin screen several dozen times in a few short hours; I knew Lucas was talented, and I admired his well-deserved success.

However, there was something very uncomfortable watching your own flesh and blood on the screen, thrash around between the sheets with a woman, even if she was an attractive one. Lucas in bed with another woman – even a stranger – forced images of him and April to my mind that I had been trying to banish for months.

It didn't help either that I was on my way to Australia, for the first time in my life. I was flying to Sydney for a few days to meet with a prospective client but couldn't shake the knowledge that somewhere nearby, within my reach, April existed: alive and in the flesh.

One of the waitresses paused to watch a close-up of Lucas' face, her eyes held the yearning of every other woman I had observed over the years when they did the same. Even Penny, when I thought about it honestly.

"I'll never get tired of that face," the hostess giggled, before glancing at me. "Oh! Mr Forrester! I beg your pardon. I didn't realise it was you, sir. Would you like some Tawny Port?"

"I would, thank you…no offence taken."

I smiled at her to let her know she wasn't going to be reported for her comment, saluting her with the shot glass before drinking it swiftly.

I chastised myself again for allowing April's image to possess my mind so often, knowing that a sensation with that kind of force would be causing her corresponding undue pain. I clenched my fists to stop my fingers lingering upon the ring, and placed an uncomfortable pair of headphones over my ears and turned up the volume of the first station that played, desperate in my attempt to rid her essence from my mind.

I spent two demanding days and evenings with my potential high profile clients; visiting, assessing and scaling by day, wining, dining and designing by night. I was under greater pressure than usual, having only a few days to leave a prevalent impression of my work upon them, since the distance was far greater than I usually travelled when liaising with clients. I met the hotel pillow in the early hours of the morning each day, working as thoroughly and as swiftly as possible, refusing to present them with less than my customary professional best.

On the morning of the third day in humid Sydney town, while I was taking my usual pre-breakfast run, along an unfamiliar route, I was interrupted by a series of people carrying the morning paper from a nearby news cart.

"Hey, you're Emerus Forrester," a man in a suit declared, motioning to me with his Styrofoam coffee cup. "I'm just reading about you."

"Hey, nice work with the Sheehans. I'm a big fan of your family," a second suited gentleman voiced.

"Thanks," I said awkwardly, wondering how I could have made the papers; the Sheehan case wasn't supposed to be public knowledge. This could ruin the liaison before it had officially begun. I jogged over to the stand and paid for the paper, reading the caption on the cover, which referred to the main story in the business section.

I supported the paper beneath my arm as I paced back to the hotel. My routine dictated that I always read the paper over breakfast, when I was the most focussed. According to the paper I had been identified with the controversial and prominent Member of Parliament, Clive Sheehan and his wife, while dining at one of Sydney's finest brasseries. One of the waiters had taken a photograph on her phone and sent it to the paper, assuming that the Sheehans were the reason for my surreptitious visit to Australia.

I cursed the media for their frequent and meddlesome interferences in private affairs of the business world. My line of work did not warrant trespassing, despite who I may engage in business with.

This automatically triggered an image of another journalist in my mind, who was not so bothersome in her work…so much as with the frequency that she occupied my mind…

"Bollocks!" I cursed out loud, holding a shaking hand up to my head. April's attention would no doubt be alerted to my business in Sydney, and I wasn't entirely sure how I felt about that idea. Would the news frustrate her and cause her angst? Or would she welcome my presence as an old friend would?

As though to answer my question, the golden ring burned with a sudden intensity, deepening to a becoming shade of fuchsia. I stared at the ring with incredulity: the ring had turned this colour only on a handful of occasions, the last time had been a month ago, when *Shirtless* had toured Australia; and I had later discovered that Darius had met with April.

My pulse raced at the notion that April could possibly hold me as dearly as she held Darius; more than brotherly, perhaps even with great affection…If the journal was correct, then she was apprehensive about my visit, but eager all the same.

I was still lost in my thoughts when a knock on the door sounded. I had forgotten to turn the door sign onto *Please do not disturb* on my hasty entrance with the paper. "Coming!" I called, making my way to unlatch the door for housekeeping.

"Oh!" she gasped. "It's really you!"

Before I had time to steady my skittish heart, she was in my arms, holding me with a desperation that I couldn't hold back in returning. I closed the door behind her and returned the embrace with a ferocity of my own, stroking her silky brown hair and planting a kiss upon her forehead.

And then her tears began, followed by wrenching sobs into my chest. Once more I convinced myself that I didn't deliberately have this effect upon her; that I was not the force behind unleashing the water valve that seemed to explode in my presence. I led her to the comfortable hotel lounge, holding her gently until the tears subsided.

"Oh, M! I'm so sorry! I'm always such a mess whenever you see me," she fussed, reprimanding herself.

"April, you don't need to apologise," I soothed. "I'm glad you decided to visit."

"Why didn't you tell me you were coming, you great oaf!" she retorted, nudging me with her elbow in mock chastisement.

"I'm here purely on business," I replied lamely, too fearful to tell her the entire reason. "I thought it would be too…difficult…for you."

"Too difficult? I'm dying to see you!" she cried. "I've missed you all so much! And then Darius came…and went so quickly. Of course I want to see you too! I just want to go back."

I tried to harden myself to her implication, that we were all equally as important to her as Lucas; but I had accepted the truth months ago, and couldn't let myself hope otherwise. It was enough that she was here now, with me.

"Can you hang out with me today?" she pleaded, an irresistible light of hope illuminating from her opal coloured eyes.

I examined her dress, noting that she was suited up for work, and probably on her way when she had read the paper. "Don't you have somewhere to be?"

"Yes, but I can feign…other business," she replied, searching for an excuse. "Maybe you'll let me set the story straight…? Write about your surprise trip to Oz when you tell me all about it?"

I hid a grin behind the deep breath I took as I glanced away.

"Ha! The ring is red! That means you're pleased," she teased proudly.

"So, you've read the journal?" I mused.

"No. The journal seems to be M.I.A. at the moment. I just remember the few things *Penny* said," I fumed. "Sorry…I know she was your girlfriend and all."

I winced at the mention of Penny's name. "Don't be. I'm not."

"So, can we hang out today?"

"Honestly, it depends on the Sheehans."

"Yes…that was unfortunate. Glad it wasn't my paper that ran the leak. Although I bet our readers will have a field-day with it anyway. I don't think Sheehan will mind though. He likes those sorts of stunts. Your liaison with him will boost his profile."

Her optimism gave me hope.

"How did you know where to find me?" I asked.

"That was easy; you boys all stay at the same hotel chain," she replied confidently.

"We do?" I asked amused, raising an eyebrow.

"You mean, it's not a Forrester signature to stay at the *Radisson*?" she teased.

"Not that I'm aware of. One of those strange genetic phenomena," I mused, alleviating myself from the lounge now that April had gathered herself together. "Anyway, I'm going to keep going with this proposal. You're welcome to stay for as long as you like."

"I've never seen you work," she said curiously, following me over to the table where my laptop lay in temporary hibernation.

"It's riveting stuff," I laughed, sure that she would be deathly bored.

"No really, I considered studying architecture at one point," she revealed, to my amazement.

"It's a pretty big leap to journalism," I pondered aloud.

"Yes, and definitely where my true talents lie. You'd laugh if you actually saw my drawings," she mused, leaning over my arm to view the outlines on the desktop from the chair beside mine. "Sorry, I won't breathe down your neck for long…these are great."

I eyed her from my peripheral vision, trying to gauge the level of her curiosity. Her eyes intensified as she examined the details of the drafts, commenting at will, and asking questions for the larger scale designs. I was pleased that she seemed to appreciate my work.

"Emerus Forrester, you are a creative genius," she breathed, a pleasant smile lighting her countenance as she glanced from the screen to me, placing an encouraging hand upon my arm.

"I don't know about that," I laughed quietly, far too aware of the warmth of her hand. "But I do love my work. It doesn't really feel like work; so much as a hobby that I get paid to play with."

She nodded in agreement. "I think I'm okay to go now. I'll leave you in peace."

"What time do you have lunch?"

"Really? You'll have time?" she asked, piquing my hope.

"April, you're a strange girl sometimes. Of course I'll make time for you. Where do you want to meet?"

"Pick me up from work," she replied matter-of-factly.

"From work? Won't that implicate you in tomorrow's gossip column or something?" I joked, stunned that she was even considering a public liaison.

"I am the gossip column! Besides, I don't care, if you don't," she replied.

"I'm used to the scandals now," I laughed, knowing that the only scandal I would stand for involved the woman standing before me.

"I'll be the envy of the office; the girls will be chomping at the bit when they see you!" she laughed softly.

"Well, I doubt that. But if it humours you, I'll pick you up from the office," I replied simply, desiring only that *she* would find me as appealing.

"M, did I offend you?" she asked quietly, slipping an arm through mine.

"Not at all. I'm glad to see you smile."

"You know I'm proud as punch to have you as my dear friend, right? Even my phantom husband?" she mused, raising an eyebrow in earnest.

"Now *that* would make their chins wag," I laughed in amusement. "You know, I missed our six month anniversary a few weeks ago."

April groaned and placed her arms around my waist, her lower lip pouting as her brows came together. "I don't want to get a divorce."

"I wish it didn't have to be this way," I replied, brushing a soft strand of hair from her eyes. *More than you will ever know.*

"I wish this whole silly thing didn't happen at all," she sighed, resting her head against my shirt. "How am I ever going to explain it? And then every time I look at you, I'll think about us as legally *divorced*. Friends shouldn't have to go through this."

"You know, I never apologised to you for that day at Erravilla," I began.

"M, please don't. I don't want to talk about it."

"Can't I at least say sorry for the way I treated you?"

"I think we were all at fault that day," she replied, turning her face away. "I wish that had never happened either."

"I was at fault, April. I had no right."

"I understand why you did it…why you came in. It's inbuilt in you to protect those who need help. It was a misunderstanding."

"Does that mean you forgive me?" I hedged, giving in to the yearning I had held onto for so long.

"Of course," she replied, turning to meet my gaze, her brilliant eyes revealing a pool of regret. "Let's forget it ever happened."

"Deal," I uttered, unable to control the impulse to bend my head and place a gentle kiss upon her upturned forehead. "Sorry."

She smiled ruefully, colour tainting her round cheeks as she slipped from my embrace. "I'll see you soon."

I watched her go until the door had sealed back into its resting place, taking several deep lung-fulls of breath before resuming my work. *Focus. This is important too.*

Oh, the pleasure and the pain...

32. Ghoul of the Heart

April Falls

I doubted if I should ever come back…

M had done a little homework before taking me to lunch, escorting me in to a small, inconspicuous, but delectable café in the historic and enchanting *Rocks* district, beside Sydney Harbour. We mostly discussed work related topics, talking casually as good friends do. I enjoyed his presence so immensely that I couldn't bear to leave when he insisted I must.

"But you're leaving tomorrow," I protested, unable to meet his gaze for fear he would see the desperation in mine.

"I don't have to," he replied slowly.

"Really? You can stay for an extra day?" I asked, snapping my head up in anticipation.

"I don't have to get home to anything in particular. I'm going to take a couple of weeks off over Christmas and New Year. Lucas wants us all to celebrate Christmas in France this year. He just bought a chalet in the foothills of the Alps and the forecast predicts a nice snowfall."

My resolve threatened to crumble at the mention of Christmas. I swallowed hard. "You mean that Alex…will be staying with you guys…in France?"

"I think so."

I winced as though he'd stabbed me and he automatically reached across the table to cover my hand with his. "We'll figure something out. I promise."

"Come for dinner tomorrow," I said. "At my place, in the mountains."

"Okay," he replied nodding slowly. "I'll be finishing up with the Sheehans tomorrow, if all goes according to plan. I'll come over after that. I'd like to see your place, "in the mountains", as you say."

I was almost nervous as I shook out the tablecloth onto the outdoor dining suite on the patio, laying cutlery, condiments and lanterns across the covering. The sultry summer air lay still, as though it too were holding its breath while the evening was blessed with the soft murmuring of crickets as the sun lingered upon the horizon. I had chastised for an hour over what to wear, before finally settling on a casual white and red summer dress, which I hoped drew out the natural olive hues in my skin.

I then chastised myself for worrying over what I was to wear to dinner with the brother of my practically estranged boyfriend! *It's not a date*, I kept reminding myself, despite the constant fluttering inside my abdominal area. A pleasant aroma filled the still evening air, and I was glad that I had taken some effort with the meal for the first guest, apart from Darius, that I had prepared in three years.

It was still too early to be expecting M, and the three courses of prepared food were perfectly in line with the expected time of his arrival. A knock resounded at the front door, startling me from the kitchen. He was early. *Never mind; we could start with the wine and entrée*. I clicked on a soft record before striding delicately to the door, flattening the non-existent creases out of my skirt along the way.

My heart leapt into my throat at the form awaiting me on the front stoop, and I instinctively made to close the door. A large foot wedged itself between the door and the wooden frame before I had the chance.

"Aren't you going to invite me in, April?" he drawled.

"What are you doing here, Andy?" I demanded, hiding my trembling fingers in the folds of my skirt.

"Why, I'm guessing you forgot to tell your mum about our little visit last time? She was all too pleased that we were catching up again," he said casually.

"What do you want?" I demanded.

"Just a chat," he smirked, pushing the door aside and striding into the house. "Seems to me like you've gone to a lot of effort for me."

"I'd like you to leave," I said, still holding my post beside the open door as the nausea swept over me at will.

"Now why would that be?" he pondered, his eyes seeping with venom.

"Because I have nothing to say to you," I replied, my breathing shallow and light in my chest.

"Well, I figured it was time for a catch up, since your fiancée died and all. Sorry about that."

"I don't think you're sorry, Andy," I said between gritted teeth.

"And then that big shot movie star boyfriend dumped you. Seems like all the men in your life just end up leaving you," he said. "That's why I've come back."

"That's very thoughtful," I remarked, not hiding the sarcasm. "But I don't need your help."

"Close the door and come and sit for a while," he said motioning for me to join him on the patio. "Like old times."

I glanced at the mantle clock. M would be here in about half an hour. I had to get rid of Andy before M arrived; I still remembered the threats Andy had made towards Hugh years ago.

"So, Andy, what brings you all this way?" I said, feigning pleasantries, feeling the veins in my neck tense and patting my stomach as though to self-settle.

"I've been monitoring you, which isn't hard, considering how public your life seems to be these days," Andy said thoughtfully. "And everything seemed back to normal. Until a few days ago when that jack-arse Forrester showed up in town."

"You mean Emerus?" I corrected, wondering what interest it was of Andy's.

"I knew he'd find a way to you," Andy said, shaking his head vehemently.

"He's not the Forrester I was with before," I said, in an attempt to diffuse the conversation away from M. "That was Lucas."

"Yes, but you had lunch with this one quite publicly yesterday, his hands all over yours," Andy recounted. "I saw *that* online this morning and knew it was time to step in."

"Andy, what has this got to do with anything? I thought you had a great new life up the coast somewhere," I deflected, sensing his irritation rise.

"I moved back recently and thought that maybe we could…see each other again." I cringed at the way he inferred that we *see* each other again. "You know I've missed you. You were the only woman for me."

I inhaled slowly, frantically thinking of a way to lure him back to his car. "Do you want to take a walk?"

"Here's fine…what's that sound?"

His ears had been alerted to the same sound as mine: the distinct motion of wheels along gravel, and then a hasty halt, followed by a car door.

M.

"Andy, didn't my mother tell you that I'm married?"

I watched his face twitch at the edges of his jaw line.

"We did talk about it, yes. She didn't seem to know much about the sham."

"Look at my hand if you don't believe me," I said, trying to maintain an even breath, despite the current of anxiety that welled within me as I held out my left hand to display the fiery blue ring.

Andy grabbed my hand and tried to reef the ring from my finger, to no avail. I screamed as I forced my hand away from his. "It doesn't come off!"

M

I had sealed the contract with the Sheehans, who had been, as April had predicted, delighted by their liaison with my work and were more than pleased with the draft prints that I had produced in three short days.

I drove with deliberation, fleeing the city in anticipation of seeing her again. I had felt as though I were soaring as I rode the wind all the way towards the mountains, defying speed limits in a frenzied desire to reach her; and with the knowledge that I had secured my first Australian clients; where there was one, others would follow.

I was more than pleased to create an Australian nexus for my business, providing a healthy basis for my frequent future travels to the southern continent. I was an estimated twenty minutes from her home, when I was gripped by a sudden scorching on my left hand. The ring glowed an iridescent bright blue, sending my feet into a frenzy on the accelerator, with the knowledge that she may be in danger, or at the very least, distressed or fearful. Blue was not a colour I appreciated in relation to April's emotions.

I approached the unfamiliar house with caution, though there was no definite sign of disturbance. I noticed a dark blue skyline parked to the side of the house; its dark windows and menacing body alterations did not fit the description of a vehicle that April would drive. Her car, a modest looking small black SUV, was stationed appropriately beneath a carport attached to the far side of the home with her personalised plates attached.

The ring still blazed against my skin, and I was sure it was due to her unknown visitor. I crept through the front door, pausing behind the lounge room wall and strained to hear the conversation. Experience with April had taught me to never rush in, even against my natural instincts.

April Falls

"So, it's true what that old diary says about the rings?" Andy sneered. "Oh yes, I borrowed your journal while you were at work. Very interesting."

"That's called stealing, Andy!"

"I know all about those rings," Andy said stepping to block my path with his arm, clawing his fingers into my bare flesh. "I'm not finished with you yet. Does Forrester know that you really belong to me?"

"Andy, take your hand off my arm; you're hurting me," I commanded, wondering if I had the strength of will to damage him as I would had he been a stranger in a dark alley. Could I hurt him when I still felt a guilty, age-old obligation to him?

"You better hope Forrester has the good sense to get back into his car and drive away."

I glanced around, panic seizing me as I wondered where M had gotten to.

"Andy, what do you want from me? I told you, I'm a…happily married woman now. What could you possibly want from me?" I said, wincing as I forced the pain aside.

"What you owe me," he ground out ferociously.

"I don't owe you anything," I hissed.

"You were willing once, and I'll take it when I please."

"Why are you really here, Andy?" I asked, sensing an overwhelming bitterness in his claim. "This isn't who you used to be. Don't you remember; we were friends once?"

"Until you left me," he returned bitterly.

"Only after you neglected me!" I cried hysterically.

"I tried! I tried to do it again and you refused!"

"What was wrong with it the first time?" I demanded, closing my eyes to the anguished images that flooded my mind.

"You didn't do it right," he replied, accusation lacing his tone. "I didn't feel anything."

"What do you mean?" I asked suddenly stunned by his revelation. "I felt everything."

"Nothing. I felt nothing. And I've never felt anything since!"

I stared at him dumbfounded. "What are you saying, Andy…?"

"No!" he bellowed so violently that I trembled, flinching away from him. "You did this to me!"

"No. Andy, I didn't do anything to you," I replied, feeling a sense of inexplicable closure for the first time in years. Andy had been what? Gay? Asexual?

"You did! You weren't good enough and now I can't…" he broke off, choking on his own words. "I just want a family of my own…"

I winced; holding back the flood of emotion attached to that little life he would never know and trying to concentrate on the rest of what he'd said…

I couldn't believe what I was hearing, though I felt a strange peace about Andy's initial revelation. I was not going to take the fall for his refusal to take responsibility for his own issues.

"Shut your mouth! Do you hear me?" I cried, suddenly finding my voice. I gulped to prevent the wall of tears that had built up as he'd spoken. He dug deeper into my arm, but I couldn't feel the pain through the rage and shock. "You want to try and prove yourself as a man, is that it?"

"No, I want you to take it back, whatever you did to me. I hate feeling this way: not being normal! I want to be normal!"

A familiar, authoritative voice broke through the turmoil. "April, is everything all right?"

Clearly it was not, and I wondered how M could stand motionless, hands in his pockets, wearing his best poker face.

Andy instantly drew me against his chest, my arm behind my back, and his elbow holding my neck in a tight hold as I faced M. M's face tightened ever so slightly, the veins in his temple rising from his forehead. I could see his eyes now, powerfully in control of the anger that simmered below the surface. A threatening brooding crept into his blue eyes as he watched and waited. His body was tense, apprehensive.

"So, this is the great Emerus Forrester…the great drunken alcoholic I've read so much about!" Andy all but slurred. "Your husband, you say?"

My line of sight travelled across the pavement, right up till I held M's with my own, feeling the question in my brow. I'd never heard M referred to as a drunk before…only Lucas having mentioned a possible drinking problem once…I searched his eyes but found nothing.

"Show him your ring, M," I said through the stranglehold grip of Andy's arm.

M held up the radiating blue metal ring, his eyes darting from Andy to me, searching no doubt for a gauge in Andy's hostile temperament. "How about we all sit down and talk."

It was a command, not a request.

"There's nothing to talk about. I'm not leaving without what I came for," Andy replied fiercely. "So you'd better step out of our way, *drunk*."

M's hands clenched until the veins stood out in 3D on his fists.

"And what exactly is it that you want from my *wife*?" M asked curiously, his eyes smouldering.

"The same thing she gave me years ago," Andy announced, wild defiance lacing his voice.

"Why now?" I asked through gritted teeth.

"Because I've read the book, and I know it's the only way to break that ring's curse," Andy answered, a fierce determination projecting through his voice. "Just to make you remember who you really belong to. You're going to be *my* wife. I cannot live with any other woman because they'll know about my...condition. I can't have anyone else knowing. It'll ruin me."

I felt my eyes grow wide in horror. "You can't just make me marry you, Andy. Believe me, I would die first. I don't love you anymore. Besides, I'm already happily married, as I've just told you."

A muscle jerked in M's jaw and he glanced at me momentarily, holding my gaze with an unreadable expression upon his face.

"I know the marriage was a sham. Otherwise it would have been in every magazine and newspaper from the North Pole to Tasmania. I know you haven't slept with anyone since that ring's been on your finger, or it wouldn't still be there. Think about it, April, we can set each other free."

I twisted to gauge how firmly Andy had a hold of me, and he tightened his grip around my throat. I chortled beneath his force. "It's okay, M. Just do what he wants. He won't hurt me."

The same thing I had said about Penny, just before she had me knocked unconscious...

"Just for you to know, the police are already on their way," M said stiffly, his face now a grim reflection of the horror I felt.

"Isn't this what you wanted? To be set free from the overbearing Forresters, once and for all?" Andy whispered. "I can do that for you."

"Not like this," I murmured, unable to meet the desperate inquiry in M's face.

It could be so easy, I thought. It could all be over in moments. Then I really would be free…but it was still my choice. And this was not how I wanted to break the curse.

I could hear the determination in Andy's voice and I could feel a hard metal object through Andy's vest: *the last I heard he was a Security Guard up the coast somewhere*…he was armed with something, but I couldn't tell what. I also knew that he would be capable of great harm if his anger was unleashed. I wanted Andy as far away from M as possible.

"Let's have some privacy," I whispered. "We'll go upstairs. Just you and me."

M's eyes grew wide with incredulity; the lines around his jaw strained. I decided that I would have to endure his wrath to protect him. He would just have to wait until I could explain. I prayed for the police to arrive, so that I wouldn't have to attempt what I felt resolved to do.

Forgive me…I wanted to say, but couldn't. *It's going to be okay*…

"Just wait here, M," I said, meeting his gaze and looking him fully in the eyes, a ghost of a smile upon my lips as I began to climb the stairs to the loft.

"So this is what you want, April?" M asked, his face crumbling like an avalanche as he watched me go willingly. "It doesn't have to be this way. I can file for a divorce as soon as the twelve months are up."

"No. This is better," I replied, trying desperately to reach him through my resolve while trying to make sure he wouldn't follow Andy and me. Whatever happened to me I wanted M to be no part of it. "You have to let me go."

I turned away as his very core shattered before my eyes. I pulled Andy by the arm, encouraging, afraid that he would provoke M if I gave him time.

"If you hurt her, I'll…!" M bellowed after us as I closed the door, turning the lock behind Andy.

<u>M</u>

She was gone.

Willingly.

A single sound echoed down the rafters after her, sealing her fate and mine: the lock. I combed my fingers through my hair so vigorously that I thought I had pulled chunks of the brown waves out. I paced rigidly. April's behaviour was incomprehensible and unbearable! I began to churn through the possible explanations for her choice: *Was she mad? Did she want me out of her life so desperately? Did she think she owed Andy something? Was she sentencing herself a penance for whatever had gone on between them years ago? Anything was forgivable…wasn't it?*

And then it struck me: it wasn't April who had wronged. It was I. She *knew.* Andy had just spelt it out for her: I was a drunkard. Somewhere floating around inside me was the drunkard…always there…always ready to pounce at every opportunity. Oh, and the things it could make you do… And she would have nothing to do with that blackness.

My mind toiled back over the last few minutes, desperately searching for the key to win her over, to talk her out of the fate she had given herself...all to free herself from the monster inside who stalked my very core.

But…

…Didn't she realise by now that I would never be free of her? Ring or nought, she could not free my mind of her, my heart or my very soul of her. There had to be a way to reason with her…

<u>Spring, 1861, rural Gloucester, England</u>
<u>Sir Walter Finnegan, last Earl of Erravilla Court</u>

Maisy was so shaken by the actions of Mr Shillingworth that she did not invite me to her room for weeks. Instead she would seek me out for a moment every day, when she thought no one was around, and we would talk. Sometimes we would take a walk down to the pond now that warmer weather was on its way, or simply sit by the old fire place after the maids were in their quarters, and she would smile as she talked about her parents, and her life as a child. I told her select information about my up-bringing in Ireland: the infrequent happier moments of my memories. I shielded her from the darkest times, times I would rather forget completely. And women, especially Rosie.

I was becoming more endearing towards my wife each time she would flicker that appealing smile of hers, which sent a warm flush through her cheeks, all the way to her pretty pale blue eyes. I became more and more impatient with the physical distance she maintained, despite the enjoyment I took from our conversations and her knowledge of many things previously unknown to me about her proud country. I saw the way she looked at me from beneath her long lashes – the way she first had the day I arrived at Erravilla.

I walked her to her room one evening, my heart in my throat, although I did not know why. We had been together many times before; it should have been a simple task now. I could not look her in the eye, and I stammered like a young fool at her door. Why didn't she ask me in, even though I could see the longing right there in her eyes? Did she no longer desire a child the way that she used to? What had changed? I could not find the words I needed and I bid her good night, furious with myself as I walked into my suite next door and stood with my back up against the closed door.

Her door clicked shut softly and I stood there for minutes listening. But there was no sound of her footsteps upon the floorboards. She was standing right beside me, on the other side of the wall...

The next night I almost broke out in a nervous sweat by her doorway as I contemplated asking her if I might come in. I shook my head and bit down on my teeth as I bid her good night again. What kind of strange illness had taken over me? I had never felt nervous with a woman before, least of all Maisy, whom I already knew intimately.

Could it be that I no longer felt assured with a woman whom I now knew personally? I had not known Rosie this well, for our time together had been short, without time for the niceties of conversation. Her father owned one of the largest potato plantations in the county, and it was only in my few minutes afternoon break each day during harvest that we would meet in the old stables out of eyesight of her looming father. We had met in that way for months...

On the third night I awoke again in my bed, and I simply could not bear to be so far from her...every brush of her hand and turn of her delicate head lingered in my mind; her very voice had begun to torment me and sometimes I thought I heard her cry out to me deep in the night. I would wake up in a sweat after dreaming about being with her, my breathing laboured and my body shaking from exhilaration.

I heard a door open nearby and I threw on a pair of long-johns, striding to the door and stepping out into the dim corridor. She gasped as I ambled straight into her, catching her before she hit the wall.

"Walter!" she said surprised.

"I'm so sorry, Maisy. I didn't mean to—"

"I heard you cry out," she said. "You called for me, Walter."

"I did?" I replied breathlessly, overly aware of her proximity in my arms.

"Yes. Are you all right?" she asked, seemingly unaware of the effect of her soft hands upon my arms.

"Yes. I mean no. Maisy..."

"Walter, would you like to come and sit with me for a while? I haven't been sleeping too well lately, and I could do with some company," she said quickly.

"It would be my pleasure, Maisy." She could not see the smile on my face, but I had not concealed it in my voice. I wanted to be near her. So very near...

She led me to the lounge before the hearth, where the remnants of an evening fire had burned, and she sat beside me, staring into the dying flames. She shivered and I instantly moved close enough to place an arm around her, pulling her to my side, where she melted into the warmth of my bare chest.

She giggled off-hand, turning to gaze up at me with those alluring blue eyes. "I wonder what Mrs Connolly would say right now?"

"I should think she would be happy," I replied simply, leaning down to place a kiss upon her upturned forehead.

I felt her body rise at my touch as she drank me in, the heady breath from her mouth resting on my throat. She moved her hands up to lie on my chest and I wasn't sure if it was a gesture of offence. But then she lifted her mouth to mine as I slowly kissed the tip of her delicate nose and then pressed my lips to hers. I had to concentrate not to allow my hunger for her to envelope me too soon, taking each step with her gently and carefully, always sensing her response to me before taking my initiative.

When I was certain that her thoughts mirrored my own, I lifted her gently and placed her upon the thick hearth rug. Her body was aflame now to touch as her eyes searched me with awe and wonderment, reflecting the emotions that sang through my very being. I had been intimate with many women, many times before... So why did I tremble with elation like it was the first?

"Walter...love me, Walter...love me..."

And I did. Her response to me awakened the call of my core being, to love her and please her with all that I had. I was barely aware of the frightful warmth upon my finger as the ring shone a bright purple. Maisy tore down all her defences in an instant, unlocking every door and handing me the keys to her very body and soul. I could not have prevented the hole that she tore open in me and then crept straight into, singing through every vein in my body as she went...

Oh God, this was good...so very, very good.

33. If I Could...

<u>M</u>

I couldn't very well do *nothing*. I wasn't about to sit around and put my feet up while the woman I loved was upstairs with another man, whether it was of her own volition or not. I strode to the front door, raking my hands through my hair in sheer frustration. For the first time in my life, I was at a loss. I always knew what to do in a crisis; I was always the one the others came to – the *dependable* one, they said. But now, when things were heading so very wrong for *me*, I didn't know what to do! *Bollocks!*

I knew what I *wanted* to do: climb those stairs two at a time, break down that door and rip her from his arms, tearing him to pieces with my bare hands. I slammed my fists against a wooden cabinet in aggravation, hearing the sweet chinking of bottles as they jumped – the wine rack. I felt the thirst arise hand in hand with my worries like old lovers and was desperate to undress the saturation.

I needed a distraction.

I forced myself to walk for the door.

Where were the police?

Was there even a crime?

Could Andy be arrested for *pressuring* someone into what he was doing up there? He had threatened her at the very least; assaulted her I was sure; maybe up for battery after leaving red indentations upon her arm...I couldn't even be sure that he wasn't armed...

Was he up there with her and armed!?

I remembered that look that had suddenly entered her eyes before she floated up those stairs and the familiar sound of her voice washed through my mind: *Let me go.*

How could she just march up there and look fate in the eyes?

I stilled at the voice of logic and saw that look in her eyes as if for the first time. The realisation rendered me into a state of overwhelming comprehension – April had not been happy to go with Andy; she had been at great peace.

A resounding *thud* came from overhead, followed by a second, more vigorous pounding, and then an aggravated roar from Andy. The ring on my finger burned ice blue with her fear; then black with her anger. I could hear the sirens in the distance, creeping closer with every beat of my pulse, checking into my present reality as I took the staircase two steps at a time. The side of my body slammed into the door with an angry crunch as the vigorous movement continued to reverberate from within.

"April! April, open the door!"

My fists collided repeatedly with the door.

"You bitch!" Andy's pathetic sounding voice rang in my ears, followed by a piercing female shriek.

I stood back, bracing myself for impact. The sirens were blearing in the foreground as they entered the property. Another piercing, threatening screech sounded, followed by a heavy *thud* as the sound of what was most definitely a human body, was slammed up against an internal wall a few feet from the door.

"Stand back, April!" I cried, slamming the flexed sole of my shoe against the door with all the force my body could produce. The door swung free from its frame, careening against the adjacent wall with an almost splintering force.

A pistol lay across the room on the floor boards.

April sat crouched, inches from my feet, holding Andy's head in her cupped hands. Her hair was ruffled, from a hard yank I surmised, and she had a gash beneath her eye. Andy's forehead was covered in blood from more than one wound; his eyes were closed and his body limp. Blood marred April's hands as she held one up to me pleading.

I stared at her for moments, my ears ringing with the sound of police sirens as car doors opened and closed outside. Within seconds they were on the stairs. April didn't move; she sat gazing at Andy, broken and overflowing with tears.

"I've killed him," she murmured. "I've killed them both…"

A police officer shoved past me and knelt beside Andy's limp form, placing two fingers against his lower neck. "You haven't killed him. Not yet anyway. Get the medic!" he ordered. "You need to step aside, Miss Falls. The two of you need to go downstairs with the other officers. Sir, are you the one who placed the call?"

"Yes," I replied, nodding slowly, unable to take my eyes from the expressionless face of Andy. "Come on, April. Leave him with the officer. There's nothing more you can do for him."

"I should stay," she cried weakly. "He might hear my voice…I didn't mean to…hurt him. But he wouldn't stop." She stared up at me beseechingly.

It was clear that April had cared deeply for this man before her, her former friend, who, in turn, had wished her harm; and I had let her go to him.

"It's over now, April, baby," I soothed, placing an arm around her shoulders as she came to me and I guided her from the room.

April Falls

I shall be telling this with a sigh; somewhere ages and ages hence:

Andy had guessed my intentions the second I hadn't followed through on my assurance, and had quickly lunged for the pistol as I made to block his path. I hadn't believed that he would actually hurt me and I still don't believe that he would have if I hadn't reacted as hastily as I did.

Andy had collided with me forcefully, knocking me against a bookshelf. He would have reached the gun if I hadn't sprung off the floor and tapped his ankles, sending him careening into a desk, head first. A fire had ignited in him then; the full force of my betrayal unleashed in a fury of fists and shoves. Only then did his form alter from the friendly face that I had known since childhood to the figure of a dangerous foe: one who had deserted me, blamed me, and then left me to carry a burden alone that should have been *ours* to share.

He had turned me into a murderer, and I had given over to the rage that had been simmering below the surface for more than five years, allowing the brunt of my fury towards both Andy and Penny, to be unleashed like a wild thing.

It had taken less than a couple of minutes to bring him down and silence him. I didn't volunteer the final moments of the fight to the authorities, for those moments were not merely self- defence. I also didn't need to explain those moments to Justice; I knew he already knew that part.

M refused to leave Audenlea, even though I was sure he must have hated me for what I'd put him through. He gave me my space, but eyed me wearily from his peripheral vision. I knew he must have thought me far more foul things than a *hussy* after my behaviour with Andy. I was repulsed by my own admissions that I had, even fleetingly, considered that Andy's offer was a plausible option for escaping the curse of the ring; that I had been willing, for a spilt second, to forego my own dignity again, and force M to sacrifice his own, for my own selfish desires that I had dared to label *freedom*.

I wanted to throw myself at his feet and beg for his forgiveness; to do anything he wanted, if only he would forgive me. I wanted to wrap myself around him unendingly if it would fix things, but Justice kept his distance. All I wanted was his forgiveness and his friendship and an appropriate response. But how could I expect him to hold me and forgive me now…

I woke up on the lounge in Audenlea, the sunlight streaming through the large bay windows and gently stirring me into consciousness. M sat partially reclined in an adjacent armchair, where I had no doubt he had stayed all night, his haunting stare fixated upon me.

I groaned as I was freshly assaulted with the havoc I had reaped upon us both the evening before. M stiffened slightly, glancing at the band upon his left hand before relaxing again; he knew that I was not in physical pain, and so he maintained his distance.

"When is trouble going to stop finding me at every turn?" I groaned, thinking of the vast string of events that had cursed my life for years. His eyes searched mine afresh, confusion shuffling through them. "Oh, M, I don't mean the ring…or you. I also don't blame you if you hate me."

He motioned as if to speak, but refrained, sinking back into thought momentarily. "I don't hate you, April. But if you'd rather, I leave you to your space; I'll go."

"I don't want you to leave," I said quickly, no longer caring if he heard the desperation in my voice. I was guilty as charged. I knew I was being selfish. I wanted him to be my stronghold, even though I was undeserving of his loyalty. "But I won't force you to stay."

"What do you want from me, April?" he asked in earnest.

"I don't know," I replied honestly. *Anything. Everything. Just don't leave.* "I'm supposed to be going to a wedding tomorrow. I know I have no right to ask, after what I've put you through but I would love for you to come with me, please!"

He stared at me, his eyes darting from side to side as though he was watching a Roger Federer and Rafael Nadal Grand Slam match right before his eyes. "You want me to attend a wedding with you?" he asked incredulously.

"Yes. If you'll have me."

"Why?"

"Because I feel safe with you."

"Safe with me? April, you could have been killed yesterday. And I did nothing."

"I always feel safe with you. And what I did yesterday was stupid. I could have gotten us all killed."

"You think *you're* to blame for what he did?"

"Of course. I took him up there. I thought I could stop him."

"You did stop him. Why did you let him take you up there in the first place? I've been over it a thousand times in my mind but nothing makes sense. Do you want me out of your life that badly? I meant what I said yesterday: as soon as I can, I'll have those papers drawn up for you to sign. You can have your life back. You don't need to put yourself through…sleeping with someone else to get that. I would never expect that of you."

"Oh, M! You can't honestly believe that? Do you think so lowly of me that I would do such a thing so easily? You heard Penny: I couldn't even bring myself to be with Lucas!"

He winced.

"Sorry…I'm an awful friend…" I thought of Andy and of M and Lucas. I had caused them all grief since I had known them and I wondered how much heartache would have been avoided if I'd made different choices…thought about my options before making rash choices; if I had taken the path less taken…

"April, there's a lot we don't know about each other. I don't even know what your relationship was with Andy, and frankly I don't care. But I couldn't think any less of you for anything that you've done…or haven't done," Justice said with such fierce sincerity that my heart broke all over again at the thought that I had betrayed his friendship so deeply.

And he really didn't know what he was saying: I was a murderer!

"I am a far greater monster than you could ever dream of being," he said quietly.

"I very much doubt that, Emerus Forrester."

…drunken…alcoholic…

I pushed Andy's sing-song voice aside, saving that curiosity for another day.

"Let me tell you about Andy. And then you might understand the reason behind my strange relationships with these people in my life…including Lucas," I offered.

I felt drained by the time I had finished and lay my head back against the lounge. I knew Justice would be a fair judge of me, and I would accept any conclusions that he came to about me, knowing they would be well deserved, and more so.

But I still hadn't told him about the life I had taken after Andy had left…

Justice was silent for a long while, his steady deep breathing audible from across the room like a grieving sigh.

"Well, it appears that you have some decisions to make," he stated, his calm voice revealing nothing.

I sat up to meet his steady gaze.

"You need to let go of the hold each of these people have over you, April. I think you have the power to do that now."

I left my chair and padded swiftly across the room, landing in his lap with the greatest feline delicacy that I could muster and burying my head into his shoulder. I revelled in the strength and security of his arms as they enveloped me, and I thought that this must be the closest thing to having the Almighty Himself hug me.

"Hmpf," I grunted playfully. "I will have to watch myself around you, for it appears that nothing gets past you!"

"You must know by now though, that it sounds like Andy has his own demons to fight that were there long before he was involved with you, April," M said seriously. "Perhaps they just didn't manifest themselves until that night he was with you. His sexuality…has nothing to do with you, no matter what he thinks. April, you did not *turn* Andy into anything he wasn't already before then," he said fiercely. "I don't want you to carry that burden around with you. Everyone has tendencies and emotions and feelings that they don't like to live with. It's what you do about them and how you live with those actions that matters."

If only I had known Justice back then…would I have behaved differently? Or had I needed to make the mistakes to know right from wrong?

"That was a bombshell if ever there was one. I feel sorry for Andy in a way: having to live with something you don't feel like you've chosen, but feel all the same…or *not* feel in his case. I feel responsible in some way, because it was with me that he realised this…manifestation. At the same time I feel relieved, that in some way there's an explanation for Andy's response to me that night, and I feel like I've gotten some closure for the first time since then. I know that it wasn't me."

M took my face gently between his hands. "April, after we're officially divorced, you may want to reconsider the friendship," he said, balancing me at a relative distance upon his knees.

I stared at him in alarm, panic seizing me at the thought of having my mentor forever absent from my life.

"For now, it's safe to say that I would really like you to come with me to this wedding tomorrow," I replied, distracting myself from the anxiety.

"Okay then. And I would be more than happy to accompany you," he said simply, the hint of a smile returning to his handsome face.

Family and close friends took to the dance floor to join the bridal party as the bridal waltz came to a close. I was surprised when M stood from his chair and held his palm out to me. I hesitated, frozen by the thought of dancing before what was sure to be a couple of hundred pairs of curious eyes.

"I know you used to love to dance. Your school friends here have been telling me lots of interesting stories," M mused, a slow grin relaxing his jaw.

I glared at the girls seated around the table, coaxing me to the dance floor, out of M's line of sight. I ignored their banter as I accepted his offer, taking his hand as he led me through the dense crowd now circling the wooden floor. They seemed generally unfazed by our presence, caught in the rapture of the new bride and her husband.

The music faded just as M found an inconspicuous niche in the crowd, as far away from our table as possible. I stood facing him, feeling awkward now that the music had stopped. I self-consciously flattened the silver cocktail dress with my hands, which had grown moist in apprehension as the opening bars of a favourite ballad played.

"This…is a great song," M said, with a curious smile upon his lips as he took my right hand in his and then softly placed his left hand in the curve of my lower back.

I had recognised the song instantly, and knew that I shouldn't have been surprised that M loved this song too; after all, 1927 were more his era of music than mine, even though I had seen the band live in concert in Sydney. There was so much I realised I didn't know about him: like the fact that he could sing. It seemed that just about all the Forresters could sing.

He leaned in closely to me, gently nudging my body into his as he moved to the rhythm. I felt the warmth of his hand as he wrapped an arm snugly around my waist. I brought my hand to rest upon his shoulder and felt the bristle of his jaw against my temple. He seemed to enjoy the haunting melody of the song as he sang in a low, barely audible voice.

"If I could paint, I'd paint a portrait of you,
The sunlight in your eyes, a masterpiece of truth…
…If I could do anything at all, I'd do it for you…"

I was struck by the power in his humble voice, the way that each word told a secret of its own as he sang, a beautiful, soothing sound to my yearning soul. I closed my eyes and listened as he continued, leaning my entire body into his.

"…And a million words, couldn't say a thing,
That won't be said in three words,
Where love's the central theme…"

My heart hammered in my chest as a deep searing pain ripped through my core; I couldn't breathe for the nearness of his voice and the astonishing reaction that it caused as he crooned the words to me.

"…Darling can't you see, you mean the world to me,
Anything that I can do, I'd do it for you…"

I pulled back gently from his face, watching his features and feeling the warmth of his breath on my face as he sang, his eyes now locked on mine with an intensity that cleared the room of any other presence other than him.

"…Sometimes I feel so second rate,
Seems loving you was my greatest mistake…"

I didn't understand how he was still breathing. The force of his chest against mine as he held me made it difficult for me to breathe. I was conscious only of M as he continued to serenade the room with the aura of his voice, a sadness akin to yearning overwhelming his features as the words reached my ears.

*"...Every whispered sound would touch your heart,
And maybe for a moment I could be your favourite star..."*

*"...And darling can't you see,
You mean the world to me..."*

I wanted to tell him that he did; that he did reach my heart; that I knew he would give me the world if I let him…

I didn't want the song to end; didn't want him to stop singing to me; and I wanted to believe that there was a love like that, not out of my reach. I didn't care that the room had stopped or that M and I were dancing freely, intimately, as if all else were invisible. I didn't care that they stared and whispered as we were locked on to one another.

I could feel the ring on my hand quiver, announcing that it had changed colour again. But there was no pain this time; and I knew without a doubt that it illuminated a deep burgundy.

Emerus Forrester meant every word.

Oh Lord, what was this?

34. A Chalet Reunion

I had more than enough for my heart and soul to consider for the week after M left Sydney the following day; I felt an inexplicable bewilderment when I was in his company. He had encroached upon my life and my emotions without me even realising the extent, and I wondered when it had all began.

I felt clearer, though not content with M gone from Audenlea. I needed time without him so that he couldn't interfere with my being in any way. I was confused, frustrated, and inexplicably aggravated, but I wasn't sure at whom. I needed an outlet – someone to blame for the tumultuous state of affairs that my life had become.

But I could no longer blame Andy; he would be safely behind bars or in a psych institution when he was released from hospital. I had only fond memories and heart-felt affection for Hugh; and my concerns were no longer in a state of disarray when it came to grievances triggered by his passing.

When I thought of Lucas, my mind seemed to spin uncontrollably, with a deep sense of longing to see him again, and the injustice over having been separated against our will. Months ago I would have admitted that absence had made the heart grow fonder; but now I couldn't be sure. Had it been too long to know? Had the burning desire that I had once had for him been replaced for another?

M phoned on his way to the airport. I knew he wanted to know about my emotional well-being. I could only imagine the hours of pain that he would have endured from the ring, caused by my night of emotional disarray.

"I think I've figured out a way around Penny's *restrictions*," he enlightened me. It always amazed me that after all she had put him through, Justice never said a bad word about her to anyone, except to her, and even then he had been amazingly civil.

"Oh?" I asked, eating my breakfast from the kitchen as I watched the summer rain splatter down through the back patio, as though it too were ducking for cover.

"Penny said that you were never to return to England, and that Lucas wasn't allowed to follow you to Australia. She didn't say you couldn't meet in, say…France," he suggested thoughtfully.

"Maybe," I said slowly. I dared not hope, despite the longing in my heart. "She also said she'd be watching Lucas and me."

"How could she possibly know that there's going to be a Forrester Christmas reunion in France?" M challenged.

"I don't know, but she's been able to access information about us that wasn't public knowledge. And she got hold of the journal," I said, my agitation burning anew.

"At worst case scenario, you and I fly in to France together, and play the happy married couple for a week," M suggested with such neutrality in his voice that I could barely believe he was the same man who had declared his deep affection for me yesterday.

"M, I'm trying to be objective here, but won't this be a very difficult week for you…if I spend the week with Lucas, right in front of your eyes?"

He was silent for a minute, and I wondered if he was going to hang up on me.

"April, I'm a selfish man. But I would never keep you from your happiness. That's in your hands, not mine."

I felt a sorrow rise from deep within me, almost a mourning sensation; and I wasn't certain if it was for M, or for me.

"You know that I'm absolutely dying to go to France," I confessed. "I want to share this close family time with you all…each and every one of you."

"I know," he replied simply, his voice hinting at a mind full of emotion. "And we want you to be a part of us, too. It wouldn't be the same this year without you."

"Then it's settled; I'm booking a flight for Christmas Eve. Can you meet me at the airport in Geneva?" I asked, wondering why I always wanted so much from him, more than anyone else; and why he always obliged…

"I wouldn't have it any other way."

Geneva, French Switzerland

So far no bombs had gone off, and no one had been kidnapped at gunpoint, but I couldn't dispel the anxious feelings when I thought of the Scottish fugitive who was still at large, more than six months after she had fled London. I tried to contain the nervous energy, which roamed through my body at will. I maintained a tense guard at all times.

I was not prepared for the freezing blizzard that greeted us in Geneva after enjoying the Australian summer. It was like the seasonal variant of *The Lion the Witch and the Wardrobe*, except that the fawns who would greet us on the other side were far better looking and a little less hairy. I worried about M, as I thought of him driving through the harsh conditions for our benefit, and wishing that, like the White Witch, he too had a sleigh and drivers for the conditions.

I immediately disengaged myself from my luggage, leaving a bewildered Alex standing by the arrivals gate as I sighted two familiar figures in the crowd. I reached them in seconds, wrapping my arms around them both simultaneously, and burying my face between them.

M placed a gentle arm around my waist and laid a kiss upon my forehead before extricating himself from his brother and me. In an instant I was swept from my feet and swung through the air, crushed against a bear size chest.

"I know it wasn't that long ago, but I'm so happy to see you!" a gruff voice sounded in my ear.

"Oh," I groaned, feeling nauseous from the flight as I whirled through the air.

"Put her down, Darius, she's going to be sick," M chastised.

"All right, all right. Now where's my other favourite Falls sister?" Darius mused, searching the crowd for Alex.

Panic froze me momentarily as I scanned the crowd for Alex, who I'd vowed I wouldn't take my eyes off. I followed Darius as he shoved his way through the busy throng, straining to see where I had left her.

Alex stood where I had left her by the ramp, an expression of irritation marring her face as I approached her, breathing heavily with relief. *"Thank God, thank God."*

Her expression altered swiftly as she laid eyes upon Darius, a few paces behind me. I watched with curiosity as he greeted her with even more enthusiasm than he had me, and then kissed her fully on the mouth.

I looked away to shield myself from the not-so-private moment. I would have to analyse my thoughts on that one later…

"Come on you two, let's get out of here," I announced, interrupting the reunion. "This place is making me nervous."

Darius automatically carried Alex's luggage for her, which she gladly accepted. M had already collected mine, against my protests. "Really, M, they're not that heavy. Besides, I'm stronger than I look."

"I know, I've seen your aftermath," he replied with a grin, no doubt referring to the condition he had found Andy in at Audenlea.

I shot him a wary glance before placing an arm firmly through his, unable to contain a grin of my own. "Just don't you forget it?"

"No, Ma'am."

We watched in silence as we followed Darius and Alex to the car park. They were like a couple of school chums, arm in arm, incessantly laughing and chatting the entire way, catching up on the few weeks that they had been apart. I couldn't help but smile at how happy they both looked.

M and I sat in silence as he drove the hour-long trip across the border into France, listening to our siblings' banter behind us, occasionally being cajoled into their merriment.

"So, any word about…Penny?" I said in a hushed voice.

"No word. I think it's a non-issue," M said, briefly glancing in my direction, with a pleasant expression upon his face.

"Good. Let's hope it stays that way," I replied, meeting his warm gaze with a satisfied one of my own.

I could roughly gauge when we were approaching Lucas' villa in the Alpine region of Chambery, in the East of France. M became ever so slightly more withdrawn and his hands tightened around the steering wheel, as though he were bracing himself. I wanted to reach out and take his hand, to assure him that I had no intention of hurting him, but knew that it was inevitable. All it would take would be a look, a touch, a word between Lucas and me.

How could we all live this way indefinitely? If I disregarded Lucas, then I would hurt him. If I embraced him, then I would surely injure M. Why was he doing this to himself? He had done nothing to deserve his wounds other than to have unrequited love.

The blizzard had lessened as we drove towards the snow-capped peaks of the French Alps. We drove past sleet covered fields and winter kissed vineyards in hibernation, along winding rural roads and through climbing pine tree forests. This was the infamous mist-shrouded cradle of Eastern France, nestled at the foothills of the towering Alpine meeting of France, Switzerland and Italy.

I felt anxious and frayed before I had even laid eyes on the chalet; as though I were leading myself to the gallows with each step that I took. There would be no true happiness in any camp while my feelings remained confused. The fate of us all seemed to rest on my shoulders alone.

We pulled into a property at the end of a muddy laneway, greeted by a series of old weatherboard buildings, which M explained were originally built to house the prized animals and vast amounts of servants for the Lord who had occupied the residence in the early seventeenth century. The main residence was a large stone mansion, in the shape of an L, which spanned several stories and was set upon the overhang of a sheer cliff face, overlooking the rolling valleys below.

The sides and rear of the house had been re-constructed with large round oak trunks supporting an almost solid glass frame, with an old style thatched roof.

"How on earth did Lucas come across this place?" I asked in awe as I surveyed the captivating residence.

"It used to belong to a client of mine," M supplied.

"Did you redesign this place, M?" Alex asked as she climbed from the car. Neither of us was able to tear our eyes away.

"I did a little bit of work here, yes," he replied modestly. "It was one of my earlier solo projects, but I've returned here on several occasions. She was one of my favourite clients," he added fondly.

I studied his face momentarily; M rarely spoke of his clients personally. I wondered what it had been about the woman that had sparked his interest. Did M have a partiality to wealthy aristocrats? I laughed at the idea – I was far from that.

The front door opened and my heart trembled at the sight of a familiar face; one that I had begun to believe I would never lay eyes on again. I stood motionless at the sight of Lucas, at the way his eyes held mine with a pleasant yearning as he strode across the grassy mire that separated him and me for what I hoped would be the final time.

In an instant the torrent of emotions that I had battled with for so many lonely months came crashing to the shore as he collected me up in his arms and held me to his heaving chest. I barely felt the burning ring upon my finger as I breathed in the familiar scent that was Lucas Forrester, snaking my arms around his neck and through his tousled hair, and resting my face against his smooth cheek.

"You have no idea how much I've missed you," I breathed, pulling myself to within inches of his lovely face and examining his mystical green eyes.

"You're not the only one. I don't think I've worked so hard in all my life, just to live for this moment," he crooned.

"Well, you can dedicate your next Oscar to me if you like," I mused urgently, overcome by the mere sight of Lucas Forrester, whose face I had studied two dimensionally on a television screen for over six months.

He chuckled his deep resonating laugh, the one I had replayed over and over in my mind; the sound that had woken me in fits of despair during the long days and nights after my exile from London. I would never tire of the sight and sound of him, that much I knew.

The front door closed and I realised that we were alone, standing in a court-yard of tasteful archaic statues, and soaked from the steady rain that fell.

"Let's get you inside where it's warm," Lucas suggested, leading me towards the house with his arm still firmly curved around my waist.

He led me along a corridor of fine European ceramic tiles and into a similarly designed formal lounge room, where the entire Forrester family had communed. I gathered that Alex had been introduced to the family, for she was seated quite closely to Rick Forrester, who was midway through telling her about his latest stage production at London's West End as I entered the gathering.

I was both surprised and delighted to see the Chisholms amidst the family, dressed more closely resembling dear friends than hired hands. I examined Geraldine as though for the first time, noticing the cheerful half-moons her eyes had become as she perused my hand snugly resting in Lucas'. Her light coloured hair hung loosely around her shoulders, and she wore a hint of make-up, which I had not seen her wear before. She wore a long elegant dress, which swept the floor as she walked, and I wondered what the occasion was.

Geraldine appeared noticeably attractive for the first time since I had met her; but knew somehow that this was not usual practice for her, as she constantly fidgeted with the frock and wound her fingers self-consciously through her hair. She was locked in an intense conversation with M, whom she sat very comfortably beside, like a sphinx guarding a prized tomb. Her face glowed with colour as she spoke, her eyes never leaving his for a moment. Usually Geraldine never looked M directly in the eye; previously I had wondered why…

Now I needed no explanation and wondered why I hadn't noticed her unyielding affection for him before. I considered whether M had been aware of her fondness before, or if indeed he even noticed it now…

"April, darling, it's so good to see you!" Rick Forrester cried, leaving a bewildered looking Alex on the lounge as he rose to embrace me in traditional Forrester fashion.

Olivia, the picture of elegance once again, followed cautiously, taking me gently in her arms and placing a chaste kiss on either of my cheeks. She held me at arms' length to appraise me in her usual fashion, noting that she thought I was by far much thinner than she had remembered, and that she wasn't going to let me leave France without stuffing me with a traditional gourmet of French cuisine each day.

It was my turn to feel suddenly overwhelmed, and Lucas stole me gently back from his mother's perusing clutches, folding me into his arms and laying a possessive kiss upon my forehead. I eyed Geraldine again from my peripheral vision, noting that she had placed a delicate hand upon M's arm as she attempted to coax him back into conversation from his momentary distraction in this direction.

"Isn't this just completely divine?" Olivia asked motioning her arms out through the air around her as she lifted her wine glass towards the cathedral ceiling. "It's rare for us to actually see M's work first hand."

I was momentarily speechless as I stared at M over Lucas' shoulder. He stood hastily and changed the subject. "Who would like more wine?"

"Um, I'm going to take April on a tour," Lucas announced in response.

"Oh! I'd love a tour," Alex piped, hastily retreating from her place beside the charismatic Rick Forrester. Darius rose to follow her as we headed through to the formal dining area. I gathered that Lucas had wanted some time alone with me, without Alex.

Darius seemed to come to the same conclusion, or he desired the same of Alex, and volunteered to start the tour at the far end of the house.

"Of course, M would be able to give you a more *informed* tour of the house," Darius muttered to Alex as he guided her off through to the kitchen. "You know, all the boring stuff…"

Lucas channelled us through to a small living area at the furthest corner of the house, which provided spectacular scenic views of the undulating hills and valleys below. He didn't give me a commentary of any description, instead leading me up a polished oak stairwell, then through an original looking stone archway to a finely furbished study and library.

Lucas locked the door behind us, taking my hand and leading me over to a leather lounge. I felt strangely anxious in his company: as though I was meeting a high profile celebrity for the first time. I smiled awkwardly as I remembered the first time I had laid eyes upon him in person.

My palms sweated and I almost wished we weren't alone as I struggled to encounter his brilliant emerald eyes which, I admitted, still held great power over me. They searched me with a minor frenzy; his heart so clear upon his face that I wanted to reach out and stroke his soft skin.

"April," he said tenderly, his velvet voice capturing my attention with every breath. "I don't want to place any expectations upon you, and I'm sorry I haven't given you any time. But I haven't stopped thinking about you since the day you left Erravilla last summer."

I raised my eyes in expectation, knowing that there was more to follow. He needed me to hear his appeal, even though I wasn't ready for any more pressure right now.

"I don't expect an answer now, and I know things are still crazy between you and M," he continued, looking out to the scenic glass display below.

I panicked fleetingly, wondering what exactly he knew of the craziness between M and me.

"But, if you still feel the same way about me as you did that evening, before I was unwillingly taken from the apartment in Park Lane, I would like for us to try and make this work."

I could scarcely believe my ears, which thundered from the excess blood pumping through my body as I inhaled his words.

"You want us to become serious?" I confirmed, daring to search his exquisite face.

"Only if you want to. I understand if it's too soon. I know you've had a lot to deal with lately," he said as the edges of his mouth dipped in concern. "I don't want to make things worse for you."

"Lucas, you couldn't possibly make things worse for me," I replied, smiling into his promising face. "I'm just glad to be here and to see you again. I thought I would go mad if I had to hold out any longer."

"You have no idea how glad I am to have you here for Christmas; it was the best surprise in the world. Good old M, always saving the day!" he mused.

"Yeah, good old M," I replied with strained enthusiasm, unable to meet Lucas' intense gaze any longer. "So, are you going to show me this house, or what?"

I stood to leave the room and Lucas followed my lead, turning me instead to face him as he stood. My heart thundered in its cage as he tilted my chin to meet his gaze. "Not so fast," he murmured as he slowly bent his lips to mine, holding my eyes until I could see him no longer. My mouth was hesitant at first, struggling against the myriad of emotions that swam through my mind, desperate to locate the time in the past when my heart longed only for him.

The feel of his lips on mine and his hands compressing me to his body was enough to make me forget the disorder in my mind, and return his kiss with an eagerness that I had longed to maintain for a short eternity.

"April," he breathed, the explosion of headiness fusing in the meeting of our bodies. "Do you remember, before I was taken that day, you said that you wanted to make our time together memorable? I asked you if you knew what you were doing; and you said, you hoped so."

His hypnotic eyes implored mine and I felt a dizzying heat rise to my cheeks at his insinuation. I remembered that moment instantly, coaxing him to the lounge at Park Lane, yearning to completely surrender myself to him at that very moment. He had been more than willing except that we had never sealed our intentions before Lucas had left to sign for his parcel that had never arrived.

"I remember," I replied, my pulse racing with divided anticipation. Every molecule in my body raced with desire to release the pent up tension that I had endured for so long.

"I'm not going to ask it of you, April," Lucas said fervently, gently running the curve of his fingers along my left hand, lingering deliberately upon the crest of the unique wedding band. "But I want you to know that if you need me for anything, anything at all, I'll be more than happy to oblige."

I swallowed hard at the blatant offer, afraid to look into his face lest he read my own desires.

35. The Curse

Lucas was offering me my freedom: a simple way to solve a number of problems. He was giving me everything that I wanted, and all I had to do was ask. It didn't have to be now; we had all week.

And everyone would know.

I cringed. My personal life on public display once again.

"I appreciate it," I said, trying to sound casual, changing the conversation with a gentle squeeze of his hand. "So, are you going to show me around this masterpiece or what?"

To say that the house was a structural tour de force was an understatement; M had created a modern wonderland within a previous world, utilising the original structures of the mansion to their utmost, and then incorporating the very cutting edge of modern expertise so that the cosy atmosphere appeared timeless.

"He must have travelled the world to find these artistic ornaments and designs," I marvelled, unable to refrain from reaching out to handle the multi-dimensional art works and motifs.

"Well, he's constantly searching for the unusual in his travels," Lucas agreed. "I don't know how he gets them through customs nowadays though. Some of these pieces are very exotic and look like natural…"

"Vegetation?" I supplied, fingering the rough surface of a wall mural mounted along the second floor landing, subconsciously covering the quivering ring on my hand.

"That one's from Malawi," a familiar voice interrupted.

I turned instantly at the sound of M's voice, which I suddenly realised had become my safeguard during the last couple of weeks. Instinctively I wanted to run to him and throw my arms around him to chase away all of my fears and anxieties. But I knew it was selfish; I could not have my cake and eat it too; it simply wasn't fair to M or to Lucas.

"Mother's sent me to find you all, to let you know that she is having dinner served," M announced. "Where are the other two?"

"I have no idea; we lost them before the tour started," Lucas said with a knowing grin.

I glanced at M, neither of us sharing Lucas' humour at the insinuation.

"Do you want me to help you find them?" I asked.

"No, I know this place well. I'm sure it won't be difficult to locate them," M replied, already heading up the wide corridor.

Dinner was a merry occasion; everyone sensed the thrill that Christmas provided, especially when united with family and friends. I considered with surprise how relaxed and light-hearted M appeared under the circumstances. He was taking the situation with apparent ease, more easily than me, who had struggled from across the room to throw my arms around him as I had gotten used to doing. I had to let go; it was becoming too hard to manage being around Lucas and M simultaneously.

Why couldn't I just be happy with one; the way Alex and Darius seemed to be scarily besotted by one another; and the way that Geraldine had eyes only for M. My twisted and confused heart wanted Lucas for physical comfort, as well as my dearest friend, M, for emotional support.

Christmas was a charismatic affair in the Forrester household; no less. We had all decided to give a secret Santa gift to a name randomly drawn from a box, which proved to be quite a hilarious affair. I was informed that it was a Forrester tradition to find the most unique gift for secret Santa each year.

"It's pretty predictable in the end," Aggie informed Alex and me as we waited for Lucas to open his surprise gift. "M always wins."

I sent him a silent smile across the room, where he sat in quiet anticipation for his brother to open his gift.

"Go on, explain it, M!" Lucas exclaimed in wonderment, holding up the pendant for the gathering to observe. The pendant was shaped like a cross, except that all four sides were the same length. In the centre was a bright white crystal.

M smiled curiously, amused by his most recent acquirement. "Actually, I found this one hugging one of the headstones in the family graveyard at Erravilla."

"You mean, you're giving me something I technically already own?" Lucas mused.

"Yes. But…I was curious when I first saw the designs on the ivory; they were unlike any I had ever seen before and I wanted to find out where it came from…originally," M continued. "So, I took it to a contact in Dubai—"

"That seedy guy from—"

"Yes, Darius. He said he had seen similar designs come from the native tribes of South America. So, I took it to South America and—"

"You went all the way to South America to find out about—"

"Yes, Aggie, for work. I tracked it to somewhere near Buenos Aires in northern Argentina," M interjected. "I was informed by a very reliable, if not completely scary looking, *Holy Man* that it's supposed to protect your loved ones from harm. So you take very good care of that pendant now, Lucas," he mused.

I was speechless at the efforts this man was willing to go to in the name of Architecture.

"You have clients in an Argentine Indian village?" Aggie asked.

"Not quite," M replied vaguely.

"Then what were you doing all the way down there?" Aggie pressed.

The entire room grew silent with anticipation.

"Well," M began slowly, deliberating his response. "I was chasing a lead from an acquaintance in Dubai…about the rings. And it too led to South America…via other continents."

"What did you find out?" I asked imploringly.

His brow furrowed in thought momentarily. "It's not unheard of."

"What's that supposed to mean?" I demanded.

He shrugged offhandedly. "These sorts of *mystical* – if that's what you want to call them – artefacts…exist from time to time."

"If it's so *mystical* then why didn't the *Holy Man* want to keep it?" Aggie pressed.

M took a steady breath as a brief smirk crossed his face, as though he were debating whether to laugh or bawk. "Well, he said objects that bring blessings…also bring curses. He actually called this lifeless piece of ivory *the Curse*."

"Great! So you thought you'd just…give it to me?" Lucas joked, although a gleam in his eye bespoke of a wearisome fear as he glanced at the ring on my hand.

"Well, brother, as I don't believe in voodoo and therefore don't see any harm in the gift, and I didn't pick your name out of that box by *choice*…that small piece of cursed ivory belongs to you," M mused.

"It sounds a bit potty to me. Are you sure there's nothing else?" Aggie persisted.

"There's nothing more to tell, really," M replied.

Really?

I would press him for more information later.

"Don't open mine next; it's completely lame compared to that," Alex laughed, cringing.

"Or mine," Aggie agreed.

After lunch Lucas handed me a small box in the privacy of the library. I was anxious as I opened his gift, afraid that my gift for him would pale in significance, and that his gift might be somewhat more personal than I was prepared for.

His gift was a simple but elegant wrist-watch. Something I could have with me at all times. The defensive walls around my heart began to soften at his attentiveness. "It's stunning, Lucas," I managed, staring at the precious keepsake that he had sought and bought especially for me.

"It keeps the time in every country in the world and has a digital map so that you can locate where we are, even when we're apart," he offered. "Oh, and you can Skype."

I wrapped my arms around his waist and held him tightly, wondering what was wrong with me that I still felt dissatisfied, even when he was in my arms, and cherishing me above all others. I still wanted more than I felt he could give me.

In the evening Aggie suggested that we all play a round of three-part charades, apparently another Forrester family favourite.

"You want me to play charades…with a room full of performers?" I asked incredulously.

"You'll get over that; their bark is worse than their bite, I assure you," Leicester said encouragingly. "Just meet them at their game, you'll see."

"What's three-part charades?" Alex asked, looking around the room as though she was scouting the wilderness for a cave.

"We each write the names of two celebrities on a piece of paper and pile them into a box. The teams take turns to guess as many names within a time limit. There are three rounds, the points get tallied, and the one with the most wins," Aggie declared.

"But why are there three rounds if the names are the same?" I asked, hoping I didn't sound as clueless as I felt.

"Ah-ha!" Aggie cried mysteriously. "That's the fun part. In round one, you can use as many words as you like, without saying what's on the paper. So if my celebrity was say, Lucas Forrester, then I could say: he's a young British actor who played Ethan in the *Seasons* saga and has won two Oscars, fourteen MTV and Teen Choice Awards, and has been nominated for two British Academy Awards, etc. In round two, you can only say one word. So you might say "actor". And in round three, you have to mime."

"The only exception is that you can't name anyone who's here: it gets really annoying," Darius offered.

Urland Chisholm offered to sit the game out, allowing an even number of people for two teams of five. He split the teams accordingly: Rick, M, Aggie, Geraldine and me, against Olivia, Lucas, Leicester, Darius and Alex.

The Forresters proved to be a very competitive family when it came to winning for glorification and the tabs had been recorded in their minds since they were children. And they knew how to have fun with a challenge. The celebrities were at times so unusual that I had never heard of them; and if Rick or Olivia had chosen the celebrity, then often *only* they had heard of the person. There were musicians and authors from centuries ago; stage and film actors past and present;

cartoon characters; politicians mostly British; so I had no clue –
sporting heroes and mythological characters.

After the first round I was bewildered by the vast array of
names that had been thought of under the banner of "celebrity", and
amazed at how quickly the Forresters scanned their brains to find
names hidden deep within their creative literary minds. Round two
wasn't as easy, and I began to chuckle at the flimsy mistakes that were
sometimes made when choosing just one word: any sound was
classified as a word, and a poor fleeting choice could ruin the entire
round. I had never realised how often the utterance "um" is used to
begin speech in everyday conversation…

By the end of round three we were all in hysterics, trying to
guess the humorously ungraceful and creative bodily contortions used
to imitate our notable characters. I doubled over as I observed Rick
Forrester's imitation of Mr Ed as he flayed about on all fours
pretending to talk like a horse; and at Aggie's insistence that Michael
"Air" Jordan was in fact pronounced "Air Gordon", while her siblings
riled around on the floor in stitches at her less than accurate sporting
trivia knowledge.

At the end of the game, I felt so relaxed that I was ready to
begin afresh. This time Aggie suggested that we play in pairs. Rick
suggested that we be paired with the person whose birthday was closest
to our own.

"Damn," Alex hissed under her breath, bewildered by the idea
of being paired with Rick after the teams were announced.

"You have to be sharp if we're to be a team, Darius," Olivia
crooned, resting an arm around her youngest son's shoulders
encouragingly.

"Just don't pick weirdos," Darius replied, his face scrunched.

"Does that mean she can only choose people born in this
century so that you'll know who she's talking about?" Aggie teased.

"Whatever, Haggis," he hooted in reply.

"That means Lucas is with Leicester," Aggie directed, causing
an eruption of cheers from the boys as they clapped each other across
the back. "I'm with Geraldine, and M, you're with April. We always

find a different way of sorting pairs, April, because everybody wants to be on Lucas' team."

"Speak for yourself," Darius mocked good-naturedly. "He doesn't always win."

"Yeah, sometimes your mother wins!" Rick snorted.

M raised an eyebrow and I grinned quietly to myself as I took my place beside him on the floor. I felt the light touch of Lucas' hand as it rested upon my shoulder from the lounge behind me.

"Nice watch," M said quietly, genuinely admiring the watch, even though I knew he must have known who gave it to me.

"Thanks," I replied, unsure how to react. For some reason I still felt the need to protect his feelings, while wanting to show off the special gift for Lucas' benefit. "It's stunning, isn't it?"

"It suits you perfectly," M replied, nodding in affirmation to Lucas above. "Good find, brother."

"Thanks, I bought it in L.A. last week," Lucas replied, seemingly oblivious to my awkwardness.

I stared into M's eyes for long, searching for a hint of discomfort, and was amazed to find none. He was completely at peace. The ring on my finger hummed with a soft yellow glow all evening. Geraldine wrapped her arm daringly through M's across from me, paying little attention to Lucas and me as she waited for the game to begin.

I couldn't believe that this was the same woman, who previously couldn't even look "Master Emerus" in the face. *Why now?* And why did I care? He was my friend, nothing more. He had made his feelings known for me and I had refused. It had been my decision. He was free for the taking whenever he wanted…

But not in front of me! A small voice cried out from within, shocking my conscious mind.

I stared at Geraldine; I couldn't believe what I was thinking.

"Och! Tha' thing's burning my skin!" Geraldine cried, her brown eyes growing wide as she unwound her arm from around M's. "Does i' always just *do tha'*?"

"Only when April's deeply in thought about something," M replied, his brows dipping in thought.

"So, wha's so interestin' tha' you burnt him?" Geraldine asked rubbing her arm, a surprising irritation lacing her tone. "I don' remember wha' all the colours mean."

Geraldine *blamed* me for hurting M? Did other people think I did this deliberately?

"I would never hurt you," I whispered, holding his incredulous gaze.

"Well, it's a pretty shade of green," Aggie chimed leaning over Geraldine to examine the iridescent ring. "What does it mean, April? What are you thinking about?"

"Are you okay, April?" Lucas asked, wrapping an arm around my shoulders and leaning into me from above.

"I'm fine. It's nothing. Let's just play the game, okay?" I replied, flustered that the entire room had intruded upon my privacy. What *had* I been thinking to make it turn that colour? *I should have read the book!*

"It's like a crystal ball or something," Darius piped up, a childish thrill enveloping his voice. "Like your own secret language."

I shot him an exasperated glare, hoping he would take the hint and change the conversation.

He leapt to his feet on cue. "Who wants a drink?"
Subtle.
"I'll help you," Alex offered.

"Yes, yes, time for a refill!" Olivia announced clapping her hands with glee. Anyone would have thought she was about to open the Christmas crackers.

The room cleared as if on cue, even though I knew most of them were oblivious to Darius' true reason for the drink break. I cringed as I noticed that Geraldine had remained behind with Lucas, M and me. I felt as though her very presence suffocated me and I sought some fresh air.

"Are you sure you're okay, April?" Lucas resumed, thankfully oblivious to my true state of emotions, even though I could not quite explain them myself.

"Really, I'm fine. I just need some air," I replied, heading briskly for the back door.

Oh Lord, this is harder than I thought it would be!

"Lucas, I'll go. Please…" I heard M's persuasive voice behind me.

"She gets light-headed some times," Lucas offered in a reserved voice. "I think it makes it hard for her to breathe."

"That's not what's wrong with her," M replied.

"Then what's the matter with her?" Lucas asked in a more pressing tone.

"She'll be fine. But it's up to her to tell you," M's voice trailed off as I closed the door behind me, bracing myself for his scrutiny. No, M would never scrutinize me: he was really concerned. And he knew something about me that I did not. I paced in anticipation like a snow leopard.

The door slid open and closed behind me. Justice approached lightly, standing beside me, his arms folded across his chest in the cold night air.

"You're going to freeze out here; you're only wearing a t-shirt," I said without turning to him, remembering the casual fitted grey top he wore that accentuated his lean form in a far too appealing manner.

"I'm used to the cold."

"You didn't need to follow me. I'm a big girl, you know."

He chuckled in a low hum. "I know you're a very capable woman who feels threatened easily, it seems."

"What are you talking about?" I asked, almost snapping at him.

"April, I'm not criticising you, it's just an observation. So far as I can tell, the ring doesn't lie," Justice replied gently. "It kind of sucks that way."

"It kind of sucks in *every* way," I retorted more sharply than I had intended.

I felt the physical blow that rocked through his body and hated myself for causing him grief. I was reacting very strongly to a heavy foreboding that had settled itself upon me this evening, and I couldn't shake it. I lifted my chin heavenward.

Lord, give me patience.

M took a deep breath beside me and waited moments before he exhaled; I knew he was picking himself up from the blow.

"April, I will always be your friend, no matter what happens in the next few months. But you need to sort yourself out. You can't keep living like this," he offered carefully. "Or else you're going to implode."

I turned abruptly to demand what he was insinuating but Justice had already retreated inside. I considered his warning for a few chilly minutes before following suit, taking my place beside Lucas upon the lounge and nestling into his welcoming arms. I gave him an assuring smile and squeezed his hand without an explanation.

"Dad, you and Darius are up first," Aggie instructed. "And no cheating!"

M and I were third in queue, and I channelled all of my energy into focussing on the game; ignoring Geraldine's enthusiastic perusal of M beside her as he guessed with determination and accuracy, five of the celebrities that I pulled from the box. I had known little about some of the characters, but described them as well as I could and left the rest to M. His accurate intuition was enough to win us the round.

Lucas and Leicester were a hysterical partnership, bringing everyone to their knees in laughter as they, sometimes crudely, and always wittily, verbalized their way to the finish line ahead of the rest. They were a close partnership indeed, well matched in intelligence and humour; and much to my astonishment, sharing one another's juvenile hilarity with ease.

The way M and I worked was noticeably different from the one Lucas and Leicester adopted, participating in the game with a more keen interest and earnest competitiveness, equally suited in spontaneity and verbal theatrics. I was pleasantly satisfied with our progress, sitting equal on the leader board with the boys, and waited with eager expectation for the final round. Perhaps the constant ebb of wine was also easing my exasperating anxiety.

It looked as though Lucas and Leicester were streaking home again, until Leicester failed to identify Lucas' quite humorous portrayal of Reverend Lovejoy from *The Simpsons*. M drew the final three from the box, two of which I recognised and the final one I remembered because it was the only name to not have been played already in the round. It was enough to win us the game.

I practically leapt onto the theatre floor and threw my arms around my partner-in-crime, dancing with glee at our co-operative success. It was the first time I had wrapped my arms around him since he had left Australia and I savoured the moment, holding him close to breathe in the familiar scent of Old Spice.

"I bet they cheated with those rings," Darius snickered.

I threw him a mock glare over M's shoulder and realised that I was still holding onto M as though he were a life raft and sighed as I released him, wondering when I would have the chance again.

"You make a great team," Rick encouraged, refilling his wine glass for the umpteenth time.

"How about some Sing Star karaoke?" Aggie suggested, apparently exuberant with the family festivities.

With the groaning that followed you would have thought she had suggested a nudie run through the snow.

"Maybe tomorrow night, Aggis," Lucas suggested.

"For the thousandth time: Please don't call me that. It makes me sound like an undesirable Scottish food," Aggie droned.

"Aggis the Haggis!" Darius chanted in his finest Scottish accent.

"I'm calling it a night," M announced, giving a slight nod of his head before heading up the stairs.

"Sounds like a good plan," Leicester agreed, wrapping an affectionate arm around Aggie and pulling her to him playfully.

"Okay you two, there are rooms you know," Darius protested at their open display of affection.

"Hey, your sister's a great *affecionado*," Leicester taunted with a satisfied grin upon his face.

"And that's information I *don't* need to know! She's my sister, man!" Darius cried in mock indignation, pulling Alex to her feet and guiding her to the stairs.

Instinctively I went to stop her; the ever-protective insecurities I held were always attending to *her* security. I still hadn't come to terms with her increasing familiarity with Darius, and I wanted to deter her from making fatal mistakes…from making the same fatal mistakes I had made with Andy.

Lucas pulled me firmly to him, bestowing a gentle kiss upon my forehead. "Let her go. He won't do anything that will hurt her."

"How do you know?" I demanded, trying to maintain a low voice.

"Because M and I have already warned him," he said simply.

<u>Summer/Autumn, 1861, rural Gloucester, England</u>
<u>Sir Walter Finnegan, last Earl of Erravilla Court</u>

We spent our nights together for weeks in this manner, inseparable.

One morning a thought struck me like a bolt of lightning as I lay there examining her blue eyes. A content smile lingered upon her face as she lay curled up against my side. It had been many weeks...

"Maisy, my precious wife...are you with child?" I asked cautiously.

She nestled deeper into the ridge of my neck so that her soft voice was barely audible. "Yes, Walter. We are finally going to have a child."

A knock resounded upon the door and Mrs Connolly announced her presence before stepping into the room. I pulled the sheets a little higher across Maisy's bare back and smiled pleasantly at the older woman, whose eyes were all but rolling out of her head at the brazen sight before her.

"Good day, Mrs Connolly. Would you be so kind as to bring my wife and me our breakfast upstairs today? And please fetch a doctor too," I asked pleasantly.

"Why, whatever is the matter, Mr Finnegan?" she asked curiously, barely containing the disconcerted note in her voice as she looked anywhere but at Maisy and me.

"My wife is going to have a baby," I announced, gazing directly at the blonde haired beauty cradled into my side.

Mrs Connolly's mouth fell agape. I knew I had offended her by my bluntness, lying there with my naked wife, and speaking of the wonderment that had passed between us recently.

For weeks Maisy virtually sang her way about the grand house, even stopping to embrace me when she thought no one else was nearby.

And then the pains began. She lost ounces of blood, the Doctor said, and would need permanent bed rest. This did not remedy the situation and all was lost to her...

Three more times Maisy carried a child for but a short time only, and three more times the outcome mirrored the first. She gave up completely and returned to the despondent Maisy I had tried to forget. In the early days she would still allow me to comfort her at night until morning. After months had passed, I was not allowed near her at all...

Two years passed and we had been married for five years. Something deep and unsettling had taken hold of Maisy. I knew that loving me was not enough for Maisy. I was surprised to acknowledge how much this recognition stung me. I had never expected more from her, and I was fooled into believing that I could provide her every dream. We had been happy but for a brief moment in time...

And then one day, seemingly out of nowhere, and with no warning, she arrived...

"Mr Finnegan, there is a woman and a child at the door. She says you had cordially invited her to Erravilla as a guest some time ago," Ms Hayes announced, unable to conceal the curiosity in her eyes.

Maisy rose with me from the guest dining lounge, with a confused expression upon her features as my heart leapt into my throat. Surely it could not be...

Maisy followed me without invitation into the foyer, standing firmly beside me as she eyed the woman speculatively.

Her faint blue eyes almost protruded straight out of her head as she beheld the small child holding Rosie's hand. One glance at the boy, and I didn't need Rosie's confirmation as to who the child belonged to.

I was speechless, staring at the brown-eyed, curly haired boy, a smaller image of myself. He was nearly five years old.

"Walter...I'm so sorry to intrude upon you. But you did say that if I was ever in need, I would be welcomed at Erravilla," Rosie announced meekly, with desperation in her once-bright eyes.

I beheld her properly for the first time and noticed a hollowness in her high cheek-bones and a yellowness that seemed to seep out from beneath her usually porcelain-like skin. Her clothes were worn and outdated, as though she had taken them from a dumpster and worn them for months without changing.

She was also not a woman who usually asked for favours. She turned to Maisy, addressing her directly. "I'm sorry, my name is Mrs Rosie O'Donnell, and this is Rupert, my son. You must be Walter's wife."

"I am...Mrs Maisy Finnegan," Maisy replied, still staring at the boy as though she had seen a ghost. "What is it that we can do for you, Mrs O'Donnell?"

"You were married, Rosie? To the politician O'Donnell from Dublin?" I asked, scarcely believing the absurdity of the situation. Robert O'Donnell was an older leading statesman in the capital, whose wife had passed away a decade earlier, leaving him with no heirs. I could certainly see why a woman such as Rosie had taken his fancy for a swift wedding. She must have known she was with child and hastily made the arrangements to give the child a name.

"May we come in? We have travelled a long way, and are very weary," Rosie asked hopefully.

Maisy looked to me for a guiding answer, but I was still at a loss for more words. "Please, Mrs O'Donnell, won't you and your boy come in?"

Maisy did not ask about the boy; she didn't need to. She just sat there beside me staring at the child.

"The truth is, Walter, I had no place else to go. Even after five years of marriage we were unable to produce a child and Robert became suspicious and started asking around. When he found out that Rupert was not his biological child..." she bit her lip, "I didn't know where else to go."

"He threw you out?" I asked, outraged.

"Walter, you must understand. A man of his position cannot have skeletons lurking in the closet. He banished us," Rosie stammered. "And my father could not stand the humiliation if word got out. You know how he is."

"You knew about me?" Maisy asked suddenly, her eyes barely focussing on Rosie's a few feet away. "Walter has not mentioned you, Mrs O'Donnell.'

"That's as it should be," Rosie swallowed. "We were young and foolish years ago. I would expect that Walter would have forgotten all about me. He is obviously very happy here with you, Mrs Finnegan."

"Young and foolish indeed," Maisy repeated, still gazing at the small boy nestled into his mother's skirts. "But you can stay. For as long as you need."

"I don't have much longer left," Rosie replied. "A few months at most. It is Rupert I am concerned about...I was hoping..."

My eyes snapped up at her boldness. "A few months?"

"I am dying, Walter. I have developed Cholera, I'm certain. We lived on the docks for months before we were able to catch the boat across to England. I gave Rupert all of our food, and ate only the remnants from the allies nearby. I ask only that you look after the boy until he is of age. Perhaps he can play with your children and in time earn his keep..."

I knew it must have nearly killed her to ask for anything, especially this. But it was clear she was devoted to the boy, and for all of their troubles, he looked well enough.

"We have no children of our own, Mrs O'Donnell. I'm sure we can work something out for your boy," Maisy offered, to my amazement. Was she thinking of her father's illegitimate brother whom he had taken under his wing when no one else would?

I did not even know how to begin to explain Rosie to Maisy, so I did not. For all of the indignation Rupert would have caused Maisy, she seemed to enjoy the company of the quick-witted and bright little boy, who smiled with a ghostly imprint of my own. I watched day by day as Maisy tutored the boy eagerly, examining his every response and poise. She looked upon the boy with yearning, but appeared to hinder no jealousy towards Rosie, who had the one thing from me that Maisy did not.

"We will say that you are my sister, Rosie, and the boy will call us Uncle and Aunt. We will adopt him and give him a good home and upbringing," I offered, knowing that Maisy would not disagree.

It was the only way I could think of to make up to them both what I had done: by giving them both what they wanted from me. A child for Maisy; a name and a guardian for Rosie's child.

"Thank you both. It is more than I could have hoped for, Walter," Rosie breathed, the shallowness in her cheeks evident as she smiled. "Thank God for you both."

A curious thanks, I thought, considering I felt like I had ruined both of their lives...

36. The Power of One

April Falls

Two roads diverged in a wood, and I, I took the one less traveled by,

I slept fitfully for the first part of the night; unable to contain the fears that crept into my dreams, dredged up from the recesses of my memory. I woke constantly, sweat beads covering my forehead as though feverish, sometimes startled or disoriented – once when Alex returned to her bed. At three 'o' clock I tiptoed from the room and managed to find my way down to the kitchen.

At Audenlea I rarely woke anymore or ate in the darkness as I used to after the accident. *Something about these Forresters seemed to lead me on midnight sustenance trips*, I pondered as I stumbled into the kitchen, groping for a light. I found the switch for the range hood, which provided the perfect level of illumination for my weary eyes.

M

I stood against the rear glass doors facing out into the winter yard, watching as the first early snow of the season descended upon the lawn. The moon shone brightly through the haze of thick snow as it fell, creating a silhouette backdrop for the white droplets. It was pleasant and satisfying to behold such a private and haunting sight, alone in the wee hours of Christmas night.

I savoured each mouth full of the warm European chocolate that I sipped, remembering the many nights I spent in foreign countries, drinking for company as I worked into the small hours. The drinks never compared to the one I drank now, which only tasted this good on the Continent.

A dim light flickered on behind me and I could see her reflection in the dark glass without turning. I took a deep breath to steady my disrupted sentiments before I greeted her.

"Tough night?" I asked, sensing her response from the weary lines beneath her eyes. She gasped.

"You scared me half to death, M!"

"I have that effect sometimes," I mused, still gazing out into the thick blanket of snow that was forming.

"Is that snow?" she squeaked, padding swiftly across the tiles to stand beside me.

"Sure is." She looked so joyful that I wanted to reach out and fold her into my arms but I didn't.

"It's beautiful," she whispered, placing a hand upon the glass as if to grasp the soft sensation of the cool ice flakes.

"Would you like a drink? This stuff is incredible."

"Oh? Sure. What do I do?"

"Come and watch," I grinned, walking back into the kitchen.

"You couldn't sleep either?" she asked, padding along behind me.

I grimaced to myself. *If only she knew how little I* did *sleep.*

"I'm always thinking about work, I guess," I replied, beginning to pour the sweet dark liquid into a mug.

"Is it that time consuming, your job?" she asked.

"It has been. But I'm working on some changes," I ventured, unsure how much I was going to reveal. That would depend on how interested she was in my long-term prospects.

"Oh?" she prompted, her unusually dark eyes glancing from me to the bench as I worked.

"Yeah, I don't think I can manage it all on my own anymore," I volunteered, watching her response carefully from the corner of my eyes.

"What do you mean? You aren't going to sell your business, are you?" She seemed mildly disturbed by the idea.

"No, just take more of a backseat."

"But how? You work alone."

She was interested.

"Not any more. I hired another architect, six months ago," I replied casually, handing her the mug and standing with my back up against the breakfast bar facing her.

"Wow, that's great. How come you didn't say anything?"

"I wanted to see if it would work out first. I've worked alone for years now and wasn't sure if I could trust anyone else to work alongside me. But it seems to be working out so far, and he's agreed to start taking on most of the international client appointments. Initial appointments, that is," I explained.

"M, this is huge! Your business sounds like it's thriving. You must really need the help."

"It's going well," I replied slowly, wondering if I should tell her the real reason for the change. "The travelling takes its toll after a while though. I love it. But I'm never home for more than a couple of days at a time. I want to find a base for my life. More continuity."

"Oh. That sounds great. So you'll stay in London and do all the local side of things?" she inquired, seeming slightly aloof. She must be more tired than she looked.

"I haven't decided yet," I replied taking a deep breath as I drank. She was hedging closer.

"What do you mean? Your apartment's in London."

"I don't know where I'll base myself, yet. It might not even be England." *Depending on how things developed in the following few months, it would hopefully be Australia...*

"Oh." Her appealing blue eyes frowned at the ends. How had I managed to increase her apparent gloom? "So you'll move farther away...and stop travelling?"

"That's the plan," I replied, an air of peace settling upon me at the notion.

"Well, that's great for you," she replied, not sounding altogether pleased at all. "If my father had done that twenty years ago, he'd still be married to my mum. I think it's great that you're going to do that. You can...move on with your life I guess. Settle down and all of that."

Was she planning my life for me? I was growing more confused by the second. Last night the ring had indicated that she was *jealous*. I presumed it was from Geraldine's sudden close affection, which I had noticed with increasing concern. That Geraldine triggered feelings of jealousy in April had blown my mind. And now she wanted me to move on with my life and settle down?

"Tell me what you did before you worked alone," she asked, changing the conversation.

"After college I landed myself a position in a Philadelphian Design firm, which was supposed to be prestigious and cutting edge, and all of that," I began, remembering back to the more adventurous years of my early twenties. "I completed an internship there and spent the next five years working my way up the ranks within the firm. The problem was, the higher up I climbed, the more battles I faced. It turned out that the partners weren't as "cutting edge" as I had hoped. They thought my ideas were too eccentric, too unconventional for the general marketplace of their clientele."

"So they fired you?" she asked incredulously.

I couldn't stifle the chuckle that escaped my throat at the sight of her wide blue eyes. "No, no, I left. I was convinced that there *was* a niche market out there; clients who would entertain my *unconventional* concepts."

She laughed with apparent relief, grinning at my charade of self-confidence.

"Well you sure showed them! I bet they're licking their wounds now!" she crooned.

I grinned at her assurance: *She had faith in my abilities.*

The smile faded from her face as she placed the empty mug upon the island bench. "M, I'm sorry for how I spoke to you last night. I shouldn't have snapped like that. I don't know why I get so frustrated sometimes. You were right…what you said. I have to sort myself out before I implode."

April looked up at me through her long dark lashes and I gripped the bench with my fingers to stop me from taking her in my arms and letting her know exactly how she made me feel. *If only she knew what she really wanted…*maybe then I would stand a chance.

I reached out to hold the side of her face in my hand and she rested it gently against the curve, still holding my gaze. "I miss you, Emerus Forrester."

A chemical reaction surged through my veins at the mention of my name upon her lips, a sound so powerful that it would bring me to my knees if she asked. I thrilled at her touch; and my heart thundered in my chest. Her proximity was intoxicating. I suddenly understood how she found it difficult to breathe at times; only *her* reaction was not motivated by me. I yearned for her to see me the way that I drank in her very presence.

"Did I miss the midnigh' tea-par'y?" a familiar voice chimed from the doorway.

I returned my hand slowly to my side, turning only slightly to greet Geraldine. "We were just having an early drink," I replied in greeting. "You're welcome to join us."

"I'm actually going to head back up now," April retorted, the discomfort of Geraldine's presence apparent on her features. "Good night, Geraldine. Night, M, thanks for the chat…and the marvellous drink."

"Any time," I replied, enjoing her every lithe movement as she strolled out of the kitchen without a second glance.

"Well, she's cer'ainly a strange girl," Geraldine clicked, moving to rest where April had previously stood. April's replacement seemed uncomfortably close. "Very good a' wha' she does though."

"Oh?" I felt my eyes narrow in mild scrutiny.

"You know, with all the work she's been doing for Lucas. She seems to have done wonders for him. I don' just mean professionally," Geraldine mused. "Have you noticed the way he dotes upon her now? He must have really missed her all those months, poor dear."

"Hmm," I replied, wondering where Geraldine's sudden prying had emerged from. She had always seemed a quiet, unobtrusive woman. Now I wondered if I had misjudged her. "Well, that's between them, Geraldine. Now if you'll excuse me, I'm going to hit the sack."

I woke to get dressed for my run and remembered the snow outside. I didn't have the right gear to go jogging through the snow, so

I decided to head down to the gym instead. To my surprise Darius was pumping some iron by the far window, steadily lifting a set of dumbbells to an old Linkin Park album, and dressed in his traditional regalia: his bare torso.

"Isn't it a little early for you to be pumping iron?" I taunted.

"Nope."

"Come on, Dario, it's before midday. You're never even out of *bed* before midday!" I pressed.

"I've got to work a little harder nowadays to keep this awesome chest of mine," he strained.

"It wouldn't have anything to do with a certain girl, would it?" I pried.

"Yes. What's it to you? You and Lucas have already said more than your fair share."

"Hey, hey, don't get touchy. I happen to like Alex. For you."

"Just like you and April," he shot back.

I froze. "You better be careful about repeating things like that around here," I warned.

"Come on, it's so obvious. She's got it bad for you."

"Darius, I'm warning you."

"I don't understand why you don't just ask her about it," he continued. "Everyone knows you have feelings for her."

"Yes, I do," I conceded, knowing that the truth had been revealed at St Paul's back in June. "But if you haven't noticed, she's our brother's girlfriend. I would never do that to Lucas."

"He's going to notice sooner or later. I wonder if he'll fall down dead with shock…he's never had a girl break-up with him before!"

"Darius! She isn't going to break up with him," I forewarned. "Not on account of me, anyway. Just drop it."

"Who's breaking up with who?"

I groaned inwardly. *Good work idiot!* I wanted to throw something to clip Darius across the head.

"No-one's breaking up with anyone, Lucas," I said, glaring at Darius from across the room. "Except maybe Alex when she comes to her senses."

"And it's "whom" not "who", FYI," Darius offered smugly.

I intensified the glare in Darius' direction.

"Steady on, since when have you become a grammar Nazi?" Lucas asked with a flick of his fringe. "So I guess it's a Forrester boys' work out. Who wants to spot for me?"

"Wow! If I could take a picture right now, it'd be the highest selling photo of the century!" Alex chimed some time later. "All three, half-naked, Forrester boys!"

Darius sat up to meet her overwhelmed expression.

"Sorry, did I say that out loud?" she asked, her face turning crimson as she turned to leave, camera in hand.

Darius and Lucas fell into fits of hysterical laughing, making their way across the floor to slap the other across the back in lively banter. Their playfulness slowly turned into an all-out playful brawl, throwing one another across the room in between convulsions of hilarity. I smiled at their amusement, suddenly nostalgic for the younger years in my memory of the same foolhardy banter.

"Ick! Get some clothes on! It's almost lunch time," Aggie announced. "Scrap that…take a shower!"

"Ohhhhhh! You aren't getting away that easily," Darius growled, hunched over as he slowly made his way towards her.

"Oh, no you don't! I'm far too old to rumble with you boys!" she protested, a mixture of alarm and amusement encapsulating her features.

Darius had her locked around the waist in an instant, carrying her over his shoulder to the centre of the floor and dropping her straight down onto the mats. I cringed with delight, waiting for her reaction. With a lithe flick of her foot she tripped Darius straight onto his backside and launched herself at him, her face a look of mock revenge. Lucas crouched beside them in glee, coaxing Darius to return to the fray. I stood a safe distance away, intrigued by the sudden interest of frivolity.

"You asked for this one, Aggie!" Lucas hooted.

"My money's on the Aggis," I howled. "Darius' going to get whooped!"

With one arm around Darius' neck in a fierce head-lock, Aggie swooped out with her foot and rear-ended the unsuspecting Lucas; who howled with mock indignation and pulled her out from beneath Darius. I found myself clapping in support as Lucas lifted her across his shoulders and began to spin her through the air, much to Aggie's horror.

"That's not fair!" she bellowed. "I'm always outnumbered!"

"Not always, my dear!"

I barely had time to notice our newest visitor before I was tackled from the side and thrown roughly onto a startled but lively Darius.

"Oh! You have to get your husband to save you now?" Darius taunted as he clawed his way out from beneath Leicester and me.

"When you *children* are done, lunch is ready," Mother announced above the chaos.

"Thank heavens for that!" Aggie cried, finally being flung back onto the mats after her long flight above Lucas' head.

"Naw, you love it!" Lucas chanted. "You know you want a rematch!"

"Only if you stinky boys have a shower first!" she retorted as Leicester helped her to her feet. "And for crying out loud you Forrester boys, get a shirt on! I don't need to witness every movement of your show-pony flexing biceps!"

"Oh, you're just jealous!" Darius taunted, making a great display of flexing each individual muscle across his robust chest.

I laughed at Aggie's irritation and grabbed my shirt, flinging it across my shoulders as I headed up stairs to follow my sister's advice and take a shower. I was still smirking at the earlier banter, and so distracted by the morning thrill of horsing around and feeling like I was fifteen years younger that I failed to notice Geraldine until I collided with her at the top of the stairwell.

"Oh, sorry," I muttered, holding out my hands to steady the person I had just rammed off the top step. I winced as I looked up to meet her amused face.

She stared at me for far too long, her keen eyes travelling the length of my bare torso before she flashed an eager smile at me.

Geraldine did not remove her hands from my forearms, which she pinned quite firmly. She blushed slightly as her gaze returned to my face, an expression of hopeful inquiry illuminating her brown eyes.

I went to excuse myself abruptly and retrieve my arms from her grip, when April stepped out onto the corridor from her bedroom across the landing. At first her eyes grew wide with astonishment as she appraised me with her opal coloured eyes; then her face flushed a becoming shade of pink and she averted her gaze to the floor. The ring on my finger burned with an intense mauve hue and I stared at her in disbelief and wonderment. *Did I really have that effect on her?*

April regained herself and held up her chin, her long elegant neck poised almost defiantly: *she was fighting it*. Then she noticed Geraldine as if for the first time, standing just feet away from her, facing me in close proximity, with her hands wrapped around my arms as though in an embrace.

I was still entranced by the idea that April found me appealing at any level at all, even at a base one, that I hesitated to remove my hands from Geraldine's grasp. In that instant April's face slowly transformed to an expression of disbelief, her eyebrows furrowing across her brow in confusion, before finally raising them in astonishment at the sight before her.

I hastily removed my arms and took a step to pass Geraldine, heading for April, as I felt the change in sensation of the metal upon my skin, the iridescent glow of vivid green reflected from the ring as I tilted my face to meet hers, and I was stunned to encounter the impact of her fierce loathing, so evident upon her face. *Jealousy.* For some inexplicable reason, she felt jealous and betrayed. I couldn't fathom what to say to her: how could I assume so blatantly her feelings for me and reassure her it wasn't true?

She lowered her eyes, stepping lightly past Geraldine and beyond my grasp, hastily making her retreat downstairs. I inhaled deeply before allowing the breath to slip from my lungs slowly. This was crazy…I must be hallucinating. I had to get out of here and fast.

I threw myself under the shower and dressed swiftly, taking the keys to Lucas' bike from the foyer on the way out the front door. The roads would be too slippery for a car, but the snow had melted enough for a steady bike ride through the ridges of the foothills. I dressed swiftly and kicked the Yamaha R1 into gear before quickening out the gate, letting the biting wind whip about my face through the helmet visor.

I rode through the cutting wind and icy conditions, along narrow windy roads and through dark channels cut into the sheer mountain ledges, absorbing the wintry enchantment as I gazed out into the valleys and frozen snaking rivers below. I climbed higher into the Alps, passing wooden lodges and glass chalets, and admiring the unique landscape and infrastructures of the Alpine regions.

The wind whisked against the bike with a throbbing force, and the air began to feel lighter as I rode through the lifting altitude. The road narrowed further still until the visible signs of humanity disappeared, where the snow obstructed the road and I was forced to pull up the bike where I could no longer continue.

The view from my vantage point was incredible as I stood to engross myself in the majestic scenery. I surveyed across the ranges, whose snow capped peaks stretched for miles in every direction, disappearing into a shroud of mist and clouds above.

I reached into the lining of one side of my inner jacket pocket and retrieved a small glass decanter, removing the lid and throwing back a mouthful of the warm liquid, feeling the sensation burn down my throat and into my belly. I tilted my head back for more, holding the flask to my pining lips. Why was the insatiable quench always so much worse when my heart was on the grill? Just like those dark non-ending days after Penny had left well over a year ago…

And then a ray of light had entered my life. I stared at the flask and wondered what April would think of me if she saw me slaving away to this amber liquid…

I felt the cool glass against my lip and tasted its tempting remnants like water in the desert.

Then closing my eyes, I threw the bottle far out over the ledge, listening to it whistle as it was carried out on a passing gust along the mountainside.

I opened my eyes and reached into the other side of my jacket, retrieving a small velvet box, opening it gently to admire the single ring inside. I admired the perfect craftsmanship of the near identical design to the ring upon my finger, and its partner, some miles away through the snowy peaks, on April's finger. This golden band would never change colour, or burn the flesh as the original rings had the power to do; but I hoped that it would fit perfectly beside its twin upon her hand.

I had found a jeweller in Dubai who specialised in the remodelling and design of antiques. He had not disappointed with his final product, complete with a flush sitting row of diamonds across the shoulders, flanking the central masterpiece: a single opal stone, the same colour as her eyes.

Originally I had planned on waiting for as long as it took for her to make up her mind, but I could see that she fought it more than ever. I would lose my chance if I waited much longer.

My fists clenched by my side; this would mean stepping into territory that I had never dared to allow myself to go before. The impact any action that I would take had the potential to take its toll on Lucas in ways that I couldn't be responsible for. But he had to realise it soon that he would have to give her up. I knew without a doubt now her feelings for me, and I had given her time to accept them for what they are. But could I take the wheel and drive her to realisation with a selfless heart? *No.* I couldn't do it.

I remembered back to that night just two weeks ago, as I had poured my heart out onto the tray of revelation for her to see on that dance floor. She had not shied away, had not forbidden my love, and had not banished me from her life. To my utter astonishment and gratification, she had laid out her own inner response, without even the slightest awareness.

My left hand had been resting on the curve of her lower back, and she had not borne witness to her own betrayal, as the enchanted ring had quivered with a fierce intensity, but had not burned my flesh at all. I knew that it had glowed burgundy.

How did she still not realise that she loved me?

Was I expected to stand by forever and watch her life pass by without me in it?

I replaced the box back within the confines of my pocket, beside my heaving chest and wildly beating heart.

37. That's When I Think of You…

April Falls

And that has made all the difference. – Robert Frost

"A few of us are going for a light trek through the snow, now that the sun's out," Lucas announced. "Do you want to come?"

"Oh. Ah…I think I'll stay where it's warm," I replied, wrapping my arms around my body as though I were cold, despite the enveloping warmth I enjoyed from the heat of the open fireplace in the lounge room.

"Are you sure?" he asked, his lovely mouth dipping slightly at the ends to form a frown. He strode across the room to where I stood near the window, watching Leicester, Darius and Alex throw football sized snowballs at each other beyond the pane glass. Lucas tilted my chin up to meet his gaze, searching my eyes with his inquiring green ones. My heart flipped lightly at his touch. "Are you sure you're okay?"

"I'm fine, really. I know this is a holiday and all, but I'm in a writing mood and I would like to work on your book for a little while. I'm supposed to have a first draft ready before February," I replied, sincerely wishing to bury myself in the task.

Lucas nodded, although I detected his doubt in my response. "You're worried about M."

I shrugged, caught off guard by the sudden mention of his name and averted my eyes back to the hooligans outside.

"I know he's been gone for a while, but he'll be fine," Lucas coaxed, pulling me to his chest for a light embrace and stowing a kiss upon my forehead. "He does this sort of thing every now and then to clear his mind. His job takes a lot out of him, you know."

"I know," I replied quietly, grateful that Lucas couldn't see my face right now, buried into his chest.

I sighed heavily: Lucas had no idea about the depth of my connection to his brother lately. It was more than just the paranormal rings that now bound me to M. I couldn't even explain it to myself. But I did worry about him, constantly, and especially now, out in the volatile elements, with nothing but a bike for protection. I hugged Lucas fiercely, desperate to chase away the unbridled fear that I harboured at the thought of him never returning…just like Hugh.

"Stay safe," I managed to say, pulling myself free from his hold and smiling up into his angelic features, which comforted me only somewhat as he turned to leave. "Watch my sister, will you?"

"Of course," he replied over his shoulder, and I could tell he was amused by my over-protectiveness. "I wouldn't leave her all to Darius' safe keeping."

I typed furiously for an hour, pouring my energy and concentration into the narrative that would be Lucas Forrester's life account to date. I grinned to myself infrequently, admiring the dominant and enchanting traits that were Lucas as well as the many exploits of his busy and manic lifestyle.

I felt exhausted after the hour, wondering how Lucas maintained any semblance of normality, until I encountered the traces of his strongholds and support: his family. Only then did I realise how important these few moments of solace were to his existence, the only place in the world where he was treated as Lucas Forrester, affectionate son and brother. I realised how much he thrived in both worlds, as though one needed the other to balance his quest for success, and just how perfectly for Lucas the forces of each world held him up the way they did.

Lucas would never be free of the screaming fans, the obsessed Pennys of the world, and the inability to walk down a road and filter through unnoticed. But that's the way he wished it. He was fulfilled in all that he did, and he wasn't going to give it up. And nor should he. This was who Lucas was: the entire package, to be taken or left the way that it was offered. I admired him for his persistence to be received by the entertainment industry and fans of the big screen.

I more than admired him; I felt honoured to be called his friend and colleague. I loved him. *But not as a woman loves a man*, I realised. Not as someone who wants to spend her life with, and grow old with him.

The absolution astounded me.

I sighed and hid beneath the covers of my bed, burying my head amongst the pillows. How could I do this to Lucas? I would have to tell him, and soon. How would he react? Did his feelings run deeper than mine in a romantic sense, or did he really love me as a dear, precious friend, the way that I held him?

The sound of a motorcycle approaching lifted me from my pondering and I tore across the room to watch as M drew near to the house through the muddy sleet upon the cobbled driveway, and then disappeared inside the old stable house. Without a second thought I stepped into my shoes and almost floated down the stairwell. He hadn't even stepped out of the thatched enclosure, replaced the helmet upon a shelf and turned straight into my open arms before I reached him.

"Oh, I was so worried!" I crooned, closing my eyes tightly as I took him in, through layers of protective bike wear.

He didn't reply at first. He seemed a little overwhelmed by my eager reception. *Maybe I was a little over the top sometimes*. I was just glad to see him alive.

"Because I was on a bike?" he hedged.

"Mm-hm."

"Of course I was going to come back," he said matter-of-factly.

"You don't know that."

He stroked my hair momentarily and went to step around me, as Geraldine walked in to the stable. I groaned quietly; however, I knew M heard me, because he stifled a chuckle into his fisted palm.

"I heard the bike and though' I'd come to see tha' you're okay, Emerus. I've kept some lunch back for you, and desser', of course, since you skipped breakfast! I'll return to the kitchen and warm i' up for you, shall I?" she asked pleasantly. She barely noticed me anymore.

Emerus. Geraldine always called him by his full name, as though she alone had the privilege to do so. I noticed him wince when she had said his name, as though he bawked at the sound of it.

"Thank you, Geraldine," he replied, although I detected a sense of apprehension in his tone. Had he finally noticed her overt display of attention this week?

I waited while he undressed from his outer layer of protective clothing and then linked my arm through his as we began the trek across the sludgy snow. We were about to enter the main entrance of the house when M gently withdrew his arm from mine, pausing in the grand entryway. I stared up at him in confusion, bewildered by his sudden withdrawal. He didn't meet my gaze, although his displeasure was locked in amidst his gentle features.

"April, I'm sorry. I'm finding this more difficult than I thought I would," he confessed, finally meeting my eyes. "I don't think this is appropriate any more. Not when there are other people involved."

Other people? I froze at his insinuation. *Geraldine!* Surely he didn't mean Lucas, for Lucas already knew of my friendly affection for M…to a degree.

"Are you saying we can't be *friends* any more?" I felt like I was twelve and in the school yard again.

"No. But I think it's only fair for all those involved, to have a little space between us," Justice replied slowly. "You are my brother's girlfriend, after all."

I understood what he was saying, but I thought that we were past that…or exempt from that. They were both my dear friends, in their own ways, and I needed them both. I wasn't prepared to let either of them go yet. I knew I was being selfish while he had placed Lucas, Geraldine and me above his own feelings for so long now. I had expected too much of him, and now he was past patience with me. I knew I deserved his rejection.

I nodded in understanding. I would do this for him if he needed it. And what lay between M and Geraldine was none of my business.

"Fair enough. Then I'll see you at dinner," I replied simply, turning and heading back to my suite.

Try as I may, I couldn't keep my eyes off M and Geraldine, whom he seemed to find welcome company over the meal. The more she looked up at him from beneath her long lashes, and lightly brushed his arm from time to time, the more I sought Lucas' affection for comfort, even though I was not listening to his conversation with Leicester and Rick across the table.

Evening meals always finished late at the Forresters, which kept with the traditional European custom; and after several courses of progressively strong alcoholic beverages, Aggie was well prepared for her promised Sing Star karaoke. I groaned silently, thinking desperately for an excuse to leave early for bed.

Lucas must have sensed my foreboding and quickly scooped me up into his arms, carrying me the entire way to the lounge room to prevent my escape.

"I hear you're quite the karaoke queen when you get started!" he teased. "Darius told me all about it!"

"Oh, did he?" I asked, glaring at a bemused Darius, who had maintained a safe distance.

"That was another time and place," I said meaningfully. "And with far more wine in me than this!"

"Well, we can remedy that!" Lucas hooted. "Who's up for another glass?"

I groaned, this time out loud, covering my face with my hands.

"She used to be the real life of the party, once," Alex chimed, with a challenge in her glance. "Not that you'd be able to tell nowadays."

"Hey! I'm doing just fine, thanks!" I retorted, mildly irritated by her lack of sensitivity. "How about you being the first one to show us all just how to get the party started, Alex?"

Her expression turned to one of mortification at the suggestion, her face colouring brightly, and she gripped Darius' arm for support.

"Sounds like an idea," Darius chortled. "How about a duet?"

"Me? First?" Alex stammered.

"You and me, babe!" Darius confirmed, lifting her to her feet and sauntering over to the mic.

"*Now* I'm starting to warm up," I mused, raising an eyebrow at Alex as she grimly accepted the other mic from an eager Darius. I settled back into Lucas' arms, resting my back against his chest. These Forrester boys aren't lacking for a sturdy chest, I admired, feeling the outline of Lucas' trim figure beneath his shirt; and remembering the same sensation when I had fallen asleep on both M and Darius. I would probably be the most envied woman on the planet if *that* piece of information were ever leaked…

"Your turn will come, sister," Alex warned, though the humour had begun to return to her voice.

I realised quickly how little sleep I had had the night before. The entertainment had only been in full throttle for an hour when my eyelids began to close. I was comfortable and warm against Lucas, and appreciated the lively atmosphere that the Forresters provided. I sank slowly into a restful doze, listening within the recesses of my mind to the mostly tuneful, but sometimes woeful, charade that continued around me.

"…she has a habit of doing this." *Darius.*

"And she hasn't even sung yet!" *Leicester.*

"Wake her up and make her sing. I've missed her Cold Chisel and Leanne Rimes." *Darius.*

"She really sang those?" *Lucas.*

"Pitiful song choice, I know. But she can wail when she warms up!" *Darius.*

"It doesn't quite look like she's up to the challenge tonight, though, Dar." *Lucas.*

"Awe, shame. Next time, she sings first!" *Darius.*

"Who hasn't had a turn yet?" *Olivia.*

"Oh, Mum! I believe that my eldest brother has not yet serenaded us with one of his good tunes. It's not karaoke if M doesn't sing!" *Aggie.*

"Emerus?" *Olivia.*

Groan. "I'll put you all to sleep if I sing now!" *M.*

"Come on!" *Aggie.*

"You're a sucker for punishment, Aggie." *M.* "Alright, I'll sing. What've we got?"

My breathing shallowed and I hoped that no one noticed I was more alert than I had been before. I wasn't going to miss the opportunity to hear M sing again. His voice had been husky, almost haunting, in a very appealing, masculine sense, and I remembered thinking that I could have listened to him sing all day.

"Well, for our Australian friends, this one's for you," he said in mock dedication. "A little more of *1927*."

My breathing almost ceased in anticipation: it was all I could do to keep my eyelids from springing open to drink in the atmosphere.

The rock beat began immediately, and I was familiar with this number now as well.

"When I'm lost in a strange place
Scared and alone
When I'm wishing for home…
That's when I think of you…"

"…When I'm caught in the cross fire
Of wrongs making right
When I wake in the night…"

I opened my eyes and met his instantly.

"That's when I think of you…"

I felt my body stiffen at his words; the memory of seeing him in the wee hours of the night this morning had haunted me all day. I always woke in the night when I was near him but not with him. I dared to hope that maybe he had done the same…

"…If not for the thought of you
The promise of dreams come true…
I'd go mad…if it wasn't for you…"

I couldn't tear my eyes away from him, even though he did frequently throughout the song.

*"...When I'm a long way from loving
So far from home
When it feels like I'm in the twilight zone
And I just can't make it through..."*

I hoped that Lucas couldn't feel the drumming of my heart beneath my shirt as I stared out from beneath my haven of Lucas' arms. No one noticed that I had opened my eyes…no one except the man with the glorious voice holding the microphone. I found myself longing for his words to be for my ears alone, as they had on that day two weeks ago.

If I could clear the room and be alone with him while he sang from his heart to mine, meaning every word as he had before! I suddenly yearned to be all he thought of, just like the words of the song. His gaze hovered on me only briefly as he continued to thunder out the bridge, mesmerising his audience.

*"I'm always thinking of you
It's all that I can do…
I'd go mad…not being with you…"*

I stared at the shaky hand resting on Lucas' shirt and folded my hand into a fist to conceal the iridescent burgundy ring from Lucas lest he notice that I was awake. As M sang the final words to his song and handed the mic back to Aggie, who was clapping furiously with the rest of the spectators, I stared in utter amazement at the ring upon M's finger as he conspicuously retrieved it into his trouser pocket.

He had seen the colour of his own ring: Burgundy.

I swallowed at the realisation as M took his place on the lounge beside Geraldine, as calm as a cucumber; he didn't even acknowledge me. *How long had he known?* A thought occurred to me and I shook at the very idea: *had it turned that colour before?*

"Hey, sleepy. Did we wake you?" Lucas asked in a low, tired voice, tightening his grasp on me in a small gesture of comfort and apology.

I swallowed hard before answering him, afraid that my mild hysteria might be noticed. "No, no. I was listening to your brother sing. It was beautiful."

"He's not bad, old M. Not bad at all," Lucas complimented, nodding to his brother across the room.

"But I think I'll call it a night," I said, yawning uncontrollably and then covering my mouth in horror at my poor manners.

"Awe, just one song?" Darius pleaded.

"No, I really need to sleep," I insisted, standing to leave.

"Come on, Apes! Just one for the road!" Darius appealed.

"Enough, Darius. If she wants to leave, then let her go," M interrupted, every façade of his face a testament to the fact that he was the directing hand of the Forrester family, and whose word was final.

Darius ceased his entreaty immediately, reclining back against the couch beside Alex. I gave a courteous nod of my head before I left. Lucas squeezed my hand firmly, with an imploring curiosity in his eyes. I knew what he wanted to know. I saw the yearning in his being as he breathed heavily with expectation. My heart crumbled within my chest. The fall was going to be a big one.

In an earlier time I would have felt obligated, like I had with Andy. But I knew with certainty that I did not owe it to Lucas to leave him with a bittersweet memory for the road. I wasn't sure of the future, but I trusted that someone knew what was best for me, and I was sure now that it wasn't a future with Lucas.

I smiled at him with a bittersweet farewell of my own, reaching out to trace the outline of his strong jaw line and cheek, resting my thumb against his lips to press in return. "I'll talk to you later," I said with an audio level for his ears alone.

As I climbed the stairs I traded one burden for another; my mind was set in my decision regarding Lucas, which alleviated the first burden. How was I going to tell him my decision, while allowing for the least possible casualty rate? And a third conundrum presented itself as I climbed: what was I going to do about M? Was the choice still mine to make, or had I foregone the opportunity already?

38. *Confessions of the Heart*

I had sensed that Alex was still enthralled with the entertainment downstairs and wouldn't be up to bed for some time yet. I knew I wouldn't be able to sleep either. I opened the curtains that looked out into the mystic courtyard, now blanketed in a soft fall of snow. The moon shone brightly, illuminating the historic sandstone cottage that housed Lucas' emerald green Porsche and motorcycle.

My mind replayed M's rejection this afternoon. *I'm finding this more difficult than I thought I would…I don't think this is appropriate any more…Not when there are other people involved…*

I fumbled for my laptop and began typing, slowly shifting through the pile of confusion in my mind. *Emerus Forrester*: The ever-dependable, directive right-hand, and stronghold of the Forrester family. The sword in battle, and the shield in defence. The turning point in times of crisis. The hand to hold for comfort; and the caring, nurturing hand during times of illness and grief.

Emerus Forrester: The older brother, who would die for his family; and even for a stranger – *me*. The one who pushes his own will and agenda aside for those who need his assistance. The one willing to give up a life of travel and displacement, in the hope of settling down to find a true home for his heart.

But where was his true home and heart? Was he prepared to give it all up…for another…for me? Was that what he meant when he said he wanted to settle down, and didn't know if that place would be England? Could I hope that he was prepared to move indefinitely abroad…as far away as the southern continent? Could I ask that of him?

He loved me…I was sure of it. I was awe-struck by the very notion. I left the laptop by the window and lay down upon the large four-poster bed that was mine for the week. I lay upon my side and held a pillow to my chest. I felt so small upon such a large surface, balling myself up as I cradled the cushion. I knew it wasn't Lucas that I yearned to be near during these moments of isolation…it was M: my friend, my comfort and my husband by legal default. And I wasn't prepared to give him up so soon. If I divorced him at all, I would be divorcing my true other half, and I may never get him back. I wasn't prepared to lose him for the world now. There had to be a way to make it work…

Oh Lord…what do I do?

A fond image intruded upon my thoughts and I tried to shake it away lest it be my complete undoing. But there he stood, atop the stairwell, looking altogether glorious in not much at all – a shirt swung casually over his brawn shoulders. I buried my face into the pillow. I had to get out of here!

M

I turned the ring on my finger in a clockwise rotation, holding it out slightly from my skin – which only succeeded in burning the fingers on my right hand as I did so. I gave up and waited for the burning to end. In truth I had become resigned to the sensation of blazing heat on my finger; I felt strangely at ease with its nuptial representation.

"That colour's most becoming on you, M," Aggie mused, leaning over my shoulder to examine the unusual violet hue. "What does it mean? What's she thinking?"

"Wouldn't that be kind of personal, Aggie?" I asked, raising an eyebrow at her sudden interest.

"Well, it can't be that personal, if *you* know," she replied.

Lucas threw me an inquiring glance. The notion that I could read April's heart seemed to disturb him immensely.

"I don't know what she's *thinking*," I replied, standing to excuse myself for the night. "I only have an idea what she's *feeling*."

"And…?" Aggie persisted.

"You'll have to ask her," I replied.

"You won't give up anything?" she persevered.

"Not this one. Night." I strolled from the room, glancing quickly at Lucas, who returned my fleeting look with a perplexed brow.

"What does purple usually mean?" I heard Aggie ask innocently as I climbed the stairwell.

I grinned as the hysterical voices of Darius and Leicester reached me on the landing.

"What?...Oh...Really?" Aggie's strained voice trailed off as I headed for my room. "I thought that was just a myth."

The digital clock beside my bed read midnight. It didn't feel that late. I must be acclimatised to witching hour from the consistently late nights...or early mornings. I surveyed the bed I had been sleeping in. *Why did they make them so large nowadays?* I thought of April down the hall in hers and was grateful for the hundredth time that she had chosen not to share a room with Lucas.

I gave the bed a miss and set up the laptop to peruse over some progressive drafts for the Sheehans.

I hadn't been working long when a light knock sounded on my door. I turned in surprise to greet the late hour visitor and groaned inwardly. *Geraldine.* She was dressed in a sheer night-dress and gown.

"Geraldine? Is there something the matter?"

"No. Nothin's the matter, Emerus. I was hoping we could talk?" she asked shyly, a grimace playing at the edges of her mouth as she closed the door behind her.

"It's kind of late. Can't it wait until morning?"

"Emerus, I've never been one for sweet words, or a pretty face. But I like to think that we're good friends," she said, averting her eyes from mine and chewing on her bottom lip.

I drew in a deep breath, not liking the sound of where this was headed. I had dealt with unrequited persuasive women before, but usually in bars, or clubs, or restaurants, never under my own roof. This was going to be a delicate mission.

"I always think about you lying up in your room all alone. The truth is; I understand what it's like to feel so alone."

She walked slowly towards me, her eyes glancing at me intermittently. I was not feeling inclined to deal with this right now.

"Geraldine…" I sighed, absently running a hand through my lengthening hair.

"I know I'm only a house hand, Emerus, but I think we can help each other. Wha' tha' Penny McClellan did to you was an absolute disgrace. I'll never forgive her for betraying us like tha'," Geraldine said vehemently.

I stood very still, allowing her words to resonate.

"How did Penny betray *us*, Geraldine?"

"She was supposed to be my friend. I was supposed to help her, and she said she'd help me in return," Geraldine said quietly, swishing across the floor in her slippers.

I creased my brows in contemplation, allowing her to come closer, in the hope that she would divulge more.

"How was she going to help you, Geraldine?" I pressed, encouragement lacing my tone.

"She said tha' if I gave her Lucas, she would give you t' me. Instead, she gave you to tha' *Joey* down the hall," Geraldine replied, bitterness resounding in her thick voice.

I eyed the sudden twitch in my forearms.

"And did you give her Lucas?" I asked slowly.

"She wanted the journal, and the rings. But it was too late. She saw them on your finger and April's that night at the club where Darius was playing."

The Dungeon.

"How did she know about the journal and the rings, Geraldine?"

"I showed her the journal when she used to stay at Erravilla…when she was supposed to be together with you. I told her tha' someday I hoped I would find the rings and be able to use them. She had already guessed my affections for you, you see; and told me of her true feelings for Lucas."

"But Geraldine…*you* introduced me to Penny…"

I struggled to contain the fury that simmered just below the surface.

"Aye, tha's wha' she asked me t' do. She didna' know how else to get close to Lucas…an'…" Geraldine averted her eyes, the guilt burning red across her cheeks. "She said you'd be the easier one to win over…I hope you are no' angry with me, Emerus."

I sat back against the bedpost in disbelief. I felt the biggest fool that had ever lived. To have fallen for Penny and her wicked games…And I'd blamed Lucas too.

"No, Geraldine, I'm not angry with you: I'm angry at myself. Go on," I coaxed, barely able to look at her.

"She found the rings in the attic just before Lucas banished her from Erravilla and lef' them there for safe keeping, planning on returning to fetch them and trick Lucas int' wearing one. She took the journal with her so tha' no one else could read i'. She threatened me no' t' tell anyone. Penny was so mad tha' the reporter had beaten her t' them. She said she wanted her dead. She thought tha' was the only way to keep her from Lucas forever."

I winced at the notion, pumping my palms into fists by my side.

"She made me tell her all sorts of information about Lucas and April: where they were going, wha' they did, wha' they talked about. I knew it was wrong but she said I would never see my brother and little nieces again if I didna' obey her. Penny became so obsessed; I didna' realise how derailed she was in the beginning. Och, I never would have hur' you."

I hung my head between my hands, trying to make sense of the information. "What about the abduction?"

"I didna' know what she was going t' do. All she asked was when Lucas was going t' be back a' the fla' in Park Lane."

"And you told her?" I surmised.

She nodded sheepishly. "Aye. I had no idea tha' nigh' where you and tha' reporter were going, or tha' she planned on marrying you to her for life! Tha's why I'm here…I can help you break away from the curse."

This was worse than I had imagined: all these noble *people so eager to help April and I break the* chains *of matrimony…* What they failed to comprehend was that I did not want to be freed from these *chains*! I would do almost anything to remain tied to her for life.

"Geraldine, you and your father are the only ones who keep the master set of keys to Erravilla. Did you give the key to Penny that night…the night she spent with Lucas?" I braced myself for her response, unsure if I wanted the truth.

"Aye. She though' she could seduce him. I know I shouldna' done it; bu' I couldna' stand to see how she treated you; and you were so unaware…so in love with the idea of who Penny was. I wanted you to see wha' she was really like so tha' you'd le' her go. Instead, it only caused a great big fight between you and Lucas. I'm so sorry, Master Emerus."

I groaned. *Lucas had been telling the truth.*

"When I confronted her about her betrayal to me, she said tha' there was another way to break the enchantment of the rings." Geraldine looked up into my eyes with determination and expectation, and I felt a deep pity for the woman. Penny had used Geraldine's innocent feelings for me and had turned her into a fool too.

I gathered her into my arms for a chaste embrace. "Thank you for telling me this, Geraldine; you've been a true friend to me."

The door of my room opened as I stood there, my arms lightly around Geraldine as she crooned softly into my chest.

April Falls

I was simply humming as I ran lightly down the corridor, padding quietly along the stone tiles as I made my way towards his room. The house was dark, lit only by the occasional wall lamp, but I listened for other signs of human activity; I wanted my presence and whereabouts to remain anonymous.

I paused just outside M's door, my heart hammering in my chest, and rested lightly to slow my rapid breathing before gently turning the old brass doorknob. The door was heavy set, like all the others in the timeless house, and opened slowly as I snuck around the door.

I inhaled instantly at the scene before me, shaking my head in dismay and scurrying back against the thick wooden door like one of the blind mice meeting with the Carver's wife. M met my glance over Geraldine's threadbare shoulder, where her long chestnut hair had fallen loosely. His arms held her to him as she embraced him with fierce determination. I thought I heard soft murmuring coming from his chest, but I didn't wait for confirmation.

I tore myself back along the corridor, passing my room across from the landing and headed straight towards the door adjacent from mine. I braced myself momentarily, preparing myself single-mindedly for what I was about to do, before letting myself in. I swiped at the flyaway tears with the back of my hand, which burned my cheek on the way through.

If he can break the enchantment so easily, then so can I! Why let him have all the fun doing it?

I slid myself beneath the covers lithely, throwing off my wrap as I turned myself in. His breathing was light; he wasn't asleep yet.

"Lucas…"

"April?"

I wrapped my arms around him and rested my cheek against his warm back.

"Are you okay? Your face is wet."

"I'm fine," I replied curtly.

"I thought you went to sleep a while ago," he said, covering my hands with his own.

"I couldn't sleep…I tried to type for a while…I've been thinking about what you said…"

His body went rigid; his breathing was shallow as though he would cease to inhale oxygen at all. I softly kissed the ridge of his shoulder blades, feeling his body respond instantly to my touch. He turned to face me, cupping my face with his large hands, his features indeterminable in the darkness. His lips brushed mine gently; the warmth of his breath fused with mine.

"Is this what you really want?" he whispered, his mouth meeting mine again, this time with more urgency.

"Yes," I replied simply, melting into his acceptance.

M

I pulled myself free of Geraldine's embrace, furious at my lack of insight and timing. April hadn't even waited for an explanation; I saw her own conclusions bare on her face.

"Who was tha'?" Geraldine asked, dabbing at her tears.

I strode towards the door without a glance or explanation.

"I' was April, wasna' i'?" she called after me. "You love her, don' you?"

I halted in my pursuit; my hand already upon the door handle. "Aye. With all my heart."

I headed straight for her room but it was empty. *Bollocks!* She couldn't have gotten far. I took the stairs swiftly in pairs, heading straight for the kitchen. There were no lights on at all; the only illumination was provided by the soldiering firelight from the lounge room. She was nowhere to be found. All the internal doors were still locked. *Where could she be?*

A cold shiver ran the length of my spine and in one moment of revelation, I knew the answer: *Lucas.* I had driven her to his eager arms. The ring upon my finger quivered violently, and I dared not to look at the omen. I knew it wasn't burgundy, for the heat seared from the metal upon my flesh, leaving an emotional mark far deeper than the physical one I would see tomorrow. She didn't love Lucas; she was purely seeking consolation for her distressed heart. In no time at all, she would be lost to me forever. This time there was nothing I could do. It wasn't like the time with Andy; this time I had to let her go…

Fool! I chided myself. *Why didn't I confront her tonight after the song? She would have heard me out, I was sure. It had all been so clear…Why did I let her go?*

I knew that I could not charge into my brother's room and take her from him this time. I had stepped in before without warrant, and I would not do that to him again. This was her choice now.

I grabbed a bottle of 60-year-old Macmillan Scotch and took a seat in an armchair in the corner of the large living area near the fire. I watched the flames dance their Highland jig as I rocked gently, and sipped straight from Macmillan's fine Scottish glass neck. I could not sleep. And I did not stop drinking until she was gone. Every…last…drop.

I remember sensing the first light of dawn when the front door opened, and two sets of footsteps hastily exited, and somewhere in the weary recesses of my mind, a car had driven out of the property on this frosty winter morning…sometime later, one set of footsteps returned.

"M? Emerus?"

Mother.

"It doesn't look like he's slept much."

Aggie.

"He looks like hell."

Leicester.

"And he's been drinking again! Look at this empty bottle of Scotch! Pew! He smells like a homeless wreck!"

Aggie.

"The 1950 Macmillan!"

Mother.

A gentle hand pressed against my forehead. I kept my eyes shielded from sight, savouring the nurturing sensations of childhood, when the same cool hand had been placed upon my brow during bouts of sickness and tantrums.

"Are you unwell, Emerus?" Mother asked, her clear voice waking me sharply. "Well, I suppose that's obvious…"

I opened my eyes slowly to meet three sets of concerned gazes. "What time is it?" I asked, straining to read the mantle clock above the fireplace.

"Nine o' clock. We thought we'd let you sleep. You don't look so good, Emerus," Mother replied, eyeing me like I was a sick puppy.

"She's gone, M."

I hadn't noticed the fourth body standing somewhere behind the others. I strained to meet Lucas' sunken gaze.

"What do you mean, gone?" I demanded, rubbing my throbbing temples.

"She left early this morning, when I was still asleep. She left a note," Lucas offered, holding out a neatly folded piece of paper.

I've gone to return the keepsakes to their rightful place.
My love to all,
April

Lucas' words suddenly resonated in my mind: *she left early this morning…when I was still asleep.* I grabbed at the ring on my left finger, panic-stricken. *It was still there.* I threw Lucas an astonished glance. He slowly shook his head.

"It's not me she loves, brother," he said slowly, returning my glance with a sombre one of his own. "She eventually told me what had happened with you and Geraldine. She couldn't go through with it."

"What happened with you and Geraldine?" Mother inquired, her eyes narrowing.

"Nothing. Nothing at all," I replied. "But April would know that now anyway. If I'm still wearing this ring, then so is she."

"What does the note mean?" Aggie asked.

"I assume she intends to take the journal and the ring back to Erravilla," I replied. "Where's Geraldine?"

"But how can she leave the ring? I thought you couldn't take it off?" Aggie asked.

"Only death…Geraldine!" I called, straddling myself upright and doing my best to stride from the room without looking sea-sick.

"What's this got to do with her?" Mother persisted.

"Everything!" I retorted, cornering Geraldine in the kitchen. "Geraldine, does Penny know that Lucas and April are both here?"

The downcast expression on her face confirmed my fears. "Aye. Tha's why I told her to leave. You're all safer if April's no' here with you."

"What's Penny going to do to her?" I demanded, laying a firm hand upon her forearm.

"Nothin'…now," she replied, her guilt-ridden eyes examining the floor.

"Did you tell her where April's gone now?" I pressed.

"No. I just informed her tha' April has left indefinitely, and tha' she doesna' need t' worry abou' a thing. I explained i' all t'… April…on the way t' the airport," Geraldine replied. "I even told her about me coming to you las' night. I also told her tha' you love her still."

"And what did she say?" I asked.

"You wouldna' believe it, but she said she forgives me, an' understands why I did wha' I did," Geraldine confessed, finally meeting my gaze.

"Geraldine, do you have any idea where Penny might be?" I pressed.

"No. She never told me much at all. She said tha' if she told me, her life would be in danger. Which never made much sense t' me, Master Emerus."

"*Her* life would be in danger?" Lucas repeated in disbelief, raking a hand through his dishevelled hair. "That means…"

I sighed. "Someone far worse is behind all this."

"But why?" Lucas pondered out loud.

"It explains why Penny's been so elusive to the police," I mumbled. "Was it all a lie? From the very beginning?"

"How did she get involved with these people?" Lucas wondered, shaking at the thought. "And to think she was at *my* house for so long!"

"Never mind that now," Mother interjected. "Geraldine, dear, we have to get the police involved, you understand?"

"Aye, Ma'am," the younger woman replied sombrely.

"Lucas, I owe you an apology…or two," I admitted, meeting his incredulous stare. "About Penny…"

"Tha' was my fault, Lucas," Geraldine rushed. "I gave her the key t' your room tha' night."

"I was wrong, brother. You were right about her all along. I was a fool," I confessed.

He nodded simply, the betrayal evident from the intensity that had manifested in his sombre green eyes. "But you need to get to an airport, and fast. I don't trust Penny; and April's now an open target."

I searched his face for understanding, needing his approval before making my next move. "Your presence will endanger her, Lucas."

"It's not me who she wants, brother," he said gravely. "Go."

"Are you going to be all right?" I hedged.

"I'm gonna go shoot some darts," Lucas replied with the determination of a soldier heading for the front line, and turning on his heel.

I knew he was already bleeding, and I would speak with him again as soon as I could. "I'll call as soon as I reach Erravilla," I promised.

<u>Sir Walter Finnegan, last Earl of Erravilla Court</u>

I watched much over the next few months. I watched the way my son grew to delight in his new surroundings, realising that the boy had most probably been discontent in Ireland with his bore of a father. The curly haired child called Rupert grew in strength and stamina and had his early studies under Maisy's watchful eyes. There was no denying the child was mine in every way, except for the youthful healthy glow about him that had once been his mother's.

Rupert applied himself early to the teachings of Erravilla and its ways, ways that I hoped were not completely English, but also of the old ways I had known of home. The home, I realised, that I no longer wished to return to. It felt complete with my son running about its hedges and forests, riding the gallant stallions and swimming in the great pond beyond the fringe of the estate.

Maisy took full responsibility for the child as though he had always been there; perhaps part of her had been expecting a child all along, and was content to grasp what chance she had to rear one. She was more than a governess in his studies and social tutoring and more than a nanny for his sleep times and meal times. Indeed, I watched as Maisy dedicated her entire energy to the child's care and nurture, and felt an overwhelming sense of satisfaction knowing that I had finally given her something of value after these long years of existence together.

Maisy was strict yet compassionate in her tutelage; dedicated yet gentle in her nurturing. There were many times when she thought I was unaware of her with the boy, and I caught her gently stroking the boy's hair or kissing his forehead in comfort.

In the last month we distracted Rupert from his mother's condition, not allowing him to see her in those final weeks. He did not cry or get into a tantrum as I might have expected a boy of his age to do. Instead he tarried on with his life and interactions at Erravilla, with what I sensed was a profound knowledge about his mother's imminent departure, having learnt the hard lessons of life from those treacherous months by the docks and aboard ships from Ireland.

Maisy would sit by Rosie's bedside many an evening and hold her hand. The women barely conversed, each probably attempting to save the other from getting crucial knowledge about her life with him. Instead, Maisy would read to Rosie until she slept, often from the Psalms or Proverbs. I used to wonder why she would read of such hope when death waited just inches away in the flickering shadows of the hearth fire.

I watched Rosie sleep after Maisy had left each night, listening to her staggered breathing and the light rise and fall of her chest. I wondered what would have become of her life had I not infiltrated it in such a brutal way all those years ago, and left her alone as I knew I should have done. What a fool I was to have thought I could have run away with her at all! She deserved much better than a broken woman's death at my hands. But I would always be grateful to her for her gift to me in bringing home my son. I would always be able to see her there, from somewhere deep inside of him, with him completely unaware that it was not him I saw at all sometimes, but she.

One evening, just days before Rosie left us, Maisy came to stand beside me in the doorway. She linked her slender wrist through my elbow and laid her head upon my arm, watching me watch Rosie in silence.

"Why don't you tell her, Walter?" Maisy said quietly.

"Tell her what?" I asked, stifling my surprise.

"Of your feelings for her."

"That's bold of you to say, Maisy," I admonished, annoyed that she was too perceptive at times.

"She hears you, Walter. You won't have another chance," Maisy continued, taking her chances boldly.

"And pray, Maisy, what am I supposed to tell a dying woman?" I asked gruffly.

"That you're sorry...that you still love her..."

"You tread where you should not, wife."

"Walter, you're burning with something. I've felt it day and night since she's been here," Maisy said gently, holding up the flaming ring for me to see.

I shook my head in defiance to her admission, my breathing heavy as the burdens I carried.

"Walter, I know you love this woman."

"Not as I have loved you, Maisy," I replied roughly, rebuking her more than I meant to.

"Yes, but Walter, never enough. While you have loved us both, you have loved neither of us enough."

"What are you talking about, woman?" I demanded, agitated that she would dare continue this line of private talk.

"Don't you see, Walter? I always wondered why this ring never turned burgundy, the colour my mother told me symbolises true love. Not the love of a passionate kind, but a soul deep love, like the kind my mother had for my father. But since Rosie has returned, I have my answer. I know I have never been enough for you, Walter."

I was stunned by her revelation but knew she spoke the truth.

I turned to her, nodding absently and placing my hands firmly upon her arms. "As I have not been enough for you, Maisy!" I said, searching her pale blue eyes.

"No," she whispered, as though realising this for herself for the first time as well. "I wanted your love so much when we were first married, but realised very quickly that I would never have it. And then I wanted that baby more...more than you...and more than Him. But I know He has forgiven me of this; and blessed us with

Rupert instead. I have kept you at arms' length, Walter, because I could not bear the pain of losing you again. Do you forgive me, Walter?"

I was dumbfounded, as one staring at an angel who called herself a demon. "Maisy, Maisy, it's I who should be asking for your forgiveness."

"I already forgave you, Walter," she whispered, placing her palm over my heart and smiling faintly up at me.

I nodded, holding her gaze. "I want you to know that I do love you, Maisy."

She shook her head in despair. "But you aren't in love with me, Walter. The ring tells the story of your heart."

"I wish I shared your fervency, Maisy."

"So do I – more than anything, Walter."

And so it was in this way that we continued. For the next fifty-five years. Not with an indifference to one another, but rather with a companionable silence and understanding of the level of our affections.

Rupert grew as he was groomed to be: a fine upstanding member of the social community, fulfilling his role as Master in training to become the next promising Earl of Erravilla Court. I was proud of my son and the endearment he had achieved for his political associations and entrepreneurial expertise with the trading industry and imported merchandise, increasing the value holds of the estate tenfold.

Maisy doted upon Rupert the same as any mother would, perhaps even more so, being ever grateful for the opportunity to parent at all, introducing him to his peers and prestigious women in London, Edinburgh and Wales. She took great pride in watching the finer ladies turn their heads ever so delicately in Rupert's direction, what with his thick curly brown hair and Rosie's rich brown eyes. He had all the characteristics of a promising Earl and aristocrat.

And he shared his mother's faith with as much enthusiasm as she did. It was her legacy to him and she cherished the time we spent together – me watching on as they read together, their mouths moving in unison. I longed for their comfort, but could not find it within me to join them on my knees…

The day Rupert buoyantly told Maisy and I of his plans to sail for the Americas left a hole in our lives far greater than anything we had experienced, past or present. As he told us of his plans to establish new trade routes to the south, and make his niche in the global market through taking his knowledge to all the World, we knew we would never see our son again. Maisy wept and begged for him not to go. "It is too dangerous!" she had wailed, knowing of the many ships that were lost to the depths of the clawing straights between the continents. "Walter, stop him! You must stop him!"

But it did her no good. Had we not raised the boy to be such? Had we not taught him of economics and geography and politics and religion? Rupert had a mind for the adventures of capitalism and sought to gain a foothold in the fast changing global markets and help lead the way into modernity of his own volition. And we had fostered him to be so. He was no longer a boy. He was twenty when he left.

It was also the day when I began to pray for him. For his purpose and safety, and return.

He sent letters frequently for the first few months, which Maisy read again and again in the attic. The letters became infrequent as he set sail for the challenging waters off Cape Horn; and then there were no more at all.

And yet I prayed even more: for a sign of Rupert's deliverance, and for deliverance for my wife, whom I could not bear to see return to the despondent woman she had been all those years ago. And lastly for me: that I would learn to love her as I had always meant to.

I found Maisy often in the years that followed in the dark little attic above the old library, sifting through pictures of her family and re-reading the first of Rupert's letters after his departure. She always held a hope that he would return. Since she would not venture from the oppressive little room, I had several large glass skylights fitted into the roof of the attic: better that she lived in the light of hope than died along with her other ghosts in complete darkness.

I knew that Rupert had been lost to us long before the ocean had claimed him for herself: so fixated was he upon the adventures of the world that I knew he would have never returned even by choice. The world was too big a place and he had to find his own bearings. He never had gotten over his mother's demise at her husband's hands: the man O'Donnell, who, for all intents and purposes, had been his father.

I researched in vain for any hope of hearing about the ship that he had boarded from London to America: The SS Rosales. There was no further mention of its journeys; indeed no one had heard of her at all. To what manner of death had my son succumbed to in the end?

And now I pondered our own ends...

The inscriptions had read: Till Death Do Us Part. For fifty-eight years I had not taken it seriously. But now I stood, a widower at last. Maisy died this morning at 6:55, at the noble age of seventy-six years. She died peacefully in her sleep, in her twin bed across from mine. At the very moment that her heart ceased to beat, the rings that had held us united for nearly six decades had finally thawed from the fiery ice blue and cracked open, springing from her hand and mine, which were held as one, onto the bed covers below.

Just before the colour had wavered and died with her, both the rings had seared with a fierce shade of burgundy: signifying the true love that coursed through her veins and mine, one for the other. I had smiled at this realisation, knowing that she had died with the knowledge of my deep commitment and affection for her. And I thanked God for the life she had lived, and for the precious jewel she had been to me for all of these years.

I began to realise all the things that had been given to me that I had not truly seen before as gifts – the day Maisy had been given to me as an eighteen year old girl: the qualities she exhibited as a person and wife, the rings that had told me of her hopes and fears and the months we had loved in our youth. I was now thankful for delivering her from idolizing the babies she had lost and given us Rupert instead. The fact that she had loved me at all was enough for me forever. And I realised that I had been the greatest sinner of them all.

I placed the rings together in the small keepsake that I had created for Maisy all those years ago, and placed them in their final resting place until the next set of hands came upon them. The steps up to the old attic were steeper than I had remembered, and I had had to pause many times before reaching the landing, rubbing these old knees as I journeyed.

I had kissed the ceramic box with the hand-sculptured designs before laying it upon Aunty Jane's vanity desk for the final time. I had not lingered in the cold dim attic, instead made my way back down the iron steps, passing closed off drawing rooms and the magnificent dining hall, which was now shrouded in large white sheets.

And so it has come to pass, that upon Maisy's death and my imminent end, and with the world on the brink of a large scale and devastating war, I am to be the last Earl of Erravilla Court.

39. Two is Better than One

<u>M</u>

"This is fine," I instructed the cabby as he drove around the turning circle of white gravel, halting in front of the magnificent sandstone structure of Erravilla Court. I handed him the fare and headed straight up the giant size steps to the hardwood oak doors. The house lay eerily silent, and there was no sign of human activity as I pushed through the large oak doors.

"April?" I called, my voice returning to me in the hollow tiled foyer. I left my bag at the foot of the stairs as I took them two by two until I reached the landing on the third floor. Her door was open, but once again I was greeted by silence.

The curtains were open and the pale sunlight streamed in through the window panes. A thick film of wintry frost glistened in the early afternoon sun as it illuminated the scenic greenery below.

I returned to the stairwell, taking the dimly lit corridor off the parlour that led through the kitchen. I paused in the place where I had first laid eyes upon her, her opal eyes glistening with the ghosts of Erravilla, on the day she had discovered the rings.

I headed for the narrow spindly stairs at the end of the corridor, taking greater care as I held onto the wrought iron structure, which I'm sure must have been a hazard, even in its first years after construction. I had to allow my eyes to adjust to the darkness before I felt my way along the line of antiques to the white wooden dresser at the end.

The journal was resting inside the wooden keepsake that the rings had emerged from nearly ten months ago. April had returned the treasures to their original resting place but she was nowhere to be found. I stared at the journal, whose contents had revealed so much for a select few people over the ages, and they were the ones whose story we knew, and I pondered how far back the trail of peculiarity led.

I had been mystified all morning by the strange object upon my finger and further baffled that the journal could not provide the answer to my query. Since I had woken this morning, the ring had hummed its usual tremor but there had been no pain associated with the changing colour. The ring had not turned burgundy, and there was no pain. The journal had not mentioned the bronzed yellow that had tainted the metal for hours now.

Was there a colour Sir Walter had failed to mention? Or one he had never experienced himself? *What was April's current mood?* I pondered, descending the rickety stairs as hastily as I dared.

The gym was unusually empty. The curtains were still drawn, and the usual paraphernalia of mitts, towels and gym bags that were often strewn across the floor were absent. It would take a while to search the entire house, I realised, and began calling out her name, receiving another hollow reply as my voice reverberated off the wooden cathedral ceilings.

I took out my phone to call Lucas, wondering if he knew of any favourite places within Erravilla that she might have ventured to. I strolled into the ceremonial dining hall, pacing by the French doors, looking out onto the garden and the forest beyond.

My thoughts turned instantly to Maisy Finnegan all those years ago. *The forest. The pond. She wouldn't...* I snapped my phone back into my pocket and turned the door handle. It was open.

I threw myself into a steady sprint along the pebbled stone path, sprinting towards the garage house and retrieving my ice skates, knowing that the ice would be slippery if I had to cross it. I threw the skates into a bag and returned to a sprint towards the mass of pine trees along the boundary, not allowing myself to be overshadowed by fear and doubt. Her words echoed through my mind as I proceeded.

I've gone to return the keepsakes to their rightful place...

I reached the edge of the clearing of reeds and gripped the nearest pine trunk, scanning the frozen pond as my breath could be seen before me in gusts of white puffy air. The pond was frozen over, with no signs of a break on the ice. I felt a momentary sense of release, but sat down to don the skates as a safeguard.

I stood on the edge of the great ice rink; and there, standing on the far bank, a few feet from the shore, was April, on the frozen ice. I was conscious of not startling her as I ambled across the ice, approaching her swiftly, my eyes not leaving her for a second.

Her face was serene, the calmest I had ever beheld her glorious features. A soft smile played upon her lips as she stared through the white ice below her. She looked free, uninhibited, and not bound by the chains that I had seen her in previously. She looked almost radiant, and ever so beautiful. I caught the breath in my throat as I rounded the perimeter near her, yearning to take her very much *alive* form into my arms and never releasing her.

"You worry too much about others, Emerus Forrester," she said simply, without lifting her chin to address me directly. "This ring's been burning me all night and all morning."

"Well, strangely, mine's been silent on the matter," I replied, gliding slowly towards her. "I see you returned the journal to the attic."

"Yes."

She paused thoughtfully, her opal-coloured hues searching the blue sky above. "I read it in transit between Geneva and Erravilla."

She knew it all now.

"You're not bad on those," she mused, examining the pair of skates strapped to my feet, before finally meeting my gaze, her face composed with tranquillity. "You didn't bring a pair for me?"

I laughed softly at her humour, always in the face of my fears. "I didn't know you could skate."

"There's a lot about me you don't know, M," she said with a smile.

"That's true," I responded, smoothly sashaying over to stand in front of her. "But I'm beginning to realise there's not much you can't do."

"Oh, there's lots I can't do! You'll realise that in time, too."

"Such as?"

"Draw, sing, paint, knit, cook, play a musical instrument. The list goes on," she said with a crooked grin, unperturbed by her confessed limitations. "Luckily, you seem to be quite adequate at some of those things…so we'll survive."

I smiled in hope at her insinuation, daring to believe that she wanted me to be part of her future.

"Would you like to skate?" I asked, holding out my hand to her.

Her eyes grew wide in bewilderment. "I thought you didn't bring me a pair of skates?"

"I didn't." I watched as her eyes grew wilder still in realisation, and her breathing grew heavy in her chest.

She walked slowly towards me, almost slipping twice on the ice before she reached my hand and steadied herself. "How are you going to…?"

I lifted her gently until her feet were even upon the ridge of my skates and placed her arms around my neck, holding her tightly as I placed my arms around her waist and pulled her to me. I stared down into her clear eyes, finding the answers that I had longed to know for so long.

"I hoped that you'd come," she whispered.

"How could I not?"

"I've been so blind," she uttered, closing her eyes, a pained line forming across her brow, "about lots of things."

"So was I," I replied, thinking of Penny, void of emotion for the first time. I had all I would ever need right here in my arms. I ran my thumb softly beneath her eyelashes, removing the sole tear that escaped from her eyes.

"You're so perfect, M. I'm afraid that I'll never live up to your standards…that I'll never be good enough for you," she offered.

I shook my head, perplexed that she could exalt me to such levels. "That's not true. I'm far from perfect, or even good, April."

A shadow briefly crossed my path of a memory buried far beneath the surface; and one she must never know. It was the dark past, one I had left behind years ago now, and would have no bearing upon our lives in the future. I would protect her from it at all costs.

"My faults are many, April, but I conceal them well, which is a fault in itself, I suppose. And you have me on a pedestal that I should not be on. It means that I have that much farther to fall when I do. You are far more than my equal, April. You're the pinnacle to me."

"So, you can accept me, faults and all?" she asked, smiling faintly.

"If you'll accept mine. I love you just the way you are. I wouldn't change a thing."

She looked up into my eyes, searching them for the truth, and finding it there, mirroring the utter surprise and joy in her own.

"Do you trust me to skate with you like this?" I asked playfully, moving slowly into a waltzing rhythm around the edge of the pond.

"Of course. I trust you with my life…and my heart."

"I don't think I can kiss you and skate at the same time," I chuckled.

She laughed, and the sound echoed through the clearing like the chiming of silver bells. "Then you'll just have to take me back to land."

"As you wish, Miss Falls."

"*Mrs* Forrester," she corrected, a satisfied gleam in her eye.

My feet nearly gave way beneath me at the sound of her admission, and I stared at her incredulously as I glided her backwards across the ice to the bank. "April, I have something to ask you…officially."

She disembarked from her flight across the frosted water, almost stumbling onto the riverbank. I hastily removed my feet from the skates, locating my shoes by the pine fringe. She stood before me, and I held both of her petit hands in mine, a smile of contemplation forming across her lips.

"Yes?" she coaxed.

I took in a large breath of frosty air and removed the small box from my jacket lining, descending to one knee. She inhaled heavily at the sight of the corresponding ring to her own.

"An opal?" she whispered.

"I've never told you…that from the first time I met you, I thought your eyes looked like opals. Sounds kind of corny, so I never told you," I confessed.

"I've never been told that before," she said in wonderment.

"Can I ask you now?"

"Please do."

"April Forrester, of my own volition and desire, I would like you to be my wife, accepting me just as I am, and knowing that I will love you only, until death do us part. Will you accept this ring, as a symbol of my devotion and adoration, and take me as your husband, from this day forward…forevermore?"

"Wow…that's some speech, Emerus Forrester. I want nothing more than what you offer. Nothing could make me happier."

I slid the ring up against the other… the eternal connection that we shared, hoping that the metals wouldn't suddenly repel one another, or worse, somehow burn her finger off altogether at the gesture. The original pair of rings quivered momentarily, before turning a deep shade of burgundy.

I stood and gathered her into my arms, snaking my hands around her lower back as she cupped hers around my face and pulled my lips to hers.

"I love this five-o'clock-shadow by the way…very sexy," she mused, still moving her lips against mine.

April Forrester

In that moment I saw the fear that I had been holding onto since I was seventeen, disappear; I had been petrified to take the risk of loving someone after Andy's betrayal. He had been my best friend and had held a part of me captive after what he had done. I realised that it had been that same fear which had prevented me from even loving Hugh completely.

And finally, the same fear had led me to take the easy path with Lucas, who I always knew would never be the perfect match for me. So I could pass the time with him, without either of us having to commit to one another. Lucas' life and mine would have separated at the next fork in the road, with him unable to give up his lifestyle for any permanent fixture, and me unprepared to follow him to the end of his road without giving up my own desires.

Love was a risk, and there were no guarantees of a forever; death would visit us all one day. But just maybe, God willing, M and I had the chance of a future that might stretch for fifty-eight years, just like Walter and Maisy Finnegan. Theirs had been a life begun by the force of a hand; and had taken an entire lifetime together to find one another. M and I had already been given a head start, and I intended to make the most of it.

He swooped me up into his arms, his lips never leaving mine, and began to walk through the thicket. I chuckled at his determination. "You can't walk the whole way back to Erravilla carrying me."

"There's a lot you don't know about me," he reminded me with a grin.

"Okay, suits me," I replied, tracing the perfect bone structure of his face down to his prickly chin. "I'll just stare at you while you walk."

"Now that could become tiresome," he pondered.

"Not from my perspective, *husband*."

That one word was his undoing. He stared at me as though I were the end of his rainbow, his penetrating blue eyes looking straight through mine with a yearning that I could feel through his trembling arms beneath me.

"Can you run?" he asked suddenly.

"Yes. Why?"

"Because I want you, *Mrs* Forrester," he declared, placing me lightly on my feet and pulling me into a hasty jog. "I think it's time we obeyed Penny before our time runs out, and abide by *all* the legal requirements of a marriage."

I grinned following his lead, keeping pace with his speed, which I knew had been reduced for my benefit. When we reached the landing to the dining room he stopped and swept me into his arms again, carrying me across the threshold into the house. He climbed the stairs with an ease I thought would be impossible for most people, and then I remembered his elite physical form that I had observed recently at the Chalet.

"Does this mean you desire what I desire, wife?" M mused, resting me upon his knee while he held up his left hand to indicate the purple hue emanating from the ring.

I held up my hand in response, entwining it through his. "Strange: the rings no longer magnetise together," I mused, having half expected the rings to lock together as they had done previously when they were in close proximity.

"I'd like to explore that theory more," M mused, gathering me to his chest again. "Which room would you prefer me to take you on this fine winter's day?"

"Yours," I replied. "I've never been to your room. You know, I've never even been to your home in Fulham."

"Well, we'll have to change that too," he replied, pushing open the door to his suite, "since it's now your home too."

I lay back casually as he placed me upon the bed, leaning back on my arms beside him, admiring his form. He must have felt my eyes burning his very flesh, and turned to meet my gaze brazenly.

I blinked and blurted out the first thing that came to my mind. "M, what did you mean about not knowing where you're going to base yourself, now that you won't be travelling as much?"

He smiled before answering, pulling me close to his side. "I was hoping that you wouldn't mind if I come and live in Oz for a while…indefinitely?"

"You'd move to Australia?"…*for me?*

"For most of the time. Occasionally I'd have to meet with Mario, the new Architect, in person. So I'd probably have to fly to London for those meetings. But I really want to stay grounded as much as possible…with you."

"Can that work with your business? Is there enough of a client base in Oz?"

"I'll work on it. All it takes is one, for word to spread. That's why the Sheehan project is so important. But I can extend to the Oceanic if I need to. And that'll be day flights or the occasional over-nighter."

"*You*, are already a wonderful husband!" I said, cupping his already familiar face with my hands. "So long as it works for you, M. I'm happy to live in London for as long as you need. I can take my work anywhere," I offered, surprising myself at what I was prepared to surrender for him, for us, remembering that I had not been so ambitious when Lucas had asked.

"We'll see. For now, there are more important things on my mind. Like getting to know my wife a little better," he crooned, closing the remaining gap between his warm lips and mine, revelling in the fact that we now had all the time in the world to be together.

My hands never left him, searching every fraction of his body for any untold mysteries, and finding every one of them joyously and earnestly. I craved his touch, holding him closer than I had thought was humanly possible, until he seeped beneath the confines of my very flesh and we moulded into one. He was my perfect match in every way; and I was his: never to wander the earth alone again…even if this life were to end. He was a part of me now, and that was all I needed to take with me each day.

In the small hours of the night, I listened to him hum softly to himself, his chest vibrating softly below my cheek with each note that he purred. "You often hum," I observed.

"Only when I'm happy," he replied, bestowing a kiss upon my forehead.

"I know this one. It's another *1927*."

"Yes, I seemed to have revived my old music collection since that wedding we went to. I used to listen to those guys all the time."

"Will you sing it to me?" I asked, knowing he would.

"It seems I've sung to you on several occasions now," he chuckled softly. "But if you don't mind the husky morning voice…"

"Even better," I chimed.

"Well, this one's for you…

"I guess I never told you
What you mean to me,
'Cause every time I hold you close
Words get in between.
There's nothing more that I can say
Than just the simple truth…
Darling, I'd die for you…"

He continued the lullaby momentarily, until I cut him off gently, distracting him with my response to his words, kissing him with vehemence. Kissing him for the precious times that lay ahead, erasing the pain and memories of Andy, who I knew I could not help, and locking away deeper still the secret of our baby, the one I had murdered the day I had had the abortion…because I still couldn't face the shame and guilt.

I would never tell a soul.

Epilogue

Three Months Later: Warner Brothers' Studios, Los Angeles

Lucas Forrester

"And….that's a wrap! Good work Lucas. Playing the villain actually suits you: it's possibly your best work yet! Take a break and be back here in thirty," Marty, the Director of my latest film shoot, *Crooners,* hollered.

"Sure thing, Marty," I replied flatly, fatigued after another gruelling ten hour shoot. I headed for the doors to the studio, grabbing a bottle of Coke and a chocolate bar on the way. We were almost at the end of the ten-week shoot. *Thank God. Literally.* Playing the bad guy didn't feel so much like work, more like a vent for my on-going frustrations in life: it came easier than I had expected.

"That stuff can't be good for you," an unfamiliar voice interrupted.

I spun on my heel as I reached the exit.

"So? What's it to you?" I demanded, irritated that people thought they could give you their advice all the time just because they recognised you.

"Nothing. I don't care how you kill yourself. You look like crap, that's all. And that new hairdo isn't helping things. That's your regular caffeine fix," she said nodding towards the Coke. "I think it's your fifth bottle today," she crooned in an undetectable European accent.

"Excuse me? Do I know you?" I asked, trying to hide the vibes of vexation that seemed to arise whenever strangers approached.

Was she stalking me? How did she get into the studio?

"No. But *I* know *you*, Lucas Ricardo Forrester. Very well."

"And you are…?" I pressed, looking casually out of my peripheral vision for security and running a nervous hand over my scalp where my hair used to be.

She reached into her pocket and I took a step out of the door, preparing to make a run for it if she took out a weapon of some kind.

"Relax, Forrester. If I wanted you dead, you already would be," she said flatly, folding open a federal badge. "I'm a Detective with the French *Surete Nationale*."

"Aren't you a little out of your jurisdiction?" I asked, eyeing her wearily.

Don't trust anybody. Even cops.

I was still pissed-off that they hadn't come through on their word that they would have this mess cleaned up already. Nine months on and I was still looking over my shoulder everywhere I went. I hated the idea that I might have to hire body-guards again, like I had to do six years ago. That had been one shitty gig.

Where was a dartboard when I needed one?

"I've been assigned to handle your case, in conjunction with the British Federal Police and, when permitted, the FBI," she replied casually, prompting me to walk with her from the studio building.

"My *case?*" I asked, mildly unnerved.

"Yes, Mr Forrester, we have reason to believe that Miss McClellan has detoured England via France, to the U.S."

"That's where I've flown from," I replied, my thoughts running a thousand miles an hour.

"Exactly. We think she's trailing you, cross-continental. Your family will be informed of any movements."

"Why? Are they in some kind of danger?" I asked, anxiously running a hand across my shiny head.

"It's a precaution, Mr Forrester. We just want them to be…aware, especially since your sister-in-law is about to launch the biography she wrote about you. It's tipped to be a best seller. You should get a wig for the occasion though. The ex-con look won't be good for book sales."

I winced at the mention of April, and at her attempted bleak humour. The hair comments I could take; I'd had hundreds of them since it had all been shaven off for the new role. But April: she was one wound I was not prepared to discuss.

"You don't sound French or British," I said warily, changing the subject.

"My mother was French, but I grew up in England," she replied dismissively. "I've spent a lot of time across the French and British borders."

She had led me to a quiet corner of the court-yard, out of ear shot and of prying eyes.

"I don't understand how Penny's so difficult to find. She's not a Houdini, or an Osama Bin Laden! How is she slipping through?" I demanded, raking my hand over my prickly scalp again.

"She's quiet. She doesn't have many contacts. But we're catching up to her; It's only a matter of time now," the woman assured me.

"That's what I was told nine months ago! I mean, what am I supposed to do, huh? Put my life on hold until someone does their job properly and finds her?" I was outraged.

"Mr Forrester, let me make one thing clear: *I* do not want to be here anymore than *you* want me here. I can think of far more useful ways to spend my time than baby-sitting an ego-driven movie star!" she retorted, her thick accent almost a growl.

I stared into her face, my shoulders squared as though I was steadying myself for a fight. *Ego-driven?*

"You need to calm down and pull yourself together. No one is asking you to stop your work – if that's what you call it. You do *your* job, Mr Forrester, and I'll do mine. I was only assigned to your case recently. I'm cleaning up, so to speak. I'm good at what I do. But as I said, I believe there are more important things in the world to save than your pompous arse. And so, I hope for all our sakes, this mess gets cleaned up quickly," she retorted.

"You haven't even told me your name," I replied with a false calm.

"Detective Bronte Hastings. We'll be in touch. Oh, and don't try and leave the country early. I know you're going to the book launches next week."

With a flick of her finger she turned and walked away. The only thing I noticed about her was that she wore a pair of knee-high ugg-boots. I would never understand ugg-boots as a fashion statement.

I caught glimpses of her over the next few days, stealing in and out of the studio. Occasionally she would wander up to the edges of the set and observe me in action. She never spoke to me. By the looks of things she was just checking on me. *Baby-sitting*, as she had called it.

"You're on for shot, Outrigger. Take it now or we'll lose her!"

I clutched at the pendant around my throat and it quivered in my hand. Odd, I hadn't remembered putting it around my neck.

I glanced across at Bronte, her face only inches from mine as she closed one eye and looked down the barrel through the target lense. The grouchy voice ordering her to shoot frustrated me as I listened through my ear piece, knowing Bronte heard the same from hers. But the voice didn't seem to distract her: her eye was focussed and her hands perfectly still on the trigger.

I could feel beads of sweat pouring down my face, but Bronte's was flawlessly smooth and dry. She was a pro, and I winced at the thought that she'd probably done this a dozen or more times before: taken someone's life without so much as flinching.

"Outrigger! What are you waiting for?" her handler growled through the ear piece.

I glanced at her slender neck as a fine muscle jerked below her jaw. *So, she wasn't completely inhuman after all.*

"No go, Murray, if this goes one centimetre either side, April will die," Bronte replied to her handler, seemingly calm, still resting as perfectly still as a snake up on her elbows in the long grass. "Don't move an inch, Lucas," she breathed, without so much as a glance in my direction.

Detective Hastings spoke to me with a familiarity that surprised me: she had always called me Forrester.

It was then that I noticed a faint white mark on the ring finger of her left hand, the one that held the barrel level. I raised my eyebrows in surprise: she didn't strike me as the marrying type. Far too independent and emotionally distant. That could explain why there was no longer a ring there, *if* she had been married at all.

"Target's on the move! Take it now, Outrigger!"

The pendant shook violently in my hand as moisture ran from my palm.

Three shots rang out across the abandoned industrial site. From our vantage point up on the hill I saw both women fall to the ground.

"You shot her!" I cried at Bronte as I moved quickly to my feet. "You just shot April!"

I woke up in a fever, wiping the sweat from my forehead with the back of my hand. I had to concentrate hard to steady my breathing.

It's times like these when I wished I'd have taken notes on April's calming techniques...

This was the third night I'd woken up from a similar dream, fear and adrenaline pumping through my body at a throbbing rate. The dreams had started the first night I had met Bronte Hastings, and I hadn't thought anything of it: just my twisted mind trying to piece together the absurdities of my life from the past year.

But after three nights of lying awake into the wee hours, I was getting fed up with the nightmares. Grown men don't have night terrors, do they?

April I had dreamt about for months. Bronte was just a royal pain in my arse already. The two didn't even know each other and they were both taunting me in my sleep!

I turned over to read the clock and was struck once again by the fluorescence radiating from the small white crystal on the pendant M had given me for Christmas. It had given off the rays of light each time I had woken up from the dreams, as though it glowed in the dark or something. But it hadn't glowed any other nights since Christmas, apart from the last three. *Weird.*

M surely did find some kooky stuff in his travels.

I was left feeling edgy and uncomfortable after the dream again. And I wanted so desperately to hop straight on a plane to Australia, just to see if she was all right.

One more week. Then filming would be finished and I would arrive home in London for April's book launch.

I placed a t-shirt over the glowing pendant and rolled over the other way. I didn't believe in superstition but the next night that pendant would be in another room.

About the Author

Reba A. Ritchie was born in 1982 and lives in the Blue Mountains, West of Sydney. She is the busy mother of three boys, and has a keen interest in travel, soccer, history and music. Since childhood she has been writing novellas, poems and stories - going on to publish several journal articles. Reba graduated from Macquarie University with a Bachelor of Laws and a Bachelor of Media in Writing.

Hosts of Erravilla is Reba's debut novel.